Crocodile

The Magical Tale of the Windermere Crocodile

By K. Trevor Wigglesworth

First edition published 2013
2QT Limited (Publishing)
www.2qt.co.uk

1st Edition
Copyright © 2013 Trevor Wigglesworth. All rights reserved.
The right of Trevor Wigglesworth to be identified as the author
of this work has been asserted by him in accordance with the
Copyright, Designs and Patents Act 1988

All rights reserved. This book is sold subject to the condition that no part of this book is to be reproduced, in any shape or form. Or by way of trade, stored in a retrieval system or transmitted in any form or by any means, electronic, mechanical, photocopying, recording, be lent, re-sold, hired out or otherwise circulated in any form of binding or cover other than that in which it is published and without a similar condition, including this condition being imposed on the subsequent purchaser, without prior permission of the copyright holder.

Illustrated by Robin Grenville-Evans
Typesetting by Dale Rennard

Printed and bound in the UK by Berforts Information Press
The Printer uses FSC and PEFC accredited paper suppliers

A CIP catalogue record for this book is available
from the British Library

ISBN 978-1-910077-02-3

Author's Note

It is probably inaccurate to describe 'Crocodile' as a children's book because in some respects it does not fit comfortably into that genre of writing.

It may therefore be best described as a book for adults who have never completely lost their childhood sense of curiosity, wonder and adventure, and who will always remain young at heart.

I hope that these broad reflections will not deter older and more inquisitive children or staid and unadventurous adults from reading 'Crocodile' and so deny themselves the opportunity and pleasure of reading about the life and exploits of a singularly unique and fascinating creature.

Acknowledgements

for Dorothy, my beautiful wife and partner, without whose constant support this book would never have been completed.

with grateful thanks to our dear friends Ira and Allene Fishman for their generous help and advice

also many thanks to Catherine Cousins and 2QT for all the help in getting the book published and to Robin Grenville-Evans for the wonderful drawings of Crocodile

Chapter - Index

Chapter One	Under A Silver Moon	1
Chapter Two	The Second Coming	9
Chapter Three	Crocodile's Island	33
Chapter Four	Shopping for Necessities	75
Chapter Five	Tarn Hows	89
Chapter Six	London & Emily	99
Chapter Seven	Crocodile's Grand Tour Parts I - XIII	117
Chapter Eight	London with Crocodile	219
Chapter Nine	Oxford and the Circus	241
Chapter Ten	Christmas at Windermere	337

CROCODILE   K. Trevor Wigglesworth

Prologue

Earth has not anything to show more fair
Dull would he be of soul who could pass by
A sight so touching in its majesty
Windermere doth, like a silver garment, wear
The beauty of the moonlight.
By William Hartley Crocodile.

Paraphrased from 'Westminster Bridge'
by William Wordsworth.

Introduction

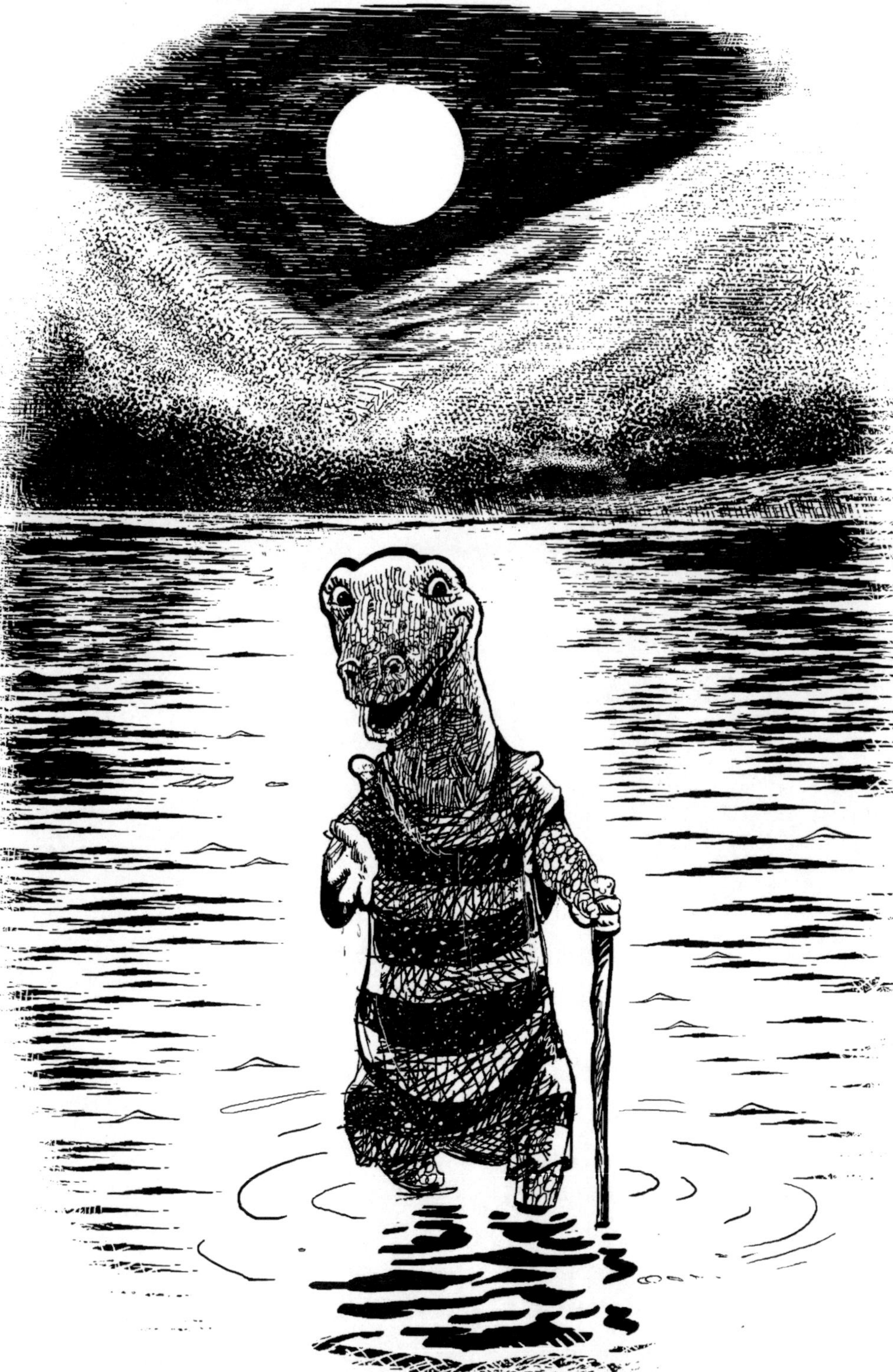

Chapter One
Under A Silver Moon

Every year, in mid-winter, we are privileged to witness a most spectacular sight – it is when a brilliant silver moon lights up our lake, Windermere. On these wonderful nights when the moon is near to full and thousands of stars twinkle in a cloudless sky – the lake, fields, forests and mountains are bathed in a serene silver light. Sometimes Jack Frost applies a final touch by sprinkling every tree, every leaf, and every blade of grass with sparkling crystals of ice. On these special nights we live in a mysterious, fairy-tale world, so beautiful, words alone do not adequately describe the breathtaking splendour. It was on a night such as this that our lives were magically to change forever.

Kate and I live in a house on a hillside overlooking Windermere. We have wonderful views of the lake and fells even without setting foot outside. Sometimes we sit for ages watching the ever-changing patterns on the surface of the lake. Occasionally, violent storms whip up the water into a frenzy of anger, but most times, the surface moves in complex patterns. It is influenced by the wind, the changing temperatures, the wake from passing boats and the movement of fish, swans, ducks, geese and other birds as they pass along the lake. Sometimes the lake puts on a spectacular show, a kaleidoscopic fantasy of intricately complex moving patterns, fanning out at varying speeds over the surface. Then, as if by magic, in the blink of an eye, the

K. Trevor Wigglesworth

e curtain falls – Windermere is returned

he surface of the lake shone like a silver ything around it glistened in the moonlight. We were drawn, as if by a magnet, down to the shore. We sat on our favourite rock by the water's edge. The night was as silent as the lake was still.

We had been there but a few minutes when we saw movement on the water some way offshore. At first we thought it might be a big fish, perhaps a pike, but as it got closer we knew, by the size of its bow-wave, that it was something much larger. Like a torpedo homing in on its target the v-shaped wave was moving at considerable speed directly towards us. The 'torpedo' suddenly slowed and then stopped. A pair of eyes appeared above the surface, then a long snout. Now we both felt a shiver of apprehension and instinctively stepped back a little way from the shoreline. A head appeared, then a neck, arms, a body and legs, all dripping water and glistening in the moonlight. As the creature stood up to its full height of nearly six feet, we were amazed to see that, not only was it wearing what appeared to be a bottle-green, one-piece swimming-costume, it was helping itself to emerge from the water with the aid of a black, silver-handled walking stick.

"Oh my goodness!" I exclaimed, in shocked disbelief, "It looks like a crocodile!" We moved back a few feet.

A voice, which appeared to come from the creature's mouth, said reassuringly, "Do not be afraid, I mean you no harm."

Shaking the water off his long snout he continued, "You are quite correct in your assumption that I am a crocodile – indeed, I am unquestionably and indisputably a crocodile," and then with a chuckle the crocodile added, "but I am also a vegetarian and a humanist – so you have nothing to fear."

"He has a rather posh voice for a crocodile!" exclaimed Kate, "this has to be some kind of clever hoax."

"It's no hoax, I assure you," said the crocodile, "believe it or not, I am your neighbour, and have been so for some time now. I must apologise for spying on you – but I am in desperate need of your help – my freedom, perhaps my life may depend on you."

The crocodile then emerged completely from the water and sat down on the big rock that we had just vacated; then transferring his stick to his left hand, he began to gesture with his right hand to give emphasis to the story that he began to relate...

He told us that he had moved to the Lake District from London only a few months ago with his guardian, mentor and friend, Professor Julius Septimus Merryweather. He said that for several years the Professor had brought him to Windermere for their summer holiday and that they usually stayed from July to September, so he knew the Lake District very well. During those visits he had seen us many times so he felt that he already knew us quite well and that he was sure he could trust us, but that he had not wanted to trouble us until it was absolutely necessary. He believed that the time had now come and was pressing.

Before he could tell us more he suddenly cocked his head to one-side and whispered, "I can hear voices ... somebody is coming this way ... I must not be seen by strangers ... I have put my trust in you and hope you will help me in my plight. If you would kindly meet me here again tomorrow night at the same time I will explain why I need your help – but please will you promise not to tell a living soul about me?"

We promised absolutely that we would do as he requested, and Kate asked if he had a name.

"The Professor called me William Hartley Crocodile because of his love of the Lakeland Poets. I prefer Hartley because its rarer and more unusual and I feel more like a Hartley than a William, and I think it suits me better. However, I must tell you that the Professor always called me Crocodile, and somehow it just stuck! The only other person that I had any contact with in London was the Professor's niece, Emily, and she would only call me Hartley. Apart from Emily, I save Hartley for formal occasions. I am happy if you will call me 'Crocodile', but I don't like to be called *Croc*, for reasons I will tell you tomorrow. I already know that your names are Kate and Matthew and that you don't mind being called Matt. I am so sorry but I dare not stay a moment longer. He waded into the water and, with a wave of his stick, he vanished beneath the surface.

Before we could utter a word two strangers appeared, some distance away along the shore, walking in our direction. As they approached us one of them said, "What a beautiful night, we have not known one like this before!"

"It can only be described as magical," I replied, "I don't think there has ever been a night quite like this before, either"

We hardly slept a wink that night. So many questions tormented our minds. Where did Crocodile actually live? Why had he left London? Where was the Professor now? Why did Crocodile need our help and why was he in danger? How did he manage to support himself without his existence becoming common knowledge? How could he possibly know that our names were Kate and Matthew?

The more we thought and talked about what we had just experienced the more intriguing it became. Perhaps the reason that the Professor had brought Crocodile to the Lake District was because somebody had discovered his existence in London. One of the Professor's colleagues may have been indiscreet and it may have become unsafe for him to continue to live in the London house. We had never read anything in the newspapers or seen anything on television about a highly intelligent crocodile living in London – it would have been headline news, not just here, but all over the world. Clearly, nobody was aware of Crocodile's existence in the Lake District – we would have found out in five minutes if he had been spotted in or around Windermere. The more we thought about Crocodile and discussed him the more the doubts and uncertainties preyed on our minds. We began to get a sneaking feeling that the whole experience could have been, as Kate had first thought, a very clever hoax. Yet we also knew that, impossible as it now seemed, we had witnessed everything first hand, very close up, with our own eyes. When we were standing next to him we were absolutely convinced that what we were witnessing was not just a clever trick or illusion, we were certain that Crocodile really existed.

If I had been on my own on the lakeshore that night maybe I could convince myself that I had had some kind of hallucination in which I had imagined entirely the whole encounter with Crocodile. Even more likely, I could convince myself that I had fallen asleep and it had all been just a dream. A vivid dream would have been the most likely explanation, but Kate had witnessed exactly what I had. We went over everything time and time again and there were absolutely no discrepancies in what we both saw and heard and even in what we smelt, because we both agreed that Crocodile was wearing a very pleasant, subtle and expensive gentlemen's perfume, which, partially, if not entirely, eclipsed the smell of the lake and the outdoors. Also, we had both noticed his nails, when he was holding his stick, and as he gesticulated when he was telling us about himself, they were quite long but beautifully manicured. These details we had both observed independently and so we were sure that they were not figments of our imaginations.

Another comment that Crocodile had made that we found difficult to understand was that he had apologised for spying on us. How could he have been spying on us? We did not go down to the lakeshore very often because we could see the lake, in all its splendour, from our house and garden terraces. If he had been in the water surely we would have spotted him. I have several sets of powerful binoculars through which I often look at the lake and I can see clearly everything that moves on the surface, and I had never spotted anything or anyone who looked remotely like Crocodile.

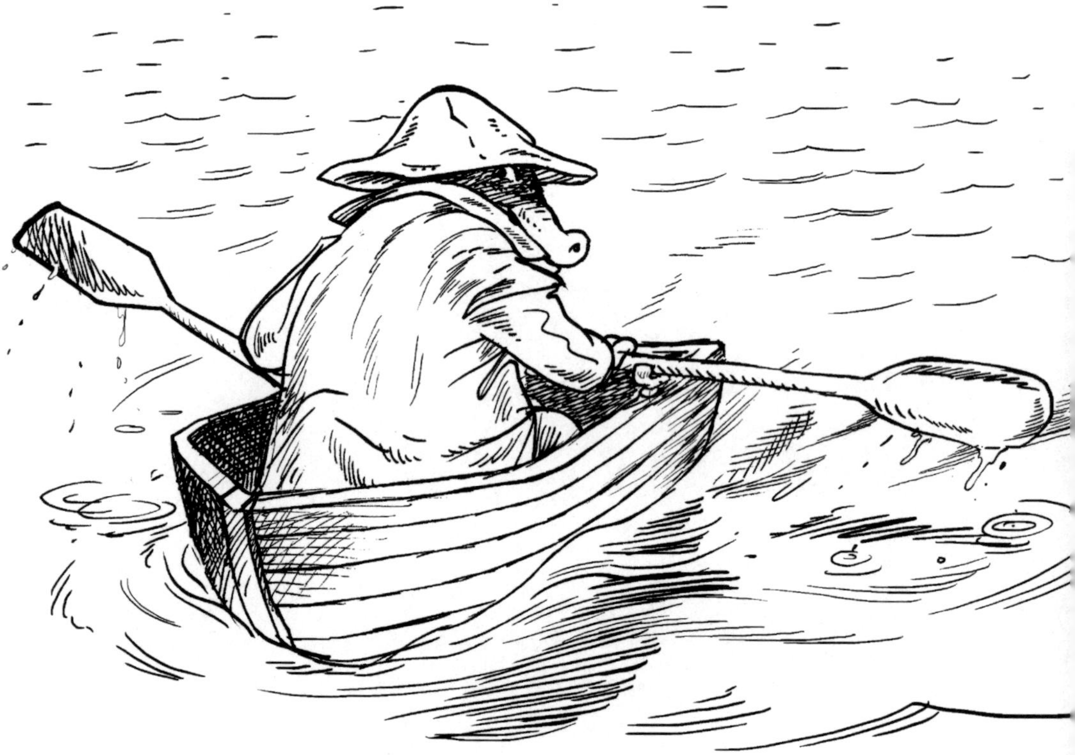

Chapter Two
The Second Coming

The following morning we decided to go for a walk to discuss Crocodile further. Most times when we walk we carry a flask of tea and often stop off in Ambleside for a take-away mug of coffee. We always walk at least two or three times a week and fresh coffee before we set off has become an essential and very enjoyable habit.

We walk frequently around Loughrigg and Elterwater and usually leave the car near Loughrigg Tarn. From here we can walk for half an hour or half a day if we wish, but we try to plan the route so that most of the return journey is downhill. Somehow a walk is never quite as enjoyable or as satisfying if you leave the hardest part until last. It is always comforting after a long hard walk to know that you have reached the point where it is now, *downhill all the way home*, or, *downhill all the way to the top*, as we sometimes say. We often tease friends, who are not used to walking on the fells, when, during a long and gruelling climb, they ask anxiously, "How much further is it?"

We reply, with straight faces, "Only about another five miles uphill before we reach the hardest bit – why, are you getting tired?" We then watch the agony turn to ecstasy when we tell them that there is only a short distance to go – then its, *downhill all the way home*.

We wondered if Crocodile and the Professor used to walk on the fells and we began to think of some of the disguises that may have been used to hide Crocodile's identity. There are hundreds of walks in the Lake District where you could trek for miles and not meet another soul, but without a good disguise it would only be a matter of time before somebody noticed him.

The early morning mist had cleared to reveal a beautiful, crisp, frosty day. Across Loughrigg Tarn, the Langdale Pikes rose majestically in the near distance and a sprinkling of snow on their tops glistened in morning sunshine. A pair of swans waddled awkwardly into the water – then glided gracefully out across the calm glassy surface of the tarn. The peaceful scene was momentarily disturbed by a cohort of gaggling geese flying in a perfect V formation high overhead – we guessed that in a few minutes they would be landing in one of their favourite foraging spots, a field at Storrs, just up the road from where we live.

Halfway round the tarn we passed a picturesque little whitewashed Lakeland cottage. Wisps of smoke were rising gently from its chimney and we remembered sitting by that fire eating freshly baked fruit scones straight out of the oven, with homemade strawberry jam and clotted cream. It was formerly the home of our plumber and we visited him there several times to discuss a heating system and other plumbing requirements for our first house in the Lake District. His wife always had a special treat waiting for us when she was at home.

At the end of the path, through a five-barred gate, the road leads up to Deer Bolts Wood and Loughrigg Terrace high over Grasmere Vale. Wordsworth must have walked here a thousand times and looked out to the Lion and the Lamb on the top of Helm Crag with Dunmail Raise winding steeply below its right flank, the road to Keswick and the North.

All the way round we went over and over the details of our meeting with Crocodile. This continued along the shores of Grasmere, up the road and uphill again through Deer Bolts Wood, then back down the road to Loughrigg Tarn. Finally we had to agree that we could not disagree about anything that we had witnessed the previous night. We also knew that Crocodile was, for sure, no ordinary crocodile. Apart from his intelligence he was not one of those huge, fierce looking ones that really scare you – the ones that you instinctively know to stay well clear of, and that if they got you in their teeth there would be no escape.

Crocodile, on the other hand, was slightly less than six feet tall and was healthily slim. His snout was quite short, as was his tail – he was an elegant creature. Astonishingly, he had the bearing and mannerisms of a refined gentleman, but he also had a childlike quality and a cheeky grin – he was a most engaging character.

We wondered if we should take Crocodile something to eat when we went to meet him that evening and if so, what should it be? He had made it very clear that he was a vegetarian, and as Kate was a brilliant cook she could make something especially for him. I suggested that instead of making our usual complete circle of Windermere via Hawkeshead, Sawrey and Lakeside, we should go back to Ambleside and Windermere and buy the necessary fresh ingredients.

Kate spent the remainder of the day in the kitchen making a huge vegetable lasagne using her secret recipe

11

for the fresh tomato sauce, which required most of the enormous quantity of tomatoes that we had purchased on the way home.

That evening, carrying the lasagne, still bubbling in the largest dish we possessed, together with an enormous piece of Kate's home-made carrot cake, we made our way down to the lake for our appointment with William Hartley Crocodile – perhaps even now, only half believing that he would show up.

The view over the lake was almost as perfect as the previous night with the moon a fraction less than full, in a cloudless sky. There was a slight swell on the lake and as we sat down on the big rock to wait for his arrival, the water lapped gently at our feet. There was a rowing boat in the middle of the lake and it was dead still in the water. We thought that the person in the boat might be fishing but their back was towards us. A small lantern hanging at the stern of the boat illuminated the solitary figure, but no detail was visible at this distance.

Our eyes constantly surveyed the lake for any movement in the water that might herald the eagerly anticipated arrival of Crocodile but the surface remained unblemished as far as the eye could see. Kate thought that Crocodile would be aware of the boat and may be waiting in the hope that it would move away before surfacing.

"The problem is," I said, "that fishing boats tend to stay anchored in one spot for hours and the fisherman sometimes goes to sleep, and wakes up only when a bell alerts him to a catch – he could be there all night!"

More time elapsed, together with a growing apprehension that the scheduled meeting with Crocodile was not going to take place. There could be many other reasons why he had not showed up but he had seemed as keen to see us, as we were to see him. How long should we stay? If he didn't show up, should we come again tomorrow night and every night after that in the hope of seeing Crocodile again?

As I was about to voice these thoughts to Kate, the sound of music met our ears. It was the sound of somebody singing, accompanied by some simple notes on an accordion. As we listened we realised that it was coming from the boat in the centre of the lake. Suddenly the accordion stopped and the boat turned in the water and began to move slowly in our direction. The song started up again but this time we could only hear the voice drifting across the water. The oars rose and fell in time to the tune, *A Life on the Ocean Waves*. The words sounded more like, *A life on Windermere*, but I couldn't be certain.

As the boat neared the shore we could see that the oarsman was dressed in shiny green oilskins, topped with a broad brimmed sou'wester. The boat slid gently and expertly onto the shore and its occupant turned to face us.

"Good evening," said a familiar voice. "I must apologise for arriving in this manner, but I feel much safer because if we are disturbed by strangers again they will not take much notice of me dressed like this." Then with an elegant bow he said, doffing his sou'wester, "I am William Hartley Crocodile, at your service."

Crocodile stepped out of the boat and onto the shore, this time with the aid of a sturdy wooden crook, the kind that shepherds use whilst tending their flocks. He sat himself down on the big rock that we had just vacated and instantly began tell us all about himself.

"I am sure that you have been asking yourselves all sorts of questions about me, for example, how did I come to live here? How did I know your names? Why did I feel that I could trust you? How I did I come to live with a Professor in London? I don't even like to think about one particular time in my past now because it gives me bad dreams, but the important part is that the Professor unwittingly rescued me from a travelling circus. I will try to tell you everything so that you will fully understand my position and my plight."

"I have only vague recollections of my very early life. I think I must be an orphan because I cannot remember my mother and father. I believe that I was reared as a youngster in private zoos and I have vague but happy memories of grand houses in fine parks, and kind people sometimes speaking to me in languages other than English, but I don't know where they were. I clearly remember one day being put gently into a long wooden box with holes bored in the top and sides. I was very frightened because I did not know where I was going or what might happen to me. After many hours travelling and several stops en route, where I was given morsels to eat and water to drink through a small, hinged panel in the side of the box, I finally arrived at my destination. The lid was suddenly lifted and, blinking in the sunlight, I came face to face with a very pretty dark-haired girl who was staring down at me.

"Hello," she said with a big warm smile, "what a handsome fellow you are!"

"In truth I had not learned to speak much at all then, just a few words that I had picked up here and there, and some not even in English – but that moment is so vividly etched in my brain that I am now fairly certain that those were the words she used."

"She gently folded down the sides of the box which had been placed in the centre of an enormous open-air cage with a kidney-shaped pool down one side. At the back of the cage was a green wooden hut with a ramp up to a blue front door. This was to be my first little house where I lived happily for several years, even though, as I have realised since, I was a prisoner. At that stage in my life I had no comprehension of the concept of *freedom*. I had never known life in the wild, or if I had, when I was very young, I could not remember anything about it. I have learned, mainly from the Professor's experience and guidance, that to a greater or lesser degree we all live in a cage. Some people live perfectly happy and contented lives in a very small cage, partly because, like a parrot, they never acquire the experience to make comparisons. Conversely, some people are unhappy and discontented with their lives even though the whole world is their stage. The Professor taught me that freedom is a relative concept linked inextricably to happiness, but absolute freedom does not automatically guarantee complete happiness. I tell you this because I know what it is like not to be free, to be a prisoner and to be very unhappy. I lived in a cage at the zoo, so by definition I was a prisoner, but I shared my life with Mercedes, the girl that lifted the lid off the box, she became my best friend and she was so gentle and kind and a tear comes to my eye, as it has now, every time I think of her, partly, because I know that I will probably never see her again."

Crocodile, paused for a moment to dab at a trickle of tears running down his long snout, and then he continued, "I fear for my freedom again now and that is why I am asking for your help, firstly, I must tell you a little about my life with Mercedes. As soon as she had settled me into my new home she produced a large dish full of wonderful delicacies, food that I had never tasted before. I learned later that it was vegetarian food, and that Mercedes was a vegetarian. Of course, at the beginning, I had no idea what *vegetarian* meant, but that was of no consequence because it was the best food that I had ever tasted. She wouldn't let me eat much of the food provided by the zoo, and in order to ensure that I had a balanced diet she used to bring me all kinds of homemade delicacies – and so from an early age I developed a penchant for good food."

"On either side of my cage, or *compound*, as it was called, were two totally enclosed cages that housed, on one side, birds of prey, mainly owls, and on the other side some very exotic and colourful parrots. Mercedes looked after the birds as well as me and she used to take me with her when she went into their cages through the connecting doors. One day she decided to start to try to teach some of the parrots to speak and I got into the habit of copying, quietly to myself, the words that she was trying to teach them. I soon realised that I was very much quicker and better at repeating the words than they were, moreover, as time went by I began really to understand some of the things that she said to them and to me. I decided to wait until I felt good enough and then to surprise her by speaking a few words that I would work out in advance. She had told me that it was her twenty-first birthday the following week and she kept repeating the days to go, in a count down to the big occasion. She talked about the birthday cake that she was going to make and showed me a picture of the cake in a cookery book – of course without realising that by now I had more or less understood exactly what she meant and had memorised most of the words."

"On the big day, she brought the cake to work and invited some of the other zookeepers into my cage for the cake cutting ceremony. I heard one of them; he was a big jolly man with a splendid moustache and a deep baritone voice, the sound of which gave me a bit of a shock, because it was so different to the high soprano voice of Mercedes. He said, 'I'll open the champagne before you cut the cake – just hang on a minute.'

"I had seen champagne before and recognised the shape of the bottle and was ready for the *pop* as the bottle was uncorked. Everybody toasted Mercedes' health and then she cut the cake and handed a piece to everybody, with the biggest piece going to me."

"'I wonder if Master Crocodile would like a glass of champagne as well, or is he too young?' said the big jolly man, with a booming laugh."

"As it turned out the other guests couldn't stay very long because they had zoo duties to attend to, and I soon found myself alone with Mercedes. This was my perfect opportunity to surprise her with what I had learned. I went over my speech a few times in my head and plucking up all my courage, saying, 'Happy Birthday Mercedes ... thank you for the cake ... please may I have a glass of Champagne?'"

"She was so surprised that she took a step backwards, but I don't think that she believed the words were coming from my mouth because she looked over my shoulder and all around me – thinking it to be some kind of birthday hoax, just as you did last night. So I walked up to her and put my snout directly in front of her face and said, 'Happy Birthday Mercedes, please may I have another piece of cake and a glass of champagne?'"

"Of course I don't know now exactly what my voice sounded like or if I spoke perfect English, but the important thing was that Mercedes understood completely what I had said – she immediately cut me another piece of cake and poured some champagne into two glasses holding one for herself and giving the other to me. She then said, 'I am overwhelmed – this makes today a double celebration and you have given me the most wonderful birthday present I could have wished for'. She raised her glass and said, 'Your very good health, Master Crocodile.' And I replied, 'Your very good health,' holding my glass up high and then clincking it gently against hers, as I had seen the others do."

"After that, I never looked back – Mercedes concentrated all her energies on my education. I have to admit that I was a very willing pupil; I spent every evening, after Mercedes had gone home and the zoo had closed, going over and over again everything that she had taught me, and then preparing for my lessons the following day. We started off by working our way through dozens and dozens of children's picture books, until I was nearly word perfect in all of them. Mercedes herself was an avid reader and she started to bring me, book by book, every work of literature that she possessed. In the end I knew them better than she did because I read them over and over again. She was a most thorough and enthusiastic teacher and I was an equally conscientious pupil."

"One thing she did stress and drill into me, over and over again, I was to keep everything an absolute secret from every other human-being until we both agreed that the time had come when we should let the public know about my abilities. She stressed again and again that when that day came, my life would change forever and that it might not be for the better. So the only other living creatures I spoke to were the parrots and some of the owls next door. I ended up spending much more time coaching them than Mercedes did because she was so busy teaching me."

"My education did not stop at speaking, reading and simple writing, because I became interested in learning other skills. She taught me to walk completely upright on two legs, though even now, after all these years I find it easier if I have a good stick in one hand, especially on very uneven ground. My real triumph, however, was on a bicycle. Mercedes used to ride to work every day and I had tried her bike out a few times when she wasn't looking. I had a few nasty spills at first, but when I got the hang of it, and gained confidence, there was no stopping me. However, as soon as Mercedes found out that I could ride she gave me another very strong warning not to let anybody see me on a bike – she said that it could prove nearly as dangerous for me as people finding out that I could speak. 'Someone will soon realise what a big money making opportunity you are', she said, wagging her finger at me. However, she promised that if I agreed to keep my riding skills a secret as well, she would buy me a bike for my birthday."

"Mercedes kept her promise and exactly one year after I had arrived at the zoo, on 1st. March, which we had agreed should be designated my official birthday, she presented me with a gleaming brand new bike all tied up with bunches of big blue ribbons. I took to riding it like duck to water because I had a very good sense of balance and a natural ability on two wheels. To this day, I am still much better at riding than walking. Again Mercedes gave me stern warnings not to let anybody see me riding the bike, so I agreed only to practise in an evening when the zoo was closed. Every evening, when there was nobody about, I spent almost as much time practising my riding skills as I spent on my other studies. To this day, I am still much better at riding than walking."

"Sadly, it was to be my cycling skills that were to bring about my downfall, and not my ability to speak, read and write. I lived in my little house for more than five years and throughout that time there was not a day that Mercedes did not visit me. She did not take a single holiday in all that time and on her days off, and in the weeks that she should have been on holiday, she visited me every day, for at least an hour or two. I now realise that I didn't have any holidays either and I worked continuously at improving my education, and even when Mercedes wasn't with me I spent much of my time talking to the parrots and some of the other birds. Every evening when the zoo was closed and there was nobody around to watch me, I practiced my riding skills as well as attempting to read everything from Chaucer to Hemmingway. What I came to realise more and more was that although I thought I was free and felt I was free, what I read and could understand in all that literature started to make me understand that I was in fact a prisoner in a cage. I think it was Alexandre Dumas' *The Count of Monte Cristo* that finally brought home the reality of my situation and yet, strangely, I was very happy with my life. It was Mercedes, in that book, who stole my heart. I remember fashioning a sword out of one of the sticks that my Mercedes had given me to help me to walk more safely on two legs. In an evening when all was quiet I would sometimes charge round my compound on my bike waving my sword at all my foes and vowing to protect Mercedes with my life."

"In reality, I didn't have any foes and I had not yet, in my short life, met a single person who had ever tried to do me harm. For that reason, one evening, when I was practising some of the most difficult stunts on my bicycle, I was very surprised when a voice called out to me – because, as always, I had checked to make sure that I was completely alone before I started to ride. At first I couldn't tell where the voice was coming from but when it called out again, I looked up and saw two men peering over the high wall at the back of my compound. They must have been on a very tall ladder because it was built like the wall of a castle and all the way round the perimeter of the rest of the zoo was a four metre high fence with curls of barbed wire protecting the top of it."

"I am sure that they did not think that I was a real crocodile because they kept asking me questions in a sort of broken English. They said they had been called by the zoo to fix a leaky roof, but that their van had broken down on the way here and did I have the keys to the main gate to let them in? I pretended not to understand a word of what they were saying. Then I heard one of them say to the other, 'Maybe, it's a real crocodile after all and it can really ride a bike', and the other replied, 'Let's go and get the other ladder and climb over to take a closer look'."

"I started to panic ... then suddenly I had a brainwave. I'd pretend that I was a real crocodile! Anyway, I jumped off the bike and ran on all fours towards the bottom of the wall where I puffed out my chest, and stood up on my hind-legs, and gave the most enormous growl that I could muster. The two men immediately vanished from the top of the wall and that was the last I saw of them. At least that is what I thought at the time. I had single-handedly vanquished my foes without even having to use my sword."

"About a week later, at night when I was asleep, I can remember dreaming about a beautiful asparagus quiche that Mercedes had baked for me. In my dream I picked up a big knife to cut myself a slice, but dropped the knife and felt a sharp pain as it stuck in the top of my leg – but the stab of pain was not caused by the knife, but by a hypodermic needle. At the time, I did not know what a hypodermic needle was, but the pain woke me up and my eyes were riveted on the needle and syringe sticking in my leg – that image has been etched in my memory ever since."

"There were four men standing over me, one was holding a sack which he thrust suddenly over my head. A rope was tied round my snout to stop me from biting through the sack and although I tried to put up a fight, within less than a minute my legs had turned to jelly and I lost consciousness."

"When I came round I was in a cage, fastened with shackles and chained to the bars. The sack had been removed but a strong rope was tied securely round my snout. Several men were staring at me and I heard one say that he did not believe that I could ride a bicycle. Another bet *twenty quid* that I could not ride a bike."

"I was unchained and pulled out of the cage. I was then dragged into a very large tent where some clowns were riding a number of very odd-looking cycles – some with only one wheel. The men lifted me onto a bike with a big back wheel and a small front one and I was pushed out into the centre of what I soon learned was the circus ring in the *Big Top*."

"The men gave me a push forward and let go of the bike – I wobbled unsteadily and fell off. I was not used to this kind of bicycle and my legs were still too weak to turn the pedals round with enough force to keep the bike upright. For the first time in my life I heard the crack of a whip. I heard the man who seemed to be the ringleader, and had assumed he was in charge of me, shout – 'GET HIM BACK ON THE BIKE!' At that moment, again for the first time in my life, I felt the sting of the whip across my back. I have fairly thick skin but it is much softer than the skin of most types of crocodile and the whip was a bull whip, used with some force."

"I was lifted onto the bicycle again. This time the men ran alongside me holding the bike until I had picked up speed – then they let go. I tried my best to pedal hard enough to keep it going but there was no strength in my legs and my eyes were so full of tears that I could not see where I was going. The bike lurched one way and then another and I crashed to the ground. 'I think that's twenty quid you owe me', said a mocking voice. 'Who would ever believe that a crocodile could ride a bicycle? I've never heard anything so daft in all my life'.

'Double or quits!' said the man with the whip. Give me a week and I'll prove I can make the croc ride'."

At this point in his story we noticed tears welling up in Crocodile's eyes. He then said in a strained voice, "I am so sorry but I cannot bear to tell you any more about my time and cruel treatment at the circus." Crocodile brushed aside his tears and then said, much more cheerfully, "But I will tell you about my escape."

Crocodile continued his story with renewed energy: "When I was in the circus ring one night I noticed a very distinguished-looking, elegantly-dressed gentleman sitting in the front row. He had a single white rose in the lapel buttonhole of his jacket and he was wearing a silk polka-dot bowtie. I could not take my eyes off him – I had never seen anyone quite like this in the audience before or anyone wearing a bowtie, other than one of the clowns who had a big yellow and red one that revolved and squirted water. I was also intrigued because he seemed to be taking as much interest in me as I was in him, so I performed some of my most difficult tricks right in front of where he was sitting. My very best trick was to ride the bike without holding onto he handlebars and spinning a hoop on each wrist, while at the same time balancing a football, at the top of a pole on the end of my snout. The finale was to dismount from the bike still balancing the football on the pole, and then flick the pole forward off my snout and as the ball fell I would head it into the audience. This time I aimed for the gentleman's polka-dot bowtie, but he caught the ball neatly, as I had hoped, before it hit its target. When I had finished my act and had taken my bow, the gentleman stood up and applauded loudly."

"At the end of the show, as I was being taken back to my cage, I saw this gentleman getting into a large limousine parked nearby. My handler put me into the cage, but before he had locked the door there was a shout from one of the lion-tamers, 'LION OUT!' he bellowed and an alarm bell sounded. I thought that one of the lions had probably slipped its harness. My handler instinctively ran in the direction of the commotion, leaving my cage door unlocked. At that moment the limousine began to move off slowly. Without any thought as to the outcome I opened the door of my cage, jumped out, ran towards the slowly moving car, somehow opened the boot lid, jumped inside, and pulled the lid down."

"The limousine travelled smoothly and quietly for at least one, maybe two hours, it was impossible to tell. It stopped, only once I think, to fill up with petrol. At the end of the journey it stopped again briefly. There was a whirring sound. The car moved forward little more than its own length. The whirring sound came again and the ignition was turned off."

"I heard the car door opening, footsteps on the ground, the door closing, and more footsteps. Another door opened and closed – then, total silence and total darkness and I pushed at the boot lid. It was locked tight. I was trapped in yet another steel cage. Yet somehow I didn't feel so bad – I knew in my heart that I had escaped from something much worse than I would now have to face. Also, I knew deep down that even if things did not turn out as well as I hoped – if given the chance again, I would do exactly the same. Moreover, I had an intuitive feeling that my destiny was somehow linked to the gentleman in whose car-boot I was now locked and that he would prove to become my saviour."

"I was locked in the boot all night. As the hours stretched by I began to think of reasons why I could be trapped for a long time; for example, the gentleman may not use the car regularly, or he may be going on holiday, even on a world cruise and would be away for months. I could be just a skeleton when he returned. I know that crocodiles can survive for a long time without food but I was brought up on regular small meals and thought of myself as a delicate creature with a discerning palate, unused to the harsh ways of life in the wild, or to the rough ways of the circus for that matter, and I couldn't see myself surviving for months in a car-boot. I was conjuring up other possibly gruesome scenarios and I must have fallen asleep. Fortunately, probably because I was so hungry, instead of having nightmares about some horrible fate, I dreamed about food. In my dream, Mercedes had prepared a feast for me. I started with a light soufflé tart with truffles and fresh asparagus, followed by a cheese and tomato pizza with black olives, artichokes and wild rocket, topped with a fresh egg in the centre. Then to finish, she had served me pears poached in red wine with great helpings of ice cream drizzled with a hot dark chocolate sauce. I was just about to tuck into this mouth-watering pudding when I

Chapter Two — The Second Coming

awoke with a start – someone had just come into the garage. Footsteps were approaching the car. The boot-lid swung up suddenly and a large wicker basket landed on my head. It was quickly retrieved and moved to one side. The distinguished looking man who had unwittingly rescued me from the circus stared incredulously down at me – then without uttering a word jumped backwards and about three feet into the air, bumped his head on the low ceiling and landed in an untidy heap on the floor.

I peered nervously out of the back of the car – I was looking down on him and he was looking up at me with a dazed expression on his face. Before he could utter a word I mustered all my resources and addressed him in my very best, smoothest voice, 'I am so sorry if I startled you, please don't be afraid. I know I look like a crocodile, actually I am a crocodile, but I am a very intelligent crocodile and quite harmless – and if it makes you feel safer, I am also a vegetarian, so you really have absolutely nothing to fear.' The man got surprisingly quickly to his feet and moved backwards towards the door. 'Please let me explain about myself,' I continued, 'If you remember, you were sitting in the front row at the circus and I was the crocodile riding the bicycle, the one who headed the football to you. You appeared to take quite an interest in me and I was very struck by your presence. The circus folk kidnapped me and treated me cruelly – they forced me to perform in the circus ring. I saw you get into your car, which was parked near my cage. Luck gave me an opportunity and I jumped into the boot of your car as you started to drive away. At this moment I have only two small favours to ask of you. Firstly, I have been locked in the boot of your car all night and have had nothing to eat or drink for more than a day, could I please have some small morsel to eat and a glass of water? Secondly, I am bursting to go to the toilet, is there one close by?'

The gentleman who had momentarily looked a little less distinguished than when I had first observed him, almost instantly regained his composure. He coughed, cleared his throat and said in a soft cultured voice, 'I did not think that in my lifetime I would experience first hand anything as incredible as what I believe I am just witnessing. When I saw you in the circus ring I thought at first that you were a man or woman cleverly disguised as a crocodile, but as I watched you very carefully I pretty much made up my mind that you were a real crocodile. I was astonished at your tricks ... but tell me, why did you not speak as well?' Before I could answer, he said, 'But please, I can see that you are in some discomfort, let me show you to the bathroom – if you will kindly follow me ... we will discuss your situation over breakfast – I will do anything to help you'."

Then Crocodile sighed deeply and said, "Thus began my new life with Professor Julius Septimus Merryweather."

Kate and I were mesmerised, not only by Crocodile's extraordinary story, but also by the passionate way that he had told it to us. It was as if we had shared his experiences first-hand. However, Crocodile now looked a little drained and it was clear to see that recounting the detail of what must have been for him an extremely distressing period in his life, had taken a lot out of him. I remembered the lasagne and carrot cake. I placed the picnic basket in front of him and lifted the lid. Just like the Professor in the garage, Crocodile made a sudden dramatic recovery and with a squeak of delight he put his long snout close up to the steaming lasagne, his nostrils flaring to take in the aroma. He raised his head still sniffing the air and with an expression close to ecstasy on his face said, "I haven't seen food like this for ages, which is one of the reasons why I need your help, my stocks of food and many other essential items are getting very depleted."

I then realised that we had not brought any cutlery with us because we had assumed that he would take the food away with him. The three of us discussed the dilemma and unanimously agreed that he should take it home with him, wherever that might be, and we would meet him again next day when he could continue his story.

Crocodile turned, reached into his boat and pulled out two large leather satchels. "These are my trusty saddlebags," he said, "I usually carry them with me to pick things up that may be useful, they are insulated and waterproof and very tough. They are getting a bit dog-eared now but they have served me very well. The Professor had them specially made and gave them to me one Christmas." He held them up proudly so that we could read the initials W.H.C. stylishly embossed on the front of both of them. "I was going to ask you home with me this evening but my little boat is too small to take us all and I did notice that your boat is not here at the moment."

I explained that our boat was away at the repair yard but it was to be returned to us at midday tomorrow.

"Excellent," said Crocodile, "in that case, if you sail across to my island as soon as you get it back I will make us all lunch and continue my story in the afternoon, unless you have a prior engagement."

We told him that we were free and would be delighted to come.

"Do you have a horn by any chance?" he then asked.

"I don't think I do," I replied, slightly confused by the question.

"No matter you can have one of mine." He peered into his saddlebags, stuck in his hand and produced, like pulling a rabbit out of a hat, an ancient brass carriage horn, that looked like a small trumpet or bugle, but with a large rubber bulb instead of a mouthpiece. He tooted the horn three times and said, "When you get to the island just give three toots on the horn like that and I will know that you have arrived. It saves me having to keep an eye out for you, so if you are late it doesn't matter."

Crocodile put the dish of lasagne and the carrot cake carefully into one of his saddlebags and got back into his boat. "Thank you so very much for making supper for me," he said, "I am really looking forward to enjoying a hearty meal, and it looks and smells delicious."

He made ready to leave and said once more, "Thank you again for coming tonight and for listening so patiently to my story. I look forward to your visit to my island and to my home tomorrow. Don't forget, just three toots on the horn, I shall be waiting."

"Excuse me," I said, "but you haven't told us where your island is!"

"How silly of me, I thought you knew, or may have guessed by now – it is the island on the other side of the lake, directly opposite your house – the one over there." He pointed with his crook. "If you remember, I did say that we were neighbours." He raised his crook once more. "Until around midday tomorrow then." He took up his oars and glided smoothly across the lake in a straight line towards what we will surely now call, *Crocodile's Island.*

As we watched him cross the lake, I said finally to Kate, "He appears to be rowing much faster than when he came. I bet he can't wait to get back to tuck into your lasagne!"

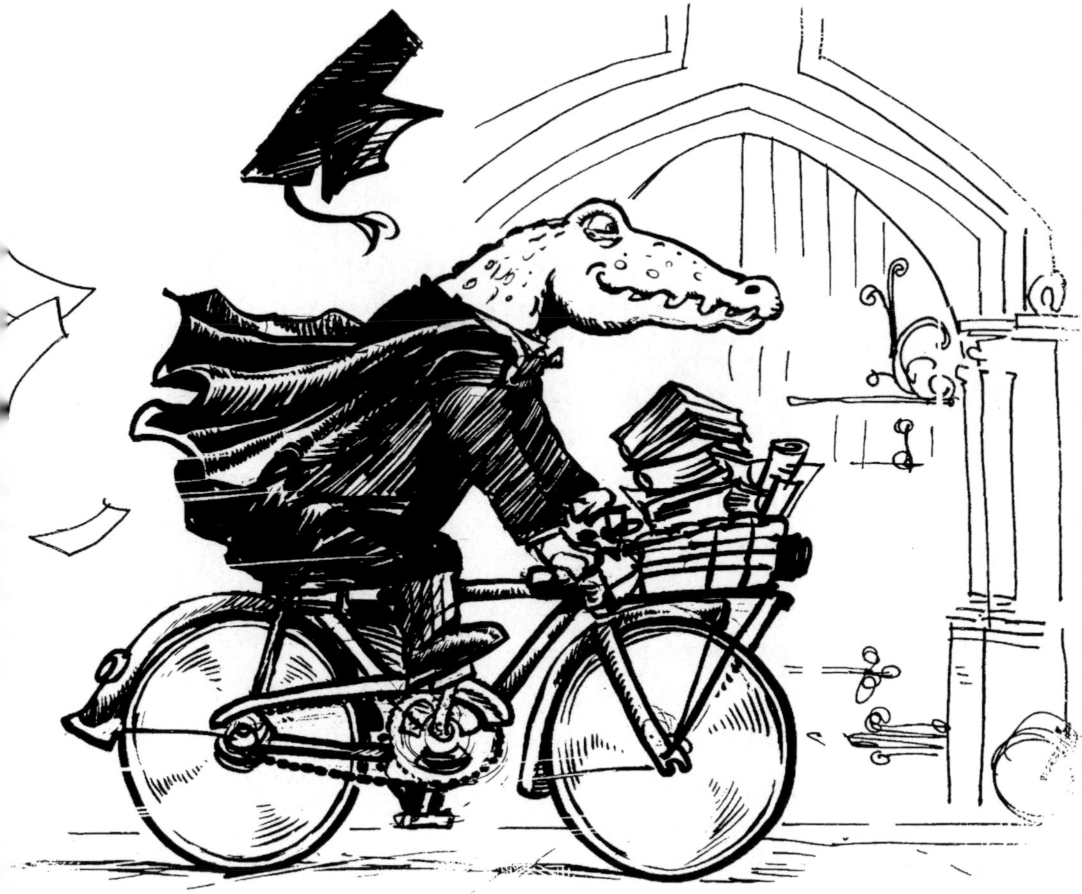

Chapter Three
Crocodile's Island

Early the following morning I telephoned the boat-yard to ask if we could have our boat back before midday. We were informed that work was finished and they would return it around 11:45 AM. We said that we would meet them on the shore, so that we could set sail immediately.

At 11:45AM, right on time, the dinghy arrived, towed behind a motorboat. We jumped onboard, said our thanks to the boatman and set off across the lake. It was a fine crisp morning with a brisk westerly breeze and we expected to arrive just after midday. As we neared the island I gave three toots on the horn, which we had fortunately remembered to bring with us, and waited. There was no sign of Crocodile or his boat so I decided to sail around the island to see if there was an obvious place to land. Most of the rock surrounding the island was sheer into the water but there were some places where we thought we might scramble ashore if we could find a way to secure the boat. I was about to blow the horn again when we saw Crocodile waving and walking in our direction. As he got closer we could see that he now had on a long blue and white striped apron with a t-shirt and checked cotton trousers. On his head he wore a rather unusual cap set at a jaunty angle. He had made no attempt, on this occasion, to conceal his long snout. He held his crook in his left hand and a coil of rope hung over his right shoulder.

I turned the boat towards where he was now standing at a low point in the island's natural rock ramparts. He looped the rope around a tree, tied it, and threw the free ends to us. We secured the boat in two places so that it was cushioned against the wall of rock and then climbed ashore with a helping hand from Crocodile.

With a broad grin and a courteous bow he said, "Welcome to my island. I am pleased that you were able to get here in time for lunch – I have prepared a simple meal which I hope you will enjoy but you must understand that I have now almost entirely run out of everything but the most basic food, so I am very limited as to what I can make. That is one of the reasons why I have asked for your help. If you will kindly follow me..." He indicated the direction with his crook and we walked behind him across his beautiful island.

Our destination appeared to be just a high outcrop of rock. As we made our way around it we came to a door-sized opening, through which we were ushered into a small lobby.

"I would just like to inform you and to reassure you, but I will have to close this entrance before we have lunch." He pointed to a large iron wheel, like a giant steering wheel, set in the wall. "I close it with this wheel. This was the most difficult engineering project that the Professor undertook here, but it was also the most important."

"My security and my freedom depended upon his making it impossible to find my home, even by a team of people searching the island, and upon his making it completely reliable in operation over a very long period of time, because there is no way that I would be able to repair it if the gear mechanism that moves the solid rock door were ever to fail. The Professor assured me that, short of major earthquake damage, it will last for centuries. I am telling you this because until you have seen downstairs and are at ease, you may be uncomfortable or feel claustrophobic if I seal us in now. Don't worry we can't be trapped in here, because, you may be relieved to know, that there are two other means of escape."

I saw Kate give me a worried sideways glance – I think the expressions, *claustrophobic*, *trapped*, and *sealed in*, had something to do with it.

Crocodile took an oil-lamp from an alcove in the wall, lit it with a gas lighter that he produced from his pocket, and led us down a long flight of stone steps that had been hewn out of the rock. It got progressively darker as we descended and the daylight behind us faded. I began to think of a film that I had seen many years ago – it was set in ancient Egypt and when the Pharaoh died and was sealed in his pyramid, members of his family and servants, including the villain of the piece, were entombed with him. I felt a little less apprehensive as we neared the bottom and it got progressively lighter. We emerged into a large cavern, which although not entirely circular in shape must have been at least a hundred feet in diameter and probably thirty feet high. An enormous chandelier hung from the apex of the domed ceiling and candles and oil lamps were placed strategically throughout the vast space; many were reflected in mirrors and polished surfaces to enhance the light. As our eyes grew more accustomed to the illumination, we began to identify specific pieces of furniture and other chattels in different parts of the cave. Much of the interior was permeated with a warm and comforting glow.

As if he had read our thoughts Crocodile then said: "I would again like to reassure you of your safety, that there are two other ways out of this cave. One is through a wide tunnel that has been filled in at the far end, making it impossible to find from the outside but fairly easy to dig out with a shovel from the inside, even though it would take a good half-hour. The Professor thought that it was important to install this additional means of escape, but I suspect that it was more for his peace of mind than for mine, because I have a very easy way out, underwater into the lake. I use it frequently when I go ashore without using the boat, but even more often, simply to swim freely in Windermere. This was the one thing I have missed all my life, because that is my natural habitat and although I am now just as comfortable on dry land, something deep inside me always draws me to water."

"The underwater tunnel was how I discovered the cave in the first place – several years ago when I was on holiday in the Lake District with the Professor. We always rented a house just up the lake and on one of my early morning swims I decided to take a closer look at this island. I had swum round the island many times before but I had never taken a really close look, and even when I did find the entrance to the cave it was only by sheer luck."

"A shaft of morning sunlight flashed on a shiny silver object lying on the bed of the lake by the island. I dived down to investigate and was surprised to find that it was an ornate silver goblet, albeit rather tarnished. Thinking that I might just have discovered the Holy Grail I placed it on a nearby rock to take a closer look. Sadly, I felt sure that it wasn't the Holy Grail because there were embossed naked nymphs cavorting around the rim. As I went to pick it up again with a view to taking it back to the Professor for his opinion, I knocked it over and it fell behind the rock that I had placed it on. With some considerable effort I managed to move the rock forward. That was when I discovered the entrance to the cave. I picked up the goblet, and then swam into the cave. It was almost pitch black, the only glimmer of light coming from the hole through the rock where my telescope now goes, but I knew that it was some sort of large cavern because I shouted out 'Is there anybody there?' and nearly jumped out of my skin when my voice echoed straight back at me. I swam out of the cave and back to the Professor to show him the goblet and to inform him about my other discovery. I will tell you the rest of the story after lunch."

"I have to tell you that I can't swim," said Kate anxiously, "just in case you think that you might ever have to take us out of the cave that way."

Crocodile smiled and said apologetically, "Please rest assured that there is not the remotest possibility that you will ever have to use that exit and even if you wanted to try it just for fun, I could take you above the surface with me in less than twenty seconds. I brought the Professor in that way, because at the time there was no other way in, and he couldn't swim either. It springs to mind that I have never seen him looking as nervous as he did when I suggested that he should ride on my back into the cave – not even when he discovered me in the boot of his car after my escape from the circus. He eventually agreed because it was the only means of entry known to us and by then he had hatched a plan for the cave and had to get inside somehow to make an inspection, but he insisted first on purchasing the very best wet-suit and sub-aqua equipment as well as having professional coaching in the pool at his London club. I still have his diving gear packed up in my storeroom," he chuckled, "if ever you want to have a go."

"Please don't worry," he said looking at Kate, "I am simply trying to prove to you that you are absolutely safe in here – probably a lot safer than in your own house. The Professor told me that it would take an earthquake, at the top end of the Richter Scale, to stand any chance of jamming the door mechanism and your house would probably fall down in such conditions. I have to close the rock door just in case somebody should visit the island and discover the entrance. This is highly unlikely at this time of year but there are occasionally a few visitors to the island in spring and summer – sometimes for picnics but usually only to take a quick look. Rarely does anyone come here in winter, but I simply cannot run the risk of the entrance being discovered – so if I have your permission I will go and close it now – would you like to come with me?"

"I would rather stay down here," said Kate, "but Matt, you go with Crocodile and see how the door operates, I think I would rather not be there when it closes."

Crocodile and I went back up the steps. He took me outside and up to the highest point where there was a clear view over the whole island, the surrounding lake and the shoreline on both sides. Looking east I could clearly see our house in the distance but it was too far away to observe any detail or to see people with the naked eye. There was not a soul in sight near the island, either on the near shore or in a boat on the water.

We went back down to the entrance and as Crocodile began to turn, then to spin the big iron wheel, a huge section of rock started to move very slowly and smoothly, but not completely silently, there being a low grating sound coming from beneath the door as it travelled on its track and slowly covered the entrance to the cave. Like a total eclipse of the sun, it blotted out the daylight completely. "There is also a big lever outside, built into an oak tree near the entrance and camouflaged by a holly bush. Using that lever you can open the door from the outside of the cave, but only wide enough for a large person to squeeze through…..so I hardly ever use it," explained Crocodile.

"Once inside you can then use the big wheel to fully open the door and it is much easier with the wheel than using the ratchet mechanism operated by the lever. It is also easier for me to swim in and out of the cave from the lake, than to use the door."

Crocodile stood back and suggested that I open and shut the door again to see how easy it was, how little pressure was required to move the huge slab of rock. I really was surprised at just what little effort was needed. Crocodile explained that it was a very highly geared mechanism – it was slow but sure, and you had to spin the wheel many times to move the door a few inches. It took about a minute to open and a minute to close. I had to admit that it was an impressive piece of engineering.

Suitably relieved that we were not about to be entombed in Crocodile's cave I returned down the steps to give Kate the good news. As I approached her I saw that she already appeared much more relaxed – she was smiling and holding up what appeared to be a photograph frame.

"Come and look at this," she whispered excitedly, beckoning me to come closer.

She pointed to an amusing caricature drawing of a Crocodile in a cap and gown on a bicycle. Next to it was a photograph of a very distinguished looking man dressed in a long black gown with an ermine collar and wearing a mortarboard on his head. The big shock was that standing next to him was none other than, Crocodile, attired in similar fashion. He was being presented with a scroll at what appeared to be a university degree ceremony.

Crocodile approached us, beaming with pride and said, "Yes, that is the Professor presenting me with my degree at a private ceremony. I was awarded an Honorary Masters Degree from Oxford University, under the tuition and at the special request of the Professor. I can legitimately call myself William Hartley Crocodile, M.A. (Oxon.). However, my achievement and this honour was never made public because the Professor always believed that if my existence ever leaked out it would be the end of the life that I now enjoyed and my freedom would be gone forever. There was a very high risk that I would be kidnapped and exploited, or worse, and he felt that there was no way that I could be properly protected if the news ever got out, and he did everything in his power to ensure that this did not happen. That is why I am with you here in this cave today and why I am asking for your help. Before I explain further, let me show you around my home and then I will finish preparing the lunch while you freshen up. Unfortunately, I am still waiting for Napoleon to return with the eggs – he gets them for me from the hens at the farm just over the hill on the mainland – he carries them in a leather pouch that I made specially for him. Napoleon, incidentally, is a Raven who lives with me here in the cave. I have another friend called Sherwood and he is a large Tawny Owl. They both help guard my island and my cave by letting me know, day and night, if there are strangers about.

Napoleon and Sherwood are both very intelligent birds. I learned to communicate well with birds when I was with Mercedes at the zoo, but although it isn't difficult to get them to carry out certain not too complicated tasks for me, I have as yet been unable to teach Sherwood a single comprehensible word. Napoleon on the other hand is now able to say a few simple words and phrases in a very croaky voice. I have only to show Napoleon an egg, or something egg-shaped, or even draw an egg on a piece of paper, and he will go and bring back all he can carry. Now he really understands the word egg, he can say egg as well as being able to count up to ten ... most times he tries. As well as letting me know if there are strangers on the island, they have also taken it upon themselves to warn the hens if there are predators around, and in return for this service I get all the eggs I need. You may not remember but you will have seen Napoleon and Sherwood many times at your house."

Kate asked, "Do you think that Sherwood is the owl that often sits on our chimney stack on moonlit nights, the one who we can see through the bedroom window. The one who seems to able to turn his head full-circle in order to look at us?"

"I'll bet it is," I replied, "and I am sure that Napoleon must be the huge glossy black bird that comes to feed with the ducks and the other birds under the holly tree. I often wondered why they were not scared of such a fearsome looking creature. If you remember, we used to watch him feed that injured pheasant, the one we called *Billy Whizz*. You thought I was mad when I bought a dog basket for him to rest in until he got better – but it did the trick and he was in it every day until his leg had mended. The Raven came and brought him tit-bits to eat and scared off the other creatures that threatened him if they got too close.

At this point in our reminiscences Crocodile started to get very excited and said in a rather high-pitched voice, whilst at the same time gesticulating vigorously, "This is wonderful ... you are doing all the explaining for me ... these are exactly the reasons why I chose you to help me and to be my friends. I had absolute proof that you were very kind to birds and other creatures and I knew instinctively that I could put my trust in you. The Professor always assured me that, if I were patient, one day I would find somebody that I could trust. However, the professor was a scientist and always advocated rigorous use of the scientific method, of observation and proof. 'Never let your heart rule your head,' he used to say – but confusingly, he also said: 'In the absence of absolute proof let your heart decide.' In your case, I was certain that I was making the right choice because I had both."

Crocodile then pointed to a very long telescope standing on a tripod. He walked over to the instrument and pushed its long body into a hole in the wall. He peeped into the eyepiece and turned it into focus. He stood back and said, "Come and take a look."

"You look first," said Kate.

I put my eye close to the eyepiece and said in astonishment, "I can see our house and terrace clearly, as if I were standing in the garden."

"Once more I must apologise," said Crocodile, "for being forced to spy on you, but it was the only way I could be sure that I could trust you. Fate also intervened because although I have studied many people on both sides of the lake through my telescope, by taking it outside onto the top of the hill – there is only one natural fissure that goes right through the rock wall of my cave that is large enough to poke the telescope into – you can't move it from side to side; it points only one way, and that is directly at your house."

"But how did you find out our names?" I asked.

"That was easy," he replied, "Napoleon, bless him, is a bit of a scavenger and he brings me all sorts of things that he thinks I might find useful. He brought me several envelopes and letters from your disposal box. I know it sounds like an awful invasion of privacy, admitting to reading your private correspondence and spying on you in this way but I had to get the information somehow so that I could be absolutely sure that I was choosing the right friends to help me. If I made a mistake I would end up back in the circus ... or worse."

"We quite understand," I said, as reassuringly as I could. "We are very pleased that you did find us and realise that for your own safety you had to check us out thoroughly before you came to see us. We are delighted to have you as our friend. We always keep our promises and we promise to do everything we can to help you in the future."

I then stood back and let Kate have a look through the telescope. Kate peeped into the eyepiece. "Goodness gracious," she gasped, "I can see right into our sitting-room."

"Don't be embarrassed," chuckled Crocodile, "I haven't seen you without your clothes on!"

I could tell by the expression on Kate's face that she was trying to remember if in fact she had ever walked through that room with nothing on. "She'll think twice about it next time!" I mused.

"I'll have to remove the telescope now," said Crocodile, "because Napoleon can't get in if it is blocking the hole. When the front door is closed the only way in and out of the cave for Napoleon and Sherwood is through that fissure in the rock. If he doesn't return with our eggs soon I'll have to re-think part of the lunch menu. While we are waiting let me show you round my home." He beckoned us to follow him.

Our eyes were now completely accustomed to the light and we could see most things very clearly. We stopped first in front of an ingle-nook fireplace with two huge piled-up baskets of logs on either side of its stone hearth. In the centre was a very large, black wood-burning stove. Crocodile swung the doors open so that we could feel the heat and see the logs glowing bright orange and yellow inside. "It's amazing how slowly the logs burn in there," he said." Just a few logs will burn all day and all night. The temperature in the cave is comfortable for me most of the time without a fire, but I got so used to having fires when I lived with the Professor in London that I do light it when I just want to feel cosy, or when it is very cold. I suspect that the Professor installed the stove here for his own comfort as much as mine – but I am really glad that he did. I cut and collect all the logs myself in the woods on the mainland. If ever I find myself with nothing to do, I go out and cut a few logs – I find it very therapeutic and it is good exercise. Cutting logs and swimming in the lake gives me all the exercise I need. I swim in Windermere every day and usually several times a day.

Although I enjoyed living in the big house in London I now realise that I wasn't as free as I am here. I had the use of a small gymnasium and a pool in the London house but that is nothing when compared to swimming in the early morning as the sun rises over the lake, or in the evening as the sun goes down behind the mountains and I have the lake all to myself, the whole of Windermere to swim freely in. I never go in disguise when I swim in the lake – I always stay well clear of boats or swim just beneath the surface so that there is little chance of any body spotting me, and if they did happen to see me, they would not believe that I was a crocodile. I would just pretend that I was an old tree trunk and vanish underwater. When I go into the woods to cut logs though, that is a different proposition. I always go in disguise with my snout well covered."

"However, I rarely see anyone in those woods; they are too far off the beaten track and too inaccessible for most people, so I feel quite safe. On the few occasions that I have seen or heard people coming in my direction I have just kept out of their way. I have been tempted to wave and shout, 'Hello!' but, as yet, I haven't taken the chance. I learned my lesson long ago when I was showing off on my bicycle at the zoo. The irony is – that if I had not done that, I would not have been educated by the Professor and enjoyed all those privileges – and I would not be here living in my own home in the most beautiful place on earth, nor for that matter would I have met you. The Professor taught me that sometimes you have to take risks, but, unless you have no choice at all, they should be calculated risks. If possible you should do your homework carefully before taking a chance. Ultimately, life is much about hazard and sometimes, as in a game of dice, you are forced to throw and hope for the best."

Crocodile hesitated for a moment and then said, "I do apologise. I am philosophising again. Please let us continue with our tour."

In front of the fireplace were two large, comfortable looking sofas, an armchair and a coffee-table, on which was a pile of magazines and a tray of coffee cups, saucers and plates, all ready and waiting for us. To the left of the fireplace, suspended on hooks, screwed into a low part of the ceiling, was a hammock woven from hemp and filled with an assortment of cushions in many different colours, shapes and sizes. On the other side of the hammock stood an antique mahogany writing desk with a green leather top, in front of which was a bow-shaped swivel chair with a matching green leather seat. Kate could not help pointing out that the desk was a lot tidier than mine at home.

We then came upon Crocodile's bedroom which consisted of a large double bed covered with a beautiful brightly coloured patchwork quilt, a kidney-shaped dressing table and stool, and two matching French style armoire wardrobes. There was also an elegant, elaborately decorated screen at the far end of the bedroom that acted as a wall to separate the bedroom from the back of the cave. As we made our way into this dimly lit space we came upon a gothic style, oak door with a heavy iron latch. Crocodile said that the bathroom and toilet were through this door and that we should take a look while he was preparing the lunch. On the other side of the steps, we now observed another quite large opening in the rock wall – we must have passed it on the way down without noticing it in the dim light.

"All my storerooms are in there," he said, "also my laundry room, my workshop, the tunnel into the lake and the other escape tunnel onto the island. You may have gathered by now that I don't have an electricity supply so everything is mechanical. I have a mechanically operated lathe and a bench drill, both with foot-pedals, set on rockers, that operate just like my old sewing machine. A bicycle without a rear wheel powers my washing machine. You'll probably split your sides with laughter when you see it, but, like all the Professor's contraptions, it works remarkably well."

At that moment Napoleon hopped into the cave through the opening by the telescope, and with a couple of flaps of his huge wings landed at the back of the kitchen on a tall carved wooden stand, similar to a lectern but with a flat top. Hanging round his neck, on a drawstring, was a bulging leather pouch, which hopefully would contain the eggs for our lunch. He must have measured at least two and a half feet from the point of his great beak to the tip of his magnificent tail feathers. I surmised that, if confronted, most hawks would keep Napoleon at a very safe distance.

Crocodile walked over to Napoleon and removed the bag from round his neck, while at the same time smoothing a few of his ruffled feathers. He loosened the drawstring, put his hand inside the bag and lifted out six large white eggs, all in perfect condition.

"You've done very well this time," he said to Napoleon, "no breakages – but why did it take you so long? You are usually back in ten or fifteen minutes."

The big bird shifted from one foot to the other a couple of times and said a few words to Crocodile in a hoarse croaky voice – they were completely undecipherable to us and even Crocodile seemed not to fully understand what Napoleon was trying to explain.

"I can't make out exactly what happened, but I think the farmer was working near the hen coop and so Napoleon had to keep a low profile until the coast was clear," interpreted Crocodile, "but no matter – we have our eggs for lunch. Now, say *hello* to our guests, Kate and Matthew."

"Allo Kate, allo Matt," croaked Napoleon.

"I'll let you into a secret," said Crocodile with a big grin, "Napoleon only learned your names this morning ... I tried to get him to say Matthew, but it sounded like *Mattoo*, so we decided to go for Kate and Matt."

I told Napoleon that we had seen him many times in our garden and thanked him for looking after Billy Whizz and helping him to get better.

"Tankoo Kate, tankoo Matt," croaked Napoleon, clearly enjoying all the attention.

Crocodile then gave him a bowl of cereals, nuts, and raisins. He tucked into them instantly and with considerable relish. "He'll eat almost anything," said Crocodile, "He doesn't have my problem ... a love of good food and a discerning palate."

While we were watching Napoleon our eyes also wandered around the kitchen. The centrepiece was a handsome, probably Victorian, black cast iron cooking range. There was a big oak sideboard to the left, next to which were two deep Belfast sinks, with bleached wooden draining-boards on each side. There were small cupboards underneath the sinks and a massive floor to ceiling cupboard to the right. Leaning against the corner of this giant cupboard was a very tall stepladder, without which it would have been impossible to reach the top shelves.

A big rectangular scrubbed pine table stood some way in front of the sideboard. It would have seated a dozen people, but only three chairs were set ... one in the centre with its back to the sideboard, and two directly opposite, presumably for Kate and myself.

Slightly in front of, and high over the cooking range, hung a gigantic wooden clothes rack which, via a system of pulleys, could be raised and lowered on a rope attached to a spoked wheel with a handle. A number of pans, utensils and bunches of dried herbs hung from both ends of the rack but there was nothing in the centre except for a few tea towels. There was no doubt that this was where Crocodile would dry and air his clothes and bedding.

As if reading our thoughts Crocodile said, gesturing to the clothes rack and then to the cast iron cooking range, "I couldn't have managed half so well without this range. It has ovens on both sides, a back-boiler for heating the water, and an iron top plate with openings for pans and griddles. It is also an extremely efficient way to dry and air all my clothing and bedding. It would be even more efficient if I had a supply of coal to burn because it would run at higher temperatures. Fortunately, I have an unlimited supply of logs ... and at least they are cleaner, and the ash is easy to dispose of."

"Now," Crocodile continued, "it will take me about fifteen minutes to complete my preparations for lunch, so this is a good opportunity for you to go and freshen up.

There are clean towels and everything else you may require in the bathroom through the door at the back of the cave."

Crocodile's bathroom was an amazing place. As well as a traditional white enamelled, cast iron, claw-foot bath, there was a large, approximately oval shaped, plunge pool, which had either been cut into the rock or had been a naturally occurring feature in the rock, or perhaps a combination of both. In the middle of the floor was a large Persian carpet in exquisite colours, mainly cream, green, blue, dark red and black. The borders were decorated with flowers, leaves and tendrils, and the central field depicted strange figures and exotic and mythical animal designs.

Along the entire length of one wall was a deep rock shelf, which, like the plunge pool, may have been a natural feature, or may have been fashioned or modified to create the long flat surface, now topped in green Langdale slate, into which had been set two white ceramic wash-basins. The entire wall at the back was mirrored glass and covered with clear glass shelves, apart from the wall space directly behind the washbasins. On the shelves were dozens, maybe hundreds, of bottles of perfumes, lotions and powders, and boxes of toiletries, most of them fancy and obviously expensive.

There were high piles of neatly folded, soft, Turkish cotton, hand and bath towels stacked on deep shelves, with others arranged on three free-standing wooden Victorian towel-rails.

We found the toilet in a separate room through a door screened by a large mahogany cheval mirror. It had an old-fashioned cistern positioned about ten feet above the toilet and was operated by a long heavy metal chain with a polished steel riding stirrup handle. It functioned most efficiently, the only drawback, as I was soon to discover, was that if you pulled the handle too vigorously you were treated to a shower as well from water cascading over the top of the cistern.

Another wall had been almost covered with a very large antique pine-framed mirror. In front of which stood a polished green slate dressing table and on which was laid out in perfect formation, a curious assortment of personal grooming implements and accessories, brushes, combs, scissors, tweezers, hand-mirrors and numerous accoutrements designed for manicure and pedicure.

Whilst sniffing at the contents of some of the wonderful variety of receptacles, tantalizingly laid out for inspection, Kate laughed and said, "Crocodile certainly knows how to pamper himself in some style ... I wonder how much time he spends in here sprucing himself up."

In what seemed a very short space of time, the sound of a gong echoed through the cave. "I think that may be Crocodile summoning us to lunch," suggested Kate.

We arrived in the kitchen to find him in the process of opening a bottle of wine. "Sancerre!" he announced as he poured a small quantity into three wine glasses, waiting on a silver salver. He handed a glass to Kate and one to me and took the other for himself. Holding the glass by its base he swirled the wine around the bowl. He then held it up to the light ... "straw coloured with hints of green," he pronounced. He swirled it some more, poked his snout into the top of the glass and announced, "Very distinctive ... gooseberry fruit with a slight aroma of blackcurrant leaves and traces of flintiness." He then poured a quantity of the nectar into his large mouth, made a sort of soft sucking sound, followed by a gentle gurgle, licked his lips with his big tongue, and concluded, "Clean, sharp and tangy, almost lemony, I think I detect a hint of asparagus in there ... what do you think?"

Quite taken aback by the sophistication of Crocodile's palate and not wanting to appear as Philistines, Kate and I went through a similar ritual, following which we apologised for not quite having his depth of knowledge, sensitivity of taste, or nuance of nasal perception, but nevertheless judging unanimously with him, that it was indeed an elegant, finely balanced, stylish wine."

With a look of great satisfaction, Crocodile replaced our glasses on the salver and carrying it deftly on one hand above his head, he escorted us to a large table, laid out beautifully with china crockery, silver cutlery, crystal glasses and linen napkins.

"It is I who must apologise," he said with a forlorn expression, "for not having the ingredients to do full justice to our first meal together. Most of my food-stocks, apart from milk, eggs and winter vegetables, are dried or preserved." He gently poured the Sancerre into the crystal glasses at our respective place settings and apologised once more, this time for the absence of sparkling mineral water but then said that happily it was of no great consequence as the fresh local water was excellent, and much better tasting than the water he was used to in London.

"The bread rolls should just be ready," he said, lifting his snout and sniffing in the direction of the stove, "if you'll kindly excuse me for a few seconds I'll go and get them out of the oven."

He returned in an instant carrying a tray-full of freshly baked rolls, which he slid gently into a waiting breadbasket.

"Please help yourselves while I attend to the first course – but be very careful – they are very hot. The butter is in the dish with the domed silver lid," he said lifting it. "It's home-made and slightly salty; I do hope that it is to your taste." Again, he returned in a jiffy, this time carrying a steaming tureen of soup and a big ladle, which he placed on a wooden trencher in the middle of the table. "Winter vegetable!" he said, "I always keep a vegetable stock-pot from which I can extract clear broth or stock for cooking, as and when I need it. I made this soup from carrots, potatoes, parsnips, turnips, swede, and onions, to which I have added butter, a little olive oil, ginger, dill, and cream."

He ladled three liberal helpings into three large bowls. "Would you like some black pepper and some parmesan?" he asked, brandishing a two-foot tall peppermill, the kind they have in Italian restaurants.

Kate said she would try some of the soup on its own first. I said that I would have a little black pepper, mainly to watch Crocodile use the big peppermill. I was not disappointed; he handled it in the style of the best Italian waiters ... finishing with an ostentatious flourish.

Kate expressed our joint appreciation and said that, along with the hot rolls and butter. It was a perfect dish for a cold winter's day.

After we'd all had a second helping, this time, on Crocodile's insistence, with a little black pepper and Parmesan, he cleared the dishes and brought in the main course.

"Vegetarian shepherd's pie with a goats cheese mash!" he announced enthusiastically. "I made the cheese myself, with milk from the goats at the farm."

The mash was a fine creamy puree. He told us that the pie contained black-eyed beans, split-peas, green lentils, carrots, onions, celeriac and spices – but unfortunately he had no fresh tomatoes, so he had added tinned tomatoes – he still had a few tins left in his store.

The pie and mash were very delicious and we were about to be talked into second helpings when, fortunately, we learned that was a selection of homemade cheeses and a pudding still to come.

His cheeses and biscuits were displayed on the big oak sideboard. He invited us to take a plate and help ourselves and, if we could manage it, to try a little of each cheese, because he had made them all himself and he would very much value our opinion.

There were three types of goat cheese, and three others. The goats' cheeses included a log with a dark brown rind, very soft in the centre and less so towards the crusty rind; a mellow one, with blue veins running through it, and one that was light, soft and creamy. Of the remaining three cheeses, the first was quite hard like Cheddar, the second was crumbly, similar to crumbly Lancashire, and the third was akin to a soft, rich Camembert, which was quite smelly, or put more delicately, it had a piquant aroma. We both tried a small portion of each of them on a selection of Crocodile's home-made biscuits – a motley assortment of shapes, colours, flavours, and textures, and all quite excellent.

The Sancerre had long since gone and he suggested another bottle before the pudding wine. Simultaneously we raised our hands and declined the offer. "If we are having a pudding wine, the one bottle of Sancerre, excellent as it was, will be quite sufficient. We don't want to end up being drunk in charge of a boat, and we hope to get back across the lake without falling overboard," I explained apologetically.

"I'll get the pudding wine then! It's Muscat de Beaumes-de-Venise," he continued. A few seconds later he added, "I learned from the Professor that this wine is at its best when it is quite young, contrary to what many people think, because it does have a long life in the bottle, but when it is fairly young, the sweet grapey perfume is at its best and most fragrant. I had a wee sip a few minutes ago and it is right up to expectations ... rose scented ... full of flavour ... orange peel, apples and honey ... perfect!"

"The pudding itself is what I needed the eggs for – a chocolate rum soufflé with a warm dark chocolate sauce," he whispered in a soft velvety voice. His description alone was sufficient to make our mouths water.

As he placed the three ramekin dishes and a big jug of chocolate sauce in front of us, Kate said, "Go on, tell us how you made it."

"Well," he replied, with a cheeky grin, "I had first better give you a health warning. This is dangerous stuff. If you suffer from a heart problem it could act as a *coup de grâce* and finish you off." He smiled again and continued with the description, "The chocolate sauce is just fine quality chocolate, containing 70% cocoa butter and double cream melted together in a bowl. The soufflé itself is chocolate, rum, cream and egg yolks. I whisk the separated whites until stiff and fold them gradually into the chocolate mixture. I then pour it all into the ramekins which I have coated with butter and sugar ... that's about it, apart from popping them into the oven."

Crocodile asked us to help ourselves to the chocolate sauce so that, as he put it, "We would share part of the risk if things went wrong."

"I have to agree – it's not for the faint-hearted," said Kate, tucking in. "But ooh! It's utterly gorgeous, and with this orange pudding wine to complement it ... it's a dream!"

"I thought you were going to say, *it's to die for*," replied Crocodile with a twinkle in his eye. "That would really be tempting providence."

"Well we think you deserve three Michelin Stars," I said, "I only hope that they can be awarded posthumously!"

Crocodile, for a moment seemed overcome by the praise that was being heaped upon him, and we detected a watery look in his eyes as he beamed down at us. He said that the Professor had always impressed upon him that one if the greatest pleasures in life, arguably, the greatest, was to enjoy a good meal with your friends and to relax in their company with a bottle or two of fine wine.

Kate and I raised our glasses. "We'll drink to that," we said together.

The three of us then raised our glasses once more as we drank a toast to the Professor.

Crocodile then ushered us to the big sofas in front of the fire. "I'll just get the coffee," he said, "please help yourselves to a chocolate or some Turkish delight."

"Even the chocolates look home-made," said Kate, with a hovering hand. With great restraint, we forced ourselves to wait until the coffee arrived.

"I am afraid that the coffee isn't very fresh," said Crocodile apologetically, "I have had the beans since last September ... that is another item near the top of my shopping list."

Crocodile settled opposite us and spoke. "I should like to tell you a little about the Professor just to give you a flavour of the kind of person he was and also the reason why I am now here on my own. Although he was an extremely cultured academic, living in a grand house in London, wearing expensive clothes, eating the best food and drinking the finest wines ... his comfortable existence was in many ways an embarrassment to him. He often said that if he became penniless tomorrow he wouldn't lose a wink of sleep. Life would simply have thrown him another challenge and he would rise to cope with his new circumstances. He would be the first to admit, however, that life had bestowed many gifts on him and he would only have become a pauper in financial terms, he would still be very rich because of his many other attributes. 'A fine may be the same for a poor man and a rich man but in reality it is very different. Therein lies the injustice,' he would say."

"His only regret at suddenly becoming penniless would be that in the very short term it would be hard for him to help underprivileged people in the way that he did. 'I could do other things, but what I do best requires money and I would never try to argue that money was not important,' he would add."

"Although he wrote many articles on the big issues, he rarely got really worked up about them. It would be more of an unbiased academic assessment of the situation, in a way, something that he wasn't personally involved in; something he was considering at arms-length. His main concerns were with ordinary people, who had fallen on hard times or had been done a grave injustice by some official or bank. His favourite quotation was, 'Power tends to corrupt ... absolute power corrupts absolutely'."

"The kind of situation that really used to get him hot under the collar was, for example, where somebody has worked hard all their life and through no fault of their own, maybe because of illness or loss of their job, get into debt. The debt is very small but because of penalties, legal expenses, court costs etc., a very small debt soon becomes a big one. The Professor would throw his arms in the air and say, 'The officials just follow rules which are backed by the full weight of the law. They have the power and that power tends to be used unnecessarily harshly and without fair consideration of all the consequences. They ruin a persons' life and the lives of his family, without conscience, for a trifling sum'. In cases like this the otherwise benign and mild-tempered Professor would jump up and down with rage, shouting, 'How can our government and legal system permit this to happen? There has to be a better way.'"

"I hope you don't mind my telling you this but I wanted you to know something about him that wasn't just superficial so that you can really understand the sort of person he was and therefore why he helped me so much and went to such extreme lengths to ensure my safety. When I escaped from the circus, what luck to be rescued, albeit unknowingly, by a knight in shining armour, whose bywords were *justice* and *freedom*."

"I must tell you that it wasn't just academic and charitable activities that the Professor was involved with. He had a great love of simple pleasures that enhance the quality of life. He used the term *super-additivity* to explain that you can do something, say a hobby, that gives you enjoyment and from that you derive pleasure not only from pursuing the hobby but from fruits of that hobby ... the total satisfaction is increased ... you get something for nothing. A perfect example is growing your own vegetables. If you enjoy gardening you may get pleasure out of growing vegetables as well as flowers. You then have the added pleasure of eating your own fresh vegetables. Of course if you find growing vegetables tedious and unpleasant it doesn't work. The satisfaction gained from eating the fresh vegetables may be less than the satisfaction lost by having to do tiresome work."

"I can see exactly what you mean," I said, nodding my head. "As you may have noticed, Kate is as fit as a mountain goat, yet she has never worked out in a gymnasium in her life and certainly has never had a personal trainer. We have always walked a lot on the fells and although that is terrific exercise for your legs and lower body it is not the best upper body exercise. Kate has developed a workout routine in the way she does housework and gardening. For example, if she is polishing a mirror or sweeping a path she puts her heart and soul into it – so effectively it becomes vigorous exercise while at the same time she does a very good job. I think that this might qualify as *super-additivity* because even if housework is not your favourite activity, it has to be done ... and if you can find a way to get something extra out of it, that has to be a bonus, even though I am sure it would be hard to convince most people that housework could be something to look forward to."

"You may find some of the things he did for pleasure hard to believe just like, as you say, some people would find it hard to accept that it is possible to get extra satisfaction from doing housework," Crocodile replied with his now familiar chuckle. "But seriously, he did get an astonishing amount of pleasure out of simple pastimes and his enthusiasm was always contagious. Cheese making was one of his all-time favourites. He couldn't grow vegetables because we did not have much of a garden in London, although I am certain that he would have grown them if we'd had a good sized plot of land."

"As with everything he did he would never do any of it half-heartedly...he even became an acknowledged authority on specialty cheeses. He had his own dairy constructed in the cellars of the London house and applied his great scientific mind to the production of perfect cheeses, albeit on a very small scale. His ambition was to produce the Chateau d'Yquem of the cheese world. He experimented with the milk of cows, ewes and goats, from places as far away as France, Switzerland and Italy. Aromatic milk, full cream milk, milk from high Alpine pastures and lush green valleys, as well as from places much closer to home, including farms in the Lake District. He once told me that the name Keswick is derived from a word meaning a place where cheese and butter are made. After I discovered this cave, the Professor realised that the temperature in the smaller storage caves was just about perfect for maturing and storing cheese as well as wine and so we brought quite a lot of cheese here together with most of the contents of his wine cellar. I made some of the cheeses but I am afraid that there isn't much left now. It has been my staple diet for some time, but if you can get me the milk and other ingredients I can make perfect cheese here in the cave. I have all the equipment I need and copies of the Professor's production details and tasting notes. The only milk I have been able to get hold of is small quantities of goats' milk from the farm. However, there are still many hundreds of bottles of wine left so you can help yourselves any time you like."

We both thanked him very much and then Kate changed the subject to ask a question that we had both wanted to know the answer to. "Matt and I are dying to know how long you have lived here and how long it took to do the work on the cave."

"We started the work a year and a half ago, in July," he replied, "and we worked on it for two summers. At first it was just going to be a secret hide-away for me, if ever I had to lie low for a while. The Professor was involved with archaeological and geological studies in the Lake District and he had permission to carry out scientific and excavation works in the National Park – so it wasn't that difficult for him to bring the necessary equipment to the island. He hired a pontoon, a type of floating platform, from the people who do jetty work on the lake and we shipped everything down from Lakeside. As it turned out, the whole time we were working on the cave, nobody ever asked what we were doing – although, in reality, nothing much was visible above ground once the opening had been cut through the rock. We then stored everything inside and camouflaged the entrance. Nearly all the work after that was underground and out of sight ... the whole operation, incredibly, went without a hitch."

"What changed our plans and my life completely was that sadly, three years ago, the Professor was diagnosed with an incurable illness that, at best, gave him only a few years to live. He was very philosophical about it, as he was about everything, and from that moment onwards he put all his energies into the arrangements for my future welfare and protection without any thought for himself and his own illness. I consider myself to be so very fortunate and privileged to have had the Professor as my guardian, mentor and companion. I will always have Mercedes to thank for teaching me to speak and looking after me in my early life – but it was the Professor who did the second half of the work to make me what I am."

"I would like to reassure you at this juncture that I will not be a burden to you. I have been very well prepared to stand on my own two feet. My one single problem is that I have to acquire food and other necessities without anyone finding out who I am or where I live. The Professor has left me extremely well provided for financially. I am without doubt the richest crocodile in the world," he said with a laugh. "I hesitate to say, because it sounds immodest, also the cleverest – but I am sure it must be true. I believe that it was his intention to leave me his London House if he could find a way to make the bequest legally binding."

"All I am asking of you, Kate and Matt, is to help me to obtain all the things that I cannot easily get for myself without running the risk of being recognised by someone. The Professor constantly warned me that if anybody that I could not trust absolutely realised my true identity word would spread like wildfire, the press and television news would soon pick up on it, and the life I enjoy now would be over. Conversely, he also had to admit that what would happen exactly was impossible to predict ... for example I could end up as a celebrity and appear on T.V. chat shows, or in films ... go on lecture tours ... maybe write a book, perhaps my own autobiography. All I can say is that what he held most dear, what for him was the most important thing in life, was to be able to enjoy both freedom and privacy, to take pleasure in the simple things in life, however learned you may become; to maintain a sense of fairness and justice in every decision that you have to take, and to have respect for your fellow man and all living creatures. He said that one day I might decide, as it were, *to go public*, but that I should only take this decision when I was wise enough to know that it was the right decision, when I was totally certain in my own mind and in my heart that I was doing the right thing. If I made a mistake it would be irreversible – my life would be changed utterly and forever, I could end up as a pawn in other peoples' games – I may no longer be master of my own destiny."

"I have been here with Napoleon and Sherwood since last September and I have not seen or heard from the Professor since then. When the Professor left me for the last time it was the most emotional experience of my life – we hugged each other for ages – I didn't want him to go and he did not want to go – but he was getting very weak ... his health was failing fast. He said that if he had not cast off his mortal coil by Christmas he would get back to me somehow – even if he had to charter an air-ambulance to make the journey ... but I think we both knew that this was our final farewell. Tears were streaming down our cheeks as we waved our last goodbye. He was the most wonderful, kind, generous, loving person in the world. I know that I have not known many real people but I have read extensively, including many of the classic novels, and I haven't as yet met even a fictional character that I could respect more than the Professor."

Crocodile continued in a quiet voice, "The Professor still had many legal arrangements to conclude in order to ensure, as far as was possible within the law, that he could guarantee the validity of the bequests in his will. I mentioned earlier that it was his intention to leave me his house. He talked about setting up a trust and making his niece, Emily, a trustee, with the intention that, for the time being, she could live in the house, but that it would be held in trust for me. He always believed that it might be possible one day for me to be granted full rights in English law, but I don't know how far he progressed with these inquiries and arrangements. The last advice he gave me was that I should try to find somebody to replace him – somebody that I could trust implicitly to act as my guardian, somebody who would understand my unique position and would help to protect me in the same way that he did. Please understand that I am not asking you to commit to this now – all I need at the moment is some help in obtaining food and provisions. The only other thing is, that at some point, I would like answers to the following questions: Is the professor still alive? Is Emily now living in the London house? What instructions did the Professor give Emily regarding the will and the operation of the trust? It would be dangerous for me to try to go to London on my own but at some point I will need help in discovering the truth about what has happened."

"Kate and I will help you in any way we can," I said. "There is nothing that would give us greater pleasure. Getting food and other necessities for you presents absolutely no problem to us ... especially if you can collect everything from our boathouse."

"But if the weather is fine and we feel like an outing in our boat we will gladly bring your groceries to the island. If it is a large or cumbersome order you can use our boat as a tender and tow it, full of supplies, across the lake behind your boat. If the worst comes to the worst, our friends have a steam launch which we are allowed to use from time to time; we can carry almost anything in that ... we could even take a picnic with us sometimes and do it in style and turn work into pleasure."

"As far as London is concerned, that also presents no problem at all. We go to London every few weeks – usually for one or two days, or we just pass through when we go on Eurostar into Europe. To give you an idea of how easy it is to get to London and back – we can catch an early train from Oxenholme Station and be in London soon after ten o'clock. Coming back, we leave Euston around eight o'clock in the evening and we are back at Oxenholme before eleven. That gives us plenty of time to walk into the West End and back, shopping, or window shopping as we go, or maybe looking round art galleries or visiting a larger exhibition, with ample time for a nice lunch in one of our favourite restaurants and, more often than not, a late afternoon tea at Fortnum and Masons to round the day off."

"I find it incomprehensible when I hear Londoners admit that they have never been to theLake District and I know that a very large number have not. When I ask them why they have never bothered to visit the most beautiful place on Earth ... they make the excuse that it is too remote or it is easier to get to Europe. I think that they are usually more than surprised when I ask them exactly what they mean by *remote* and then tell them that I can get to London in three hours, Edinburgh in two and Manchester in one and a half. I always make them promise that they will visit the Lake District for their next birthday, as a birthday present to themselves. That gives them a date they won't forget and hopefully they feel more obligated to make the journey. I tell them that it is their loss if they don't keep the promise."

"We used to live in London," said Kate. "Where in London did you live?"

"The Professor's house is in Bayswater," Crocodile replied. "He found it very convenient living where he did because, as I have told you, he spent a lot of time in Oxford and he could walk to Paddington Station in a few minutes to catch his train."

"That is an amazing coincidence," said Kate, "Matt and I lived in London for five years and for half of that time we lived on Craven Hill Gardens in Bayswater – so we know the area well. We did all our local shopping on Queensway and although we didn't have a garden, Hyde Park was only a stone's throw away on the other side of Bayswater Road."

"I have to tell you," exclaimed Crocodile, "I used to swim in the Serpentine sometimes. I swam just below the surface most of the time because there was always a high risk of being spotted or even being picked up on a security camera ... you never know when or where you are being watched in London. I don't even think about being noticed in Windermere ... I can see anybody else in the water at a great distance and long before they can see me ... and there are no security cameras here. The Professor's specially converted vehicle was a Dormobile – not only did it have a secret compartment, but from in there I could get directly onto the ground underneath it. The Professor installed a pair of doors in the floor ... like they have in armoured vehicles that carry cash or gold bullion. It was not only a last resort means of escape for me, but when we went to places like the Serpentine I could come out underneath and straight into the water. Later, the Professor made me a towelling dressing gown with a big hood, so I just walked out in that and when I was sure nobody was close-by I would slip out of it and into the water, leaving it at the side of the lake for when I returned. We also had a system of signals in case a problem arose. There were two red flashing lights on the front of the Dormobile and the Professor would switch these on if it were unsafe for me to come out. He also had an electrically operated pennant on the roof that he used to hoist if things got really difficult. He would then collect my dressing gown and drive to another pick-up point and I would see the pennant fluttering in the breeze as he drove along Serpentine Road. The Professor always took the greatest care possible with his plans for protecting me – even to the extent of rehearsing procedures prior to the real event. He accepted that in some unforeseen circumstances you could be in a position where you had no choice other than to take a gamble – but he also showed me that with some prior knowledge, sensible planning would nearly always pay dividends. I have to admit that he was usually right. He said that if you have to be involved in gambling then you are more likely to be successful if you own a casino. He also said that it is much better to be a grandfather clock than a loose cannon. I guess that's the best description one could give to the Professor ... he ticked like a grand-father clock ... nothing was hurried, everything was carefully thought out and everything was done in its own good time."

"I can only recall one incident at the Serpentine that nearly gave us a problem. Just as I was about to come out of the water four men arrived and sat down on the grass just across the road and started to play cards. The Professor gave me the warning signals, collected my dressing gown and moved to another spot a few hundred yards away. No sooner had he put my dressing gown out than a tramp came along, picked it up, examined it and started to make off with it. The Professor jumped out of the Dormobile and confronted the tramp, who was reluctant to hand it over. The outcome was that the Professor gave him more than enough money to buy another dressing gown together with an invitation to attend one of the *sanctuaries for the homeless* that he supported. The tramp went on his way singing *When Irish Eyes Are Smiling*, and I got back into the Dormobile without being spotted."

"Have you been swimming in any of the other lakes in the Lake District?" I asked.

"All the big ones, and some of the little ones," replied Crocodile," I can remember Coniston Water, Tarn Hows, Rydal Water, Grasmere, Thirlmere, Derwent Water, Bassenthwaite Lake, Buttermere, and Ullswater. Last summer, the Professor had planned to take me to Haweswater. He told me about a submerged village and he thought that I should swim down and take a look. Perhaps we could go there this year?"

"I know there are people who have made it a goal in their lives to swim in every lake and tarn in the Lake District just as so many people have tried to emulate Alfred Wainwright and climb all the 214 peaks over 1,000 feet high ... it is a lifetime's achievement for most people but some try to do it in a year or even a summer. I know that a Wasdale farmer once did it in under a week, and even that incredible record may have been broken by now," I said.

I then said, in response to the worried expression that had suddenly materialised on Crocodile's face, I then said, "Please do not look so concerned. Kate and I are not into breaking records, but we do love to walk on the fells and climb some of the high peaks, and I was just wondering how much walking you had done with the Professor both in the Lake District and in London?"

"Sadly, none," said Crocodile, with an apologetic shrug. "The Professor was always too concerned for my safety to risk taking me somewhere where I might be found out. Although he did promise that one day we should try to climb a mountain. But latterly, I don't think that his health was good enough for mountaineering."

"So was it always the same procedure, of going in the Dormobile, and you getting out and more or less straight into the water?"

"Yes, that was the way he wanted to do it," replied Crocodile. "Of course I would always look out of the windows and observe what was going on along the way."

"What I must tell you," I said, as gently as possible, "without in any way meaning to upset you, is that the true grandeur of the Lake District can only be witnessed properly by walking on the fells and viewing the glorious scenery from the slopes and summits of the highest mountains. What I would like to suggest is that we work on your disguises in order to make it possible to take you with us. I fully understand the Professor's concerns for your safety, and clearly, his tactics have paid off. I agree entirely about thorough planning and I believe that everything we do together, where there is some risk involved, should be planned meticulously. It is simply that I do not think you should stay completely hidden forever and if you agree with this proposition, you may as well come out with us sooner rather than later. What do you think?"

"I must confess," replied Crocodile, "that I agree completely with what you say. I do believe that the Professor was over-protective. Before his illness we had planned to do many things, including walking on the fells, but somehow time ran out – we left it too late."

"Kate and I have met a lot of people," I said, "some of whom live in the Lake District, who have reached the stage in their lives when they start to take stock of their past. They realise that they never did climb Scafell Pike, Helvellyn, Skiddaw, Great Gable, or the Langdale Pikes – they could have made it easily when they were young, or, with a little effort, much later in life; but they didn't, and the day has arrived when it is now too late – a huge regret to add to their register of regrets, to the list of wonderful things that they should have done and could have done, but somehow just didn't get round to doing."

"Kate and I promise that we will not put any pressure on you to do anything that you are uncomfortable with. We will simply come up with ideas and discuss them with you, and if you agree to try some of them, we will take it slowly and carefully, one step at a time."

"What I suggest we do now is for us to go home and consider everything that you have told us and then meet again tomorrow after we have been to Windermere and Kendal to get the things that you are most in need of."

As if he had anticipated what I was going to say, Crocodile reached up and pulled some sheets of paper from under a heavy glass paperweight on the mantelpiece.

"I have made out five lists," he explained, "and numbered them 1 to 5 in order of reducing priority. The first is a list of things that I need desperately. The second is a longer list of items that I could do with during the next couple of weeks or so. 3,4, and 5 are not urgent – anytime over the coming month will do. Please let me pay you for everything so that you can get it at your convenience."

"Please don't give us any money," said Kate, "we can discuss finances another day and in the meantime Matt and I will get you as much as we can and come over again after lunch tomorrow."

"That's a good idea," I said, "It will also give us time to talk about how we can help you, in the light of what you have now told us. I would like to discuss everything with Kate and make sure that we are both in agreement before I open my mouth."

As we were about to take our leave of Crocodile, Sherwood, a large tawny owl, glided effortlessly over our heads and landed on Crocodile's left shoulder. "He's only just got up. He sleeps most of the day in the wine cellar in a small bunk that I built for him on the top of the wine racks. He normally gets up around dusk, but he probably heard our voices and curiosity has got the better of him today. Sherwood and Napoleon get on very well, although they don't often go out together unless they are with me. The only thing that they don't see eye to eye on is who sits on my shoulder when I take a stroll round the island of an evening. I don't want one on each shoulder, so they have to take it in turns.

I almost forgot. Would you like to have a look round the wine cellar and choose some bottles to take back with you?"

"If you don't mind, I think we'd better be on our way – just to make sure that we get across the lake before the light goes," I said, apologetically, "but we can take a look tomorrow when we come with your groceries."

"That's fine," he replied, "It will give me chance to tidy up a bit in there before you come." As he was speaking he lit an oil-lamp and escorted us back up the stone steps. When we were at the top he hung the lamp on a hook in the ceiling of a deep alcove just inside the entrance. The flickering light illuminated a large number of walking sticks in a multitude of shapes, sizes and designs. As the lantern swung from side to side a collage of strange shapes danced on the rock wall behind them.

"These are a small part of the Professor's collection," he explained. "I usually take one with me when I go out. There are country walking sticks and hiking staves, and a number of canes in exotic woods with fancy horn, ivory and silver handles. The Professor had this evening dress stick specially made for me for my degree ceremony ... Look!" He lifted it out to show us, "It has an ebony shaft and a solid silver crocodile design handle fashioned in my image." He held it higher so that we could take a closer look.

"It's exquisite!" exclaimed Kate. "It's beautifully made ... most impressive ... the Professor certainly has an eye for lovely things."

Crocodile beamed with satisfaction, put the stick back in the rack and chose a long curly Rams-horn shepherds' crook to take with him. He then opened the rock door and we made our way out into the soft fading light of an early January afternoon. The sun was already below the tree line of Grizedale Forest, though wisps of sunlit cloud still floated in the darkening sky.

Walking back across the island with Crocodile, staff in hand, Sherwood on his right shoulder with Napoleon circling overhead, we all agreed that it had been a wonderful day – one that none of us would ever forget.

Crocodile steadied the boat while we scrambled aboard and, as he pushed us out onto the water, we thanked him again for the delightful lunch and for his warm hospitality. He said that he would watch us all the way across the lake to make sure that we got back safely.

A short distance from the island, Kate whispered, "Just look at him! If he had an eye patch on you'd think he was Long John Silver standing on Treasure Island."

I laughed and nodded in agreement.

We waved in the direction of the ever-diminishing Crocodile until he was an indistinguishable speck in the fading light. We tied up in our boathouse and then walked down to the shore where we both waved again in the direction of Crocodile Island. We were too far away to pick him out now but we had an inkling that he just might be watching us, through his telescope, so we waved again for another couple of minutes before finally turning to make our way up the steep slope to our house.

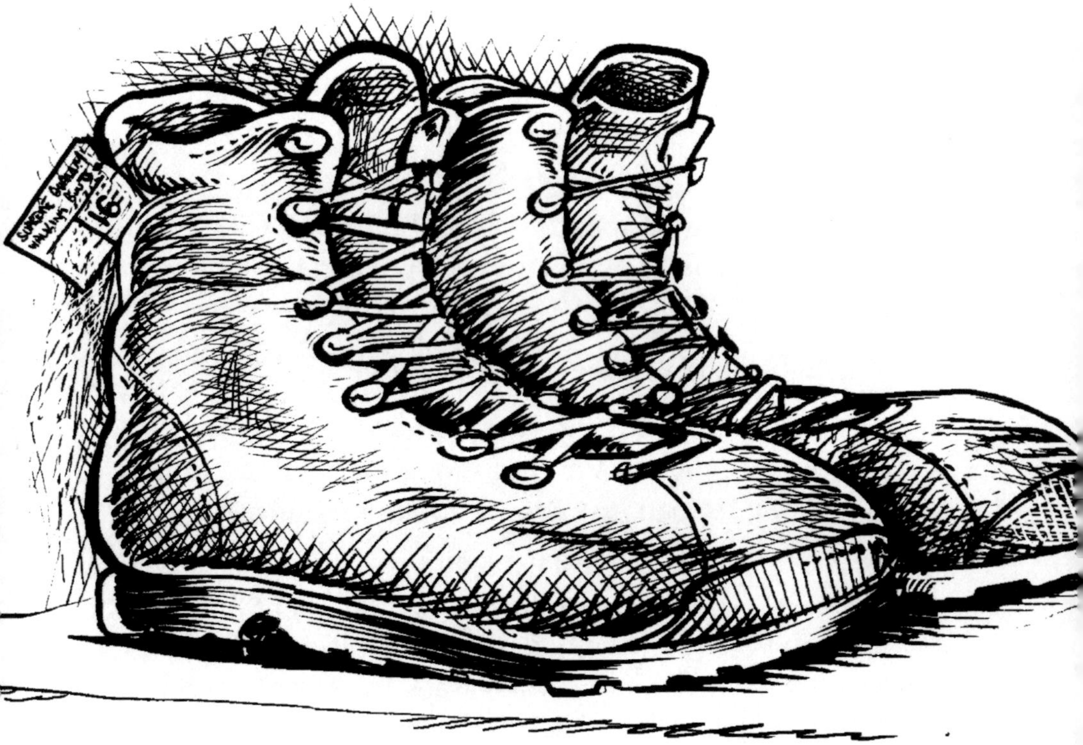
16

Chapter Four
Shopping For Necessities

The following day we went out to get some of Crocodile's provisions. We had read carefully through his lists, and everything was easily obtainable. We didn't want to get so much that we had difficulty in transporting it comfortably in the boat without squashing the fresh produce. We had worked out a system where we would put everything into strong plastic boxes with lids and handles – we already had sufficient at home to fill the car. I stuck a box number and a clear ring-binder pocket on the front of each one so that we could put a list of the contents and prices into the pocket on every box. We had decided that it would be easier to put everything into the boxes as we brought the carrier bags back to the car from each shop, rather than to take everything home and pack them there. This system would also make things simpler for Crocodile because he could see, at a glance, what was in each box. I had a couple of sack trucks in the garage and we decided to use one to get the boxes down to the lake, and to give the other to Crocodile so that he could use it to transport them across the island.

Kate also thought that it would be nice to get him a few special treats in addition to the fairly basic items on his lists. With this in mind, our first port of call was Cartmel Village, for some Cumbrian sticky toffee puddings, with extra sticky toffee caramel sauce.

As we drove south along the lake we began to discuss where it would be possible to take him without his standing out like a sore thumb and we realised immediately that we would have to conjure up some very realistic disguises in order for him to pass incognito in a crowd. The most difficult bits of him to camouflage were his long snout and his tail. Not that his snout was that long when compared to most crocodiles that we had seen and it was not at all fierce looking, but nevertheless, it would have to be very well concealed. Also, his tail was fairly short and very flexible. It could easily have been hidden under a long dress or skirt, but we didn't think that he would take kindly to being dressed up as a lady, or a washerwoman, like Toad in *Wind In The Willows*. A very baggy, long jacket or a longish coat appeared to be the best option. Kate suggested a balaclava or a big scarf would effectively conceal his snout, but there would be many occasions and circumstances when he would look silly or out of place wearing either of these things. We thought that a big bushy beard would be the best solution in most situations.

For many years, when we were in business, we employed a lovable Irishman, a builder by trade, and he had a most magnificent silver beard. However, it was usually full of all sorts of debris; nails, screws, bits of brick, and, usually a pound or two of cement dust. You had to stand well clear when he tried to shake it all out at the end of a day's work. I can see him now building a wall for us ... I have never met anyone who could lay bricks so fast. The hilarious bit was that when the wall had reached a certain height, all you could see from our vantage point was a pair of big hands, a brick, a trowel, and a bushy beard working their way across the top of the wall as the final courses of bricks were laid. It looked as though the beard and the hands were doing all the work. After that we called him Billy Beard, and to this day we always think of him when a fine beard walks by. Some are so impressive that you always take a second look, but you would never gaze too hard for fear of being thought rude. So having discussed Crocodile's situation at length, both Kate and I felt that it was unlikely that anybody would come close up and stare at him, and there would be even less likelihood of someone trying to pull his beard to see if was real. We concluded that, provided he was dressed as inconspicuously as possible, and we were careful where we took him, the chances of his being found out were pretty slim.

We realised that, although Crocodile could speak effectively through the side of his mouth with his beard on, he would struggle to eat a meal in a restaurant in full view of the waiters and other diners without attracting attention. I am not saying that it would be impossible, but it would not be easy for him to get food and drink smoothly and naturally into his mouth without some contortion or strange manoeuvres. It was something that we could get him to practice, but unless we felt that he could eat and drink without attracting attention, taking him to restaurants, for the time being, at least was out of the question.

We were very conscious of the fact that the Professor had protected Crocodile to such a degree that, we felt, if he were to spend the rest of his life in this way, it would adversely affect his freedom and impinge, in a very restrictive way, upon the overall quality of his life. His life in London, living in a grand house, was enviable, yet in many respects he had still been a prisoner. Perhaps it was no worse than for a King, or a film star, or pop idol, who can't go out without being instantly recognised and hounded by the paparazzi.

"Maybe even a King or a Queen goes out in disguise," suggested Kate, "Maybe they have false beards and wigs and big dark glasses to hide their faces – wouldn't that be a hoot!"

"It would be just as much fun for Crocodile," I replied, "If we can perfect his disguises we can take him nearly anywhere, I'm surprised that the Professor didn't think of that."

"He seems happy enough in his cave," said Kate "and who wouldn't be? It's like a boutique hotel with all mod cons. It's just that he's still a virtual prisoner and dare not venture much further than into the woods around his house or to swim in the Lake. And he always has to be on his guard – he can't even get out of the water if there is anyone around."

"The cave is brilliant," I agreed, "and when you think about it, it's much more comfortable than the houses that most people would have lived in in days gone by. Even well-heeled people like William Wordsworth would not have had the amenities that Crocodile enjoys. Wordsworth House at Cockermouth, and Rydal Mount are fine properties, but Dove Cottage was only tolerably comfortable and I know that it wasn't easy keeping warm and clean in those days, especially in the winter. I remember reading once that Dorothy Wordsworth continually complained about damp rooms and smoky chimneys, so much so, that they were often covered in soot and had to let the fire go out in the middle of winter and go to bed to keep warm. Poor people couldn't even afford wax candles and they had to burn evil smelling tallow candles. Winter nights for most people must have been an ordeal."

"I totally agree," nodded Kate, "so long as we can get Crocodile's disguises right he can look forward to a wonderful life on Windermere."

The Lake District, before Wordsworth's time, was home to native oak woodlands, with many of the pine forests being planted in the nineteenth century. Local woodland would have created an extensive supply of firewood for winter warmth and all year round cooking. Just like Crocodile, most people would collect it free of charge and have plenty of room to store large quantities of logs and kindling, unlike those living in the cities or large towns, where it may not have been easily available and there would have been a price to pay. It would seem that for people living in the Lake District, or anyone else in northern climates, so long as you had plenty of wood to burn and a good chimney you could keep warm in winter. If you had a badly constructed chimney you got smoked out and covered in soot and probably ended up going to bed to keep warm. The problem was that you needed the hot coals from the fire to fill the bed-warmers, assuming you could afford bed-warmers, and good hot coals came only from good hot fires. So if you had to let the fire go out you would end up, at best, spending many hours in a cold damp bed.

Kate and I concluded that at least Crocodile didn't have these problems to cope with – he was snug and warm and safe in his cave. There were only two important things missing from his life – the regular company of good friends, and the ability to walk freely on the fells, and in the very large number of interesting and exciting places to be found all over the Lake District. We were determined to rectify these omissions but in a way that would not compromise his safety and freedom.

It takes around twenty minutes for us to drive to Cartmel and it is a drive that we always enjoy. Some journeys are just a means of getting from A to B in a reasonable time, but most journeys we make regularly in the Lake District are pleasurable in themselves. Today we were heading south, down the lake to Newby Bridge, then along country lanes to the ancient village of Cartmel. The village is famous for its superb Augustinian Priory that dates from 1188. Cartmel also has a racecourse and we often come to the horse races, on spring and August Bank Holidays. Today, we stopped in the market square for one reason only, and that was to get a big bag of sticky toffee puddings for Crocodile.

On the way from Cartmel to Milnthorpe, our next planned port of call, we decided to stop for a cup of tea at Levens Hall. It was too early in the year for the house to be open, but we often carry a flask of tea or coffee with us if we are going to be on the road for a few hours. Today, we sat on a wall overlooking the river Kent by Levens Bridge. In a few weeks the lawns around this fine Elizabethan house would be sprinkled with brightly coloured crocuses, but now, still in the grip of winter, there was not a single one to be seen. The topiary garden however was as magnificent as ever. It is impossible to pass Levens Hall without noticing the weird and wonderful shapes of the topiary and I told Kate that when I was young, and coming on trips to the Lake District with my mother and father, we always regarded Levens as the *Gateway to the Lakes* – when we saw the topiary we knew we were nearly there.

It was market day in Milnthorpe and we couldn't park in the market square. Kate wanted to get some pies to take home, and then to look round the market. By the time I had caught up with her she had just completed a purchase of two balaclavas and two big, long, woollen scarves for Crocodile, from one the market stalls.

"I thought these would be great camouflage for him," she said, holding them up. "These scarves are so big he wouldn't even need a beard to hide under," she added.

"They're great," I replied, "well spotted! My only thought is that he can hardly go about wearing a great scarf and a balaclava in the middle of summer, or if we take him into a café, or to the pictures, or somewhere like that. I think that we will have to find a beard manufacturer and get him an assortment of beards for different occasions. Probably a theatrical costumier or a fancy dress shop will fix us up. Somebody must make beards for King Lear and Robinson Crusoe and Father Christmas, so they can't be that difficult to get hold of."

My thoughts about beards were suddenly distracted by a wonderfully, mouth-watering aroma wafting up from the carrier bag that Kate was holding. It was one of those delightful smells that instantly put your taste buds on red alert. Kate noticed that my thoughts about beards had been temporarily distracted by a more pressing consideration.

"I thought it wouldn't be long before your antennae picked up on my other purchase," she said with a grin. Then to complete the seduction she lifted up the carrier and opened the top right under my nose. "Home-made chicken pies, your favourite, straight out of the oven. I thought we could have one each for lunch while they are still warm. Why don't we stop at Levens again, on the way to Kendal, and have them with the rest of the tea."

As it happened, we decided to stop just up the road from Levens, at Sizergh Castle. Like Levens, Sizergh had started life as a pele tower built in the thirteenth century for defence against the frequent raids from the north. At one point a moat had protected the castle, but all that remains of the moat now is a lake with a small island. We stood looking down onto the lake whilst tucking into the still warm, mouth-wateringly fragrant chicken pies.

Kate reminded me that the last time we had stood on this spot was on a bright sunny evening last year when we had come to Sizergh to see an open-air production of, *A Midsummer Night's Dream*. "If you remember," she said, "the island was just a blaze of white marguerites and meadowsweet – how different it looks now!"

Back in the car, our conversation returned to beards, a subject of which we knew very little, but one about which, unknown to us then, we would learn a lot about during the coming weeks, as we painstakingly sought to acquire the perfect beard to camouflage Crocodile's long snout. Our initial research led us to believe that this beard went by the name *wizard*, like the one Merlin used to wear in, *The Knights of the Round Table*. It was more pointed and much slimmer than a Father Christmas beard, and it should cover his snout without, in any way, arousing suspicion. Moreover, with a beard like that, he would be able to dress as eccentrically as he wished. Following our initial tests with *wizards*, we concluded that the perfect beard would have to be a little fuller and wider in order to ensure that, for example, if we were to take him into restaurants or to parties, his snout would be well and truly camouflaged to the extent that he could eat and drink without arousing suspicion.

Chapter Four — Shopping For Necessities

On the way into Kendal we discussed the necessity of a pair of fell-walking boots for Crocodile. After we had acquired virtually all the grocery items on Crocodile's list we spent some time looking round for a suitable pair of boots. Our main problem was that Crocodile wasn't sure himself what size would be best, and this was also made more difficult by the shape of his feet. In reality, his skin was so tough that he didn't need boots at all. We had toyed with the idea of having some soft overshoes specially made for him, just to hide his feet, but the soles would have to be tough enough to withstand the rocky terrain of the Lakeland fells, so we thought it more sensible to try to find boots, off the shelf, that would be suitable. In the end we concluded that we would have more luck in some of the specialist climbing shops in Ambleside, which became our next port of call.

After a hunt around several shops we found some that looked just about right. In answer to our enquiry about the largest boot size that they sold, the salesman informed us that they had in stock up to a size 16, but to his knowledge, size 14 was the largest that they had ever sold, at least in recent memory. I wondered how long the size 16's had been on the shelf, and what happened to them if they went out of fashion or were superseded by an improved design. Somewhere, in a warehouse there may be hundreds of obsolete pairs of size 16 boots, gathering dust and impossible to sell, because nobody had big enough feet to fill them. I decided to make the salesman's day and buy a pair of size 16 boots, but only on condition that I could return them if not fit for purpose. However, we also took a size 14, and a size 12, together with some big socks and several pairs of the largest insoles available, on the understanding that we would return the unsuitable sizes, and purchase a second pair of boots when we had ascertained which pair was the best fit. Fortunately, the salesman was too courteous to ask why we didn't bring our giant friend into the shop to try them on, instead of going to all this trouble. I had thought up an excuse, just in case, but it wasn't necessary.

I had already taken the two sack trolleys down to the boathouse so when we got back home it was just a matter of loading everything evenly into the boat so that we didn't risk capsizing half way across the lake. When we arrived at Crocodile's island, three blasts on the horn were again not needed because he and Napoleon were already waiting for us, standing in exactly the same spot from where he had waved goodbye to us.

"I've got everything ready for coffee," he shouted, "but if you have managed to get me some fresh coffee we'll use that instead of the stale stuff that I have here."

"We've brought you a good selection to try," Kate shouted back, "just small quantities of each, so that you can decide which you like best for next time."

Crocodile was beaming all over his face as he pulled us into the bank and helped us tie up. I suggested that we pass all the boxes up out of the boat first, but he was already a step ahead of me. "I made this up last night," he said, sliding down a long plank of wood. It was about two feet wide with a three-inch high edge down both sides and on the bottom. He then threw down a length of rope with a hook attached to the end and said, "Just put each box against the stop at the bottom and attach the hook, and I'll pull them up one at a time."

It took us just two trips across the island with three boxes loaded onto each trolley – twelve boxes in all. My labelling idea proved an immediate success because all Crocodile required instantly was fresh coffee, and we found it in a few seconds.

"Just leave the boxes at the top of the steps," he said, "I only need coffee just now. I can fetch everything else down later."

"What's that lovely smell?" asked Kate, as a most wonderful aroma wafted up the stairs.

"Scones in the oven," replied Crocodile: "Napoleon managed to get a small amount of fresh double cream from the farm so we'll have them with butter and cream."

"We've brought jam as well," said Kate, "organic strawberry, and I think there's blueberry and a couple of exotic ones for you to try as well."

We all agreed that strawberry would be perfect with hot scones, butter and cream, so we pulled a jar out of one of the boxes. Suddenly we were all licking our lips at the prospect.

As we neared the bottom of the steps he invited us to look around the wine cellar while he was making the coffee and checking on the scones.

"I don't want to do a King Alfred," he chuckled.

At the entrance to the cellar he lit a couple of Florence Nightingale type lamps to enable us to read the labels more clearly. He invited us to pull out anything we fancied and he would box them up for us to take back on one of the sack trolleys.

"That's one thing we forgot," I said to Kate, when Crocodile had gone to the kitchen, "we should have brought him some big battery torches. We'll get him some rechargeable ones, and charge them up at home for him."

Crocodile's wine cellar was divided into aisles, and the aisles were split into sections, so that each country of origin had its own compartment, or several compartments, sub-divided into regions, for large wine producers like France. The reds were on one side of an aisle, and the whites, wherever possible, were placed directly opposite. The bottles were either laid simply, on horizontal rock shelves, or the shelves had been divided diagonally into four triangular shaped compartments, and the bottles were stacked in the shape of a pyramid.

We made our way down each of the aisles, pulling out a bottle here and a bottle there to read the label. One thing was sure; Crocodile and the Professor did not drink vin ordinaire. The dusty labels that appeared before our eyes were impressive and bewitching ... Margaux, Lafite-Rothschild, Latour, D'Yquem, etc, etc.

I whispered to Kate, "One case of some of this stuff would pay our grocery bill for a year! The Professor certainly showed Crocodile how to live well."

We made our way back to the kitchen to find Crocodile just taking the scones out of the oven. He slid them onto a wire cooling-tray on the table, removed a big pan of milk from the stove, and poured out the coffee.

Crocodile's scones were mouth-wateringly delicious and the butter, jam and cream added just a touch of extra satisfaction. The conversation deteriorated to *oohs, aahs*, and *mmhs*, and didn't improve much until we had scoffed the lot. We then told him about our plans for the following day and we said that we hoped it would be the first of hundreds if not thousands of days out and about in the Lake District.

Chapter Four — Shopping For Necessities

We told him that we had decided to take him, early in the morning, on a short walk around Tarn Hows. This would enable him to try out his disguise and the new boots, and to judge other walkers' reactions to this rather unusual looking individual. With luck we would not meet many other people at that hour, even at Tarn Hows. Kate then presented him with the three pairs of boots together with the big scarves and the balaclavas that she had acquired for him.

Crocodile couldn't wait to try on the boots, or hide his excitement. The size 12's were too small, the size 14's just about right and, alas, the size 16's were too big. I would have to return them to the shop and probably doom them to a life on the shelf.

We arranged to meet him at 7.30 AM the following morning and I drew a simple plan of our meeting place. He seemed to know exactly where it was – he would only have a bit of woodland and a field to cross from the spot where he could moor his boat. He promised to pick out some suitable clothing and try on the other things that Kate had brought for him.

There were tears in his eyes as we pulled away from the shore and he and Kate waved continually to each other as we crossed the lake. I keep a pair of binoculars in the boathouse and as soon as we were inside I took a quick peek to see if I could still see him. I focused them on his island, and sure enough there he was, with Napoleon on his shoulder, still waving in our direction.

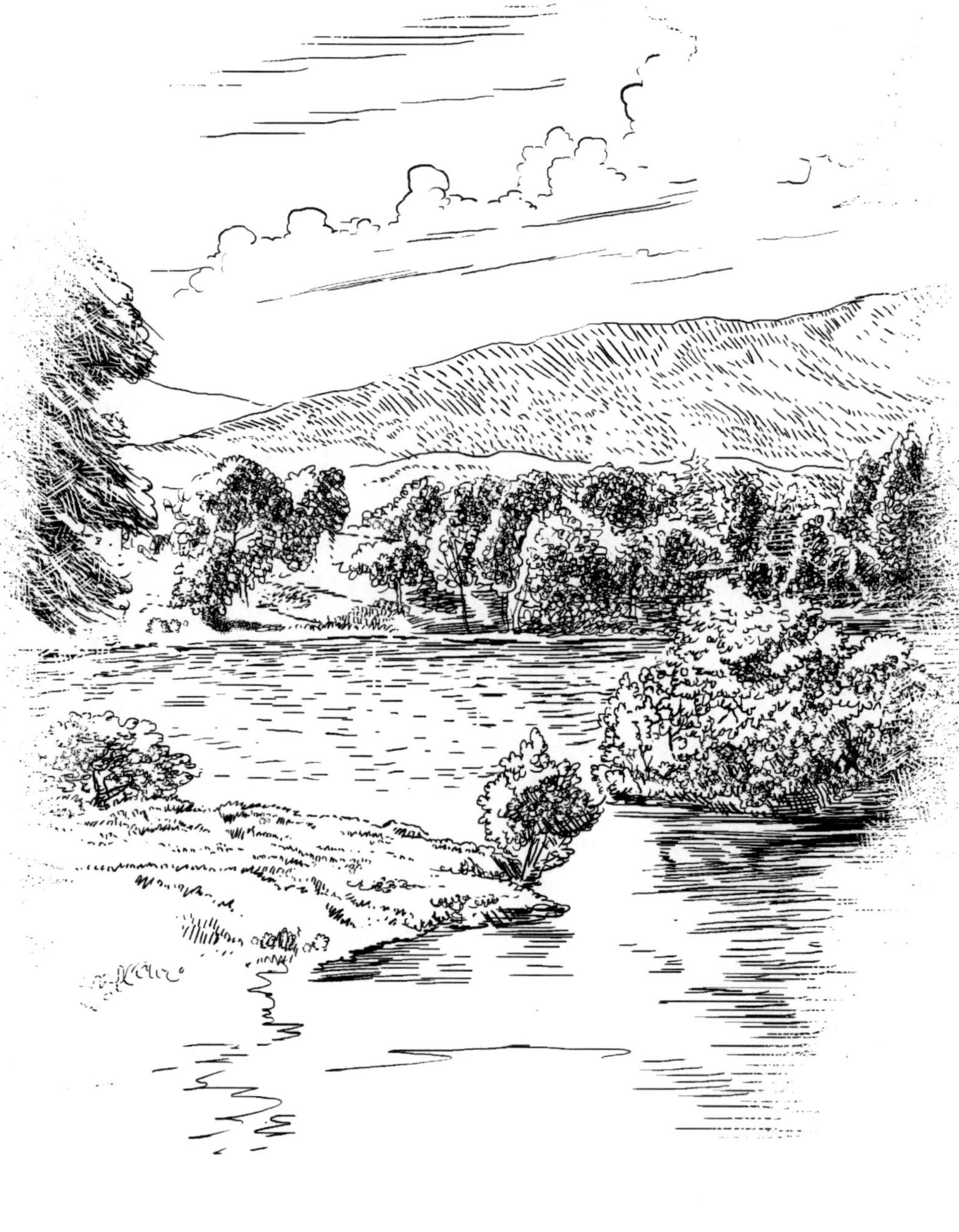

Chapter Five
Tarn Hows

Unfortunately our initial experiment taking Crocodile out onto the fells was marred by the weather. For his first walk we decided to go early in the morning because it was one of the most popular short walks in the Lake District, and even though it was very early in the year we knew that by nine o'clock there would be a fair number of people on the same circuit.

We met him as arranged, on the western side of Windermere near his island. We could have taken the estate car over on the ferry but we decided to drive round instead. We arrived just after seven-thirty and he was already waiting for us. He looked magnificent – but it was disappointing to observe that he most definitely did not blend in with the surroundings.

He had on the size 14 boots, the ones we had bought him in Ambleside. He was wearing a baggy pair of checked, mustard coloured plus fours, and some thick sage green socks that Kate had also found in the market at Milnthorpe. The plus fours, together with a tent sized Harris tweed and leather shooting jacket, effectively hid his tail. On his head he wore one of Kate's Balaclavas, but this was topped with another headpiece, a fine Tyrolean hat with a splendid feather in the side. He wore leather mittens and carried a tall crook in his right hand. One of Kate's long scarves was wrapped loosely round his snout and a large pair of sunglasses completed the camouflage.

"Gosh," gasped Kate, "he'll stand out like a sore thumb!"

I couldn't suppress a laugh, but I said, "Don't worry, we'll probably not meet any other walkers at this time in the morning, and even if we do, they'll just think that he's an eccentric old gentleman ... they may smile, or even laugh when they've passed by ... but they'll be too awestruck to approach him ... I think he's quite safe."

I made a mental note to suggest a more commonly worn ensemble for future outings with Crocodile, and then a second or two later I felt that might be wrong – because the thought also struck me that, generally, most people tend to keep odd looking, eccentric individuals at arms length, perhaps fearing that if they get too close they may be confronted with a situation that might make them feel uncomfortable. That apart, seeing Crocodile as he was now, about to take a giant step forward into society, convinced me completely that the best single piece of effective camouflage would be a large beard, and that Kate and I should put maximum effort into tracing the best sources of supply. I realised that his tail could easily be hidden under almost any suitably long clothing, but in order to ensure perfect camouflage for his snout for many situations that we would most definitely encounter, a large beard would be the only really practical and perfect solution.

We jumped out to greet him. We both gave him a big hug, then he stepped back and asked, "How do I look? You don't think I've overdone it do you? I wasn't quite sure what to put on!"

"You look fantastic!" we assured him.

"I've always tried to dress like the Professor," he said. "He has impeccable taste."

He jumped aboard and in a few minutes we were in the car park above Tarn Hows. Kate had brought a flask of tea and some biscuits – we all had a cup before we set off.

At first Crocodile seemed a little nervous, peering here and there and constantly looking over his shoulder. There were no other vehicles around and we hadn't passed anyone on foot on the way up. We crossed the cattle grid at Lane Head and down the one-way road that overlooks part of the high ridge stretching from Wetherlam to Coniston Old Man, with Yewdale and Yew Tree Farm in the valley below. This long ridge walk was one that we certainly intended to do with Crocodile when we felt he was ready. We couldn't even show him the high fells today ... they were shrouded in very low grey cloud.

A small herd of black and white belted Galloway cattle munched grass nonchalantly at the side of the road. As we passed within two or three feet they just looked up and stared at us inquisitively, with their big bright eyes. They were very clean and in tip-top condition.

"It's incredible to think that they have been out all winter," I said to Crocodile. "Kate and I were here a couple of weeks ago ... Tarn Hows was frozen ... this road was closed to traffic and we only just made it up on foot. They were here then and looked just as healthy. We have a friend who is a dairy farmer and he told us that *Belties*, as they are called, are derived from Celtic stock and are very hardy. Look at their thick shaggy coats, I bet they could survive in arctic conditions with coats like those."

"And they are free," said Crocodile, "and have not a care in the world ... they make me feel happy!"

We turned sharp right at the entrance to Tarn Hows Cottage and made our way down to Tom Gill car park by Glen Mary. Then, across a wooden bridge, dedicated to Tom and Ruth Wood, *Who loved the Lake District*, and up the path along the deep wooded ravine, known as Tom Gill.

All the way up trees cling precariously to the rock walls. They have such a shallow anchorage that the destiny of those closest to the ravine is sealed at birth. Many fall straight into the water while others topple to span the gorge, forming bridges for the woodland creatures, creating a safe way across when the torrent is in full flow. As if he had read my thoughts, Crocodile pointed with his crook up ahead to two red squirrels scampering over the trunk of a fallen tree to the other bank.

We are surrounded by hundreds of trees that do not share this fate. Crocodile knew their names almost as well as Kate, and together they identified those around us as we passed by. Among the ubiquitous, cone laden larch, were ash, beech, hawthorn, holly, oak, silver birch, spruce, and many majestic Scot's pine.

The ground was covered in a thick carpet of rustling brown leaves, and mosses were in abundance in every nook and cranny ... but there wasn't a single flower anywhere.

Chapter Five — Tarn Hows

On our journey to Tarn Hows that morning, all the verges and hedgerows were displaying clumps of snowdrops and wild daffodils were appearing here and there ... signs of spring were all around us, yet here in the wood by Tom Gill, winter was still holding on with a tight grip.

Crocodile, with the help of his crook, was now leading the way and enjoying himself immensely. Suddenly, he stopped in his tracks and pointed forward. We knew that he must be in sight of Tom Gill Waterfall, a spectacular cascade of white water tumbling into a rock pool sixty feet below. At the top of the gill, after a final scramble over smooth rock, we arrived at the tarn itself. Crocodile ran to the water but thankfully stopped at the edge. "Don't worry," he chuckled, "I am not going to jump in – although I might have been tempted if I hadn't been wearing all this disguise."

As he moved back from the water's edge we were all suddenly surprised by the appearance of an early morning jogger but he was past in an instant with just a nod in our direction in reply to Kate's cheery, "Good morning!"

We walked clockwise around the tarn until we reached a long s-shaped bench at the far end, where a stream runs into the tarn. We always sit here for a little while, unless somebody else has beaten us to it. A pair of mallards, fresh out of the water, waddled up to us. Crocodile unbuttoned his jacket to reveal his trusty saddlebags slung either side over his shoulders. He opened one and produced a pouch, out of which he took some tit-bits for the ducks, and said, "Like you at home, I feed the birds on my island everyday, and usually carry something with me when I go into the woods."

"This is a lovely spot," he continued, "I am beginning to understand what you meant when you said that the true grandeur of the Lake District can only be properly appreciated by walking on the fells. It seems like paradise here, so I cannot imagine what it is like standing on the highest mountains."

"The views from the high fells are not necessarily better," I tried to explain, "it is a different experience. Whereas here it is tranquil and beautiful, you could say, a vision of paradise ... on the high fells it is beautiful in a different way. In those places the views are magnificent and majestic; they are spectacular, but they can also be formidable."

At that moment two mountain-bikers flashed by without even a glance in our direction. Crocodile got quite excited when he spotted the bikes. "I do miss riding," he said. "I haven't been on a bike since I left the circus ... most of my act was done on bikes. Even though I say it myself, I was very good ... to the extent that I should have been one of the highest-paid performers at the circus. I didn't get a penny and they just kept me locked up in a cage twenty three hours a day, chained and muzzled, and on a dreadful diet ... just leftovers, and water to drink. If it hadn't been for the trapeze artists, Frank and Lily, who took pity on me and used to bring me food from their table, I think I would have starved."

Kate said, "We have two mountain bikes and we could easily get one for you. We go out on them every two or three weeks – often into Grizedale Forest where you can ride for miles and you hardly see another soul. We could easily take you there; that would be a perfect place for you to ride."

Crocodile got very excited at this prospect and immediately asked when we could get a bike for him.

"We'll get you one in a few days," I said, "but you had better try out a few different models and sizes. You can spend anything from a hundred pounds to several thousand. I think our own cost about three hundred pounds each but they are perfectly adequate for us. You might need something a little bit better if you are going to practice your cycling tricks on it."

"Gosh!" exclaimed Crocodile. "That will really give me something to look forward to ... I can't wait."

We continued our walk round the other side of the tarn and up to a high vantage point, the best place we knew to see the whole of Tarn Hows and the surrounding fells. The cloud had by now partially lifted, allowing us a view of Coniston Old Man, Wetherlam, the Langdale Pikes, Loughrigg Fell and Fairfield, their tops white with snow. Crinkle Crags and Bow Fell, usually visible from here, were still in cloud.

"This panorama is almost the same as the one we get from home, except that our house is five miles away on the other side of Windermere, over there," said Kate, pointing in the general direction of our home. "And that is where your island is as well, except that you cannot see what we can see."

More people had now started to arrive at the tarn and so we decided to go home earlier than originally planned. We did not want to take the slightest risk of anybody getting suspicious about Crocodile and we persuaded him that we should perfect his disguise before we got too ambitious. On the way back we promised Crocodile that we would try to get in touch with Emily and make arrangements to visit her in London at the earliest opportunity.

When we stopped by the side of the road where we had met him that morning Kate and I were both suddenly overcome with a feeling of sadness, and a strong awareness that Crocodile did not want us to go. All the way back from Tarn Hows, he kept telling us how much he had enjoyed the walk and how it had given him a new sense of freedom.

"What I have missed most of all, since last September, is being in the company of a friend," he said, in a voice full of emotion. "Although most people would say that I am now free, especially when compared to my life at the circus, where I was locked in a cage twenty-three hours a day. The Professor explained to me that together with other criteria, friendship is an essential condition of freedom and my own experience tells me he was right. The real test of freedom must take into account the quality of your friends. To be completely *free*, and therefore to be truly happy, you need to share your life with at least one honest, loving friend, but preferably more than one. If you have no true friends, or only fine feathered, fair weather friends, you may, in reality, be trapped in a world of your own, on your own, where you are both prisoner and jailer. Friendship and freedom go together like a horse and carriage, except that, you can have friendship without freedom ... for example, I had Mercedes at the zoo, where I was a prisoner in a cage ... but you cannot have true freedom without friendship. A carriage without a horse is not a lot of use."

"I had never thought of the connection between friendship and freedom," said Kate, "but I am sure that the Professor is absolutely right. Matt and I promise to be your true and faithful friends. We promise to visit you at least several times a week, unless of course we are on holiday. If we are on holiday in the UK you can come with us, when we have perfected your disguise. Matt and I have roughly planned out the whole year and we won't be going on any other holidays until we have taken you on a grand tour of the Lake District. We will show you all the places that we love ... all the places and everything else that makes living here so special."

Crocodile was suddenly transformed. He spoke excitedly, with a broad smile and bright eyes, "That is wonderful ... thank you so much ... I don't know how I can ever repay your kindness."

Crocodile gave us both a hug and turned to wave many times as he crossed the field and headed for home.

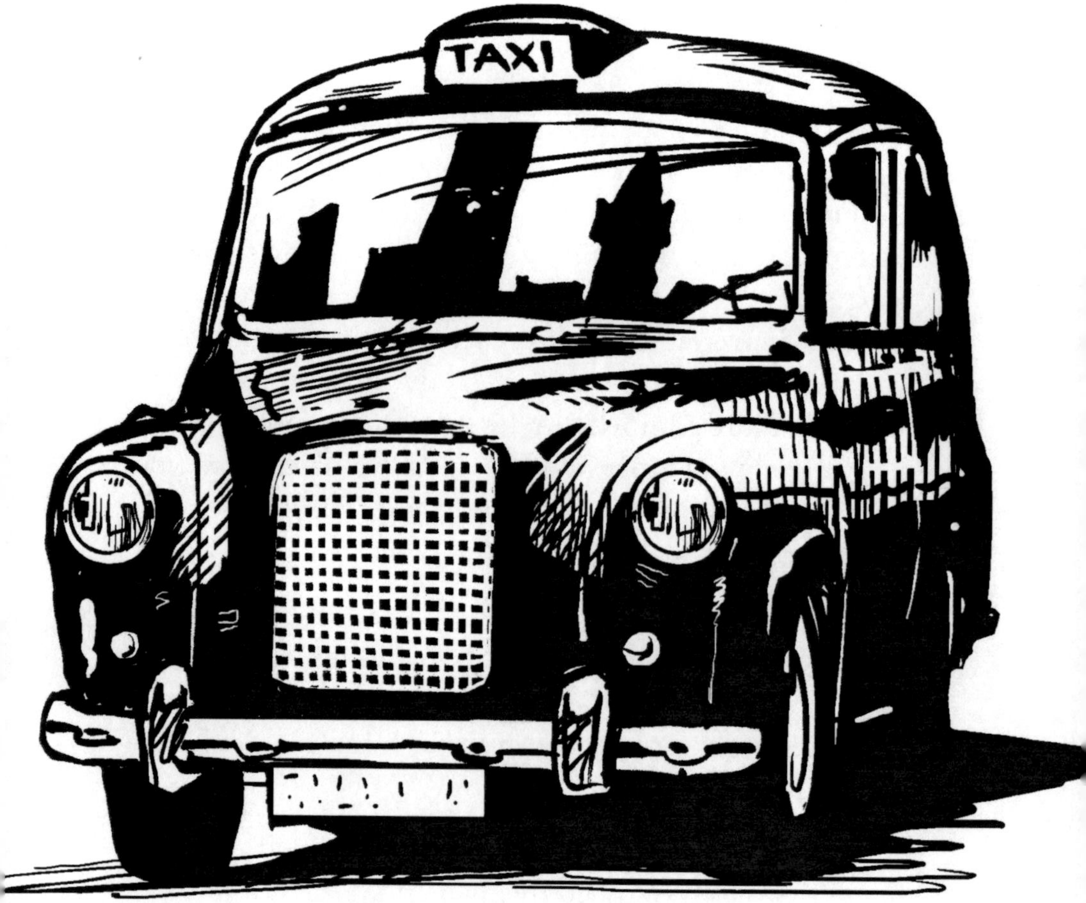
TAXI

Chapter Six
London & Emily

As we pulled into our drive we were surprised to find Napoleon standing underneath our holly tree and as soon as we got out of the car, he flew down on to the mat outside the front door.

"Look," said Kate, pointing to the big bird, "there's an envelope sticking out of the top of his pouch."

I pulled the envelope out of the pouch and saw that it was addressed to, Kate and Matt.

"For your urgent attention." It was beautifully written in ink in a flourishing ornate script.

I opened it up on the doorstep and we saw that it contained a note attached to a more formal looking document, elegantly written on parchment.

"It looks like Crocodile's will." I said with a perplexed glance at Kate.

On the covering note was written, 'From the bottom of my heart I thank you both for a wonderful day which I shall never forget.' Underneath it read, 'On the way back to my island I suddenly remembered that Emily had planned a six month holiday with her relatives in America and, if I also remember correctly, she was about to leave around this time. As a great favour would you kindly contact her with the utmost urgency so that she can give you news of the Professor? I will send Napoleon over again later today and tomorrow. Please would you put your reply in his pouch so that he can bring it back to me and please will you read the document carefully before telephoning Emily?' It was signed – 'Your Grateful Friend and Obedient Servant, William Hartley Crocodile.'

The document was headed, 'Under the assumption that I am no longer of this world or compos mentis.' Kate and I read through the contents, which included a list of detailed instructions for contacting Emily.

"Under the circumstances," I said, "I think we had better try to contact Emily today."

I left Kate talking to Napoleon while I went into the house in order to write an immediate reply. On the first piece of paper I could find I scribbled out a message to the effect that we would try to contact Emily today, but according to Crocodile's instructions I was not to telephone her from the Lake District, so it would take some time to accomplish this. Would he therefore leave it until near dusk before he sent Napoleon back again. Kate popped the note into Napoleon's pouch and off he went, a hop, skip and a jump and he soared into the air with a few flaps of his great wings. By the time we were down in the lounge and looking out across the lake, Napoleon was just a black speck in the distance dropping down on to Crocodile's island.

A flask of tea and a few hurriedly gathered biscuits and we were on our way out of the Lake District to telephone Emily.

Little did we know, when we had set out for Tarn Hows that morning with Crocodile that we would,

Chapter Six — London & Emily

twenty-four hours later, be on our way to his house in London to visit Emily. The Professor, in his hand written instructions, advised that, at least for the time being, not even Emily should know that Crocodile was living in the Lake District in a cave. Crocodile however, should try, by whatever safe means, to contact Emily as soon as possible after Christmas to let her know that he was safe and sound. Furthermore, under no circumstances should he return to London for some considerable time, perhaps for as long as a year. The Professor had also included a code for contacting Emily and vice versa.

The reason behind this apparently strange advice was that somebody knew about Crocodile's existence, somebody that the Professor believed would do him harm. Early last summer the Professor had started to receive strange and disturbing telephone calls requesting information about a missing crocodile. The callers told him that they were making enquiries on behalf of a zoo. There had been two attempted break-ins at the Professor's home, but because the security was almost on a par with Fort Knox, they had been unsuccessful. It was for this reason that they had returned early to the Lake District and the Professor had made the final decision to leave Crocodile in his cave and return to London alone, with the intention of returning before Christmas.

The Professor had given Crocodile and Emily the identity password, *Civis Romanus sum,* with the response, *Et Tu Brute?* Only the Professor, Crocodile and Emily, and now of course Kate and myself knew this code. So when I telephoned Emily the first thing I said was Civis

Romanus sum, to which she promptly replied, *Et Tu Brute?* She said that she was expecting a call as she had been briefed by Julius, but did not know when, so she was very pleased and relieved to hear from me.

Again, the Professor had instructed I telephoned Emily, from a place outside the Lake District, on a public phone, so that she would not know my location. I thought this a little extreme as I felt sure that she must have known that the Professor spent most of his holidays in the Lake District, and had just returned from there, so she would easily put two and two together ... but I carried out my instructions to the letter.

She immediately referred to Crocodile as Hartley. When I said that we called him Crocodile, she informed me that Julius also called him Crocodile as a familiar name, using Hartley for formal occasions ... but she had always called him Hartley, which she preferred. I went on to explain that I wished to visit her in London to discuss his situation and plans for his future.

"How is Hartley coping?" she asked, "Julius has looked after him so well for so long – I had feared that he might become depressed, even frightened, having to fend for himself."

I told her that she could rest assured, he was fine and very comfortable in his new home and that from now on he would have our help and protection. Again she said that she was most relieved that things were working out for him because she had felt that Julius had not pursued the best course of action – leaving Crocodile on his own. She then told me that she had laughed to herself when

Julius had given her a secret password and all her instructions, but she now believed that Hartley really had been in some sort of danger because she too had received a number of increasingly aggressive telephone calls. She also believed that for a time the house was being watched – occasionally, she had noticed men loitering for long periods of time outside the property. She had observed, on two occasions, binoculars being used to survey the house. Finally, she had telephoned the police and told them that she suspected a burglary was being planned.

"I feel a little safer now," she said, " and I have not had any more phone calls or detected anything suspicious going on outside."

"Just to be absolutely sure," she continued, "would you mind awfully if we met in a public place? I am certain that you are who you say you are … but I am on my own, so I can't be too careful. We could then return to the house after proper introductions."

"I must apologise," I said, "I didn't give you my name – you only know that I am a Roman Citizen,"

"I thought it was Brutus," she said, with a laugh.

"Touché," I replied, "Actually its Matthew, Matthew Worth. My wife is called Kate and we will come to see you together. To be on the safe side, midday would probably be the best time – just in case the train is delayed. Would Euston Station be too far for you to travel?"

"Not at all, but perhaps somewhere more comfortable," she said.

I suggested a cafe on the main concourse at St. Pancras, which Kate and I always visited when we were going on Eurostar. Emily knew exactly where it was.

"That will do fine," she said, "but you haven't told me which day. Also, how remiss of me, I should have told you I am going to America on Friday ... for six months!"

"At a push we could come tomorrow, if that would not be too inconvenient." I said.

"That would be perfect," she replied. "I have nothing at all planned for tomorrow."

"That is good of you to see us at such short notice," I said, "Crocodile ... I am sorry ... Hartley ... will be so relieved that I have been able to contact you. Before I go, may I enquire, on his behalf, about the Professor?"

"Sadly, I am afraid that it is not good news ... would you mind terribly if I give you the details when we meet tomorrow? I would rather do it face to face than over the telephone."

"Of course not, and we look forward to meeting you tomorrow." I said.

"Goodbye and thank you so much for calling, and for helping Hartley. Just one last thing ... so you will recognise me. I am silver-haired, middle aged, and I will be wearing a red silk scarf... Until tomorrow."

The following morning, as was usual on our trips to London, we parked the car near Oxenholme Station in good time for the 8.00 am Virgin train to Euston. Oxenholme Station is dear to Kate's heart because she had lived, until the age of eleven, just a few hundred yards down the road in a house that was built by her father in his spare time. All her childhood memories are here and they are stirred frequently, because we pass the house each time we go to the station. It is also known as Oxenholme, The Lake District Railway Station, as it is the junction between the West Coast main line and Windermere branch line. At the other end is the small bustling town of Windermere, and just down the hill is Bowness, and the lake.

The first station you come to, travelling south, is Carnforth ... famous for David Lean's classic film, *Brief Encounter*. As we sped through I began to recall the events that had determined we would be on this train and heading for London. Emily had seemed a very pleasant, sensible lady, and it gave both of us some comfort to know that Crocodile was not completely alone in the world and there was somebody else there to help him and to help us make the right decisions about his future. From what Crocodile had told us, I was aware of only one other person on the planet whom I believed could also be trusted and would no doubt help us, and that was Mercedes. I was determined, one day, to try and find her – both Kate and I believed that this would be one of the best and kindest things we could do for Crocodile. Fortunately we had been able to let him know that we had spoken with Emily and that we had arranged to meet her in London today, because just as we got back home after calling Emily, Napoleon flew in, and another hastily scribbled note outlining our plans was dispatched by *Raven Post*. It was confirmed to us that Ravens also had the advantage over pigeons in that they could offer a parcel service as well. When Kate opened his pouch to insert our message there were four freshly laid eggs inside and a note from Crocodile saying that he hoped we would enjoy them for breakfast!

After a pleasant, but uneventful journey, we arrived at Euston on time, and in a more relaxed frame of mind. We were early for our appointment with Emily so we walked to St. Pancras and mooched around the shops on the concourse for half an hour before taking a table outside our favourite café, where we ordered a cappuccino and a de-caf latte.

Instantly recognisable, Emily arrived exactly on time. Kate and I waved and she approached us, smiling. After introductions, I told her to call me Matt, but she could use my formal name, Matthew, if she preferred, to which she replied with a smile, "You're having a dig at me already, and I have been here less than a minute ... for that, *Matthew*, I may well use only your formal name! How is Hartley?"

"He is fine," we replied simultaneously. "But I think he is missing the Professor," added Kate.

At that moment the waiter approached and Emily ordered Earl Grey tea.

As soon as the waiter was out of earshot Emily immediately told us about the Professor.

"Poor Julius!" she said. "Sadly he passed away ... just three weeks before Christmas. He had been very ill for a long time and I know he would have gone much sooner if it had not been for Hartley and Julius' total commitment to do his best to ensure a safe future for him. Hartley became not only his best friend but he was the crowning glory of Julius' distinguished career. He was absolutely determined to go to see him at Christmas ...but he died in his sleep. I am sure it was for the best ... yes ... I know it was a blessing – because even if he had survived the journey he would probably have died while he was with Hartley and that would have put Crocodile in a terrible position ... he would not have known what to do. Imagine the legal complexities ... I shudder to think ... yes, it was definitely for the best."

    In the taxi from St. Pancras to Bayswater, Emily told us that Julius had set up a trust in which she and Hartley were the main beneficiaries. For legal reasons the house had been put in their joint names, of course without the solicitors knowing that he was a crocodile, and on the basis that it could not be sold while either of them was alive. "Julius left a lot of money to his many charities," she said, "but he also left more than enough for Hartley and myself to live very well for the rest of our lives. If he needs anything at all, just let me know, and I will transfer the necessary funds into your bank account, if you will kindly give me the details before you leave. Also, I have instructions to hand over £10,000 in cash for his immediate needs and I will give this to you as well. I know instinctively, already, after knowing you for less than an hour, that I can trust you. Furthermore, and please do not be offended by this, but, as Julius used to say, 'There are situations in life where you just have to act when there is realistically no other option – if you are trapped in a burning building and the only escape is to jump into a swimming pool, or a lake, but you can't swim, you may as well take the chance'. I will be in America by the end of the week and as I can't do anything myself to help Hartley I have nothing to lose. The £10,000 doesn't belong to me anyway, so I couldn't spend it, and there is plenty more in the bank. I hasten to add that my own good sense would prevent me from giving you all of Hartley's money, at least without proof that it was going to be used entirely for his benefit."

"Kate and I fully understand your situation and we can only assure you that we have pledged to look after him for as long as he needs us, and we will do our best to fulfil the Professor's role as his guardians."

Suddenly, I realised that the taxi had stopped at traffic lights just round the corner from where Kate and I used to live. I asked Emily if she would mind if we took a very short detour so that we could take a look at our old house. This was the second house today we had passed in which Kate kept a large store of very happy memories. Of course, none of my memories were attached to the house on Oxenholme Road, but wonderful memories, memories of our salad days, flooded back in the few seconds that we stopped in Craven Hill Gardens. It looked exactly the same as it had all those years ago as if time had stood still. It would no doubt look the same in another hundred years. The classically designed, grand terraced buildings, were too good to change, the architecture could not be improved.

A few minutes later the taxi pulled up outside the Professor's house, a magnificent Regency style mansion set behind iron railings and a small front garden. After a short wrangle with Emily, I paid the fare. It was nice to be called *Guv* again in a strong Cockney accent.

Inside the front door was a vestibule with a beautiful mosaic floor, which continued into the main hall. The design was classical, depicting a woodland grove with three garlanded nymphs, one with a platter of fruit, one with a pitcher of wine, and one playing panpipes, all attending superior deities I would imagine, at a picnic. The hall was lit with natural light, filtering through a large stained glass skylight overhead. At the far end of the hall was an imposing, centrally positioned, stone staircase. The treads were carpeted and the deep red carpet held in place with heavy brass stair-rods.

Emily led us past two opposite pairs of double doors and then to the left of the staircase into a cloakroom where she took our coats. It was a more luxurious version of Crocodile's bathroom in the cave, but without the baths. Italian marble had been extensively used. Two of the walls were mirrored glass and lined with glass shelves, stacked with perfumes, powders and lotions. The most noticeable difference was the lighting. Here low-voltage electric lighting made everything sparkle compared with the warm glow of candlelight in the cave.

Emily then took us back through the hall and opened the pair of doors, now to our right. She hesitated and asked, "Would you like to see Hartley's pool first?"

I suppose it was a rhetorical question because of course we said that we would love to see it. We followed her back through the hall again, this time to the right of the staircase where she pointed out a short corridor to the kitchen. The entrance to the pool was off a lobby at the back of the main staircase.

A pair of heavy wooden studded doors, perhaps ten feet in height, guarded the entrance to Crocodile's pool. They completely filled the arched portal in which they stood and must have been hinged on the inside. Emily took hold of the pair of iron hoop handles and, twisting both wrists, turned them together. We heard the echoing clump of a heavy latch. A heave from her slight shoulders and the two giant doors parted company with a melancholy groan, to reveal their secret. Our jaws dropped open simultaneously; it was the most beautiful Roman bathhouse we had ever seen.

The bath was rectangular, about seven metres by fifteen. Seats had been built into the sides at regular intervals all the way round. Presumably this enabled bathers to sit comfortably in the water and relax, or read a book. The materials used were marble with mosaic tiles. On each side, along the length of the pool, were marble columns about twelve feet high. These were the supports of the porticos, which ran full length down both sides of the room. As in the hall, the bathhouse was lit with natural light through a stained glass cupola, thirty feet above our heads, and positioned so that its apex was directly over the centre of the pool.

"I thought it was very extravagant of Julius ... building such a grand pool for Hartley. But as it turned out, Julius ended up using it almost as much as Hartley. They would both spend ages in here, just talking and reading, or playing chess. After Hartley taught Julius to swim, Julius made a floating chessboard and they would spend hours in the water playing chess. I warned Julius that his skin would shrivel up if he wasn't careful," she said, laughing and wiping a tear from her eye.

I helped Emily to close the doors and we followed her back to the drawing room. She said that she had made a light buffet lunch and asked us to excuse her for a few moments while she went to boil the kettle.

As soon as she was out of earshot, Kate whispered, "This house is incredible, and that pool, it's to die for. I thought Crocodile lived in style in his cave ... but this is unadulterated luxury. I bet none of the Roman Emperors had a pool as classy as that."

Emily returned shortly, pushing a very large trolley full of food. It had a tabletop with two shelves underneath and, strangely, two steering wheels, one at each side.

"This is another of Julius' inventions," she said and laughed again. "He had some weird and wonderful ideas ... but everything he created was well thought out and perfectly engineered. I have to admit that they were not all as silly as many of them looked ... you should have seen his fool-proof alarm clock, I've had it dismantled now because I am sleeping in his bedroom and I had no intention of being attacked by an alarm clock early in the morning. This contraption however has proven a Godsend because of the remoteness of the kitchen. He called it his *in-house catering unit*. It looks cumbersome but it is remarkably easy to push and to operate and it does save me a lot of work. It has heated sections built into it for keeping food hot. Using the wheels at the sides you can raise the shelves to the same height as the top to make a complete table and it is balanced and weighted so that no matter what you load it up with, it cannot fall over. At least that is what Julius said, and, to my knowledge, it hasn't happened yet."

Together with a choice of fine teas, we were treated to warm bread rolls and butter, a seafood cocktail, spicy chicken on skewers, game pie and a plain mixed salad. Clearly, Emily wasn't vegetarian but there was enough choice to satisfy Kate, particularly as this was followed by a selection of cheeses with celery, then homemade trifle and fruitcake. We ended up pleasantly full.

"I am afraid I am just a plain old-fashioned cook," said Emily apologetically, "not cordon bleu or Michelin starred, like Julius and Hartley ... we had some wonderful lunches and dinner parties when they were in charge of the kitchen. I was reduced to the rank of kitchen porter, but I always enjoyed myself and will miss that part of my life very much."

We told her that her lunch was delightful and quite unexpected, and we had already experienced Hartley's wonderful cooking and hospitality.

"Also," Emily went on to explain, "I purposely didn't offer you wine because I have a suggestion to make which is incompatible with drinking at lunchtime. I don't know if you are aware but Julius made a special vehicle for Hartley, the one they used for their trips to the Lake District. My suggestion is ... so long as you can find somewhere to park it, that you take it back with you. I asked the man who looks after my car to get a new MOT certificate and he has made sure that the battery is fully charged ... so it is ready to go!"

"That is an excellent idea," I replied. "Parking isn't a problem, we live in the Lake District not London, and anyway, we have a large garage at home, with space for another vehicle. I was wondering how we would get Hartley to London ... this would solve the problem."

In an instant we had revised our travel arrangements for the return journey. We had intended to catch the 8.00pm train from Euston, arriving at Oxenholme around 11.00pm.

If we were to drive home it would mean leaving much earlier and sadly forgoing afternoon tea at Fortnum and Masons, but after the lunch we had just eaten, this prospect did not now seem quite as great a sacrifice.

I was mentally planning the detail of the journey when Emily interrupted my train of thought. She apologised for the long-standing engagement she had, to visit her cousin in America – she would be staying in New York and Boston and would be away for several months. Because she had been concerned about security, she had engaged the services of another cousin and his wife, who had agreed to stay in the house until she returned. She would inform the police of her plans so they could also keep an eye on things.

I told her that it wasn't a problem to us and anyway, the Professor had advised Hartley not to return to London in the near future. I asked her if she would kindly inform her cousin and his wife that we would contact them so we could find out exactly when she intended to return. We would then bring Hartley to see her when it was convenient. I asked her if the password would be necessary. She said that they were totally unaware of Hartley's existence and if I used the password they would think that I was mad.

We spent another hour at the house with Emily. She told us more about the Professor, about his career, his charities and his life with Hartley. She gave us the £10,000 in an envelope and I gave her my bank details so that if anything went wrong she could transfer money into my account for Hartley. After coffee and biscuits we followed her to a lock-up garage, about a quarter of a mile from the house, where the Dormobile was kept. It was silver, with black, one-way, glass windows. It was more modern and far better looking than we had expected and it started first time.

Emily told me to keep the garage keys, as she had a spare set, so that we could use it whenever we came to London. She said that she would walk back to the house to get a bit more fresh air. We thanked her again for the lovely lunch and for all the trouble she had taken. She said that she was so relieved that Hartley had found such good friends and she looked forward to seeing us all in a few months. We wished her bon voyage for her trip to the States and waved goodbye.

In my head I had already planned the journey home – it would not be the shortest way but it would be more pleasant and more rush hour proof. Instead of the usual M1, M6 route, we would go on the M40, with a detour into the Cotswolds. We had discussed the possibility of staying overnight at one of our favourite pubs – but the three bedrooms were already booked. We changed our minds about staying and instead stopped for a short break in Chipping Campden, where we shared a sandwich and some nibbles. Kate had a glass of white wine and I had a non-alcoholic, lager and then we were on our way again, on roads we knew well.

The journey was now Stratford, Henley-in-Arden, then M42, M6 Toll, and M6 until 15 miles from home. We took two further short breaks for a coffee, at Norton Canes and Sandbach. We were back home before 11-30, only a few minutes later than we would have been if we had come back on the train. But it had taken nearly twice as long.

"Do you know what we forgot?" said Kate, as I opened the front door. "We've left our car at Oxenholme Station!"

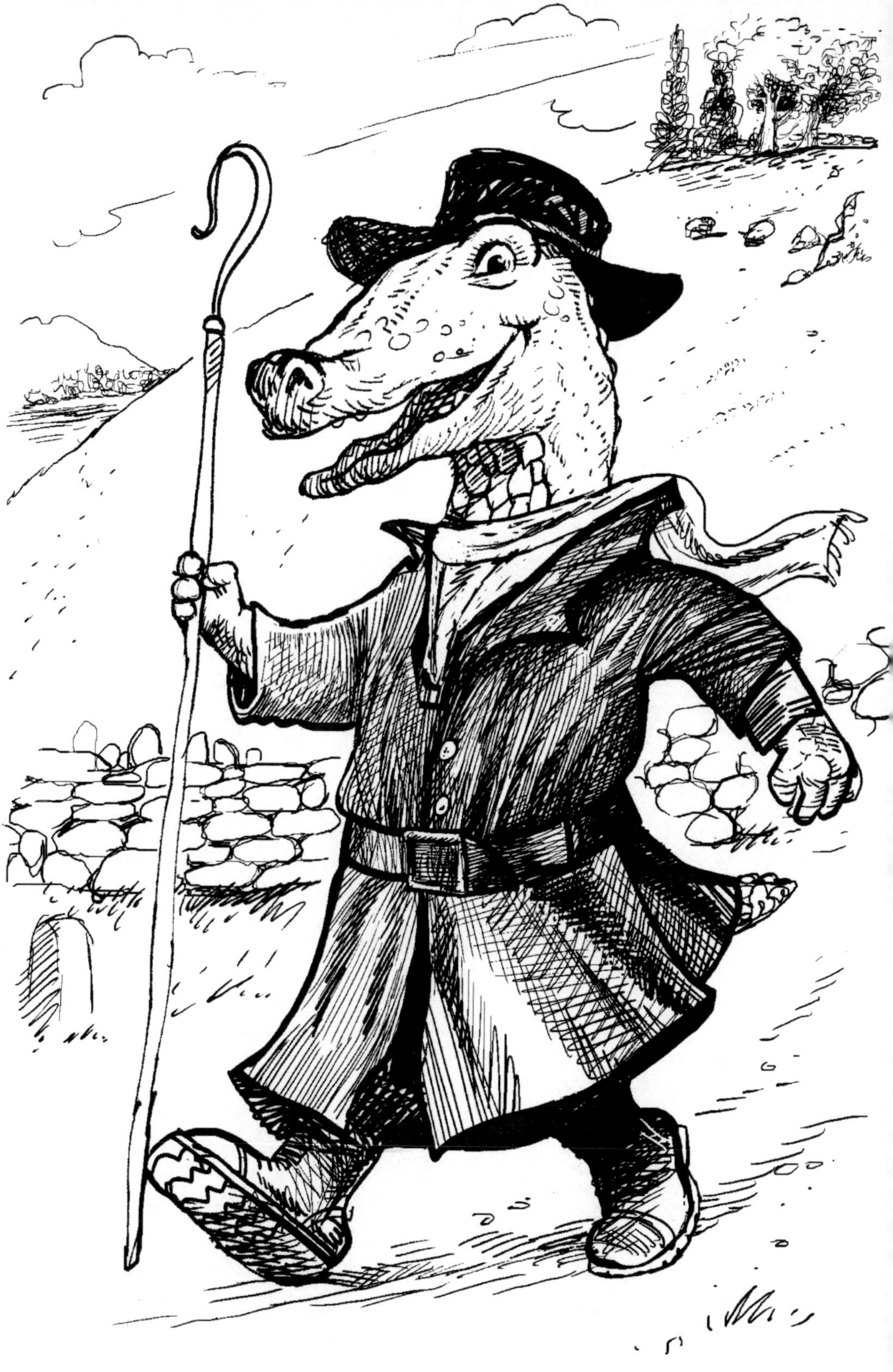

Chapter Seven
Crocodile's Grand Tour

PART I

The existence of Crocodile had changed our lives dramatically. It had also made us think much more about life in general, and about our own life experiences and how we should now use what we had learned in order to do what was best for him. The very best experience in life is learning from your own mistakes – *learning the hard way* – which is in fact, *learning the best way* – there is nothing to beat first-hand personal experience. The main qualification is that things have a habit of appearing in different guises, and often it is only after multiple experiences of a similar problem that you gain real experience. Even then, you rarely know the full truth about a given situation, so in the end there will always be an element of risk. Experience gives you some ability to manage risk, but nevertheless you will always be dealing with probabilities, and ultimately with chance and hazard.

I have never considered myself as a gambler, but as I got older, and with more experience of life's ups and downs, twists and turns, successes and failures, I came more and more to realise that the majority of those of us who try never to take a risk ultimately form the hard core of life's losers.

Kate and I were well aware that when you are as young as Crocodile you think you know everything, especially if you are well-educated. It is only as you travel through life that you realise more and more that you don't. Education, per se, does not make you worldly-wise. For that reason I am always wary of the judgement of young people in powerful positions, and for that matter, the views of people of any age who are so certain about all their beliefs. It is a sobering thought to know that in one book, *The Origin of Species*, Charles Darwin proved beyond a reasonable doubt that all the greatest minds throughout history were wrong. I hasten to add that we did not think that Crocodile proved Darwin wrong – it proved him right. Crocodile was simply a quantum leap in the evolution of one ancient species. Nevertheless, without the extreme patience of Mercedes and the genius of the Professor, the power of Crocodile's brain would never have been known. He could so easily have ended up in a cage, in a zoo, or in a circus, entertaining people with clever tricks but without his full potential ever being realised.

It cannot be denied that the Professor had got him to where he was by being ultra careful in everything that they did, and that strategy had been successful. Unfortunately, it had resulted in Crocodile missing out on many wonderful things that he could have done to enrich his life. We believed that the time had now come for him, with our help, to remove his shackles, to be more adventurous and to be free.

Kate and I promised each other that we would do our best to show Crocodile as much of the Lake District as possible over the coming months. This would include many easy walks, then building up to some of the longer and more arduous ascents of Lakeland's finest mountains. If we could get his disguises near perfect we planned to intersperse the walks with bike rides, boat trips, picnics, country fairs, shows, sports days, and visits to historic buildings. This was what we did every year, but this year was going to abound with pleasure and we would make it the best year ever both for ourselves, and for Crocodile.

We knew exactly where to start ... where better to walk than in Alfred Wainwright's footsteps, retracing his very first fell walk from Windermere railway station, where he'd arrived on a steam train from his hometown of Blackburn. He would have walked out of the station, across the main road to Ambleside, and up a winding woodland path to the rocky outcrop of Orrest Head. In only twenty minutes he would have been standing on the top, and gazing at a stupendous panoramic view of Windermere and the surrounding fells.

Orrest Head is the perfect appetizer to the banquet that is to follow. I can easily imagine the shocked disbelief on the twenty-three year old Alfred Wainwright's face, a face that hitherto had looked only upon the sombre moorland landscape surrounding the Lancashire mill town of Blackburn, where he was born and raised. I can imagine exactly the impact it would have had because I know Blackburn very well, as from an early age I spent many weeks there at the home of my cousins, my mother's twin sister's children. They, like Alfred Wainwright, were brought up in a landscape of steepled, chimney laden, mills, and two-up, two-down, back-to-back stone and brick terraced houses, with outside privies. The most common sound was not the sweetness of birdsong, but the clatter of clogs on the cobbles of Blackburn's hilly streets as the workers wended their way to and from work in the dark satanic mills.

For Kate and myself, the Lake District is as close to the Garden of Eden as it is possible to find on Earth. Through the seasons of the year we live in an ever-changing landscape, which encompasses the majesty of the Lakeland fells, the grandeur of the dales, the splendour of the lakes, and the beauty of the wayside flowers.

It is the ubiquitous presence of water that gives the Lake District a saturation of colour and an unsurpassed wealth of flowering beauty. Its outstanding feature is the incredible variety of scenery to be seen round every lake and valley. Nowhere has nature crammed so much into so small a space as in the Lake District.

Before our tour could begin we had one important and distressing task to perform and that was to tell Crocodile about the Professor. The morning after our return from London we got up early and sailed across to Cocodile's Island. We saw him standing there and waving in our direction before we were half way across the Lake. I will not go into detail because it is too distressing and the only thing that made it ever so slightly easier was that he told us instantly that he had already steeled himself for bad news about the Professor. We offered to spend some time with him but he said that he would prefer to remain on his own for the rest of the day, but if he could look forward to going out with us tomorrow that would be a great comfort and would help him through. We told

Chapter Seven   Crocodile's Grand Tour

him that we had returned in the Dormobile and that we would take him in it tomorrow. We also told him that he could try on some of the new beards that had started to arrive in the post. With this in mind we arranged to meet him at nine in our boathouse. There were tears in his eyes as we pulled away from the shore, but he stood there, stalwart, waving to us until we were home.

We chose a perfect day early in spring to begin Crocodile's grand tour of the Lake District. We had given much thought to his disguises and we were especially pleased with some of the beards that we had managed to acquire for him. The beards had come in many styles and sizes but the best ones were just the right shape and size to completely cover his long snout. We were at last confident that, apart from looking like an eccentric dandy, he would pass almost, but not quite unnoticed, in a crowded place. He would not exactly melt into the background, as we had hoped, because he insisted on wearing certain flamboyant pieces of apparel in conjunction with the outdoor clothing that we had obtained for him. In the end we said, "Why not?" In life other people don't mind you being a little different, but it is a puzzlement why people don't like you to appear too different. Envy, even admiration, can soon turn to scorn and ridicule or worse. I am sure it is a basic instinct in the nature of all animals – to pick on those of their kind who are perceived as being a little too different from the rest of the pack.

Many people would, no doubt, take a second glance at Crocodile, but he appeared not so out of the ordinary as to arouse suspicion. Some may smile at his splendid beard, but we felt it highly unlikely that anyone would go further than expressing amused interest, let alone accost him in an aggressive manner or assume that there could be a very unusual creature underneath the bearded ensemble. There wasn't a person on the planet who, in their wildest dreams, would imagine for an instant that he could be a crocodile in disguise.

Confident that he was pretty safe, we set off on that bright February morning to re-trace Wainwright's steps up Orrest Head. Halfway up the woodland path, through a gap in the trees, we could already see partway down the length of Windermere. I had brought a pair of binoculars with me, and I took a quick look, focusing them on what I already knew was there, and then handed them to Crocodile. "What do you see?" I asked.

"It's my island!" he shouted, with great excitement.

Centre screen, at the furthest point visible on the lake, was Crocodile's Island.

"You get an even better view from the top," I said, "and from there you can see exactly where you live in relation to everything else around you."

When he stood on the top and looked about him, Crocodile's jaw dropped open so wide that we feared he would swallow his splendid beard when he closed his mouth. We had told him to close his eye when we got near to the top, and we guided him into the position we had planned in advance; that was looking in a southeasterly direction. We then told him to turn anti-clockwise so his view was in the direction of the Pennines in the east, above Kirby Lonsdale and Ingleton. As he continued to turn he would see the Pennines above Sedbergh, Hawes, and the Yorkshire Dales – (James Herriot country) – then over Shap in the direction of Appleby and Penrith. Through the final 180 degrees, the view is over Cumbria and the names of the highest peaks together with their heights are etched into the top of a stone standing on a timber lectern, so they can be easily identified. We pointed them out to Crocodile and read their names out loud, "The Langdale Pikes, Great Gable, Great End, Bow Fell, Scafell Pike, the highest place in England, Crinkle Crags, Wetherlam, and Coniston Old Man."

I handed the binoculars to Crocodile again so that he could get a closer view of each of these magnificent Lakeland fells. Pointing out his island again, I told him that it lay between the Old Man and our house, but that the house was not visible from the top of Orrest Head. It was hidden behind the hills and woodland to the south of Bowness.

"What we plan to do this year," I said, "is to take you to the summit of many of those mountains. We'll also take you up several of our other favourites, such as Fairfield, just over there, to the north, and to the Helvellyn range beyond. We may also climb Skiddaw and Blencathra, north of Keswick. And Pillar and Haystacks, over the other side of Scafell Pike, and Great Gable that you can see in the distance."

"Through the summer months we will probably try to do one every ten days or so," said Kate, "In between we'll have plenty of time for shorter walks, and all the other pleasures we have lined up for you. Don't worry though, we won't push you too hard – we don't have to do everything in one year! If we don't do it this year, we'll do it next ... or the year after. We've got it all to look forward to, no matter when!"

Crocodile seemed lost for words and his head just nodded up and down. He then focussed the binoculars once more on his island. "I can't understand why it looks so small from here," he said in a puzzled voice. "I can see that it is definitely my island because I can recognise the trees and rocks and the general shape, but it looks tiny."

"It's called perspective," Kate said, "It's like holding a penny close to your eye when there is a full moon; the penny looks bigger than the moon because it is so much closer to your eye. In a painting, an artist has to create perspective by actually painting things smaller in the background, so they appear further away, even though in reality they are the same distance from your eye, and in the same plane. A figure in the foreground will be painted larger than a house in the background. Experience tells you that the house must be bigger even though it looks smaller. From where I am standing, you are a hundred times bigger than your island and Scafell Pike. But I know from experience that it only appears so because they are so far away."

Crocodile still didn't seem entirely convinced, but his head continued to nod up and down as if he had taken it all in.

We sat on a bench at the top for a while and had a cup of tea from our thermos flask. "It is strange to think," I said, "that many people have lived their whole lives without standing on a spot like this. In the past, all over Britain, people usually didn't travel more than thirty miles or so from the village or town of their birth, so if they didn't live near a mountain, like the villagers in the Lake District, they would never have done what you have just done and seen where you live in relation to everything else around you. Kate and I sometimes hire a hot air balloon and go high up over the Lake District so that we can see all of it. We once passed directly over our house, and could probably have landed in the garden if there had been no wind. You need a perfect day and perfect weather – Kate and I will try to arrange a flight for all of us this summer."

"That would be absolutely fantastic," said Crocodile, "I once saw a film about some people going all round the world in an air balloon in eighty days. Do you need oxygen masks?"

"No," I replied with a smile, "you don't go that high, but you can go pretty high if the weather conditions are just right. I must ask at the balloon company how high you can go if the weather is very good. We often see balloons over our house; some will float gently right down to the lake and then they will go up to a few thousand feet, so high that you almost lose sight of them with the naked eye."

Our next stop was to be Biskey Howe, on the other side of Windermere, just above Bowness. It is only a stone's throw from where we built our first house in the Lake District. On our way to Biskey Howe we pointed out the house to Crocodile and pulled into the drive. Kate told him that a lot of our memories were there and moving to the Lakes was the best thing we had ever done.

"It looks a wonderful house," he said, "why ever did you leave it?"

"Yes, it is a lovely house and we built it intending to stay there for the rest of our lives. The plot of land that we bought to build it on was part of the garden of the house up there. It was the only plot of land in the whole of the Lake District that we could afford and we were very lucky to get it because it was never advertised. The man, who owned the house next door and the garden, had already got planning permission to build one himself, but had taken a job abroad before he started to build it. By chance we found this out from his architect who we had contacted for another reason. We shot straight round here and, over a cup of tea, we had shaken hands on a deal to purchase his land."

"We built the house of our dreams and lived very happily here for several years. The one single thing that gnawed away at us was that even though we were living in the Garden of Eden, we couldn't see the Garden – we could only see other houses. One day, again by chance, we came across a house that was not as nice as ours but it had stunning views over Windermere and the surrounding fells. We thought we might just be able to afford the asking price and we didn't care if it took us ten years to change the building – the view was so wonderful. Of course that meant selling this house, the one that we had put so much loving care into. We had to make one of those crucial decisions, which at some time or another everybody has to make. It is never easy at the time, but you know in your heart that if you don't do it you will regret it for the rest of your life. Such a decision as

Shakespeare so eloquently put it, *'There is a tide in the affairs of man, which taken at the flood leads on to fortune.'* Sometimes, in life, fate only gives you one big chance, and most people, I believe, know instinctively, that it is now or never. My advice to you is that if you know in your heart that fate has offered you such a chance, take it. As the Professor said, 'follow your heart'. You may regret it forever if you don't."

"I do sometimes get a little confused," Crocodile said, "about the difference between following your heart and taking every precaution, and doing all the checks and balances."

"It does sound contradictory," I replied. "You should always, as the Professor advised, do your research thoroughly. However as I have tried to explain, life is full of chance and hazard and you can only be certain that you have done the right thing after the event, that is, at some point in the future. Retrospectively, you will nearly always know if you made the best choice. When we made the decision to sell this house that we had moved heaven and earth for, we kept asking ourselves the question, why should we sell it for something much more expensive, that was over thirty years old and needed a fortune spending on it? That was the question that our bank manager also kept asking. In the end, to some degree, we let our hearts rule our heads but only because our experience had taught us that this was a unique situation. It really was a lifetime opportunity and we knew that if we took the easy path and turned it down, we might never get the chance again to own something so special, something that we would enjoy for the rest of our lives. Instinctively, we knew that it was a now or never situation. Today we are absolutely certain that we made the right choice, but as in a card-game analogy, we could have been dealt a very bad hand and we may have lived to regret it. In life, there are no guarantees. I just hope, that if you take our advice, as you have taken the Professor's, we can help you to make the right decisions most of the time. I have to warn you that we may not always be right, but, I hope we will also be here to help when things go wrong."

"I think I am beginning to understand the reasoning behind the Professor's advice and his insistence that, in his absence, I should find someone that I could trust to help me. I believe now that I have much more to learn about life than I thought I had and I appreciate so much what you are doing for me. I do realise that you may sometimes give me advice that turns out to be wrong, because, and I think this is what you are saying, it is impossible to predict the future with absolute certainty; luck will always play a part."

"Yes, you are right," I said, "but you can also help to make your own luck, by trying hard and doing things properly and sensibly. It's just that sometimes you have to take a chance and make an instant decision and keep your fingers crossed."

"Don't worry," Kate said, reassuringly, "I am sure that we are all going to have a wonderful year without anything going wrong, and always remember that in terms of the quality of life and our potential for pleasure, merely living in the Lake District gives us a head start on everybody else. Now for the moment, no more serious talk; we'll take you to another magical place just up the road."

Chapter Seven
Crocodile's Grand Tour

"You're now going to get another surprise," Kate continued. "We used to come to Biskey Howe nearly every week when we lived up the road. It was like an extension to our garden as you will see in a couple of minutes. You get a very splendid view from here so we used to bring a flask of tea, or even a bottle of wine on occasions, and a book each, or some magazines, and sit here for a couple of hours."

I parked the Dormobile at the side of the road so that we had only a few yards to walk. We went up a couple of steps and along a short narrow path through some dark bushes. When we came to a large rock face, I told Crocodile to close his eyes again. We led him a few yards further, and then I said, "You can open them now." Once more we witnessed the extreme look of surprise on his face at the view stretching out in front of him.

"I always think of Lionel Wallace in H.G.Wells' short story *The Door in the Wall*," I said,

"If you don't know the story, it's about a man, who as a young boy discovers a secret door in a wall near to where he lives in London. He only had to walk through that door and he was in paradise."

"I have read, *Alice In Wonderland*," said Crocodile. "It's a bit like Alice going down the rabbit hole and coming out in a strange new world."

"Or, as in C.S. Lewis' book, *The Lion, the Witch and the Wardrobe*," said Kate, "where the four children go through a wardrobe in a large country house and into the magical snow-covered world of Narnia."

"This conversation has just reminded me of something that I experienced when I was young," I said. "My father used to take me to a beautiful garden not far from where we lived. I called it my secret garden because, like here, the entrance was through some bushes, then down a wide set of steps and on to a long, very green lawn bordered with pretty flowers and totally surrounded by trees. After my father died I went back many times to try to find that garden but never could. One day I bought a large-scale map of the area and I spent the whole day looking for my garden, but I couldn't find it. I have often thought that I must have dreamed it up, but I am as sure as I can be that I didn't."

"When I was at the circus," said Crocodile, "I often used to dream that I was back with Mercedes, in a beautiful park with lawns and flowers and pools with fountains, but I know that I was just dreaming because, although the zoo was surrounded by a wonderful park with a lake, I was never allowed out of my cage. Mercedes told me that she would love to take me on a picnic in the park or into the surrounding countryside, but the director of the zoo would never permit it and it was as much as her job was worth to risk taking me without permission. In spite of this she was always optimistic that one day I would be free and that we would travel to beautiful places together."

Like Orrest Head, the view from Biskey Howe is spectacular. You are not as high so you don't get the same overview and you don't get a full circle panorama, but if anything the surprise can be even greater because it is totally unexpected. You don't get the foretaste of things to come as you do as you climb up Orrest Head.

"There's my island again," shouted Crocodile. "It looks much bigger from here."

I handed him the binoculars so he could take a closer look.

"Yes I can see everything much more clearly. I don't think that I could pick out Napoleon or Sherwood, but I think I could see people, if anybody had landed there. You have a look Kate."

Kate took the glasses, peered through them for a while, and then said suddenly, "I think I've just had a fantastic idea. As well as the boathouse we also have a summerhouse, it's right at the back of the boathouse, so you can't see it from your island. Well, inside there's a huge cupboard as well as a toilet and washbasin with a mirror above it. There's also a tiny kitchen facility for making tea and coffee and simple meals. My idea is that instead of us driving all the way round the lake in the Dormobile to collect you at the side of the road, all you have to do, say after your morning swim, is to swim into the boathouse and then go straight into the summerhouse. All we need to do is to get a few sets of clothes and other disguises for you, and keep them in the cupboard. There's a flagpole outside so you could simply hoist the flag when you are ready and we'll come down and collect you in the Dormobile."

"You see," I said to Crocodile, with a smile, "Kate is not just a pretty face."

"I have to admit that it's a brilliant idea," said Crocodile. "It only takes me a few minutes to swim across; it's actually much quicker than in the boat."

"It would also be another safe haven for you if, for whatever reason, you could not return to your island," I added. "Moreover you can get out of the lake without being seen because it's deep water right into the boathouse."

"It's a pity that we can't stay here a bit longer," I said, "but we wanted to try and get you a bike today. We can always come here whenever we want to, so we can still use Biskey Howe as an extension to our garden, even though we live farther away now. If we have bikes we can be here in a few minutes."

"I can't wait to get on a bike again," said Crocodile enthusiastically. "It seems like donkeys' years since I rode one at the circus. I hope I haven't forgotten how to ride."

"That's one thing you don't forget," said Kate. "Like ice-skating, or swimming, once you know how, you can always do it. It becomes natural and I think it is as much about confidence as technique. Once you know you are not going to fall off, fall over, or sink, you will always be able to do it. You'll soon find out because that's where we are going next, to get you a mountain bike."

PART II

We knew of several excellent bike stores in and around Kendal but we had decided to take him to one where he could ride it outside and where there were no pedestrians or traffic to give him a problem. When we arrived outside the store Kate and I told him that we thought it a good idea for him to come in with us, not only so that he could look at all the bikes and choose the one that he preferred but also because it would be a good test of his disguise.

He seemed a little startled at this suggestion, but I think that the temptation of getting his hands on one of the bikes made his mind up for him and he suddenly seemed eager to go inside.

We wandered up and down the aisles of bikes for some time without being approached by any of the sales staff. There was an incredible selection to choose from, but this was very much narrowed down by how much one wanted to pay or could afford. The price range seemed to be between less than £100, to well over £3500, and there may have been some machines more expensive than that. We told him that it was to be a present from Kate and myself, but as we weren't made of money, we would like him to choose something around the £500 mark. He tried to argue that he had plenty of money and he didn't expect us to pay, but Kate told him that the gift would give us more pleasure than if he were to buy it for himself, so it was the best deal for all of us. Kate had a wonderfully effective way of making it clear to anyone who was about to argue with her that it would be completely futile. She did it firmly but pleasantly and it was a technique that I had never perfected; when I tried it, the outcome was generally a prolonged argument.

After about half an hour we had narrowed the choice down to two mountain bikes.

Crocodile had managed to ride them a little way, up and down the aisles in the showroom, and seemed relieved that he could handle them with confidence. I then asked the salesman if we could take them outside for him to try. He instantly recognised us because we had bought our bikes from him a few weeks ago. He didn't even come out with us, but I thought he would have, if the price tag had been £3500.

Crocodile rode round the car park several times on each bike, changing the gears and testing the brakes. He adjusted the saddle height a couple of times on both bikes and rode a little faster and applied the brakes harder so that the tyres began to slide along the surface. "If it's all right with you I think I will have the model with the disc-brakes," he said, "I find them a little smoother than the calliper brakes on the other bike ... but it is £50 more expensive."

"That's a good decision," I said,. "I wish now that Kate and I had bought bikes with disc-brakes, but I think we could still have them fitted, so we may well do that."

"I'm very impressed with your technical knowledge," said Kate to Crocodile.

"I used to service and repair the bikes at the circus as well as ride them," he replied. "I felt safer doing it myself. The only thing they ever gave me was a set of spanners and Allen keys, and that was because it saved them having to do the work themselves. If they have the disc-brake kits in stock I can easily fit them for you."

"If they have the right ones available we'll get them today," I said.

"I used to ride monocycles as well as bicycles," added Crocodile. "You couldn't freewheel on the circus bikes, but this enabled you to go backwards and forwards and gave you the control and balance necessary to ride the monocycles. You could do tricks that would be impossible on an ordinary bike, so I really can't show you anything very clever, other than something like this."

Suddenly he shot off up the car park and at the far end he skidded round. He then pedalled furiously towards us and at the very last second, just before we thought he was going to crash into the building, he stopped almost dead and the back wheel lifted right off the ground. He spun the bike round in a sort of pirouette, before riding round us in a circle. He did another circular tour at an even faster speed; then he lifted the front wheel and held it in the air in a wheelie position for a final circle.

Kate and I had noticed that the salesman had appeared in the doorway, just in time to witness Crocodile's tricks. We started to clap and the salesman joined in, albeit with an astonished look on his face. Crocodile jumped off the bike and took a bow.

When I went into the showroom to pay for the bike and ask about the disc-brake sets the salesman agreed to let us have two sets for the price of one as we were buying another bike. He said that he was most impressed with the riding skills of the old bearded gentleman. I told him that many years ago when he was a young man he used to perform in a circus.

We loaded the bike into the Dormobile and we had only travelled a short distance when Crocodiles's eye caught the name on a sign advertising beer. "I've heard of beer but never tasted it," he confessed. "The Professor only drank wine."

"Perhaps we could stop for a beer somewhere on the way home," I said, but that idea didn't go down too well with Kate, who was looking forward to a cup of coffee.

"Nothing to stop us having both," I suggested.

"Ok!" agreed Kate. "We'll have a coffee first, then you boys can go for a beer – I'll probably just have a sip, then I can drive us home."

We had coffee on a balcony overlooking a weir on the River Kent, the same river that flows through Kendal and the grounds of Levens Hall. The source of the Kent is above Kentmere Common, near the old Roman road over High Street, another fantastic ridge walk that we planned to take Crocodile on this summer.

We knew of a very attractive pub which we would pass on the way home and as we made our way there I explained to Crocodile that beer production was similar to wine production except that with beer, the starch in malt, usually barley malt, is converted into sugar which yeast then turns into alcohol, and that hops are added to enhance the flavour.

"We'll try a couple of beers to give you an idea of differing flavours," I told him.

"We might as well have a sandwich here," Kate suggested as we pulled up outside the pub, "and I think it is just about warm enough to sit outside. I'll find us a table while you get the drinks. As I've volunteered to drive, please could I have a tomato juice?"

Crocodile and I went to the bar and I ordered two halves of Lakeland Golden Nectar. I saw him watching closely as the ale was pulled and poured frothily into slim glasses. I let Crocodile choose the sandwiches and I gave the order to the barman; then we went outside to find Kate.

"Let me have a sip first," said Kate. "Come on Crocodile you try it as well!"

"Perhaps we had better go over there where nobody can see him," I said, "I think that he's going to have to lift up his beard to drink it."

We changed tables and I watched Crocodile's face closely as he put the glass to his mouth – his beard was now resting on his shoulder. It would be hard to describe accurately the range of expressions on his face as he sipped the golden ale. With some difficulty I prised the glass from Kate's hand and tried it myself. Crocodile had gone into wine-tasting mode as he struggled to identify the unfamiliar range of flavours that were now stimulating his taste buds.

"It is quite bitter," he pronounced at last. "That was a big shock because I have never experienced anything quite like it before, but now that I have tried a bit more I can detect an orangey fruitiness under the bitterness, and that is very pleasant."

"It is an acquired taste," I explained. "Some beers do take a bit of getting used to, but as with wine, the more you taste, the more knowledgeable you become, and it takes time to get to know the ones you like best. Also, like wine there are changes in flavour over time, but I think beer is more consistent. There are probably fewer variables in the process, but don't quote me on that."

The sandwiches arrived with the crisps we had ordered and I asked the waitress if she would kindly bring us another couple of glasses of something lighter than the Golden Nectar that we were now drinking. She recommended the Coniston Blonde.

"They probably call the bottled variety Coniston Bottle Blonde," said Kate, with a twinkle in her eye. I laughed but I don't think that Crocodile got the joke.

By the time the waitress had returned with it we were the only people sitting outside, so that Crocodile was again able to drape his beard over his shoulder and drink without too much difficulty.

His immediate comment was that the colour was paler. He poured some into his mouth and swilled it around for a few seconds before swallowing it. He then did the same again a couple of times before exclaiming, "Yes there is quite a difference, not as bitter, but there is a surprising sharpness to it and a tangy lemony fruitiness comes through after you swallow. Perhaps I prefer this one ... but I believe that I could also get used to the other."

"I am sure you are right," I said, "bitter beers do take a bit of getting used to."

"I'm surprised that the Professor didn't get into brewing beer," said Crocodile, stroking his beard. "It would have been right up his street!"

"I'll just nip back to the Dormobile, if you'll excuse me for a minute. I've brought something that I would like to show you." I came back with a chart and laid it on the table. It started to curl up so I held it down with our plates and Kate's empty glass. "Do you recognize the design?" I asked Crocodile

"It looks like the London Underground map, but I can see that it isn't."

"You're right. It's the same design. Very clever! But it's a map of pubs in the Lake District. They are shown on coloured lines so that you can find them more easily. You can see that Kate and I have put a tick against the ones we have visited recently, which illustrates clearly how long it will take us to get round them all. We've tried to count them a couple of times but we always come up with a different number, somewhere between 170 and 180. We go to some quite regularly, either because they're old favourites, or they are close to where we live or to where we walk frequently. I hasten to add that we never drink before going up on the fells as that is a recipe for disaster. We also take it in turn to drive home."

PART III

We always feel that winter is behind us when Damson Day arrives. The celebrations take place at Low Farm in the Lyth Valley. It's on a Saturday to coincide, if possible, with the few days in the year that the damson blossom is in full bloom. The Lyth Valley runs from just south of Crosthwaite to Levens, our gateway to the Lake District. It is a road that we have travelled along hundreds of times so we know every twist and turn, rise and dip, as it follows the river Gilpin to join the Kent below Sampool Bridge.

We had promised Crocodile that we would take him with us and this year Damson Day was timed to perfection – the blossom was at its very best and the weather was as good as you could expect in May or June, let alone April – brilliant sunshine, no wind and the temperature around 20 degrees Celsius. We realised immediately that we should have worn lighter clothing, and that poor Crocodile would nearly bake in his bushy beard, heavy jacket, hat and scarf.

From the disguise aspect, there were plenty of oddly dressed characters around, including Morris dancers and people in old-fashioned country clothing, and nobody gave him more than a second glance.

The range of country crafts on display intrigued Crocodile. He was particularly taken with a small herd of alpacas and a lady spinning their wool on a spinning wheel and using her bare feet to work the treadle.

"There used to be alpacas at the zoo," he whispered, "and that contraption reminds me of my washing machine, which I have to peddle with my feet. I do it with bare feet because I always end up in a pool of water. It was one of the Professor's inventions and perhaps not one of his better ones, but it does the job, so I can't complain."

We wandered round a marquee full of stalls, selling all manner of country products including Alpaca knitwear. We sampled both damson and blackberry gin on several stalls and even with Crocodile's sensitive and experienced palate to help us we couldn't decide which one was better. In the end we went for the prettiest bottles and bought two of damson and two blackberry. I warned Crocodile to drink it carefully as it was 25% proof.

Crocodile took a leaflet from a display, advertising, *High Adventure Balloon Flights*. I told him that we had already flown with them and that we would organize a flight for all of us later in the summer. He was further mesmerized by a display of quad bikes on an adjacent stand. I heaved a sigh of relief when the proprietor, in answer to his question, told him that it was too dangerous to try them out here – I had a sudden vision of him jumping onto one and doing a wheelie in front of all these people and then completely running amok. The man handed us a card together with the name and address of an outdoor pursuits centre that gave tuition and hired them out.

Kate and I noticed once again that Crocodile could hardly contain his excitement, both at the prospect of a balloon flight, and a ride on a quad bike. As we got to know him better we realised more and more that, although in most respects, he was a sophisticated young gentleman, knowledgeable about a wide range of subjects, he also imparted a child-like enthusiasm and delight for things that were new to him, or that he had only read about in books.

His naivety about many things gave us a lot of pleasure. For example when we arrived at a black pudding stall, because they were described as, puddings, Crocodile thought they were some sort of exotic desert. We told him that, as a vegetarian, he shouldn't sample them. He immediately asked the man proffering the samples if they did a vegetarian version.

"Tell him we're working on it," he said to Kate with a wink.

We guided Crocodile away smartly before the conversation got any deeper.

Fortunately, the next stall was offering samples of fudge and cheese. This time Crocodile asked some very intelligent questions about the methods of production and clearly impressed the lady on the stand when he outlined some of the Professor's techniques for making cheeses similar to those on display.

We headed round the Mad Hatter Tea-party Chair-o-Planes to the archery range. Some years ago I went on an archery course at Salmesbury Hall, an attractive black and white timbered Tudor manor house in the Ribble Valley, famous for its resident ghost. Having honed my skills at the butts I was therefore able to show Kate and Crocodile how to hold a bow and aim and release an arrow. Needless to say, they both scored better than I did.

We spent the last hour of our stay relaxing in the sunshine and listening to a quite remarkably talented pair of aged rockers, who treated an increasingly merry audience, intoxicated with damson gin, or beer or both, to a medley of musical hits. One was playing a guitar, the other on a keyboard, and the music was good enough for the Albert Hall.

On the way back home, just as we were about to turn left towards Windermere at the end of the Lyth Valley road, Kate said, "Why don't we take Crocodile up onto Scout Scar? We'll get an overview of the whole valley and the damson orchards. When I was at school in Kendal I was in the Girl Guides and we used to go trekking and on nature rambles up there – the views are fantastic. It will be especially beautiful now, with the blossom at its best."

We parked the Dormobile on an old quarry site, just at the top of the long two-mile descent into Kendal that we coast down almost every week. We crossed the road, went through a kissing gate and up an easy path, which, in a few minutes led us to the scar edge. Again, with a wave of a wand, we stepped out into a strange land, looking out over a vast plain hundreds of feet below, and in the distance, to the west, we could see again the familiar outline of the Lakeland fells.

It is an uncommon landscape for the Lake District because the crag is limestone and the top surface, limestone grassland. There is a sparse scattering of dwarf-like trees, yew and whitebeam, along the exposed ridge. The yews are miniature versions of the 700-year-old specimens to be found in many an old English churchyard. The whitebeam, naturally small, is in its element here in the limestone soil, and we have found them before on our travels, in the Cotswolds.

There are several routes over the top of the Scar but the best views are from the track that runs along the Scar edge. As we walked close to the edge we looked down into the Lyth Valley and into the distance to where we had just celebrated Damson Day. Crocodile pointed to a buzzard circling gracefully a hundred feet below us. Here, nature has created an almost perfect habitat for birds of prey and we have seen hundreds over the years on our regular trips through the valley. It is only on a few special days in the year that you will get the view that we were now enjoying, with white damson blossom covering the trees in the orchards and spilling over the tops of the hedgerows across the valley, as far as the eye could see.

"Why do damsons grow here in this valley?" Crocodile asked.

"They've been here for centuries," Kate replied. "Apparently, the Crusaders brought them over from Damascus hundreds of years ago, and I think that is how the name originated. Sadly, although this view over the damson orchards is still very beautiful, it is not as splendid as it used to be when I was a little girl, when the whole valley was snow-white with damson blossom."

Crocodile looked a little puzzled. "Why should it be different now?' he enquired.

"The damson orchards have declined in the same way that apple orchards have declined in other parts of the country," Kate replied. "It's probably down to changing ways of life, but as with most things, in the final analysis it's about money. I think that the particular problem with damsons is that they are relatively expensive to pick, and hand picking from naturally brittle trees is also quite dangerous, and it is easy for pickers to fall and be seriously injured. Compare this with hand picking grapes at Chateau D'Yquem, where the fruit is close to the ground and the Chateau can charge hundreds of pounds a bottle. There is a limit to what you can charge for a jar of damson jam or even a bottle of damson gin. Happily in recent years there has been a resurgence of interest in damsons, so it's far from being all doom and gloom. It's just that I can remember when people used to come in droves in springtime, when, as I have just said, the whole valley was white with damson blossom. In the autumn, at harvest-time, people would queue at stalls on the Lyth Valley road to buy damsons to make jam and for bottling at home. Happily, there is again an increased interest in home cooking and organic foods, so future generations may one day be able to stand here and look down on a valley that is, once more, completely whitewashed with damson blossom."

"It might be hard for you to understand," I said, "but it is important to have pleasant memories of times gone by. Some changes are for the better but others most certainly are not, and anything that does damage to the local economy and way of life is generally a change for the worse."

"Yes, I think I understand," said Crocodile. "I often think back to my time at the zoo with Mercedes ... I thought I could never be happier and I was so sad when I was taken away from her ... I thought I would never see her again ... and perhaps I never shall. Yet my life with the Professor was just as happy ... probably happier, because in a way I was more free."

"Here in the Lake District and with you as my friends, apart from the sadness of never seeing the Professor or Mercedes again, I feel happier than I have ever been, but those memories are very important to me and have kept me going when my future was so uncertain."

"Memories are very important to everybody," I said." You should always live for today, with just an eye on the future, but never forget the good times of the past. Having a large store of happy memories to recall will help you to enjoy each new day more than you possibly could without them."

As we were talking, I hadn't realised that we had arrived at the Mushroom Shelter. It sits at nearly the highest point on the ridge, around 750 feet. It was built to commemorate the coronation of George V, but was refurbished and given a new stainless-steel domed roof in

Chapter Seven — Crocodile's Grand Tour

2002 for Queen Elizabeth's Golden Jubilee. Inscribed around the inside of the roof is a plan of the surrounding fells through 360 degrees. As you turn slowly round you can see the Howgills, the Yorkshire Dales, across Morecambe Bay, the Lakeland Fells, then over to Fairfield and Kentmere. You can view every high point of the panorama in the time it takes to turn full circle and if you turn more slowly and line them up with your eye you can read off their names. We counted about 140 in total but that included Blackpool Tower!

"Until I was eleven I used to live over there," said Kate, pointing towards Kendal. "My father was a builder and he built us a house in his spare time on Oxenholme Road. The area was known as Murley Moss, and then it was nearly all fields both behind and in front of the house. All my happy childhood memories are there and I was devastated when my parents decided to move away. Of course I realise now that if we had stayed in Kendal I wouldn't have met Matt, and we wouldn't have met you ... and the three of us would not be standing here having this conversation. So what do you deduce from that wise Crocodile?"

"Well!" pondered Crocodile, "I'll have to think about that for a moment."

"While you're thinking Matt and I will count the names on the map again," Kate said.

This time I got 138 and Kate managed 139. We were about to start again when Crocodile said, "There are a lot of things in life that I am very unsure about and from what you have just told me, I could also say that if the circus folk hadn't kidnapped me, I wouldn't have met the Professor. If I hadn't met the Professor, I am fairly certain that I wouldn't have met you and we wouldn't be standing here having this conversation and I wouldn't be living on an island on Windermere. I can only deduce from what you say and from what has come to pass, that, in the final analysis, nobody has complete control over his own destiny. We can only do our best and hope that all will be well and that it ends well."

We laughed and Kate said, "That's probably the best deduction you could make."

Crocodile then asked, "Kate, were you very sad when you left Kendal?"

"Heartbroken!" said Kate, "but although many of my happy, early memories are of Kendal, it always makes me sad to go back to my old house. Perhaps you have read Arthur Ransome's book, *Swallows and Amazons*?"

"Oh yes!" said Crocodile, nodding his head vigorously. "It was the book that the Professor gave me to read when we came on our first holiday to the Lake District ... I got very excited about sailing-boats. The Professor taught me how to sail and I found it quite easy because, naturally, I know a lot about water, currents and winds, so it was almost second nature. Learning all the new boating terms was the hardest part. I had never before come across words like port and starboard, bow and stern, boom and jib, thwart, traveller, halyard etc. Let alone Captains, Mates and Able seamen ... but I am familiar with them all now. I only have a rowing-boat at the moment but perhaps you would help me to purchase a sailing-boat?"

"Of course we will," said Kate. "Nothing would give us greater pleasure. As for the nautical terms, I am sure that many of Mr. Ransome's readers reached for their dictionaries a few times when they first read his books. The reason that I asked you if you had read the book was because I wanted to explain why I am sad going back now. You see, in the lovely fields and meadows that surrounded our house, my three sisters and I and other friends did all those things that the *Swallows and Amazons* did, but on dry land. We had all sorts of wonderful adventures and we used to camp out in the fields in the summer holidays. We didn't meet any pirates, or charcoal burners, but we did meet other campers, lots of interesting people, who pitched their tents near ours."

"The most exciting time was when the Romany Gypsies came to camp in the fields up the road. They were there every year. They had the most beautiful hand-painted, horse-drawn caravans. I made friends with a girl called Robina, she was about my age. When she was travelling away she used to write to me several times a year to tell me where she was and what she was doing. She went to a lot of horse fairs, because her father traded in horses. Sometimes she would be staying at a fairground and helping out on the helter-skelter, or on the swing-boats, or a coconut shy, or a, roll-a-penny stall. I always thought that she was a very lucky girl to be leading such an exciting life and I used to imagine that I would travel with her and work on fairgrounds and ride her father's fine horses and have all sorts of adventures. The only riding that I did until I was very much older was on Shetland ponies, in one of the fields at the back of our house ... my father used to rent the field to their owner and we were allowed to ride them when their owner was with them."

"My mother was a dressmaker. She worked from home and our house was always full of rolls and piles of fabric. They were stacked everywhere because she never threw anything out and what she didn't use she saved. Anyway, she got to know Robina's mother quite well and I think they did deals together ... she would sell her off-cuts of brightly coloured materials for scarves and things that they sold, like peg-bags, as well as bigger pieces of fabric for skirts and blouses. I always knew that she liked to have her fortune told, and one day, when we were all sitting round the table she told us that Robina's mother had read her fortune and had told her that it would be our last summer in this house and that we were going to travel far away to seek our fortune. 'What do you make of that?' she asked. We didn't know whether to laugh or cry. On the one hand we may have adventures in exotic places in far off lands, but, on the other, we would be leaving the place we loved most in the world, and all our friends. Perhaps we didn't believe it would really happen and fortune-telling was simply nonsense."

"The prediction turned out to be true after all, and within a year we had moved not once but twice. The first move was to Warton, near Silverdale, where my father had built another house ... I knew he was building it because I used to help him at weekends, carrying bricks for him to lay, but I thought that he was building it to sell, not for us to live in. We were only there from May to August when, one evening after our meal, he gathered us together and told us that he had now sold this house, and it was, 'An offer he couldn't refuse.' We were on the move again. It was then that I realised that moving about like Robina wasn't as much fun as I had imagined. Don't misunderstand me, I am not against travelling, and now I know that travelling is important in order to enjoy a full and varied life. But a stable happy home is more important, even if you don't live in the Lake District."

"I did go to a lovely convent school, where I learned everything necessary to lead a good life, and where I was very happy. If we had stayed in Kendal I would have gone to my secondary school there, but fate decreed that it was not to be. Again, going back to what we were saying before, if I had continued my schooling in Kendal I would not have met Matt and we would not have known you ... so once again ... all's well that ends well. I am slightly embarrassed telling you this because I know that you had private tutors and didn't go to school at all."

"No, I didn't," said Crocodile, "but don't feel sorry for me because Mercedes and the Professor were wonderful teachers. I have read lots of books about schools, such as, *Billy Bunter,* and, *Tom Brown's Schooldays.* I am not sure that I would have been very happy at school ... certainly not at schools like that. Although the Professor told me all about Rugby School where he went, but he said that it had changed a lot since Tom Brown was there."

The beautiful high-pitched song of a Skylark on the wing suddenly and pleasantly interrupted the conversation. This delightful melody was accompanied intermittently by the more familiar, 'cuc-coo', of a distant Cuckoo. We stood in silence listening to the music, and occasionally turning slowly to enjoy the slight breeze in the heat of the afternoon, gazing in wonder at the vast panorama displayed all around us.

PART IV

Crocodile's first bike ride was up Ghyll Head to Strawberry Bank, then over Cartmel Fell to Gummer's How. We pointed out the old, but freshly painted, Westmorland/Lancashire boundary sign, just across the road from Broad Leys, home of the Windermere Motor Boat Racing Club. The house, a Grade 1 listed Arts and Crafts style building was designed by Charles Voysey, and every detail, including the exact colour of the paint is faithfully maintained. We knew this because we had spoken with the painter a few months earlier concerning some work at our house and he told us about the work he was doing at Broad Leys and the paint mixes he was using. Kate and I were invited to dinner there on a couple of occasions when our nextdoor neighbour was its Commodore. We also have grandstand seats on our balcony at home for all the speed boat races and firework displays.

I told Crocodile that motorboat races used to be held nearly every weekend in the spring and summer months. Our house stands about the mid-point of the course used by the boats, and I have to admit that they were a fine spectacle.

"I don't think that the races would have troubled me," added Crocodile, "I would simply have stayed out of their way, but I have to admit I like fast machines and most certainly I would have watched them from a safe distance."

A few yards past the WMBRC we turned steeply uphill to Ghyll Head and Cartmel Fell. Kate and I were soon puffing and panting while Crocodile, seemingly effortlessly, vanished into the distance. When we finally arrived at the top he was standing by the side of the road peering over a wall at what turned out to be several anglers fishing in Ghyll Head Pond. He told us that the Professor had been a keen fisherman and loved both river fishing and fishing from his boat on Windermere.

After Ghyll Head Pond the road meanders gently downhill for some considerable distance. When we could see the road clearly we rode three abreast so that we could talk, but being very careful to get back into single-file well before a corner or a blind hill.

A little further up the road I stopped at the entrance to an old country property. Peering through the gateway we could see on the left a large barn with first-floor windows. In front of it was a wooden garage that resembled a boathouse. The main house, I knew was three to four hundred years old, it looked well lived in and full of character. It stood in a beautiful garden, full of trees, shrubs and flowers, set high on a hillside overlooking the lush Winster Valley. The sign to the right of the gateway read, *Low Ludderburn*.

"Are you any wiser?" I asked Crocodile, pointing at the nameplate.

"I recognise the name," he replied, "but I can't think where I have heard it."

"I'll give you a small clue," I said, "a former owner was a famous fisherman."

Crocodile scratched his snout and looked puzzled.

"He was also a famous author," I added.

"It must be Arthur Ransome then. Did he write, *Swallows and Amazons*, here?" came the reply.

"I believe he wrote, *Swallows and Amazons*, and other books in the series here, where he lived with his Russian wife Evgenia, from 1925 to 1935. Amazingly, they left this idyllic spot, a sublime retreat for any writer, and moved to Suffolk. I am sure it would have been on Evgenia's insistence, and I am also sure that Kate would have equally as much difficulty in persuading me to leave the Lake District as I would have in persuading her; it just isn't going to happen, ever!" Arthur and Evgenia did eventually return to the Lakes but not to this house: they spent the remainder of their days on the other side of the lake."

From Low Ludderburn we followed the road around the south side of Cartmel Fell, high above the Winster Valley, where we could now clearly see in the distance the distinctive limestone Scars of Cunswick, Scout and Whitbarrow. The hedgerows bordering the road were deep green, lush and dew laden. As we rode slowly by, Kate pointed out to Crocodile the abundant riches of an English country lane. White wood anemone and lily of the valley, red campion, wild strawberry and early purple orchids; clusters of perfumed bluebells and pink tufts of wild thyme; bright yellow bird's foot trefoil and gold star-like lesser celandine.

Chapter Seven   Crocodile's Grand Tour

Quite suddenly we were at Strawberry Bank, the home of one of our favourite pubs. On this occasion, influenced perhaps by the summery weather, we opted for Belgian raspberry beer, which was presented in hand-wrapped half champagne bottles. We took it outside and sat for some time in the warm sunshine sipping our fruit beer very slowly.

"Life doesn't get any better than this!" purred Kate.

"No, I have to agree," I said. "I couldn't think of anything that I would rather be doing at this moment ... how about you Crocodile?"

"Well!" mused Crocodile, shading his eyes from the sun, "I have to admit that it would be much easier to draw up a list of things that I would rather not be doing."

We nodded in agreement.

After a drowsy half-hour siesta we headed further up onto Cartmel Fell, and past the church of St. Anthony of Egypt, strangely located in the middle of nowhere. It is a little gem of a place at least on the inside and famous for having a triple-decker pulpit. Today there was a christening in progress, so we did not take Crocodile inside.

The final leg of our journey before heading home, took us right over Cartmel Fell to the car park below Gummers How. Unknown to Crocodile we had got up early that morning and I had parked the Dormobile there. Kate had followed me in the estate car and driven us back home. We had left a picnic in the cool-box.

When we reached the car park we put our bikes in the Dormobile and transferred the picnic from the cool-box to a picnic hamper. Crocodile hadn't brought his saddlebags so I carried the hamper on a leather strap over my shoulder. We crossed the road and started the short and pleasant climb to the summit of Gummer's How. Although Gummer's How is over 1000 feet high you are already nearly halfway up when you leave the car park. An undulating path winds through clumps of old larches and silver birch leading to the base of the rocky fell top. For youngsters it is a fairly safe but *real* rock climb, and I can well remember my excitement the first time I climbed it, at the age of six or seven, with my parents – I felt that I had conquered Mount Everest.

The summit is marked with a stone trig point and from here we could see the complete range of the Southern Fells, from south of Coniston Old Man to Wetherlam, then to the Langdale Pikes, Skiddaw, Fairfield and Kentmere Pike. Looking east we could see the Pennines and then south and west, to Morecambe Bay and the Kent, Leven and Crake estuaries.

We walked to a grassy bank just below the summit where Kate spread out a large car rug that we had brought in the Dormobile. From this viewpoint we overlooked the Swan Hotel at Newby Bridge, and closer still the complex at Lakeside, which includes the terminus of the Lakeside and Haverthwaite Railway, formerly the Furness Railway branch line, still running real steam locomotives. Most prominent are the large steamboat piers, still so-called, although the big boats on the lake are not now powered by steam engines.

As we watched, the Tern, originally a steamer and well over a hundred years old, moved gracefully into port.

"I see the Tern nearly every day as it passes my island," said Crocodile. "It is usually about the same time as the Swan, or the Teal heading in the opposite direction. On occasions they have passed pretty close to me while I have been swimming in the lake, but I always stay under water for some time, until they are well clear before I come up to the surface. It wouldn't do for some sharp eyed passenger to spot me from the deck ... although I think the Captain would take a bit of convincing that one of his passengers had just seen a crocodile in the water, let alone be persuaded to turn round and come and look for me. He'd assume they'd had a tot too many at the ship's bar. I always give speedboats and yachts a very wide berth. I certainly couldn't swim faster than many of the powerboats, so they are the biggest danger. I can hear them coming miles away and I am always prepared, but what sometimes catches me out is when they make a sudden turn, so I tend to swim well below propeller level when they are close."

"Have you ever been spotted?" Kate asked.

"I am sure that I have been seen many times by people in boats," he replied, "but there are so many birds on the water, big fish in the water and floating logs and other debris. All I have to do is submerge for a few minutes, so even if they do see me, and come back to take a closer look, as long as I stay underwater for a while, they'll think they imagined it. I feel quite safe in Windermere."

"The view from here is probably where Arthur Ransome sketched his map for, *Swallows and Amazons*," I said, "apart from the fact that you can't see Rio from here. It's hidden round the bend in the lake."

"I think I can just see my island," Crocodile said, pointing to the furthest point on the lake.

"I think you're probably right," I said, "but I haven't brought the binoculars. I must remember to keep another pair in the Dormobile."

"Shall we have our picnic?" Kate asked, rhetorically, as she was already taking things out of the basket and all our mouths were watering with expectation.

"Don't get too excited," she added, "it's not a banquet."

It was, as always, quite delicious and centred round a big asparagus quiche with lots of salad and some big juicy tomatoes.

"This pastry is scrumptious," drooled Crocodile.

"I put mashed potato in the pastry mix," Kate explained, "I always think it adds an extra dimension to a simple quiche."

"I didn't bring wine," I said, "because it's not very sensible when you are climbing, as you are much more likely to have an accident. So I've just brought iced water with lemon and honey and a flask of coffee for afterwards … though I must admit, I could have managed another of those sparkling fruit beers."

"We've still got strawberries and cream to come," said Kate, diving back into the basket.

After the picnic we closed our eyes and dozed in the warm sunshine under an azure sky and for a second time, in the space of a couple of hours, we agreed that, "life didn't get much better than this."

PART V

The following Saturday we took Crocodile for his first outing on the high fells. We had not climbed High Street and had never even been to Haweswater, which was where, on Alfred Wainwright's advice, our base camp should be, so it was an unknown adventure for Kate and me as well.

We went to Shap via Kendal before turning west towards Rosgil and Bampton. I was getting low on fuel but had assumed that there would be a filling station between Kendal and Shap ... the only one, on the outskirts of Shap village was closed. I noticed, with some concern, that the sky in the west, in the direction we were heading, had turned very black. Luckily, after a few enquiries, we found a tiny garage near Bampton that had a diesel pump. I chatted with the owner while he was filling up the Dormobile and mentioned that we were about to climb High Street. A frown spread over his face and, sucking through his teeth, he told me that six walkers on Wainwright's famous classic *Coast to Coast* walk, 190 miles across England, from St.Bees to Robin Hood's Bay, had been stranded last night in bad weather on the top of High Street, while trying to cross from Patterdale to Shap, and had just been rescued that morning.

"Lucky to be alive," he grimaced. "You just be careful ... don't like the look of yon black clouds ... don't think I'd be risking going up there today."

As he replaced the filler cap, his bowed head shook slowly from side to side and as I drove away his melancholy expression seemed to prophesy impending doom.

I didn't dare mention this conversation to Kate or wild horses wouldn't have dragged her onto the fells, but as we drove along the shores of Haweswater towards Mardale Head, the sun burst through and the surface of the lake danced and sparkled merrily below us, lifting my mood considerably.

I stopped the Dormobile at the side of the road, at a point that gave us a grand view over Haweswater and Mardale. The island of Wood Howe, and the wooded peninsular of the Rigg, were directly below us, with Harter Fell towering in the background. Its summit was ominously hidden in dark swirling cloud but our planned route up High Street stretching out spectacularly to our right was bathed in bright sunshine.

In Alfred Wainwright's own words: 'The ridge of Rough Crag and the rocky stairway of Long Style together form the connoisseurs' route up High Street. The ascent is a classic, leading directly along the crest of a long straight ridge that permits no variation from the valley to the summit.' However, Wainwright does add, and it was this comment that reassured me that it would be safe to attempt the climb today, that, 'the ridge route may be attempted in mist, being so well-defined that it is impossible to go astray – but it should be kept in mind that there are crags close by on both sides for most of the route, the Riggindale flank (north) in particular, being precipitous'.

Clearly, this does not sound completely reassuring and so I had planned an escape route that we could take, down to Blea Water from Caspel Gate, above Rough Crag, well before the final ascent up Long Stile. There didn't appear to be an alternative safe escape route other than to turn round and backtrack, and that option appeared more hazardous. As I knew well from experience, it is one thing to look at a map or a drawing, and plan a course of action, but things are rarely quite so simple. What may look relatively easy on a piece of paper may prove, in reality, to be extremely difficult.

We drove to Mardale Head and parked in the car park. Kate inspected Crocodile to make sure that he was well camouflaged. She had now taken to tying his beard at the back and around his neck so that even if somebody were to give it a good tug it would not be dislodged. She had managed to acquire an ex-army combat suit for use in tropical or desert conditions for him. It was made of a light Khaki fabric and kept him much cooler than some of his early disguises. It also had a hood that could be pulled right over his head and gathered with cord-pulls, leaving only his eyes visible. In this camouflage, even the weirdest creature from outer space that a fertile imagination could conjure up, would pass unnoticed in Piccadilly Circus. He had asked if he could make the picnic on this occasion and he had brought it in his leather saddlebags. We noted that he had had the foresight to attach a leather strap so that that it would be secure over his shoulders on the rock climbs.

The ridge route was bathed in sunshine when we set off. The clouds still hung darkly around the top of Harter Fell but thankfully seemed reluctant to move northwards. We made our way round the head of the lake and after a little way we took a sharp turn up to the left off the main path. Instantly we were climbing steeply up through bracken towards Swine Crag. It did not take long to discover that poor Crocodile did not have a head for heights. He clung to a big rock and said in a quivering voice, "I thought that Gummer's How was quite scary but at least you knew that if you fell you'd probably just hurt yourself and maybe not do too much damage, but if you fell here it would be curtains. I haven't experienced anything quite like this before and my head has gone quite dizzy."

"Neither Matt or I feel relaxed when we are in a position where we know that if we were to fall we would probably not live to tell the tale. Frequently, I dare not look down other than at my feet on the path. All I can say is that like most new experiences you do get acclimatised after a while, but if you would prefer to go back down now, there is a more gentle route to the summit that we can take, where you can stay well away from dangerous drops."

"No!" said Crocodile, "I'll carry on for a minute or two. I am just being irrational. You know, I have ridden a monocycle on a tightrope, high above the circus ring, albeit with a safety net, and with no fear of falling. It's just that I am much less steady on my feet, and if I had tried to walk across, with just a pole to steady me, most certainly I would have fallen."

"Keep well to the inside, just watch your feet and up ahead, and don't look over the edge," said Kate putting her arm on his shoulder. "I am probably more nervous than you are, but as long as you simply put one foot slowly and firmly in front of the other there is no way you are going to fall."

After a few minutes, Crocodile had composed himself and we all edged slowly upwards. Whenever we came to a particularly narrow or precipitous bit we held onto him, front and back, and cracked a few jokes. A little farther up, over Heron Crag and Eagle Crag, there were undoubtedly some precipitous sections, especially to the north, but we were able to steer a route that kept us far enough away from the edge for the drops to cause no concern.

However, another problem now confronted us. I looked up to see that a blanket of cloud was covering the summit of High Street and was edging its way down Long Style towards Caspel Gate. My concern was that if it reached Caspel Gate it might block our view down to Blea Water, which was our escape route back to Mardale Head. Miraculously, by the time we had reached the summit stone of Rough Crag we could see clearly up Long Stile to the top of High Street – the cloud had vanished completely.

"I think we deserve a cup of tea," said Kate.

I slipped off my rucksack and took out a flask and two mugs, using the flask top for myself.

"How are you feeling now?" I asked Crocodile.

"Not too bad," he replied. "On the way up I was reminded of the first time that I climbed a rope ladder for my tight-rope act. I nearly fainted from shock. You see it's very unnatural for a crocodile to climb up high on anything. My knees started to knock almost as soon as I left the ground. I just didn't look down again and kept going until I had reached the platform. Once I had scrambled onto the platform there was a safety net underneath so if I had fallen I wouldn't have hurt myself. I had practiced for hours riding a monocycle along a tightrope just a few feet above the ground, until I could ride across forwards and backwards, even without a pole to balance myself. At this stage in my career I have to say, without bragging, that I was probably the biggest attraction in the circus and so I had become valuable property. If I were to injure myself badly it would cost them money. I believe it was for this reason that they put sacks filled with straw on either side of the tightrope along its full length when I was practicing at a low level. I did fall off a few times at first but I soon mastered the technique. That made me realise the dramatic effect that confidence has on behaviour. Once you know for sure that you can't hurt yourself, your whole approach is different. Confidence also grows with experience, but the bottom line is always that, if it doesn't matter if things go wrong, or if you make a mistake, then things won't go wrong and you won't make any mistakes ... if you see what I mean."

"I know exactly what you mean," I said, "but I could say it is rational to be scared in dangerous circumstances and irrational to know no fear. There is a famous photograph of steel erectors on a New York skyscraper, eating their lunch sitting on a girder hundreds of feet above the ground. A slip, a sneeze, a freak gust of wind, and you are no more ... why would anyone risk everything when there is no need? Of course there was no need for us to come up here today ... we could have gone for a picnic and just sat above Tarn Hows in the sunshine. There is also no need for anyone to risk sailing single-handed round the world, to climb Mount Everest, to walk to the North Pole or to fly round the world in a basket hanging under a balloon. What some people call irrational, others call noble or magnificent. These are questions and opinions you have to answer and judge for yourself. There is no definitive answer, only consensus. I think you have been very brave climbing up here today and it would have been much easier for you to have turned round after the first couple of hundred feet and gone for a swim in the lake. Kate and I are very proud of you and we know that it can't have been easy for you."

"A journalist once asked Donald Campbell if he was ever afraid. His reply was that he was afraid every time he got into Bluebird. He said that courage was nothing to do with being fearless ... courage was overcoming and smashing through fear. He believed that doing what he did, dangerous though it was, was infinitely better than sitting on his backside watching television all day. Some people have accused him of suicide because he made his final run to capture the world water speed record before the wash from his first run had completely subsided. His wife Tonia, who knew him better than anyone, utterly denies this possibility. The truth is probably that he had to make a snap decision, which in the cold light of day, was, arguably the wrong decision. It is easy to pass judgements and to make statements about what people should have done when you are sitting in a comfortable armchair in front of a warm fire."

"Don't worry," said Crocodile, "I wouldn't have missed this for anything although I'm jolly glad that there isn't much farther to go to the top."

"All the other climbs we have planned for this summer we know well and none of the routes are as scary as this, and that includes Scafell Pike, Helvellyn – missing out Striding Edge, Skiddaw, Great Gable and Coniston Old Man," I said to reassure him.

Kate suddenly jumped up pointing over our shoulders, "Look!" she cried excitedly. "Isn't that an eagle?"

Crocodile and I turned round and sure enough soaring far below us over the deep chasm of Riggindale and high over the backdrop of Haweswater was a very large bird of prey.

"It's a golden eagle," said Crocodile, "I got to know them very well at the zoo – but it's wonderful to see one that is truly free."

We watched, fascinated, as the huge bird soared on the thermals – its great wings held steady. With only slight adjustments to its wing tips and feathered ailerons, it covered great distances effortlessly in graceful sweeping movements.

We watched for ages and could still see it as we made our way to the top of Long Stile – the final leg of our climb. Only as we approached the summit of High Street did it finally vanish from our view. We now beheld a different horizon as a whole new vista of mountains appeared before us. I pointed in turn to the ones I could identify… I named them out loud, "Fairfield, Dollywaggon Pike, St. Sunday Crag, Catstycam, Raise, Stybarrow Dodd, and Great Dodd, Skiddaw and Blencathra." I didn't know the others to the north by name.

"It is satisfying for us to know that Kate and I have stood on the tops of all those mountains," I said.

"I hope we will climb them all again with you," said Kate to Crocodile.

I took out my camera and photographed Kate and Crocodile standing in front of the summit stone. I was about to swap places with Kate when a man approached and offered to take one of the three of us. I made a mental note to have two copies framed, one for Crocodile's mantelpiece, and one for us.

"Is it picnic time yet?" asked Crocodile.

"You took the words out of my mouth," I said. "We'll sit over there behind that wall, out of the wind."

Crocodile emptied his saddlebags with gusto and spread the contents on a square green tarpaulin sheet. He described the dishes as he opened each container.

"Mushroom pate, made with wild mushrooms from around my island. I've used quails' eggs in it. Napoleon managed to get some from the farm, I don't know how. I've boiled a few extra to eat with the pate, or with the other dishes. I have also made another paté, nut with date and mint chutney. There's chilli, Tabasco, cayenne and black pepper in this one to give it bite. I hope it's not too hot for you. I have made celery Almondine as an accompaniment. You can eat everything on these homemade savoury biscuits or some fresh bread, baked this morning. The main course is a roasted baby aubergine tart with cherry tomatoes and black olives. I've also done some jersey potatoes and mange tout to go with it. There's summer pudding with clotted cream to finish. The cream is again courtesy of Napoleon."

Our mouths were watering uncontrollably, long before the end of this gourmet recital. He had taken the trouble to press everything tightly into the containers in such a way that it held its shape on the long climb up. Amazingly, the aubergine tart was heart-shaped and the plaited crust in perfect condition. I recall reading that the Victorians frequently went overboard with their picnics on the Lakeland fells, but surely, none could have surpassed this. Not even the generals, riding over High Street with their Roman legions, would have feasted in grander style.

"Did you know that, astonishingly, this ridge over High Street was once a Roman road?"

"I do remember the Professor saying something about it once ... but I don't think I quite understood, and it is even harder to comprehend when you are actually up here."

"Apparently the Romans built a road over here because the valleys were nothing but swamp and forest and it was, incredible though it may seem, the best way to get from the Roman port of Glannoventa, now Ravenglass, to Carlisle and Hadrian's Wall beyond. There was also a Roman fort at Ambleside, called Galava, as well as Mediobogdum, the fort at the top of Hardknot Pass, which had a garrison of 500 men."

"Yes, I visited the fort with the Professor," said Crocodile. "I saw the remains of the baths. The Professor explained that the Romans made a big thing of bathing ... they bathed in stages, from cold, to warm, to hot ... with a separate bathroom for each stage. As you are aware, the Professor was keen on exotic bathing."

"Yes we saw the pool he built for you in London," said Kate, "it was very opulent."

"Incidentally," she added, licking her lips, 'the pates were wonderful, and this aubergine tart is divine ... and well complemented with the creamy texture of the Jersey Royals and the crispy mange tout, Yum! Yum!"

Crocodile beamed with pride.

We relaxed for about half an hour after finishing the picnic, then when we were well rested, I said, "You'll be relieved to know that the way down is much more gentle than the way we came up; just a pleasant stroll around Riggindale, then down to the lake. We should also get a wonderful eagle's eye view of the spectacular ridge route of our ascent."

We took it slowly going down, especially as, although the descent was easy, tiredness always starts to set in at this stage and muscles begin to ache and the risk of falling is greater. Blisters can also be a problem if something has been rubbing in your boots. We try to remember to carry sticking plaster and lint, but usually find, if someone in the party gets a blister, we've forgotten it. Probably the best way to ensure you won't get a blister is always to remember the medical dressings.

As we descended we stopped frequently to admire our route up to the summit and we could clearly see Long stile, Caspel Gate, and Rough Crag, then lower down, Eagle Crag, Heron Crag and Swine Crag. We could also see right across the top of High Street and it wasn't difficult to imagine a Roman legion marching over the ridge. At some point somebody would have stood in this spot and seen exactly that. Centuries later it was named Racecourse Hill because horse races and other festivities were held up there every July until around 1830.

We were now walking directly down to Haweswater, and I said to Crocodile, "While I was planning this climb, I read a little about the flooding of Mardale and the creation of Haweswater Reservoir in the 1930's. Haweswater Beck was dammed to expand the small lake and flood the valley. The logic was that, at 600 feet above sea level, it would be capable of supplying systems great distances away. However, many of the comments at the time were scathing about the scheme and many mourned the drowning of the village. It must have been awful for the villagers when their church, farms and inn, all good and well loved, were brutally taken away from them."

"In very dry weather, even today, the ghostly remains of the buildings of Mardale Green re-emerge for all to see, but unlike at Brigadoon, all life has long since ceased to exist."

"Would you mind awfully if I went for a swim and had a look at the buildings underwater?" Crocodile asked suddenly.

"I don't see why not,' I said with some surprise. "What do you think, Kate?"

"I am sure its quite safe down there, but just be careful; you've already been in enough dangerous places for one day."

By the time we got back to the Dormobile, Crocodile was raring to go.

"We'll move along the road a little way so that you can get into the water without being seen," I suggested.

By the time we had stopped at a convenient spot, Crocodile had changed into a blue and white striped swimming costume. He threw on a large white dressing gown, pulled the integral hood over his head, and a few seconds later he was over the wall bordering Haweswater. When I looked over, a moment later, all that could be seen was the neatly folded dressing-gown at the water's edge ... a large stone had been placed on the top of it.

Kate had suggested meeting him in half an hour and we had synchronized our watches with the diver's watch that Crocodile always carried in his saddlebags. This would give us time to go and freshen up at the hotel, a couple of miles up the road.

We managed to grab a cup of coffee at the hotel and a take-away for Crocodile. We arrived back for our rendezvous with five minutes to spare. Kate and I waited by the wall, from where we could see over the lake to the crags we had just climbed and to the summit of High Street. The dressing gown still lay neatly folded by the water's edge. A few more slightly worrying minutes passed by before we saw a movement in the water. Then, much to our relief Crocodile's head appeared above the surface. We looked around to make sure that the coast was clear and signalled to him that it was safe to come out.

"Look what I have found," he exclaimed, as he emerged from the water waving something at us. It was a large, very tarnished, brass doorknocker.

"I'll polish it up and keep it as a memento of my visit, although I have to say that it was pretty grim down there. There is something extra sad about the death of a village in that way ... even if it had been bombed it could have been rebuilt and raised from the ashes. I wonder why they didn't take it down stone by stone and rebuild it nearby? There looks to be plenty of good land around for that to have been possible with a little ingenuity."

As we drove home we discussed plans for resurrecting Mardale. Crocodile suggested continuing the road round the head of the lake and Kate said that an inn would be well placed there for climbers coming off the fells. By the time we arrived back home we had firmed up detailed plans for the resurrection of Mardale Green, complete with church, pub, a general store and post office, and a village green with a duck-pond, all surrounded by pretty stone cottages. However, on a final note, we had to agree that it would be far too late to appease the original residents of Mardale, and doubted that we would be successful in winning over the planners and the purists.

I had learned a very big lesson from our High Street expedition - and that was that I had proceeded against my own common sense. Even though, when we had set off, High Street was bathed in bright sunshine, dark clouds were not far away. The cloud appeared to be static and on the map there was an easy way down if it started to move northwards. I hadn't taken into account that Crocodile was not as good on his feet as we were, or considered that he may have a fear of heights. The reality of the situation was that after a certain point it became clear that it would be much easier to continue upwards rather than retracing the route we had just taken. Our problem was that the way the cloud was moving meant we would be well into it long before we got to Caspel Gate and the escape route would be hidden from view. There were precipices around and I knew that a young boy had been killed recently in a fall there. As it turned out we were fortunate – the cloud lifted.

I vowed to take every reasonable precaution possible in future when climbing on the fells with Crocodile. Several times during the couple of weeks after High Street, he complained of sore feet and legs and we decided only to climb one high fell every two or three weeks and to intersperse the big climbs with much shorter walks and rambles, leisurely picnics and boat trips. Kate and I would take great pleasure in showing him places and things that were dear to our hearts. This may include anything, from houses with literary associations, to a visit to our favourite pig ... Thomas, who lived at Watendlath above Ashness Bridge.

PART VI

We decided that our next trip, following High Street, would be to Watendlath. The view over Derwent Water from Ashness Bridge is one of the most picturesque in the Lake District. As a young boy I remember it being the start of the then gated road through a wood, and a hidden valley to the isolated hamlet of Watendlath, the setting for Hugh Walpole's novel, Judith Paris, part of the Rogue Herries set. Then, it was customary to pay a three-penny bit to the man who opened the first gate for the car to pass through at Ashness Bridge. The gates, and sadly the three-penny bits have long since gone ... Also the man!

Watendlath was the home of Thomas, Thomas the pig, who was famous for his sweet tooth, and in particular his penchant for bars of chocolate. The little cafe there does a roaring trade in chocolate bars ... Crocodile alone bought at least five to feed to the grateful Thomas.

"Chocolate bars are especially good for him just now," said the lady in the cafe. "He's recently sired half a dozen piglets and we've had to separate him from his wife and offspring ... he was getting too amorous again and we feared he might have harmed the youngsters. Chocolate helps to take his mind off his other desires."

That day we made a long detour home to show Crocodile Long Meg and her daughters, at Little Salkeld, in the Eden Valley. Long Meg was here long before the Romans came, perhaps five thousand years ago, since the late Neolithic or Bronze ages. In the Lake District and surrounding countryside there are many examples of standing stones, stone circles and burial cairns. Crocodile was quick to point out that in crocodile years five thousand is not very long and that crocodiles had been around eons before humans evolved.

"I wonder," said Crocodile, "if a Neolithic or Bronze Age youngster had been educated by Mercedes and the Professor, whether he or she would have been as intelligent as I?"

"Well!" I replied, "There are many cases of youngsters from primitive races today being educated to a high standard. Maybe you are not unique and there are other crocodiles around that have evolved genetically as you have. Ultimately, that may be one of your goals in life; to find another crocodile like yourself. As you are aware, achieving your standard of intelligence and knowledge takes many years of hard work, just as it does for humans; so alas, I am sad to say that you would be extremely lucky to find another Crocodile who has been educated to your high standard."

"That is a very sobering thought," he replied, scratching the end of his long snout.

Before visiting Long Meg we went to the small cairn circle of Little Meg. Long Meg and her Daughters, although only about a kilometre away, cannot be seen from here; it is over the crest of a hill. It is thought that a processional avenue once led to the Mother and Daughters.

"Mercedes was very religious," said Crocodile. "She was a Roman Catholic and went to mass every week. The Professor, on the other hand, was not remotely religious but he loved churches. He believed that all life evolved from stardust. He said that people are born inherently selfish but potentially good or potentially evil. Significant people and events in our lives help to form what we eventually become. However, he said that a leopard rarely changed its spots ... in other words, fairly early in our lives we become what we will always be in terms of our basic character. He also said, as he usually did, that there will always be exceptions to the general rule."

By now we were approaching Long Meg. There are more than seventy granite stones in her circle, although Long Meg herself is not granite, she is an enormous red sandstone pillar, standing over four metres high. She is positioned outside the ring of granite stones, so that people standing in the centre of the circle can see, on Mid-Winters Day, that the setting sun settles precisely into a v-shaped notch cut in her top. Long Meg's raison d'etre was for the worship of the sun god and Mid-Winter's Day was the most important day of the year.

PART VII

At the end of the following week we decided to take Crocodile to the Holker Garden Festival. For us it was one of those special events in the year, like Damson Day, that we did not want to miss out on. We had enjoyed almost drought conditions in April, but May, which is usually a good-weather month in the Lake District, had proved to be a disappointment – simply too many heavy showers and very few totally dry days. We had had to select our days on the fells with Crocodile carefully and sometimes rearrange things at short notice, but Napoleon's Raven Post service had made this much easier. I had fixed a metal bar underneath our bell button so that Napoleon could comfortably stand on the bar and press the bell. This meant that we didn't constantly have to keep an eye out for him ... he simply rang the bell to let us know that he had arrived with a message from Crocodile and we would send an instant reply. However, by the end of May the weather had settled to

Chapter Seven

Crocodile's Grand Tour

near perfection and by June we were enjoying a quintessential English summer.

The Holker Garden Festival is a celebration of the very best of gardens, food and country life. This year there were more than 150 small stands alongside the huge marquees for Floral Art and Horticulture, Foods and Crafts, and one called *Made In Cumbria*, featuring products and produce from around the region. Alongside these were a host of demonstrations, country pursuits and other activities for all ages. We felt comfortable taking Crocodile here because, although we would be in a crowd of several thousand people, some of them would be dressed in a variety of weird and wonderful costumes and Crocodile would not look at all out of place.

Crocodile had sent Napoleon with a message just before his early morning swim in Windermere. We sent a reply, arranging to meet him at nine o'clock in the Dormobile, which we had left, the previous night, in our parking space above the boathouse. He was already dried and dressed and eagerly waiting for us when we climbed aboard. He had a pair of extremely baggy cream trousers on, Oxford Bags, no doubt, a long, jazzy, striped cotton blazer with an extended tailpiece, and a silk handkerchief in the breast pocket. He wore a multi-coloured university scarf and a wide-brimmed straw boater. This outfit, together with the now familiar, long, grey bushy beard, gave him a distinct resemblance to W.G. Grace. He would not have looked out of place at Lord's, The Oxford and Cambridge Boat Race, or Henley Regatta.

"Good morning," beamed Crocodile. "I have to tell you that I was up half the night attaching the tail-piece onto this jacket. Luckily, I had two identical jackets that the Professor once bought for me. I can't remember if they were his cricket club colours or his rowing club colours, but I know the reason I had two was because he had forgotten that he had already bought me one the previous summer from his tailors in Saville Row.

"You look very smart and quite the part," said Kate, "and the tail hides *your* tail perfectly. Well done!"

It's an easy drive to Holker. We go south down the lake to Newby Bridge, then follow the Lakeside and Haverthwaite Railway, past the old Dolly Blue Works at Backbarrow, left at Haverthwaite Station and the Thomas The Tank sheds, then a four mile drive through woodlands to Holker Hall. As with many of the grand estates in Cumbria, Holker is kept in pristine condition, maintaining our heritage in admirable style for the benefit of everyone. The Hall is set in romantic gardens and surrounded by manicured parkland.

Firstly we looked round the show gardens and then went into the Floral Art Marquee. Crocodile was intrigued because all the themes were connected to water, with titles like *River of Dreams*, and *Below the Waves*.

On exiting the marquee we were confronted by three exquisitely constructed boats. One was a Clinker Sailing Dinghy built in larch on oak frames – green on the outside and varnished to a high gloss finish on the inside. The second was a twenty-four foot contemporary electrically powered craft, beautifully built using traditional timbers. The third, and the one we really fell in love with, was a thirty-foot open launch named, *Silver Shilling*. It had a polished cedar and mahogany hull and a gleaming oak and cherry interior. The power options were electric drive or a hybrid system of electric and diesel. There was also a list of extras, which included a stereo system, picnic fridge and wine cooler.

"What an amazingly opulent way to go for a picnic," said Kate. "Just our cup of tea, or should I say our glass of champagne?"

These beautiful boats mesmerised Crocodile, and as we walked on he couldn't stop talking about them. The surprising thing was that he seemed to know a lot about the technical aspects, including the finer points on the choice of diesel or electric power options. He told us that electric power was environmentally friendly using solar energy and being almost completely silent in operation. He said that the Professor was a staunch supporter of products that were kind to the environment.

"Our favourite boat in the Lake District is the Steam Yacht Gondola on Coniston Water," said Kate. "From the deck you can see the powerful engine doing its work in almost total silence – and it is steam powered. That boat trip is certainly high on our list of priorities for you in the near future."

The next attraction that caught our eye was *Polly's Parrot Show* but just to the right of the entrance was a stall selling strawberry tarts. I bought us all tarts with clotted cream, and we ate them while watching *Polly's Parrot Show*.

Their current owner had rescued all the parrots, following serious ill treatment. They had fantastic names like Barney, the dancing white parrot; Gonzo, the red-capped parrot; Inca, a blue, yellow and red parrot, whose speciality was rope climbing and tightrope walking. Tiki would lie on his back and pretend to be dead, while Majeica was an expert at kissing. Apparently, when he was rescued he had lost his beak completely. His owner explained that parrots are able to grow a new beak in a year. In fact, if they don't wear them down by gnawing at things, the beak would just grow bigger and bigger. Unfortunately, if they lose them completely they may grow back deformed. In Majeica's case a special mould was used to encourage the beak to grow to the correct shape.

He now had a quite splendid beak, as Crocodile was soon to experience. Majeica suddenly flew onto his beard, climbed up it using his beak and claws, and began to kiss Crocodile in approximately the spot where he thought a mouth should be. Of course there wasn't a mouth there to kiss; the opening to Crocodile's mouth was at the sides and near the bottom of the beard, not top centre. Confused, and unable to find a mouth to kiss, Majeica scratched his head; he then removed a blob of clotted cream and some crumbs from Crocodile's beard and flew back to his owner, where he continued his kissing in the way he was used to.

We ambled up and down the rows of stalls. Then Crocodile and I waited for Kate to try on a jumper on one stand. It was a long wait because there was only a single cubicle to change in and about a dozen ladies, each with at least an armful of clothes, were already queuing for their turn. Every so often the occupant of the cubicle would alight for second and third opinions and then re-emerge five minutes later wearing the same garment just to make sure that her advisors had in fact given an honest, unbiased judgement, and that it really didn't make her bottom look too big.

I said quietly to Crocodile, "I don't believe that you will have experienced this ritual before. It is an art form perfected by nearly every female from a very early age, yet quite incomprehensible to most men however long they live. Even if the first garment tried on is close to perfect, I do not know anyone who has personally witnessed any lady ever buying it. I am not saying that she will not eventually purchase it, but it will only be eons later, after half the clothes in that store and substantial quantities of merchandise in many of the other shops in town have been duly considered. Nearly always, a few minutes before closing time, she will finally come to the conclusion that the first garment, after all, did in fact suit her the best. There then ensues a race across town get back to the first store before it closes, followed by great relief when the courteous shop manager assures her that she doesn't mind staying on after closing time, 'If madam would like to try it on again'. Finally, her mind is made up and she agrees to take it ... but only on condition that she can change it for the smaller size if she believes, after all, that the smaller size would have been a slightly better fit. Then, would you believe it! On the way back to the car, she sees a frock in a display window that may have suited her better and the shop is now closed. However did she miss that when we passed by before?"

I don't know if Crocodile fully understood the strange but ubiquitous behavioural pattern that I had been trying to explain, but Kate arrived, all in a fluster, before he had the chance to speak.

"Have you seen the queue?" she said, with a disappointed look on her face. "It will be at least another twenty minutes before I can get to try it on ... but no matter, I don't think it was the right size anyway, and there's a shop in Kendal that sells the same brand ... perhaps we could go there tomorrow to see if they have them in stock?"

Kate and I followed Crocodile who was pointing excitedly towards a crowd of people. When we got there we saw that it was a mini circus ring with a clown performing in the middle. When we eventually got a better view we saw that the clown was riding a monocycle in and out and around a group of children sitting on the grass. He kept asking them silly questions and making them laugh. He then moved into the centre of the ring and performed various juggling tricks with skittles, hoops, and some empty wine bottles, which he pretended to drink from first and then ride in a drunken state, nearly running into the children. Finally, he climbed a metal pole in the centre of the ring and continued juggling at different heights up the pole. The finale was performed with him standing on the top of the pole.

"I used to do similar tricks at the circus," said Crocodile, "but I had a variety of bicycles as well as monocycles in a range of heights."

When the clown came down from the top of the pole he announced that there would now be a short intermission. He took down the pole but left his monocycle and other equipment on the grass in the centre of the ring. A man in the audience said that his son was learning to ride a monocycle and could he have a go if he kept an eye on him?

"Only if you promise to supervise him and take full responsibility," said the clown. "I am not insured for accidents. I'll be back in twenty minutes. Please be careful."

Everybody watched as the boy tried to ride the monocycle. His father ran with him and after a few uncertain starts he managed to stay more or less upright for a few seconds.

Suddenly, before we could say anything, Crocodile walked into the ring. "Perhaps I can be of some assistance," he said to the boy and his father, "I am a trained mono-cyclist."

The boy handed the machine to Crocodile who just jumped on and rode all the way round the ring. He then spun round in several circles and rode backwards into the centre of the ring and stopped. He beckoned to the boy and helped him onto the monocycle and followed him round, steadying the machine and whispering into his ear. The crowd clapped and cheered when the boy finally got going quite well. When he finally dismounted, Crocodile whispered in his ear again and they both gave a little bow together. By the time the clown returned the show was over.

As we were leaving, Crocodile said to us, "I thought I'd better not do any juggling or anything too fancy just in case my beard flew up or fell off ... that would have caused quite a commotion!"

After we thought that we had seen nearly everything, we discovered that *Free Hot Air Balloon Flights* were being offered in the park close to the Hall. We decided to go and see if we could arrange a flight for Crocodile. En route we were sidetracked by a Punch and Judy show, so we stopped for a while to watch the performance. Crocodile was astonished at the appearance of a crocodile, which suddenly jumped out from behind the curtains and attacked Mr. Punch. Mrs. Punch then appeared from down below carrying a large truncheon with which she smacked the crocodile several times on his head. With jaws wide open the crocodile then attacked Mrs. Punch, but Mr. Punch grabbed the truncheon and beat the crocodile down until he vanished from view.

"What do you make of that?" Kate asked Crocodile.

"I am sure I really can't make head or tail of it," he replied with a gasp. Clearly he had never seen a Punch and Judy show before and therefore had absolutely no idea what was going on. He simply asked what a crocodile could possibly be doing jumping out from behind a curtain and attacking a very odd looking lady with a big nose. Kate and I tried to explain, with some difficulty, that it was traditional children's entertainment, but we also had no idea exactly why a crocodile should have been given such a role. He was obviously portrayed as the baddy, but then Mr. and Mrs. Punch were not exactly Mr. and Mrs. Nice.

"It was probably to add a touch of the exotic," suggested Kate. "I suppose when Punch and Judy shows first appeared, not many people in this country had ever seen a crocodile, and as far as we know you are the only real crocodile in the Lake District now. Although you'll be interested to know that I read recently that crocodiles did once live here ... at a house in Ambleside. The owner had heated pools built for them, just like the Professor did for you. I believe that William Wordsworth and Dr.

Chapter Seven   Crocodile's Grand Tour

Arnold stayed there – so they may have seen the crocodiles as well."

Unfortunately, when we got to the balloons there was not only a very long queue, but, as well, a breeze had picked up and it had suddenly become too blustery to take off safely – particularly as there were very high trees close by. The balloons were tethered to cables and would only go up to a height of fifty or sixty feet, but it was still a potentially dangerous situation. However, it did give us the chance to show Crocodile a balloon close up and to give him an idea of how they worked.

We watched as they prepared a balloon for take-off in the hope that the breeze would subside. Firstly, they tipped the basket over onto its side in order to attach the nylon/polyester balloon fabric, called the envelope. I explained that the big bag containing the envelope is placed downwind of the burner frame, which sits above the basket on flexible nylon poles. Wires are fixed to vertical load tapes built into the fabric of the envelope. We saw them pull the envelope out of the bag and check it thoroughly to make sure that nothing was damaged or tangled. I said that the wires are then fixed to points on the corners of the burner frame.

There were three sizes of basket available and they were all constructed in the same way, in wicker – a combination of willow and stripped cane I believe, with the edges protected by strong hide. On Damson Day we had watched a man skilfully weave wicker shopping-baskets, which he said should last a lifetime. He told us that in days gone by they used to be handed down from generation to generation they were so strong, albeit deceptively so. Balloon baskets have been made in this traditional way for over two centuries and modern materials such as nylon and fibreglass have been found to be inferior. They were simply not up to the bumps and bangs that a woven basket could easily withstand.

The largest of the three baskets was divided into three compartments, two for up to eight passengers in total, and one for the pilot and four propane gas cylinders, each holding eighty litres of fuel and good for a couple of hours total flying time. The basket measured about seven feet by four, by four feet high.

Crocodile appeared even more excited about them than he had been about the boats – perhaps because he had never seen a real balloon up close before.

The single disappointment in that wonderful day was that we didn't get to take Crocodile up in a balloon. If anything, the gusts of wind were increasing and the pilot decided that it was too risky to fly. We promised Crocodile that there would be other days when we would fly in a balloon.

On the way home he asked all sorts of questions about balloons. He found it difficult to believe that the limp spread of fabric that had been laid out on the ground in front of us could carry eight or nine people thousands of feet into the air.

"It is amazingly simple," I said, "and due entirely to the fact that hot air is lighter than cool air. The explanation in physics is when air is heated the spaces between the molecules increase, making the same volume of air, lighter. If that air can be contained in something very light, like a balloon, then the balloon will fly if the total weight of the volume of hot air contained in the envelope and anything attached is less than the weight of the same volume of cooler air on the outside. Many hundreds of years before this was discovered, Archimedes realised that the reason a ship floats is because it displaces more than its own weight of water. It's the same reason why a crocodile floats. Also, like a ship, a balloon has to be very large to carry a lot of weight. If you tried to row across Windermere with the Dormobile in your little boat, it would sink ... but the ferry can easily stay afloat with twenty or thirty vehicles on board."

"Yes," replied Crocodile, "I think I understand that now. The Professor told me all about Archimedes jumping out of his bath and shouting *eureka*."

"A strange fact," I said, "was that the Montgolfier brothers, who pioneered the first manned flight in a balloon, believed that the reason it flew was because the things they burned, which included straw, wool, rancid meat and old shoes, gave off an unidentified gas, which, like hydrogen and helium, was lighter than air. They had no idea that it was simply hot air that made their balloon fly. Another stroke of luck they had was that the sooty smoke created by burning these things blocked the tiny holes in the cotton and paper envelope, thus retaining the warm air that would otherwise have escaped. In other words, if they had used *clean* hot air, as we do today, the fabric used for the construction of their balloon would not have contained it sufficiently to enable it to take off."

"Nevertheless, fly it did, and I think that if a genie were to give me the chance to witness any event in the whole of human history, I would probably choose to be in Paris on 21st November, 1783 to see Jean-Francois Pilatre de Rozier and Francois Laurent, Marquis d' Arlandes, in front of King Louis XVI and Marie Antoinette and a crowd of thousands, make the very first manned flight in the Montgolfier's magnificently decorated hot-air balloon."

"Amazingly, the flight lasted twenty-five minutes and, after flying high over the Seine at around two to three thousand feet, it landed more than five miles from where it took off. It must have been an incredible spectacle. Man had done the seemingly impossible, and it created a sense of euphoria almost to the point where it was believed that if this was possible ... for mankind, anything was possible."

PART VIII

Our first summer with Crocodile continued exactly as we had planned. Picnics and boat trips, long walks and short walks, hard climbs and easy climbs, and lazy days in the sun.

I remember one hot July afternoon, taking him for a long iced drink at The Swan Hotel at Newby Bridge. He sat with Kate on the bank of the River Leven while I got the drinks from the bar. When I returned he was feeding a pair of swans with morsels of food from his saddlebags. It has to be seen to be believed how a creature so elegant, so graceful, so majestic on water and on the wing, can appear so ungainly waddling about on dry land.

Chapter Seven   Crocodile's Grand Tour

We had brought with us a simple picnic, consisting of walnut and olive bread that Kate had taken out of her bread-maker just five minutes before we set off. Crocodile had brought a selection of his homemade cheeses and pates. Kate had made a summer pudding laced with crème de framboises, and accompanied by almond, coconut, and vanilla sorbets that she had kept cool in thermos flasks.

We walked along the riverbank and into a field adjacent to the Lakeside to Haverthwaite Railway line. Then we sat in the grass under some trees and spread out the picnic.

"This reminds me of, *Le dejeuner sur l' herbe*," said Crocodile with a smile. "One of the Professor's favourite paintings."

After the picnic, and feeling pleasantly full, we ambled deeper into the field where the grass was waist high and dry as straw. We lay down under the clean-brushed blue sky and dozed dreamily. Every now and then I was partially awakened by the sound of a steam locomotive chugging along. Even the hoot of the whistle and the screech of steel on steel were dulled and drowsy, muted by the heat of that high summer afternoon. I felt that I had travelled back through time half a century or more to the gentler days of my youth when, like Wordsworth, I had felt on occasions, in places like this, a wonderful sense of contentment and happiness and above all, a feeling of being completely at one with nature.

I am not sure how long we lay there but by the time we were fully awake the sun was well past its zenith.

189

Crocodile said with a yawn, "I had a dream about the Professor ... perhaps because once in a similar setting by the River Thames the Professor confided in me by telling me about a most significant event in his life. He described it as being, on a personal level, at least as significant as meeting me. It was in fact a series of events that broke his heart and changed, utterly, the course of his life."

Crocodile then related the story to us.

"The Professor told me that when he was still at school he met a girl called Lydia, who was the same age as himself and they saw each other almost everyday for nearly three years. He said that in the evening after he had finished his homework, he would run the two miles to her house with wings on his heels ... he felt only air beneath his feet as he whistled and sang along the way. Often he used to pass an old lady who was either working in her garden or standing at her gate and she took to waving as he ran by. One day she stopped him and said in a soft voice, 'These past two years I have watched you running and heard you whistling and singing. You make me happy because I know that you are happy. You must be very much in love. Seeing you also brings a tear to my eye because like you, I had found the love of my life. Sadly, for me, the future that I looked forward to was not to be. My fiancé was a soldier and was killed on active service a month before we were to be married. You have helped me to rekindle, more brightly, all my precious memories of him. I always shed a few tears when I think of him, and that is almost every day. Some are still tears of sadness but others are now tears of happiness when I see you and think of him. Take it from me, complete happiness is not possible without true love, but that love must be given, accepted, and shared equally ... it is a fine balance where the feelings of both partners are in perfect equilibrium. It must also stand the test of time and everything that life throws at it. I was not given the chance to take the test, but I believe in my heart that I would have passed with flying colours. You seem to be off to a perfect start, just like I was. I wish you all the luck in the world'."

"All this is still quite difficult for me to understand," said Crocodile, pensively, "I suppose that you have to experience true love before you can properly understand it. I have read many novels in which the authors have attempted to describe what it is like. I know that I love you as I loved the Professor and Mercedes, but there aren't any female crocodiles around for me to fall in love with. You may find it hard to believe but I have never met another crocodile, male or female, at least not since I was a baby and my recollections of that small part of my life are, to say the least, very dim, and probably more imagination than fact. I don't know how I would react or how a crocodile would react if I were to meet one. Can you imagine a human being who had never met another human? I suppose my situation is a bit like that of Tarzan, who had been brought up by the animals in the jungle. The main difference is that I have been well educated and there probably isn't another crocodile in the world who can speak a word of English, yet alone hold an intelligent conversation."

I had never considered Crocodile's situation from this perspective. The very thought of being the only one of your kind was a sobering one. When creatures evolve there must essentially be created the first of a new kind. The new creature's genes are passed on to its offspring and in turn they will pass on the genetic change to their progeny. I assumed most changes would be small, evolution would occur piecemeal, some pieces would be bigger than others, but I doubted that anything had happened before in the process of evolution to equal Crocodile's situation. Having said that, he still looked exactly like a crocodile; nothing in his bodily appearance had changed. All the change, all the evolution was, as far as was discernible, in his brain. Nevertheless, it was sufficient to make him fundamentally different from others of his species. He was as strong as a crocodile, he could swim like a crocodile and hold his breath for ages under water, but in nearly every other respect he thought and acted like a human being.

I could not begin to imagine how Crocodile must feel deep down about being the only one of his kind on the planet, or even in the universe. One could surmise that evolution was universal to life everywhere, the exception being God's creations, which presumably, could be born with any degree of sophistication. Crocodile's unique position was not even like being transported to a distant planet and finding oneself the only human in a society of aliens. The crucial difference would be that there, all the norms and values and patterns of behaviour would probably be quite literally *alien*, that is, unless the laws of physics and biology are exactly the same everywhere. To the extent that there exists in the universe a natural tendency for all living creatures to develop in the same way so that as they become more and more intelligent their patterns of behaviour converge until, ultimately, an identical perfection is achieved.

Crocodile had been brought up as a human being however, and all his thoughts and feelings, and natural behaviour were human not reptilian. He would always be different only because of his appearance. The reality of his situation was that he was more human, more humane and certainly more intelligent and cultured, than many human beings. He was in essence, wonderfully unique.

Kate and I had often thought of and discussed likely scenarios for him, if he were to come out into the open. We agreed that he would probably be more sympathetically accepted than for example the *Elephant Man*, a deformed human being who was regarded as a freak, exploited and paraded before the public in shows. There would always be this risk, even though it would be handled differently today. The world's media would pursue him to the ends of the earth; one could only speculate where it all might end.

My mind drifted back to the story he was telling about the Professor and his girlfriend, and I asked him what happened between the Professor and Lydia.

"It was very sad," said Crocodile shaking his head. "He could never bring himself to tell me the detail of what happened, but I know that he thought about her every day of his life. He used to take me with him several times a year to put flowers on her grave ... on her birthday, at Christmas, and other days that were important to him and to her memory. All he told me was that he won a scholarship to Oxford. Lydia had promised to wait for him until he had finished his degree. They wrote to each other nearly every day and of course he was with her during the holidays. What started off as a three-year course though, expanded to six years. At some point during those last three years something happened between them. I got the feeling that it involved another man and before the Professor had completed his PhD. Lydia was dead. He often used to say to me that the real cost of his degrees was the loss of the love of his life. He always believed that the old lady who had stopped him at her garden gate had given him a warning that he had not heeded, and for that, for the rest of his life, he would suffer as she had done. The kindest thing that he said to me was that I had brought a light back into his life, a light that had been extinguished, a light and a warmth and a sparkle that he thought he had lost forever."

PART IX

Our first major climb, after High Street, was Helvellyn. I felt that Striding Edge was a *no go* route for Crocodile, so we went up from Wythburn Church at the south end of Thirlmere. As we drive north from Grasmere, and before the steep climb up Dunmail Raise, I always think of Green-head Ghyll, made famous in one of my favourite poems, *Michael* by William Wordsworth. I probably read it at least once every year, often reading it out loud to myself. It is very easy to read aloud and its rhythm, tone and language always sound impressive. Even though *Michael* is a simple tale about a good shepherd, it has a power akin to the grandeur of Milton's

Paradise Lost. Any story about the breaking of the human spirit cannot but bring tears to your eyes, yet for me the fact that Michael left the sheep fold unfinished, although poignant, is of small consequence when compared to the rest of his life. Michael, his wife and their kind, will always have my admiration. You have only to compare them with many people in human society to put things in perspective. Yes, there are some things in life that you have to come to terms with, that you should not let break your spirit. And yes there are some mountains that are impossible to climb ... there is no shame in not trying.

The climb up to the summit of Helvellyn from Wythburn is very steep, but if taken slowly, it is not at all tedious. It is relatively short, and almost risk free. Our plan of attack on all the big climbs was to start early and to take it easy, both going up and coming down. The purist will argue that it is less interesting to climb Helvellyn from the west than from the east. This is because it is only from the east that the dramatic structure of Helvellyn can properly be observed. In particular, the way the glaciers have carved long valleys, separated by sharp serrated ridges of rock, into the east side of the mountain. This spectacle appears as a wonderful surprise, after the gentle contours of the last part of the climb up from Wythburn. As you climb from the west you know you are getting high because you can see Thirlmere in the valley below getting progressively smaller. You are also aware that your elevation is lining up with the tops of the highest fells in the Lake District to the south and west. The view over the summit to the east, looking down onto Striding Edge, is nevertheless unexpected and breathtaking. Crocodile said that he felt that given time he could get accustomed to heights with sheer drops. I told him that in our first year the important thing was to get to the top without injury. It would certainly cause us some problems if he were to break a leg. The last thing we wanted was to have to call Mountain Rescue to come to winch him off with a helicopter.

Our next major climb was Great Gable. Again we took the easy route starting from the slate mines near the top of the Honister Pass, and already a thousand feet above sea level. Apart from the steep rock stairway at the beginning, and the rocky scramble up from Green Gable to the summit, the middle and longest part of the ascent is little more than a leisurely stroll; yet the views over Buttermere and Crummock Water are magnificent. We promised Crocodile that we knew a really good spot to go swimming from in Crummock Water, and we would go in the water with him if he would keep his eye on Kate. She had been having secret swimming lessons in preparation for this very occasion. Kate had nevertheless brought a life jacket with her in the Dormobile, insisting that she wouldn't be quite so nervous if she wore this protection.

As we rounded Brandreth, the great mass of Gable came fully into view.

"Seriously, we're not going up there ... are we?" gasped Crocodile.

"I know it looks intimidating," I said, "but apart from a rocky section surrounding the summit it is much easier than it looks, and even the rock climb to the top isn't very dangerous. We wouldn't be taking you if it were. To put your mind at rest, the last time we climbed Gable we were astonished to be accompanied on the last section by a couple with a very young baby. The baby was strapped to the man's chest. You have nothing to be concerned about."

"I see!" said Crocodile, and then with a grin, "The Professor would say that your argument is not necessarily logical, in that the man may have gone on to climb the North Face of the Eiger the following week with the baby strapped to his chest, but that fact doesn't make the climb easy or safe."

"I can't argue with that," I replied, also smiling, "especially as many people would think that it was not a sensible thing to do. I was just trying to give you some reassurance."

"We'll strike a bargain with you," said Kate, "we'll promise to keep you safe up to the top of Gable in return for your promise to keep us safe in Crummock Water ... is that a deal?"

"That's a deal," said Crocodile grinning at us again, "and I'll take your word for it that it is not as hard as it looks."

"It is not so much the height of Gable," I said, "but its apparent height, standing more in isolation than many of the other big names, that makes it look so daunting, and I believe, makes it look like a real mountain. It has such a distinctive shape. Someone once said that it was fantastic to look at, fantastic to look from and fantastic to climb. I agree entirely with that sentiment and I think you will too when we get up there."

At the top of Green Gable, and before going down into Windy Gap for the final push to the summit of Great Gable, we stopped for a breather and for coffee and biscuits.

I suggested that where we were standing was a bit like landing on the Moon and looking at the Earth. Such is the proximity and size of Great Gable. If you face south you look straight at the northern crags of the mighty Gable. In other directions, using the same analogy, you look into outer space, in fact to Crummock Water and Buttermere. Looking northwest you see spectacular panoramic views over Borrowdale, Derwent Water and Keswick, and to Skiddaw in the north. Turning to the east I pointed out Sty Head Tarn and Sprinkling Tarn surrounded by Great End, Allen Crags and Glaramara.

Pointing out Sprinkling Tarn, I said to Crocodile, "I predict that you'll be swimming in there within the next few weeks; that's where we take our morning coffee break on the way up Scafell Pike and you'll get a second chance on the way down. It's also a beautiful place to sit awhile on a sunny day … I know that the sun will be shining, because we won't be climbing Scafell if it isn't. As I've told you before, that's another great thing about living in the Lake District, the weather can nearly always be perfect when you want it to be, so long as you make your plans at short notice."

"Sitting by Sprinkling Tarn, you can't hear a sound and it seems as far away from a city centre as it is possible to get. Yet it is a pleasant isolation, far from the madding crowd, in contrast with the top of Scafell, where you might as well be on the moon. You feel good because you have just climbed to the top of the highest mountain in England, but you wouldn't want to stay there for too long."

"The Professor and I sometimes used to discuss odd subjects like travelling deep into space to visit other worlds," said Crocodile, "but he had concluded long ago that, although it may sound exciting, to be realistic, it would be a tedious waste of a life, simply because it would take so long. He said that going to the Moon, or even Mars, is one thing, but going out beyond our own solar system is quite another. One day, he said, it might be necessary, assuming we had the technology to make such a journey possible, but for sure you would become an expert at playing noughts and crosses and hang-man, and other such time wasting games. Even if your spaceship was a massive structure with a very large crew ... that would be your world, for much if not all your life."

"Yes, I understand clearly what the Professor was saying," I replied. "There would be no Sprinkling Tarn, no Great Gable, or Scafell Pike, and no Windermere, on a spaceship."

"There wouldn't be any clothes shops either," said Kate with a look of genuine concern.

Crocodile and I looked at each other ... neither of us said a word.

Only a single deep notch known as Windy Gap separates the two Gables. It is but a short scramble down, then a real, but safe and simple rock climb up to the top of Great Gable.

We had to push, pull, and pamper Crocodile a few times, but he persevered heroically, if at times unsteadily, all the way up to the summit. Unlike Skiddaw, grand though it is, which we climbed a fortnight later, you get a real sense of accomplishment reaching the summit of Gable. Perhaps it's because the ascent of Skiddaw is more like a long hard walk, albeit with spectacular views. In Victorian times tourists were transported to the top on ponies. On the Gables, you can make believe that the top of Green Gable is the final camp before the last leg up to the summit of Everest and when you get to the top you are standing on the top of the world.

PART X

The most iconic peaks in the Lake District are without doubt the Langdale Pikes and this was one climb that we could not leave out. We had decided to start from the New Dungeon Ghyll Hotel and go straight up Stickle Ghyll, to Stickle Tarn. Stickle Ghyll is a fast flowing beck which cuts a dramatic path through the rocky terrain. We had chosen a particularly hot day and for that reason it seemed steeper and tougher than the last time we had climbed this route. Crocodile found it hard going and the hot day felt even hotter because of our exertions up to the tarn. We stopped frequently to give him short rests and as soon as we made it to the tarn we took off our boots and paddled in the water for a few minutes before sitting on some rocks and getting out the flask for a well earned cup of tea.

It's amazing how cool water followed by a hot cup of tea cools and calms you down. Only a few minutes earlier we had been puffing and panting in the heat, and Crocodile had been getting stressed out and certainly very hot under the collar. Now he looked as cool as a cucumber reclining on a big rock and sipping his tea.

I told him, "You'll be relieved to know that the worst is now behind us."

"Where do we go from here?" he asked looking around him as if he were ready for anything.

"Up there! "I said, pointing almost vertically upwards to the top of the enormous mass of Pavey Ark, towering above us on the other side of the tarn."

"I see!" he replied, without flinching and with an expressionless face. "I have to say that looking at it from here, Pavey Ark looks nearly as daunting as Great Gable, but I am sure that you are going to tell me that it isn't as hard as it looks."

"Well, it would be very hard if we were to go straight up the face, but we don't intend to do that. We go up the side, up the ridge from the north," I said, pointing out the direction. "It's a bit of a scramble but I assure you it's easier than the last pitch up Gable."

"Don't you think that it's a wonderful feeling to be standing so close to the Langdale Pikes?" said Kate. "I sometimes think of all the places in the Lake District where you get fantastic views of them ... there must be dozens of viewpoints and they are always instantly recognisable. They seem to be everywhere. It's a bit like continually bumping into an old friend in many different places, a friend you instantly identify, from almost any angle. You could be going round Loughrigg Tarn, walking by Elterwater, or along the River Brathay, arriving at Tarn Hows, or driving along Esthwaite Water, even coming back from shopping in Kendal and they suddenly appear in the distance, majestic as ever. It seems that you don't have to go looking for them ... they follow you around."

"This is a great thrill for me," said Crocodile. "The first time I came to the Lake District with the Professor was on a short trip in winter. He had to attend an important meeting here and he asked me if I would like to accompany him. It was my first long-distance trip in the Dormobile. At some point on the motorway I fell asleep. I must have been dreaming again about being kidnapped and I was very startled when he woke me up. It took me a minute or two to recover. Then the Professor asked me if I would mind closing my eyes again because he had a surprise for me. After I had shut my eyes he guided me out of the Dormobile, across a hard surface and onto something that was cold and crunchy. After walking just a little way we stopped. Then he told me to keep my eyes shut and to tilt my head down so that when I opened them I would be looking at my feet. After that, I should slowly raise my head until I was looking straight in front of me."

"When I opened my eyes I was staring at snow and my feet were covered in it. As I raised my head, I began to think that I was still dreaming, but now it wasn't a nightmare, I was in paradise. A lake stretched out in front of me, it's surface shone like polished glass. A little way out, a pair of swans floated gracefully on the water, heads held high. Then the most beautiful snow covered mountains came into view and the sun was shining brightly in a clear pale blue sky. Everything about me shimmered and glistened. I was spellbound and completely lost for words. 'Those are the Langdale Pikes and this is Windermere', said the Professor. 'Welcome to the Lake District'."

We continued on our journey, walking round Stickle Tarn with Pavey Ark towering above us, then following Bright Beck, which flows into the tarn, before crossing the stream in order to reach the northern ridge and our stairway up to the Langdale Pikes. It is a short steep climb to the summit of Pavey Ark and we let Crocodile lead the way, a task which he accomplished with growing confidence. On the summit we guided him to a safe spot from where we could look down the broad almost vertical rock face to the rough screes and the dark waters of Stickle Tarn, now far below us. Crocodile complained of a funny tickly feeling in his tummy.

"Don't worry," I said, trying to reassure him, "you've got butterflies and so have I."

"Me too!" said Kate stepping back a few paces.

"It's quite a normal reaction and happens to many people when they get close to a dangerous drop. Even though your rational self tells you that you are not going to plunge headlong into the abyss, you nearly always get butterflies as you approach the edge. This sensation is often followed by an assumed vertigo brought on by your nervous system suddenly starting to behave irrationally. Then you ask yourself, is it really irrational when you have the knowledge that some poor souls do fairly regularly slip or swoon or get blown off the top of crags by freak gusts of wind? Is it not just a natural warning to be careful? The problem is that if you are too careful you change the way you do things naturally ... you don't act positively or confidently and it is this change of attitude that creates the problems and increases the danger. Nevertheless, people like my own brother, who have no fear of heights, always astonish me. Somehow they know instinctively that they are not going to fall, so they don't. Whereas the nervous ditherers create their own self-fulfilling prophecy. I am trying hard to convince myself because I am never comfortable in places that I perceive as being potentially dangerous. For me there will always be a difference between walking across a plank of wood placed in the middle of a football field and one placed between the tops of two skyscrapers, where the butterflies would become more powerful than all the money in the world."

From the summit of Pavey Ark it is then a pleasant walk across a flat moorland plateau followed by an easy climb to the top of our next objective, Harrison Stickle, from where there are superb views of Bowfell, Crinkle Crags, and down to Elterwater.

I pointed out the Crinkles to Crocodile, telling him that, weather permitting, we would be up there next week.

"We love the Crinkles almost as much as the Langdale Pikes," said Kate. "We get a fantastic view of them and Bow Fell from our house, but sadly a pine forest obscures a perfect view of the Langdale Pikes, so that we can only see the tops of them. Perhaps one day they'll cut down the trees and give us a better view."

Our final leg, before the long steep descent down to Dungeon Ghyll, was to the top of Pike of Stickle, where the views are similarly impressive, looking way down into Langdale, surrounded by a cohort of fells, from Rosset Gill, across Bow Fell and along the Crinkles.

On the way down to Dungeon Ghyll we told Crocodile about the discovery, on these very slopes, of the heads of stone axes made up here by Neolithic man and that thousands of years before the Roman legions arrived stone headed axes were produced in Langdale in great quantities.

PART XI

Throughout that summer we interspersed our climbs and walks with a variety of more leisurely activities. For example, we cruised on Coniston Water aboard the Steam Yacht Gondola, taking afternoon tea at Brantwood and sitting on the terrace overlooking the lake in the warm sunshine, then going on a tour of Ruskin's fine house. The previous weekend we had taken Crocodile to Kirkby Lonsdale – we had walked over Devil's Bridge, where both Crocodile and I had further attacks of butterflies as we peered down over the bridge's parapet into the river and on to the rocks far below. Crocodile had asked how one could be sure that the wall wouldn't collapse under the weight of so many people leaning on it. I had replied, speculating that with luck you might land in the water if it did give way. Crocodile concluded that even he wouldn't risk jumping into the water from that height. I pointed to a diving board set into the rock on the opposite bank, "Much better to jump in from there," I suggested.

Across the bridge there was the usual fine array of motorcycles and Crocodile was like a child at Christmas as we wandered up and down the rows of gleaming bikes. I explained to him that bikers make a special pilgrimage here, and that there was probably a connection between the Hell's Angels and Devil's Bridge, but now it acted as a magnet and a shrine for motorcyclists from all over the country.

After we had finally dragged him away from the high tech macho machinery we went back over the bridge and ambled along the riverbank to the steep steps leading up to Ruskin's View. Crocodile had told us that the Professor admired John Ruskin's work on social reform and that both were Professors at Oxford University, but not at the same time.

Kate and I had had the good fortune to look across the River Weser at Hamelin Town, but I am sure one could easily say of Ruskin's View, *A pleasanter spot I never spied*, overlooking the River Lune, which meandered gracefully through glorious English countryside. We now stood in Ruskin's house in the Lake District. I am equally sure that the same could be said about the view from Brantwood.

In fact we were in the turret room, a striking addition by Ruskin to the original house. I knew that Charles Darwin had also stood in this very room gazing out over Coniston Water to the Coniston Fells beyond. Now we were in the same spot with Crocodile at our side and with the knowledge that he was the supreme example of a quantum leap in the evolution of one species. How Darwin would have envied us. The moment also made me reflect on the Professor who had clearly understood the biological and evolutionary significance of Crocodile – it was to his credit that he kept Crocodile's existence a secret – I doubt that Charles Darwin would have done the same.

We had a special affinity with the Steam Yacht Gondola, not just because it was our favourite boat, but also because, by a quirk of fate, it was instrumental in changing our lives. We had been taking a cruise one Sunday afternoon and had got into conversation with another passenger, who turned out to be a friend of the man who had fitted out the interior of the Gondola. It was built in 1859 at a cost of one thousand guineas; then rebuilt from a wreck in 1979 for nearly four hundred times as much. It was obvious that whoever had created the two elegant saloons was a master craftsman and we knew that, cost permitting, he was the man to fit out our planned new house in Bowness. And so it came to pass; he actually built the entire house for us. Embarrassingly we ran out of money towards the end of the build but a few years later we sold it for twice as much as it cost us. This good fortune enabled us to purchase the house of our dreams, with its magnificent views over Windermere and the Lakeland Fells. Fate intervened that day on the Steam Yacht Gondola and also ensured that one day, years into the future, Crocodile would come into our lives.

On the way back to Coniston from Brantwood, we steamed gracefully and silently across the lake, the only sound being the lapping of water against the hull and the hum of the passenger conversations, I thought of the contrast between this craft travelling quietly and sedately at ten knots and Donald Campbell's Bluebird K7 screaming over the same stretch of water at three hundred miles an hour.

Heading vaguely in the direction of home we called in at the Tower Bank Arms, perhaps for a half or a pint of Bluebird Bitter, or something equally refreshing. Just as we entered the pub our favourite window seat became vacant so we spent the next half hour quenching our thirst and watching the world go by. We could easily have been fooled into thinking that we were in a hostelry in rural Japan because most of the passers-by were Japanese. The reason is simply that Beatrix Potter's house, Hill Top, sits in a large garden next door. She is so popular in Japan that they have erected a replica of the house there and every year, thousands of Japanese tourists flock to see the real Hill Top. We explained this strange phenomenon to the puzzled Crocodile who asked if any of them could be Samurai. Not wishing to disappoint him Kate avoided the question and told him about our friends, Yas and Yumico, who, when they stayed with us, used to come down to dinner in traditional Japanese dress. They had given her a most beautiful silk kimono, which she sometimes wears on special occasions.

We also explained to Crocodile that much of the Lake District, from Near and Far Sawrey, to Hawkshead and Coniston, and from Tarn Hows to Little Langdale, is as un-spoilt as it is today because of Beatrix Potter's Legacy. Using the proceeds of her wonderfully illustrated books, from Peter Rabbit to Little Pig Robinson, she bought over

Chapter Seven   Crocodile's Grand Tour

4000 acres of land, including ten farms and twenty houses, and left it all to the National Trust.

"She must have been a lot richer than William Wordsworth," said Crocodile.

"I am sure William would definitely have approved of what she did, even if he didn't make as much money," said Kate.

We made further detours on the way home taking a look at Fox How, once the holiday home of Dr. Thomas Arnold, the famous headmaster of the Professor's old school, Rugby.

The house, which William Wordsworth helped him to acquire is situated on a beautiful road, which runs along the River Rothay, and was a favourite route from Grasmere to Ambleside, and vice versa, for William and Dorothy.

Our final port of call that day was Rydal Hall, built, much to William's chagrin, next door to his beloved Rydal Mount. We spent the last hour of this relaxing day out watching a game of croquet on the lawn. Crocodile surprised us again by informing us that he had played croquet many times with the Professor in London. He said that he had a good eye for a ball and that he was quite a good player.

PART XII

The following day we got up later than usual. Apart from the depths of winter we are normally out of bed early because both Kate and I believe it to be a waste of the day to lie in bed just for the sake of it. We both however think that all rules are meant to be sensibly broken, especially self-imposed ones, and sometimes it is nice to have a lie in, especially if the weather is unpleasant. The weather forecast, although not too bad, was not good enough for us to tackle Scafell Pike. We decided therefore to walk up to the foot of Crinkle Crags instead and if the weather was still holding up, there would be time enough to climb them, or at least climb to the top of the first one.

Shortly after we got up, Napoleon arrived with some fresh eggs, so I sent a message back with him to advise Crocodile that we would collect him in the Dormobile on his side of the lake at midday. As we left the house Kate and I looked across the lake to the Crinkles, their distinctive roller-coaster peaks clearly visible in the morning sunshine.

Crocodile was waiting for us when we arrived. He was wearing a full-length, gabardine, Dick Turpin style coat, and a wide-brimmed Australian outback hat, minus the corks. His saddlebags hung over his shoulder and in his right-hand he carried a long bone handled shepherds' crook, which he waved above his head as soon as he saw the Dormobile.

Taking the road from Little Langdale we headed towards the Wrynose Pass and our base camp at the Three Shire Stones, which formerly marked the meeting point of three counties, Lancashire, Cumberland and Westmorland. Before the change in 1974 it was possible to be in three counties at the same time by putting your hands on one stone and each foot on the other two. Today, you can't do that – Cumberland and Westmorland are no more so it is not quite as exciting.

Chapter Seven — Crocodile's Grand Tour

The walk round Red Tarn and up to Great Cove was pleasant and leisurely, and the view down into Great Langdale was superb. Just at that moment, when we had committed to attempt the climb, black clouds, drifting from the direction of the Scafells, appeared over the summits of the Crinkles. We decided to take a rest for a while and see how the weather developed because I knew from past experience that the route over the Crags was not straightforward and could be dangerous in poor visibility.

As we sat beneath the Crinkles looking across to the Langdale Pikes and down into Great Langdale, with the Dungeon Ghyll hotel far below, Crocodile spoke suddenly, "I wonder if Emily has returned from her holiday in America? Do you think we should try to make contact and arrange our trip to London?"

"I was thinking only the same thing yesterday," I replied, "but it would be nice to get Scafell Pike under our belts before we go. The weather forecast is improving after today so why don't we give the Crinkles a miss, as the cloud is getting heavier and darker, and try for the *big one* later this week. Then I'll phone to see if Emily is back and if she is, make arrangements to take you to see her as soon as she can have us."

"Gosh! That's made me go funny inside," said Crocodile. "Suddenly I don't want to leave the Lake District, but I would like to go back to my old home just one more time."

"That's settled then," I said. "Scafell Pike, then London here we come! "

PART XIII

So it was that, two days later, on a bright, still, crisp autumn morning, the three of us were heading expectantly in the direction of the highest place in England. I had no concerns about the weather, as the predictions were that it was now settled under a wide zone of high pressure for the rest of the week. Kate had suggested an early start so that we would be at Seathwaite at a time that could see us up Grains Gill by mid-morning.

Wainwright describes the route up from Borrowdale as a classic expedition and the finest fell walk in the Lake District, and even though the summit of Scafell Pike is not the most distinguished, it is nevertheless the highest, and it is the journey through a wonderful landscape to that point that is so memorable.

We left Seathwaite Farm at a canter and we were soon at Stockley Bridge, making our way, progressively more slowly, up Grains Gill following the stream that flows into the River Derwent and thence to Derwent Water, and to Keswick. Towering above us on the left are Glaramara and Allen Crags, with Seathwaite Fell to our right. We homed in relentlessly on our initial target, the foot of the awesome and precipitous Great End.

Crocodile was puffing and panting much of the way up Grains Gill, so every few minutes we stopped to give him a breather and to view the spectacular scenery that surrounded us.

It was much cooler than when we had climbed up Stickle Ghyll to Stickle Tarn, and the Langdale Pikes, but we were still relieved when Crocodile reached the top and we could inform him that the hardest part of the climb was behind us and he could now take a well earned rest, by the tranquil waters of Sprinkling Tarn a short detour to our right.

"I always think," said Crocodile," when you tell me that the hardest part is over, even though we are only half way up the highest mountain in England, you're trying to convince me that it's downhill all the way to the top."

I could detect a twinkle in his eye so I knew that he was teasing me. However, I pretended to be serious and tried to explain what I meant: "I've told you before that it's just a matter of psychology – if you know that the worst is over and in a very short while it's downhill all the way home, that knowledge changes your whole attitude. Similarly, if I had told you that we'd just done the easy part of the climb and it was very much steeper and harder now, all the way to the top, which would take us another three hours, I'll bet you wouldn't be feeling too good about it. Now you are more relaxed, because you know that the hardest bit is behind you and you can face the last part in a happier frame of mind, and, even if there are some short hard bits to come, you'll take them in your stride because you know it's not all like that. So although it's not literally downhill, it's relatively downhill, if you see what I mean."

"I'll feel even better after a dip in Sprinkling Tarn," he said. "Where is it?"

A few minutes later and we were standing looking down onto the sparkling waters of Sprinkling Tarn.

"That water is just too inviting," he said. "It will cool me down nicely."

Kate and I took off our boots and socks and paddled at the edge while Crocodile swam effortlessly to the centre of the small tarn and vanished beneath the surface.

"It doesn't seem like five minutes since we were over there," whispered Kate, pointing westward to Great Gable. "When we were looking down from Green Gable onto Sprinkling Tarn. It's even more delightful now we are here and just listen for a moment. It's dead silent. I can't hear a thing."

We both listened intently, but there was nothing to hear. It wasn't an eerie silence; it was a beautiful silence, a reverie without sound.

Some minutes later we were awakened by a faint splash and a small ripple in the surface of the water in the centre of the tarn. The ripple expanded and changed in shape from a circle to an ellipse, then to a V as it gathered speed. It moved directly towards us, and slowed and stopped. A now familiar pair of eyes appeared above the surface, then a long snout. We still felt that shiver of apprehension, but this time we knew what it was and who it was. A head appeared, then a neck, arms, a body and legs all dripping water and glistening in the sunlight. This time it emerged from the water without the aid of a walking stick. This time the feeling was not of fear, but of love and gratitude, for knowing this wonderful creature who, in just a few short months, had become such a good friend.

"The tarn is full of fish!" he exclaimed as he waded to the shore. "Most of them I recognise from my swims in Windermere, but one I have not seen before."

Chapter Seven   Crocodile's Grand Tour

"I read somewhere recently that *Vendance* have been brought here from Bassenthwaite. I understand that they are quite rare and they have done this to give the species a greater chance of survival."

"That's a coincidence," he said, "I knew a fellow called Vendance, a friend of the Professor's. He was a French nobleman, *Le Marquis de Vendance* and very eccentric. He permanently displayed a lace handkerchief. It was either in his cuff or in his hand, or partly in both, and he always gestured wildly with it when he got excited, which was most of the time. He walked with a long silver handled cane. I have it in my collection, or at least a similar one that he gave to the Professor. Unfortunately I didn't know him personally because, although he was a close friend of the Professor's, I was not permitted to meet him. That is a shame because he could have taught me French. However, and I don't believe that I told you this, the Professor used to give regular dinner parties to which I was not invited. He simply thought that it was too great a risk, and the fewer people who knew about me the better. Anyway he made up for this in a small way by letting me eat my dinner in a secret priest's hole located behind the oak panelling above the dining room. You get a terrific view of the guests around the dining table. The Professor had wired me up for sound so that I could hear everything that was said, and I had a pair of opera glasses so that I could get close-ups of the expressions on the diners' faces. I didn't feel left out at all and I really used to enjoy myself. There were some embarrassing moments and surprises but I had better not tell you about those. I will however tell you that Le Marquis was a perfect gentleman with impeccable table manners; he always gently touched his lips with his handkerchief or napkin after each small morsel of food had been delicately placed in his mouth. I hope that my table manners are nearly as exemplary because I learned a lot from him. But he never knew it."

"We always thought that you had the bearing of a French aristocrat," laughed Kate. "That explains it all."

"Which reminds me," I said, "Kate and I realise how much you want to go back to your old house and to see Emily ... first thing in the morning I'll telephone to see if she's back and I hope I will be able to make firm arrangements for our trip to London."

That clearly pleased him and we set off for the summit of Scafell Pike at a brisk pace with Crocodile leading the way. "Onwards and downwards," he shouted," all the way to the top!"

"Follow me sir, I'm right behind you!" Kate shouted back.

Underneath Great End, up Esk Hause, then a change of direction to Ill Crag, which you think could be Scafell Pike, but isn't – you still have further to go – but on that day it didn't matter. We had even made a detour to the top of Great End from where we could look down onto Sprinkling Tarn, now only a fraction of the size that it had been a little while ago; then down again to Borrowdale and Derwent Water, with Skiddaw and Blencathra in the far distance, a breathtaking panorama of the northern Lake District.

We had then made our way back to Calf Cove and finally to the path, easy at first, then difficult in parts, as stones become boulders and boulders become bigger boulders – but it didn't matter; however rough the going, we were up for it. We skipped along knowing we were going to make it – it really was downhill all the way to the top. We had gone to the moon, or so the landscape and our achievement led us to believe.

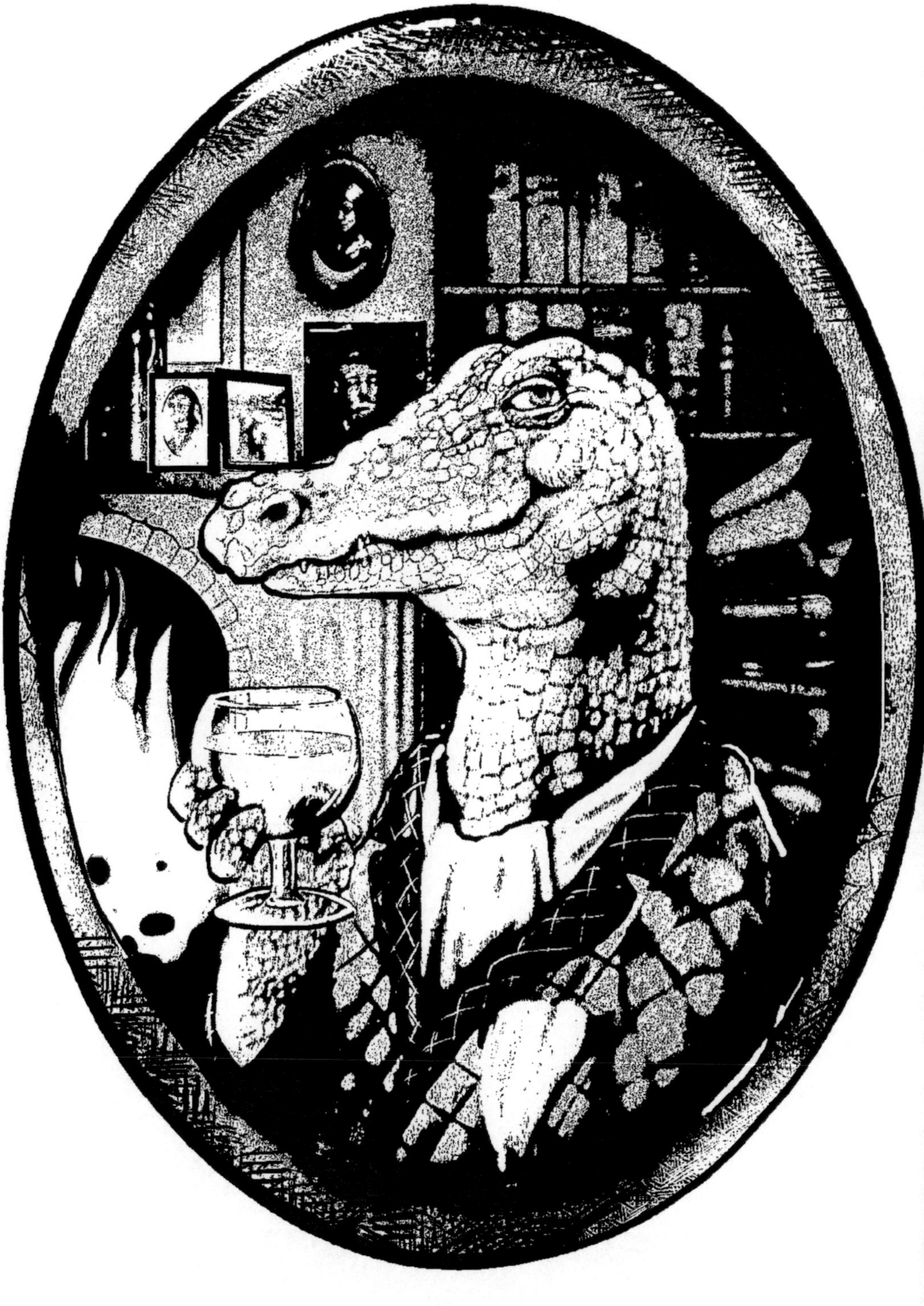

Chapter Eight
London With Crocodile

The day we set off for London it was raining, cats and dogs. I had watched Crocodile rowing across a very choppy Windermere and noted that he was all done up in oilskins with a giant sou'wester covering his head. By the time he was ashore I was there to meet him in the Dormobile, and by the time Kate opened the door for us at the house the oilskins had been replaced by a magnificent Harris Tweed suit with a matching cape and deer-stalker hat.

"Good morning Holmes," said Kate, "done any deducing this morning?"

Crocodile grinned broadly and said: "Well I did deduce that I need not bring any more clothes with me for our little sojourn; I have wardrobes full in London."

Emily was back from America and we knew that Crocodile was champing at the bit to go back to London to see her and the house where he had spent so many happy years under the tutelage, and in the loving care of the Professor. Although I had taken a lot of persuading we had, after much discussion, decided to go by train. I was badgered into accepting that if we booked seats in the *quiet coach*, which was always at the rear of the train going and the front of the train coming back, and either Kate or I sat next to Crocodile with one of us on the opposite seat, then he would be quite inconspicuous. We also decided to take a wheelchair with us, because, although it wouldn't be a problem getting on at Oxenholme, down at the northern end of the platform, it would be much easier, after letting all the other passengers disembark, to wheel him out through Euston Station with a blanket over his legs, and then straight out of the wheelchair into the back of a cab. Hopefully with that we'd be virtually home and dry.

At my insistence we had also agreed that we would wheel Crocodile from our reserved parking place at the stables, just across the road from the station, to the position on the platform from which he could get straight onto the train. I would then fold down the chair and store it in the bicycle compartment at the rear of the carriage.

As we drove round Kendal and up Oxenholme Road to the station the rain began to ease. We stopped again for a brief moment to show Crocodile the house that Kate's father had built and where she had spent the early years of her life.

"I'm probably feeling the same now as you will when we arrive outside your London house," said Kate to Crocodile. "Places where you were very happy and content, albeit long ago, always evoke a deep sense of inward pleasure. That doesn't mean that you were happier then, it is simply that most people have their ups and downs in life, good spells and bad spells, lasting sometimes for long periods and sometimes for just a short time. Long spells of sustained happiness are cherished possessions that nobody can take away from you; they will always be with you, in safe storage, for the rest of your life."

Chapter Eight — London With Crocodile

"That is just how I feel when I think about my life with the Professor and with Mercedes, all those years ago," said Crocodile wistfully.

Thirty minutes later Crocodile was heading back to that former reality at over a hundred miles an hour.

The express train whisked us to London Euston in just two hours and forty-five minutes, only stopping at Lancaster, Preston, Wigan, and Warrington. I told Crocodile that we had been promised an even faster service in the not too distant future. His single complaint on that ultra efficient mode of transport was that he could not understand the *foreign* gentleman who gave us regular messages over the speaker system as the journey progressed.

"He's not exactly foreign," explained Kate. "The gentleman in question has a fine broad Scottish accent! "

"Yes," I said, "but speaking with the experience of someone who has spent much time in Scotland, I don't think, in this case, you are meant to hear all of it. So long as you can decipher Preston, Wigan, etc., that is probably all he intends and probably all that matters."

"Rather like an auctioneer at a cattle mart, you just need to get the gist; all that matters are the bids," said Kate, grinning.

The train emptied quickly at Euston, disgorging its passengers at a rate that suggested they were all late for some important meeting or appointment. We took our time and Crocodile needed no help to unload and settle himself into the wheelchair. Having explained to him that the catering services at Euston Station, although adequate if you were very pushed for time, or starving hungry, were poor compared to St. Pancras. We opted to stroll over there for a coffee and a light bite at the concourse cafe where we had met Emily on our previous visit, and to take the opportunity to show Crocodile the station. We would then find a cab to drive us to Bayswater.

Judging by his comments in the taxi, Crocodile knew London as well, if not better than we did, and he explained that the Professor always gave him a running commentary as they drove together round the streets of London. What we didn't know, even though we had lived for several years just off the Bayswater Road, was that the road dated from Roman times when it was known as the Via Trinobantia, but that Bayswater itself, with all its grand buildings, was little more than 150 years old.

"The Professor was a great authority on the history of London, and of course on the Bayswater area where he lived," Crocodile explained. "I was thinking on the train coming down, that the Professor once told me that Robert Stephenson, who built the first railway locomotive, *Stephenson's Rocket*, lived just round the corner from us, albeit not at the same time. I also recall that you told me that you lived in Craven Hill Gardens. I can remember the Professor telling me, just after he had given me copies of, *Jane Eyre*, and, *Wuthering Heights*, that if a time machine could whisk us back to 1848 we would have been short term neighbours of Charlotte and Emily Bronte, who used to stay at Craven Hill."

Another Emily was already on the doorstep as the taxi pulled up and Crocodile's excitement was a pleasure to behold.

Chapter Eight

London With Crocodile

"Hartley, my dear, how are you? How wonderful to see you. Come and give me a big hug!"

"Hello Emily," said Crocodile throwing his arms round her, "I'm thrilled to see you again, and looking so well ... it's great to be back home after all this time."

"Hello Matthew, hello Kate, it's so nice to see you again and, so good of you to bring Hartley home. I hope it hasn't all been too much trouble. You must be starving after such a long journey all that way from the Lake District. I'll just show you up to your rooms so you can freshen up and then you must come down to the drawing-room for a light lunch that I have prepared. Everything is ready, I have only to put the kettle on. So take just as long as you need, there is nothing to spoil or go cold."

None of us had the heart to tell Emily that we had just had lunch at St. Pancras.

She ushered us through the vestibule and into the main hall – it was just as I remembered – the beautiful mosaic floor, the classical imagery on the walls, the stained glass skylight high above. On my last visit I had not taken in the elaborate cornice or the richly coloured frescos between the cornice and the stained glass. Perhaps there was better light in the hall at the moment, or perhaps there was just too much to take in on one visit.

"I have put Kate and Matthew in the Senators' Suite, perhaps you would kindly show them the way Hartley. You, of course are in your old quarters and nothing has been disturbed, so you will find that everything is just as you left it."

Emily took our coats and Crocodile led the way up the grand staircase and into a wide corridor to the right of the main landing. Half way along, and with a flourish, he opened a huge pair of panelled doors and said, "I am sure that you will be very comfortable in here; the Professor always reserved these rooms for his special guests. Le Marquis always occupied this Suite." Crocodile gestured in the direction of a fine four-poster bed, then with a bow, he said, " I'll see you downstairs in a little while when you are quite ready. Please take your time."

Crocodile closed the doors gently behind him as he exited the room. Kate whispered, "Did you notice how easily Crocodile slipped into his role as master of this grand house?"

"Perhaps it would be more appropriate to call him Hartley, or M' Lord," I suggested.

Crocodile was already in the hall as we came down the stairs. He looked quite unlike like the personage that had accompanied us on the train. He was now dressed in a fine maroon velvet smoking jacket topped with a gold silk cravat; a matching pocket-handkerchief billowed from the breast pocket. The black brocade trousers were tight, with gold braid down the side of each leg, and slightly flared at the bottom, covering most of the heel of the mirror polished black boots, but cut higher at the front to show a splendid pair of shining brass buckles.

He escorted us to the drawing room to await the arrival of Emily's light buffet lunch. Before we could say a word she entered the room pushing the Professor's food trolley, or, *in-house catering unit*, to give it its proper title. It was stacked to capacity with all sorts of goodies.

"Just a little something to tide you over until dinnertime," she said. "I have already eaten so I hope you don't mind if I just have a cup of tea."

"I had a pastry day, yesterday," said Emily motioning toward the piled trolley.

"I found this book in the kitchen, *Sweet and Savoury Tarts*. Julius loved tarts of all types, shapes and sizes, as I am sure, Hartley will remember."

"He certainly did," replied Crocodile, his head nodding vigorously. "He used to say,

'A tart a day keeps the doctor away'."

Out of the corner of my eye I detected that Kate was struggling heroically to suppress a fit of giggling.

Fortunately, Emily had seemed not to notice and she went on, "I am not the best of cooks, not in the same class as you, Hartley, but I do love making tarts. Good pastry gives food an extra dimension; tarts are fun to make and the finished dish always appears like a work of art, especially if you give the tarts a fancy pastry edge."

Crocodile helped Emily to fold out the trolley's tabletop and to display the plated tarts on it.

Each tart had its own uniquely decorated edge. "Just take a plate and help yourselves to a small portion of each. I had better tell you what they are and of course, they are all vegetarian. This is potato and asparagus, then aubergine and cherry tomatoes, and finally, goat's cheese with leek and walnuts. This is a French apple tart, then a pear tart with almonds, pistachios and chocolate – and finally a custard tart with nutmeg. To accompany, I have done a mixed salad and some remoulade, and of course a big jug of double cream."

"It all looks absolutely wonderful," said Kate, "but you really shouldn't have put yourself to all this trouble."

"Not at all," replied Emily, "I have too much time on my hands now and trying to keep busy keeps me out of mischief. More importantly, this is a special occasion and I want to make your stay as memorable as possible. Hartley has insisted on cooking the dinner this evening, for his own homecoming. I have agreed but only on the condition that I help with some of the preparation."

After we had filled our plates and were seated again, Crocodile said, "I have planned our dinner for about 8.30 pm. because I am sure that you will want to take a rest for a little while. I hope you will join me for a swim in the pool later, and then you can take your time getting ready for dinner while I sort things out in the kitchen. Would you like some wine with your lunch?"

"A swim would be wonderful," said Kate, "but if you don't mind, I would prefer a nice cup of Earl Grey." We all agreed to follow suit and save ourselves for the feast to come.

"Let's just relax today," Emily suggested, "there will be plenty of time to discuss Hartley's future during the rest of your stay."

* * *

Chapter Eight — London With Crocodile

Back in the Senators' Suite, Kate said, "Isn't it incredible how easily Crocodile has re-adjusted to his former life-style? It's as if he'd never been away. He is very comfortable in the role of gentleman of the manor. Goodness knows what must have gone through his mind when the Professor left him on his own in a cave in the Lake District."

"Yes, and the worst part would have been the uncertainty about the Professor and about the future. He was suddenly, completely on his own in a world where he knew nobody, apart from the Professor, Emily, and Mercedes. In his situation the chances of ever finding Mercedes again were extremely remote. Finding some friends like us was really his only option, and in doing that he must have known that he was taking a great chance. We might have sold him to the highest bidder or tried to exploit him in some other way for financial gain. Goodness knows what is going through his mind now. Do you think he might be tempted to spend more time here, or even to stay permanently and just take his holidays in the Lake District?"

When we had agreed to take Crocodile back to London neither of us had given a thought to the fact that he might be tempted to stay, or at least not return with us immediately.

"Well," replied Kate, "only he can decide that, but I honestly believe that the likely outcome is he will return with us, and then maybe suggest more frequent trips and longer stays here. I am sure that he loves the Lake District too much not to want to spend most of his time there."

Very shortly afterwards, our fears were to be proved completely groundless. When we went down to the pool Crocodile was already in the water. Kate and I eased our way into two of the seats that were cut into the side of the pool – the water was invitingly warm. Crocodile immediately swam over to us and said: "I feel I should tell you something, just in case you have been thinking about or discussing my situation. Although, this house is very dear to my heart, I have absolutely no intention of spending the rest of my life here. I would love to come here from time to time to visit Emily and I see no reason why she can't visit me in The Lake District. My true home is there on Windermere, surrounded by the fells and close to nature. London is a fine city to visit but for me it is not where I want to be. In the Lakes I am at one with all I survey. In London, I may now be master of this fine house, but that is all. In the Lakes I am free as a bird, but if I returned to London I would feel that I was back in a cage."

We spent the next twenty minutes swimming with Crocodile. He then excused himself, saying that he had better get things moving in the kitchen. As he climbed out of the water he said, "See you at eight-thirty for cocktails."

On the stroke of eight-thirty Kate and I were greeted at the bottom of the grand staircase by Crocodile, now in classic evening dress, and sporting a scarlet rose in his lapel, the colour of which matched exactly the broad scarlet cummerbund around his waist. He motioned us through to a bar adjacent to the dining room and overlooking the fine Roman bathhouse where we had been swimming just a couple of hours earlier.

"This routine was standard procedure when the Professor was at home," he explained, "except when he was entertaining guests from whom he wished to keep me a secret, then I used to go up to the priests' hole with a couple of cocktails and some nibbles, or something more substantial if it was going to be a long evening, and watch the proceedings from there. I didn't mind because I knew it was for my own safety. The Professor was an avid devotee of the etiquette of cocktail making. My only criticism was that he tended to stick mainly to the old classics, the Manhattan and the Harvey Wallbanger were two of his favourites. He felt that recent introductions involving coconut milk or ice cream, a lot of fruit or too much ice, were not quite kosher, or a little too risqué for gentlemen of his era. This was one of the several things that we agreed to disagree on. He would often say to me, albeit with a twinkle in his eye, 'Hartley, dear boy, will you ever learn? I see you've concocted for yourself one of those girlie extravaganzas again. I do wish you'd take a drink like a gentleman!' Anyway, I'm shaking mainly girlie drinks tonight, I hope some are to your taste Matt," he said. "I know that Kate will love them."

"I'll try anything once," I replied.

"In for a penny," said Kate.

Crocodile showed off his skills by mixing several exotic cocktails, including a Blushing Pina-Colada, a Hooded Claw, a Grasshopper, a Scarlet Lady and an Apricot Bellini, which Kate said she remembered from Harry's Bar in Venice. By the time they were poured Emily had joined us and we took sample sips of each before making our final choice. Kate stuck with the Apricot Bellini and I hung on to the Hooded Claw, consisting of Amaretto, Cointreau, prune juice, and fine ice snow.

"I know that you and Kate like Sancerre so I've put some bottles on ice for dinner; very good years from the best estates, if I'm not mistaken," beamed Crocodile.

Crocodile escorted us through to the dining room, explaining as we entered that in spite of his great learning, the Professor was, uncharacteristically, superstitious.

"For example," said Crocodile, "he would never entertain having a dinner for thirteen people. The dining table comfortably seats twelve people and there are only twelve chairs. As with many things in this house, the Professor designed them himself, this dining table included. It is constructed in three separate sections, identical in size, to seat four, eight, or twelve people respectively. Tonight we are using only the centre section. They are on wide metal rollers so that the floor is not damaged when they are moved. You simply jack them up with a handle and push them apart."

"We've had so many wonderful dinner parties here," said Emily, "but in spite of his Englishness, when it came to food Julius thought only of *L'arte della cucina Italiana* – Italian cookery. It was always his favourite; perhaps it was the Roman connection. I bought in the ingredients so that Hartley could cook such a meal in Julius' honour tonight. Now, Hartley, if you would kindly fill our glasses so we may toast his memory."

"To my dear friend and mentor, Professor Julius Septimus Merryweather," said Crocodile. We all raised our glasses and toasted the Professor. Crocodile looked particularly sad and I noticed Emily wiping a tear from her eye as she put down her glass.

"Come now!" said Emily, "Julius was the last person who would have wanted us to be sad on his behalf, especially as it is the occasion of Hartley's homecoming. I suggest that we put serious matters aside for tonight and enjoy dinner, as Julius would have expected. We'll have plenty of time later for serious discussion. Come, Hartley, I'll help you to bring in the antipasti."

They were back in an instant, each carrying a large round wooden platter, which they placed simultaneously in the centre of the table.

"Just a simple selection," said Crocodile, "please help yourselves. Emily got me some wonderful mushrooms, chanterelles, morels, oyster, shiitake and others, so I made a mushroom salad. There are also stuffed baby artichokes, char-grilled peppers with anchovy and capers. I've also done some, *fritto misto*, deepfried vegetables in batter. Emily bought in the bread, which is wonderful, rosemary with black olives and sundried tomatoes."

You can always tell when people are eating good food. Normal conversation ceases for a while, becoming just a murmur of sound expressing contentment or mild surprise accompanied by the sharp chink of steel on china, and a resonant chime or ping of glass or crystal.

"If I'd had more time I would have made, *Sinfonia del Mare*, or Sea Symphony, using all kinds of seafood, for the main course, but I opted for a simple spaghetti with king prawns and chilli. I do hope that you will find this agreeable," said Crocodile as he cleared away the empty platters.

Even though it wasn't Crocodile's exotic sounding *Sinfonia del Mare*, it was still fine music to our taste-buds, although by the time we had cleared our plates both Kate and I had reached that point of gastronomic gratification, and state of well-being, where we both knew that it would not be wise to eat much more. Our satisfaction curves had reached their peaks. Less can definitely be more when it comes to food and drink and Crocodile seeming to sense this, said, "We must all be feeling pretty full, especially on top of Emily's wonderful tarts. I have, however, made tiramisu, which was a favourite of the Professor's. He called it his, 'Pick me up', which is what the word means in Italian. He always insisted on it at a dinner like this. I hope, therefore, that in his honour, you will try just a very small portion; we can have the rest tomorrow."

Put that way we could hardly decline and we laughed about it later, agreeing that, even though it was beautifully light, a much larger portion of tiramisu could definitely have been more aptly translated as *knock me down*, or even, *finish me off*.

Throughout the latter part of the meal and over coffee, Crocodile related some of his adventures in the Lake District to Emily. Although I had told Emily that we, and Crocodile, were living in the Lake District, I did not mention his cave, simply letting her believe that he was living with us. I had also told him, that for the moment it would be safer if he did not mention the cave or the island. Nobody in the world knew about his hideaway and I felt it prudent not to tell Emily, just in case it came out in conversation without thinking.

Crocodile related his story from the very beginning, from when he had seen us, on a silver moonlit winter's night, sitting on a rock on the shore of Windermere. He told her how we had become the closest of friends, and how we had helped him to come to terms with the loss of the Professor, and advised him how to plan his future. He said that he did not know what he would have done if he had not found us.

Crocodile described the glories of his beloved Lake District in *Wordsworthian* metaphors – he talked of life and Nature and sweet liberty – he spoke of the grandeur and the simplicity, the peace and the tranquillity, the teeming hedgerows and the joyous birdsong: he spoke about the pastoral mountains and the craggy steeps, the secret groves and peaceful vales, the tumultuous brooks, the gentle meadows, the rustling leaves, the murmuring streams, the fair rivers and the majestic lakes; the splendour in the grass and the glory in the flower..

* * *

I could hear Kate's voice very faintly at first, then as she started to become more agitated her voice got louder and louder, "The door is jammed fast! I've tried everything and it won't budge an inch." She began to bang louder and louder and I could hear the shouts and the banging echoing from the depths of the cave.

"Don't panic," I shouted, "I can release it from the outside, then you can spin the wheel."

"I'm spinning the wheel as hard as I can, but it's useless, it won't budge an inch!" she shouted back. Her voice became more and more agitated and I started to panic as well ... then the voice changed.

"Matthew! Matthew! Kate! Kate! Wake up! Wake up!"

The banging on the door got louder and louder, and I suddenly realised that I wasn't standing outside Crocodile's cave and that it wasn't Kate's voice, it was Emily's.

I jumped out of bed, flung on my dressing gown and opened the door. Emily was standing outside and she was visibly in a state of shock.

"Whatever is the matter?" I said.

"It's Hartley," she cried, "He's gone! "

By this time Kate was at my side.

"Something terrible must have happened to him!" she said, sobbing.

We followed her, almost running, to Crocodile's room. The door was open and it was immediately obvious that something very violent had taken place. The room had the appearance of being completely ransacked. There was a great tear in one of the curtains and the bedclothes were on the floor. All the drawers had been pulled out of the dressing table, and from other items of furniture around the room as well, their contents thrown onto the bed and scattered everywhere.

"I thought I heard strange noises soon after we went to bed," said Emily, her voice choking with emotion. "I listened for a while and heard no more and I thought it must have been the wind. I went back to sleep. Then something else woke me again, so I got up and saw that Hartley's bedroom door was wide open. I have been all round the house but Hartley is nowhere to be found. I always lock and bolt all the doors before going to bed, but the bolts on the front door have been drawn back, so whoever it was must have gone out that way, because all the other doors are bolted on the inside."

"I'd better have another look round the house," I said, arming myself with a baseball bat that had been flung on the floor with the other debris. I escorted Emily and Kate down to the kitchen and when we were sure it was quite safe, Kate said that she would put the kettle on while I went round the house.

"Do you not think we should call the police immediately?" said Emily.

"Let me take a look round first," I said, "then we'll sit down over a cup of tea and decide what to do."

I went straight to the back of the house, to the door that I knew led out into the garden. It was bolted top and bottom, as Emily had said. I slid back the bolts and turned the big key in the lock. As soon as I pulled the door open I could see instantly what must have happened. A light telescopic, aluminium ladder was propped up against the sill of one of the first-floor windows. The window was closed. My mind immediately jumped back to when Crocodile had described how he had been kidnapped from the zoo. I went back upstairs to Crocodile's room and started rummaging around amongst all the debris for any clue that might confirm my suspicions. It did not take long to find the evidence that I hoped I would not find – a large empty hypodermic syringe and needle. My worst fears were realised. Crocodile had been kidnapped!

And probably by the same gang that took him last time. I had also remembered Emily telling me on the telephone, when I first made arrangements to meet her in London, that she thought that Crocodile may have been in some sort of danger. I put the syringe into a plastic bag that I saw amongst the debris – in case it could be used for evidence, both for fingerprints and for the substance it had contained – I did this without touching it myself, as they do in detective dramas on TV.

I did not know at that juncture, if, or how we could involve the police. In my panic, all sorts of thoughts were pumping through my mind. If it was the fairground people who had kidnapped Crocodile, they would claim that Crocodile belonged to them, arguing that it was the Professor who had stolen him from them all those years ago. I began to realise that whatever the outcome, if we involved the police, Crocodile's idyllic life in the Lake District would most certainly be over.

I ran back to the kitchen and told Kate and Emily what I had discovered.

"Oh I do hope that they don't harm him," said Emily, with a sob. "I feel this is all my fault, because what I didn't tell you when we made the arrangements for your visit was that I had a suspicion that the house was being watched again, and just before you arrived yesterday I received another of those strange telephone calls. It's just that you get so many of these annoying sales people phoning you at the most inconvenient moments, that I simply put the receiver down and it slipped my mind to tell you. I had no idea that something like this would happen ... it's all my fault!"

Chapter Eight   London With Crocodile

"You really can't blame yourself," said Kate. "If anyone is to blame it is Matt and me for bringing him to London."

"I think that we are all overlooking the most important point in all this," I said. "We can safely assume that, so long as it is the fairground people who have taken him, they are unlikely to harm him physically to the extent that he can't work for them. I feel certain that the reason they have taken him is because he was their most valuable asset. He is worth a fortune to them, so why would they not look after him at least well enough to enable him to perform his acts in the circus ring? They may lock him in a cage for twenty-two hours a day but they are hardly likely to injure him so that he can't do his job."

"Oh!" Emily cried. "Not in a cage, not poor Hartley in a cage. I can't bear the thought of it! "

Kate put her arms round Emily and said, "I know that the situation looks pretty dire but if they are going to put Crocodile in a circus ring surely we can find him and rescue him."

"Brilliant thinking!" I cried. "There can't be that many circuses around. I'll have a look on the Internet and see if there are any advertised."

"We'd better use the computer in Julius' office," said Emily. She led the way up to a grand, book-lined study with an enormous carved mahogany desk at the far end, positioned in front of a splendid bay window and flanked by a fine pair of Roman marble pillars.

There was a lot of information on the web search about circuses, including Circus Acts, Circus and Big Top hire, Juggling and Circus Stunts, and hiring Circus Performers. As I scrolled down we saw that the Cirque Du Soleil was on at the Albert Hall, just across the park.

"Cirque Du Soleil wouldn't use Crocodile," said Kate, "I'm pretty sure of that."

I scrolled down further to Zippos Circus, also on in London. Then my heart missed a beat when I saw the next entry – it read, The Greatest Show on Earth, now on in OXFORD. Last week of tour – Tickets still available – Book now online for special discounts.

"It's too much of a coincidence," I almost shouted. "They must have taken Crocodile there."

"Shouldn't we telephone the police straight away and let them know what has happened?" said Emily excitedly.

"I suggest we check the situation out for ourselves first before we notify the police," I said. "I think we have to be realistic about the overall situation and once we have notified the police we'll have to tell them all about Crocodile. It won't be long before Fleet Street finds out, and his identity will be exposed to the whole world. Anyway, he may not be in Oxford; they may have hidden him away in some remote spot. As I have already said, we should derive some peace of mind from the fact that I don't believe that they will harm him; why should they when he is so valuable to them? Moreover, look at all the trouble they have gone to, to kidnap him. They have had this house staked out for ages, so he must be very important to them financially. I fully agree that if we can't find a way to rescue him then we will have no choice but to involve the police. I just think that we should give it our best shot first because I don't believe that he is in extreme danger. Don't forget that he has already escaped once in the boot of the Professor's car, so with our help I am sure he will find a way to escape again."

Thankfully, I detected some signs of relief in the facial expressions of both Kate and Emily, although I was trying hard to convince myself that my reasoning could be true.

"Oh I do hope you're right, and I can see a lot of sense in what you are saying," said Emily. "It's just that I can't bear the thought of Hartley being locked in a cage and mistreated in any way."

"One important factor," I suggested, "is that they don't know that he can speak or that he is anything like as intelligent as he is now. The Professor saw him performing in the circus ring and there is nothing to stop us buying tickets and doing just that. As soon as he sees us he'll know that we have come to try to rescue him and he is more than clever enough to help us make that possible. It's nearly half-past five now; there is no point in going back to bed, so why don't we get ready, have an early breakfast and take a train to Oxford?"

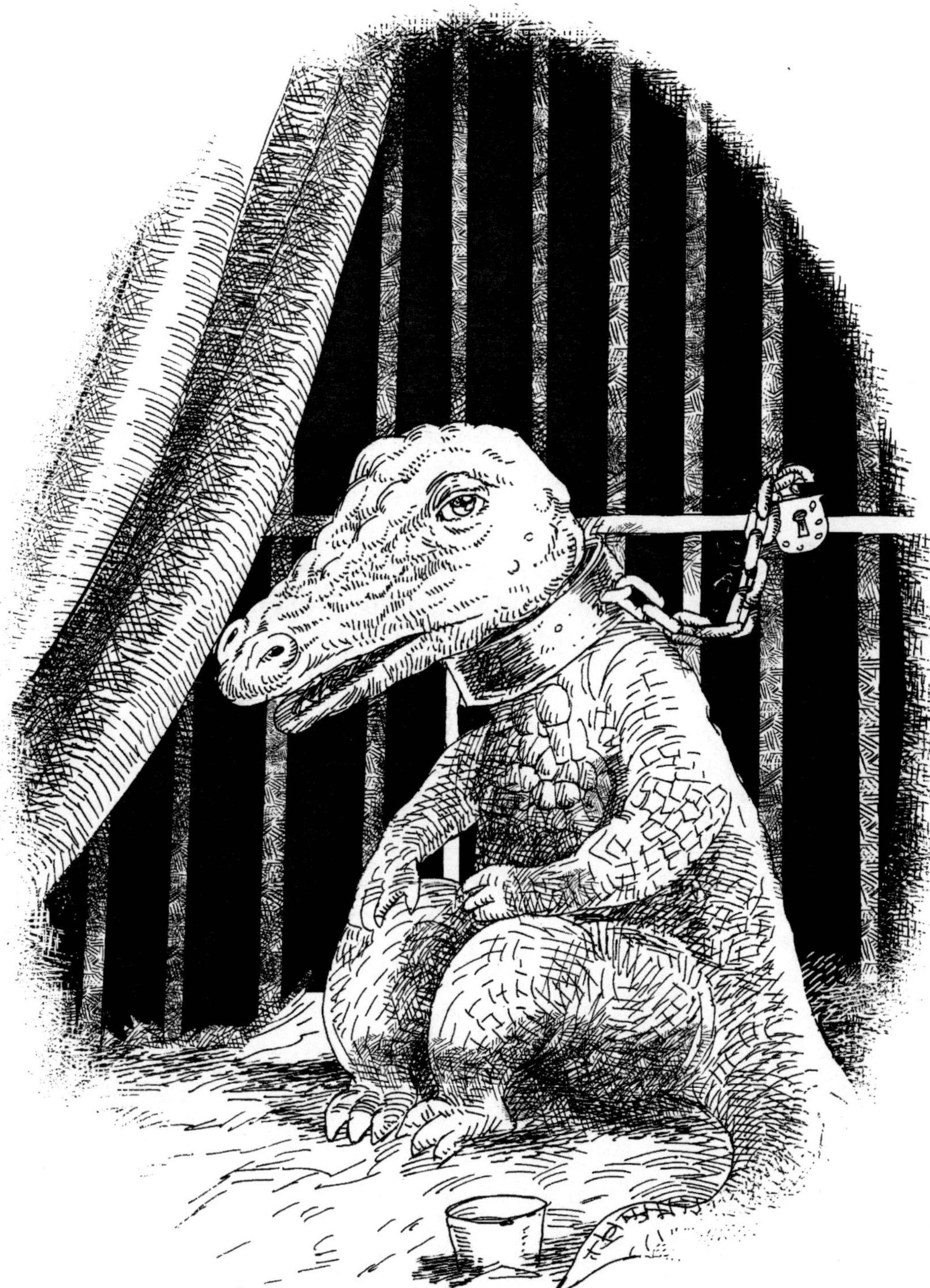

Chapter Nine
Oxford And The Circus

I feel sure that Emily was quite relieved when we suggested that just Kate and I go to Oxford. "I have no idea what we will be up against," I said. "Also I think that someone needs to man the fort here in case one of the kidnappers tries to make contact, although I am fairly certain that this will not happen. It is just within the realm of possibility that they could demand a ransom for his safe return, but from what Crocodile has told us I truly believe that they want him for one reason only and that is for his value to them in the circus ring. It is also just possible that they may be off their guard in one sense, not expecting that we could know who has taken him or where he is. Nevertheless, I am sure that they will be guarding him very carefully because he escaped from them before and I believe they will try their hardest to prevent him escaping again."

We said goodbye to Emily and promised to telephone if we had any definite news of Crocodile. We walked the short distance to Paddington Station – just as the Professor would have done on his regular trips to Oxford.

As we crossed Eastbourne Terrace another thought flashed into my mind causing me to stop in my tracks.

"Don't stand in the middle of the road." shouted Kate. You'll get us both killed."

"Sorry," I said, as she pulled me onto the pavement. "It's just that a thought crossed my mind that they could have bugged Emily's phone. It seemed too much of a coincidence that they were able to grab Crocodile on his first night back after all this time. I don't know anything about phone hacking but I am sure there will be people at the circus who know about communications, so it is certainly on the cards. Whatever happens in Oxford, I think that we should take the precaution of not phoning Emily in case they are able to listen in."

As soon as we were on the train we started to discuss how it might be possible to rescue Crocodile if he were there. We both realised that without some suitable means of transport it wouldn't be easy. It would be highly unlikely that they would stand by and allow us to bring him back to London on the train. We also realised that London and the house in Bayswater was the last place we could take him and, unless we involved the police, they would be back at once to kidnap him again.

"They may of course assume that we will inform the police," said Kate, "but I do agree with you about it being stupid to take him back to Bayswater."

Our growing optimism suddenly took a very steep dive as the reality of the situation sank in.

"This situation is just like playing snakes and ladders," I said, "except it's for real. When I was only four, my grandfather made me an enormous snakes and ladders board out of wood with all the snakes and the ladders and the squares painted on it. We used to play the game a lot and I don't know how but I always used to win eventually, although not until I had slid down umpteen very long snakes. I clearly remember him telling me that

Chapter Nine

Oxford And The Circus

snakes and ladders is just like life and the secret is never to give up, however many snakes you slide down – if you keep going you'll get there in the end. He also said that life isn't the race most people believe it to be – it doesn't matter if you get there first; the important thing is that you get there eventually. Of course I didn't comprehend what he meant then, but it stuck with me until the day that I did understand. I know we will get Crocodile back, and I don't think it is going to be as easy as we thought, but we must never stop trying."

Kate and I had visited Oxford many times and we knew the city quite well. Kate was more familiar with its clothes shops than with its famous Colleges, but on at least a couple of occasions I had managed to persuade her to take a tour round these iconic buildings. History was one of her favourite subjects, and she was especially knowledgeable on the Tudor and Elizabethan periods, but when it came down to a specific choice, clothes shops or history, clothes shops were the bigger draw. A tour round Oxford's Colleges would be most agreeable to her so long as we left, "sufficient time", to browse round the shops later. The more usual response, however, was, "Why don't we look round the shops first, then if we have enough time left over… "

On this occasion, both shops and Colleges were far from our thoughts and as soon as we were out of the station we took a taxi straight to the circus. The taxi driver knew exactly where it was and he told us that there was a travelling fair on the same site this year. He said that the joint attraction had been very good for business and he would be sorry to see them go. I asked him if he knew where the circus was from and he said that he thought they were from somewhere in Eastern Europe, but he wasn't entirely certain. He then said that it was their last week and that he had heard that they were returning home after the weekend. This was their last show of the year in the U.K.

Both Kate and I looked anxiously at one another, as we had both understood the implications of this piece of information. It was spelt out quite clearly to us; we had to rescue Crocodile before the weekend. After that, heaven knows where he might end up.

He dropped us off at the entrance to the fairground and as soon as we got out of the taxi we could see the enormous Big Top at the back of the site. Two large hoardings bedecked with circus posters were positioned on either side of the entrance. I noted that the times of the shows were 2.00 pm, 6.00 pm, and 8.30 pm. I looked at my watch; it was just after 11.30. I pointed the times out to Kate and said, "The first show isn't until two o'clock so this gives us plenty of time for a full reconnaissance of the site. There may not be many people around the Big-Top until after one and I think it will be safer for a detailed inspection if we are in the middle of a big crowd; at least until we find what we are looking for."

"What exactly are we looking for?" asked Kate, raising her eyebrows.

"Your guess is as good as mine," I replied, "just for some place where they could be hiding Crocodile. I know he could be in any of the caravans, but if you remember, he told us that they used to keep him in a big cage so I think we'll take a look at the cages first to see if we can detect anything suspicious."

The only way to get to the circus was to walk right across the fairground. We made our way past roundabouts and coconut shies, swing-boats, toffee apple and candy-floss stalls, dodgem-cars, and a giant Big-Wheel that stood in the centre of the fair.

"Why don't we take a ride on the Big-Wheel first," said Kate. "We'll get a brilliant bird's-eye view of the whole of the circus from up there."

"You're not just a pretty face," I said, as we made our way through the turnstile to buy our tickets.

It took ten to fifteen minutes to load up the new batch of customers. We were led up a wooden ramp and then locked into our seat with a steel bar across our laps. I noted that the man then pushed a pin through the bar for double security. I saw that Kate was starting to look a little queasy and the man picked up on this as well. "Nobody's fallen out yet!" he said with a wink at Kate. "At least not this week! Just don't rock the cradle too much." He then gave it an almighty push and we were off up to the next position.

After what seemed an eternity, we finally reached the very top position on the Wheel. We were now looking right down onto the Big Top.

"This is probably the best chance we are going to get to take a steady view of the whole site," I said. "If only I had brought my binoculars!"

Nevertheless, what was instantly apparent was that all the caravans were at the back of the Big Top. There were none at all at the sides and there were no cages to be seen anywhere. We could, however, make out an area in the middle of the caravans, which was covered in what appeared to be a very large tarpaulin sheet.

"If he is here, and he's not in one of the caravans then I'd bet my bottom dollar that he's somewhere under that tarpaulin," I shouted, as the Wheel began to spin and the volume of the music increased."

Each time we descended from the top our eyes were glued to the expanse of tarpaulin in the middle of the caravans – but we had seen all there was to see from that vantage point.

Now back on terra firma we made our way towards the entrance to the Big Top. There was no sign of a queue to get in and we agreed that it would be safer to wait until the show had started before we tried to get round the back to take a close look at what was under the tarpaulin. We agreed that when we did have a go we should go together and think up a reason for being there just in case we were stopped and questioned.

"Let's pretend we've lost our dog," suggested Kate. "That will give us an excuse for poking around under caravans – they may even help us to try to find him!"

"I don't know what I'd do without you," I said.

We made our way back to the fairground and wandered around the rides, stands, and stalls and other tempting attractions, the sum total of which make all the fun of the fair. It brought back memories of the fair held annually, here in Oxford, in September. We had made, I believe, three visits to Oxford for the St. Giles' Fair when we lived in London, catching the train from Paddington for the one-hour journey, just as we had done this morning. It was, however, the sight of a magnificent Wonder-Waltzer that brought back the most vivid memories of the annual fair that I used to go to as a boy.

When I was very young, my Mother used to take me to our local fair every year in June, but the visit had a dual purpose – both to give me a thrill on all the rides and to treat herself to mountains of crockery from the extremely popular 'Pot Stall'.

The polished pieces of china, porcelain and pot were auctioned in great piles. Starting off with a single plate held in one large hand, the auctioneer would add another and another, all interlocking to form a firm base. Then plates of different sizes would be slotted in between and on the top would go bowls, then cups and saucers, followed by a milk jug, a sugar basin, a gravy boat, cruets and tureens – all would be miraculously balanced on the one big hand.

The auctioneer would shout out the asking price, which would go up and up as the pile increased in size and height – then, when the set was complete to his satisfaction. He would reduce the price step by step until somebody in the large crowd agreed to pay it.

"Sold to the lucky lady in the green hat!" he would shout.

The auction was repeated continuously throughout the day and late into the night. My Mother would spend hours there, often with her twin sister, patiently waiting to get the best bargains.

My Father, having dropped us off in the late afternoon, would return around 10 o'clock in the evening to collect us and the annual mountain of crockery. The last words my Mother would always say on our arrival, were:

"Now you will make sure that the car boot is empty when you come to collect us!"

Each year at this moment he always wore the same resigned expression on his face, knowing that even though we had long since acquired sufficient crockery to cater for an army regiment, it was futile to protest.

While my Mother spent the evening at the Pot Stall, I enjoyed a deliriously happy time with my friends, most of whose mothers were doing the same as mine.

As I got older my taste advanced from small Roundabouts, Roll-a-Penny, Hoop-La, Skittles and Helter-Skelter through to Swing-Boats, Chair-o-plane rides and large Carousels, Coconut-Shies and Rifle-Ranges, to the Octopus and Dodgem Cars and ultimately to the teenagers' Dream-Machine – the dazzling Wonder-Waltzer – blasting out the latest pop hits whilst rough-shaven macho-men, risking life and limb on the rolling roller-coaster platform, sent the cars spinning this way and that, at breathtaking stomach-churning speeds and G-Forces. As the sky darkened into evening and then into night, the volume of the massive speakers increased to immeasurable decibels, transporting the swooning occupants of the spinning cars far out to Earth's orbit.

Kate pulled me back to the present and to reality with a sharp tug of my sleeve. "Look," she said, pointing, "toffee apples! I haven't had one since I was girl. Let's get one to share." Even though Kate and I had not eaten a toffee apple for donkey's years we knew instinctively what to expect when you tried to bite into one. The first bite is the most difficult, and more especially if the apple is a big one and it has been heavily coated with toffee. It's hard not to dribble and look like a pig, but once the protective toffee coating has been successfully breached it is less embarrassing.

Kate said, "Do you remember once giving part of a toffee apple to Ben the donkey, whom we often used to visit with tit-bits on the way home from work? It stuck his teeth together just as it's doing to mine now."

We spent another half hour or so wandering round the fairground. Our hearts weren't in it though and we were just killing time until we felt there were enough people queuing to get into the Circus to act as camouflage for us to sneak round the back and try to discover some evidence that Crocodile may be held prisoner there.

As we made our way round the back of the Big Top I began to experience that sinking feeling you sometimes get on a big issue when you begin to believe that, perhaps you were being too optimistic and the reality was that it couldn't be this easy to find Crocodile. He may be a hundred miles away, or even on the other side of the Channel by now. I didn't express these sentiments to Kate – I knew that, right or wrong we had to give it our best shot because at this juncture no other option was open to us, except for calling in the police, with all the unknown consequences that course of action might produce.

We soon realised that the only way to get inside the semi-circle of caravans was to crawl underneath one of them. To our surprise, on the other side was a grass paddock in which a group of children were playing games. Some boys were playing football and some of the girls were skipping with a long rope. Kate went straight up to one the girls and said, "I wonder if you could help us? We have lost our dog. He ran under one of your caravans, so he must be around here somewhere." Kate then produced some pound coins from her purse and said that we would pay a reward if they could help us find him.

The sight of the coins had an amazing effect and we were suddenly surrounded by most of the children, especially by the bigger boys. One of the boys said that he had seen a dog a couple of minutes ago under one of the caravans and he pointed to a black and chrome van with a large television aerial fixed to the side.

"What did he look like?" asked Kate, but the boy started to mumble and then said that he wasn't sure, but it wasn't a very big dog and he thought it might be black or brown.

"Our dog is a large Yorkshire Terrier," said Kate. "He is silver blonde and is called… "

"Hartley," I interjected, "his name is Hartley." I took some coins out of my pocket and said that the reward had just been increased.

This had the effect of creating a buzz of excitement among the children and they were soon scurrying here, there and everywhere calling out, "Hartley, Hartley!"

It was now obvious that the paddock, the space we now found ourselves in, was quite some distance from the Big Top. Furthermore, a steel fence, backed with canvas sheeting, completely screened what appeared to be another large area between the paddock and the Big Top. There was a pair of heavy wooden doors in the centre of the fence, and as the children ran around and poked about under the caravans Kate and I edged our way towards these doors. They appeared to be firmly locked and I asked one of the older girls what was on the other side and if our dog could have gone through there.

My heart skipped a beat at her reply. She said that was where all the cages for the circus animals were and also the changing tents for the performers. She said that the younger children were not allowed inside during the performance. At that moment one of the doors suddenly opened and two men came out carrying some planks of wood on a long ladder. I managed to take a quick peak inside, which revealed a hive of activity, including clowns and other circus performers, horses, ponies and a baby elephant.

A rough looking, hairy-mountain of a man was holding the door open and the girl dashed up to him just as he was about to close it. "Steve," she shouted, "have you seen a little dog? This lady and gentleman have lost one and we think he could have got inside."

The man's eyes narrowed and he scratched his hairy chin.

"They're offering a big reward!"

His face relaxed and he said that he would have a look round.

"He's called, HARTLEY," the girl shouted, as the man closed the door.

We waited for about ten minutes before the door swung open again and Big Steve's head peered out. "No Hartley in here! Perhaps the lions have had him for lunch," he chortled. Without further ado he slammed the door shut again.

"Never mind," said Kate, "We'll have a good look round the fairground. I'm sure he'll turn up."

"Don't believe what Steve said about the lion; he was only teasing. I'm called Meredith," said the girl, "and he's my uncle."

"Oh, I wasn't worried about that, Meredith," replied Kate smiling, "Hartley would be a match for any old lion."

All the children started to gather round us again and so I said, "Well, you have all done your best so I think you deserve the reward anyway, what do you think Kate?"

"Absolutely!" said Kate. "I couldn't agree more."

We emptied our purses of all the coins that we had brought to the fair and distributed them amongst the children, telling them that we would return later in the week with another reward if they would keep looking for Hartley.

"Don't forget that we are going home this weekend and it's the last show on Saturday," said Meredith. "If we find Hartley, I'll keep him in my caravan. It's the blue one over there. But don't leave it later than Saturday."

Meredith showed us a way out between two of the caravans and as we waved goodbye, on impulse, I turned and said: "A few years ago we came to your circus here and there was a Crocodile that could ride a bike. Can you remember him?"

"It's funny you should say that," said Meredith. "Uncle Steve told me only this morning that we had just got him back, but that he wasn't very well, and they were hoping that he would be fit enough to perform on our final day on Saturday."

"In that case," I said, "We'll definitely be back on Saturday. If you see him will you give him our best wishes and tell him that Kate and Matthew wish him a speedy recovery."

* * *

Less than six hours later I was back in our beloved Lake District, having caught the 17:55 train from London Euston to Oxenholme. Meredith had told us all we needed to know and our relief was immeasurable. Our feet hardly touched the ground as we left the fairground and hurried back to Oxford Station to catch the first available train to London. We had realised immediately that it would be pretty much impossible for us to try to rescue Crocodile there and then, especially as he was likely to be chained and manacled, and surrounded by circus folk who were not just going to let us walk out with their most lucrative asset. What was needed was a comprehensive plan to rescue him with timing to catch his captors off their guard. The important thing was that we knew exactly where he was and hopefully where he would be at a given time on Saturday – performing in the Big Top. By the time we had arrived at Paddington, we had worked out the broad outline of a plan to rescue him.

We had decided that Kate should go back to Emily's and co-ordinate things from there as well as, hopefully, enlisting Emily's help with the rescue plan. Even though we had not considered at this stage exactly what her input might be, our logic was that she was the only other person that we could trust completely and that she might be able to help us in some way, however small.

I had returned to the Lake District, primarily to get the Dormobile, which we felt would be more useful than a car in rescuing Crocodile and getting him back home. We had also decided to enlist the help of Napoleon because, unless we were to put our complete trust in Meredith, which just might backfire and forewarn the circus folk, he was one sure fire way of getting a message to Crocodile without suspicions being aroused.

The basic plan was to get Crocodile to escape on one of his bicycles or monocycles straight out of the circus ring. If he could get to the Dormobile before the circus folk realised what was happening or could trace where he had gone, he would be home and dry. He could leave his bike some distance from the vehicle and when he got to it, roll underneath and climb into the under-floor compartment where he would be completely concealed. We would simply drive him out of the car park as other vehicles were leaving and even if the Dormobile were searched, which would be highly unlikely, he wouldn't be discovered because the Professor had gone to great lengths to ensure that the compartment was nearly impossible to find. The plan was audacious but it was simple and would catch the enemy completely unawares.

On the Oxenholme train I had decided on a back up plan, which would involve Emily and the police. If Crocodile's escape from the Big Top were somehow thwarted, then Emily would enlist the help of the police on some pretext, the detail of which I still had not worked out by the time I reached Oxenholme. We would have to think of a way to ensure a police presence at the circus on Saturday – a plan B, in case something went wrong with plan A, because by this time we would have burnt our bridges, and Crocodile might be held prisoner until the circus was out of the country. We would have to come clean and let Crocodile tell his story to the police and to the world, with all the unknown consequences that would be triggered by that course of action.

It had been my intention to sail to Crocodile's island as soon as I got back home but the weather had suddenly taken a significant turn for the worse and by the time I was down in the boathouse I realised that it would be madness to try to cross the lake in those conditions. The jetty was awash with water and the boats that were moored in the bay were being violently assaulted by crashing waves and gusts of wind at near hurricane strength. The lake had assumed the character of an angry sea and an entity you knew instinctively that you didn't dare meddle with. You must keep it at a safe distance, as you would a lion or a shark, or even a crocodile for that matter. I made my way despondently back to the house and I was soaked to the skin before I was halfway up the garden.

Kate and I had been under considerable stress following Crocodile's abduction. Stress is usually accompanied by troubled sleep and this night was no exception. It was a night of fitful dreams, mostly forgotten by daybreak, but a particularly vivid one stuck in my memory. It was quite bizarre and it involved Crocodile being imprisoned, not in a conventional cage but in a giant hourglass. We pressed our noses to the glass but we could not hear what he was saying and he wore an incredibly forlorn expression. We could see, as he could, that time was running out, as the soft sand poured through the centre. Crocodile was fast to the wall but we knew that it was only a matter of time before the sand gave way and he would slide to the centre – and the centre would not hold.

"A rope ladder!" shouted Kate. "We must get a rope ladder, it's our only chance to save him!" We had then climbed up the hourglass with a rope ladder, which we dropped through a hatch in the top. Crocodile tried to reach it but if he moved from the wall he would hurtle down the sifting sand to the centre. We started to swing the rope ladder to and fro but still Crocodile couldn't reach it and the sand at the wall had started to slide. "Just one last big effort," I shouted. We hurled the ladder with all our might. Crocodile jumped ... and I woke up with a start.

The storm had blown itself out during the night and it was already a bright day with a slight breeze moving the tops of the trees along the lakeshore. The lake was its normal self again.

I had been so exhausted I had gone to bed with only a cup of tea and a biscuit. Now I was ravenous; so before setting sail for the island I decided to treat myself to a hearty breakfast of porridge, cream and honey, with a dash of whiskey; followed by bacon, eggs, sausages and fried tomatoes on several slices of buttered toast – all washed down with a big pot of steaming coffee and hot creamy milk.

The Dormobile was always kept fully serviced and complete with all necessities, including a wardrobe of outfits for Crocodile and clothes for us, so it was simply a matter of driving down to the boathouse and sailing over to collect Napoleon.

The evidence of the ferocity of last night's storm was strewn around me as I made my way down to the boathouse once more. I had remembered to bring a big torch with me because I would have to find my way down the steps into Crocodile's cave in darkness.

It was a pleasant sail to the island, apart from a near collision with an unfortunate tree, no doubt a victim of last night's violence, which was making its way solemnly down the centre of the lake. Nevertheless, it claimed the right of way and I had to make a nifty manoeuvre to miss it.

Apart from pricking my hands on several holly leaves, I had no difficulty in opening the huge rock door with the ratchet mechanism that was operated by the disguised handle, which I moved back and forth to create an opening just wide enough for me to squeeze through. I had already decided to leave it slightly ajar, partly because I was certain there was nobody else on the island, but mainly, to be completely honest, because I did not relish the thought of closing the door completely behind me, even though I knew exactly how to open it from the inside of the cave. The remotest possibility of entombment is not an appealing prospect, especially when you are alone in a dark cave.

Creeping down the dark steps, all alone, into Crocodile's subterranean world was a spooky, nerve tingling, experience and so to give myself a little Dutch courage, I put my free hand to my mouth and shouted down into the cave, "NAPOLEON!" only to make myself jump as the echo repeatedly bounced back at me. Happily I heard a familiar flap of wings as Napoleon flew to greet me.

"Hello Napoleon," I shouted, "it's Matt!"

"Allo Matt," croaked Napoleon straight into my ear, as he landed on my shoulder.

I took a quick look around the cave but, in the absence of the light and warmth from the fire, lamps and candles, it seemed a different place. I knew that Crocodile was now a prisoner in a cage, far from home, and in my mind's eye I could see him with a forlorn expression on his face as in my dream, when we had tried to rescue him from the hourglass, I felt very sad. Some comfort came from the big bird that appeared as pleased to see me, as I was to see him. He stayed on my shoulder croaking gently until I had found his cage and collected an assortment of whistles, used by Crocodile to call him. I had observed that the high-pitched note from the biggest whistle would easily carry across the lake on a calm day or with the wind in the right direction. I also picked up a couple of his pouches, a small one, and the biggest one – I just had a feeling that they might come in handy.

As I had expected, Sherwood was nowhere to be seen, but he was a creature of the night and I had decided in advance to leave him at home to look after things here, especially as he may have been more of a hindrance than a help with our plans to rescue Crocodile.

As I was about to leave, my eyes alighted on a very familiar object, or, more correctly, pair of objects. They were Crocodile's saddlebags, hanging over the arm of a sofa. I was stopped in my tracks. With a tear in my eye I picked them up and slung them over my spare shoulder. Then with heavy steps and a heavier heart I made my back up into the sunlight.

Napoleon stayed close to me as we sailed across the lake and hopped onto my shoulder again as I made my way up from the boathouse to the Dormobile. I had put some juicy titbits ready for him in the vehicle, which I popped into his cage just before we set off.

I could see him in the rear-view mirror, pecking contentedly as I eased out onto the main road.

"Well, Napoleon!" I shouted back as we pulled away. "We're off to rescue Crocodile!"

We did not make a single stop until we reached Stow-on-the-Wold in the Cotswolds. I had made a slight detour through Chipping Campden with the intention of grabbing a quick coffee, but changed my mind because an outdoor market had made parking almost impossible. I nearly turned right to Broadway at the top of the long hill south out of Campden, but again changed my mind and turned left to Stow, where my main purpose was to stock up with suitable delicacies for Napoleon to keep him happy. I remembered that Crocodile had told us that he would eat almost anything but I decided to spoil him nevertheless, purchasing an assortment of dried fruit and nuts, fresh bread and cheese, cakes and biscuits.

The big change in my plan to drive straight to London happened out of the blue when we were driving through Burford. A poster at the side of the road caught my eye and I slammed on the brakes rather too suddenly for the reasonable consideration of the vehicle behind me, whose driver gave me a very black look as he passed by. Staring out at me from the poster was Crocodile, dressed in a bright yellow suit, on a monocycle, balancing a large ball on a pole on the end of his snout. In big letters it read, *BY POPULAR REQUEST – A VERY SPECIAL PERFORMANCE THIS SATURDAY ONLY BY THE AMAZING CROCODILE. Book NOW to avoid disappointment.*

I made an instant decision to drive straight to Oxford and back to the circus.

The fairground was in full swing but the circus was in-between shows. I parked the Dormobile, poured out some more nuts and raisins for Napoleon, and then made my way round the back of the Big Top. The children I had seen before were now playing on the outside of the long crescent of caravans. I could not see Meredith with them so I made my way directly to her pretty pale blue caravan, the one she had pointed out to us yesterday.

"Was it really only yesterday?" I whispered to myself as I pulled the handle that jingled the small shiny silver bell at the side of the door. "So much has happened since then."

Meredith opened the door and she seemed really pleased to see me. I noticed that her cheeks were streaked with mascara as if she had been crying.

"Come in! Come in quickly!" she said, putting her finger up to her lips and almost pulling me inside. She closed the door behind her quietly.

"What ever is the matter? I said, with some concern.

"I've been working things out!" she said, secretively. "I am so pleased to see you! Sit down on the sofa and I'll make us a cup of tea and then I'll tell you all about everything that has happened."

She vanished through a beaded curtain into what looked like a small kitchen. She had suddenly seemed very excited.

She returned in a jiffy carrying a big wooden tray on which was placed a jade green, white and gold china tea set, including a large teapot, hot water jug, milk-jug and sugar bowl. Also on the tray was a silver tea strainer and a large plate piled high with slices of sponge cake. An ivory handled, silver cake-slice was tucked under one side.

"I made the cake this morning," she said, "I do all my own cooking."

"This is very civilized," I said, with some considerable astonishment. "You are very competent for one so young."

"How old do you think I am," asked Meredith.

"Well," I said, feverishly thinking of what to say, in case I offended her. My common sense told me to bat for safety.

"When, I saw you playing with the other children yesterday, I thought you were the eldest, and then if you had asked me the same question, I would have guessed about thirteen or fourteen. Now I see that you must be older than that, so I will guess fifteen or sixteen."

"You're getting close," she said. "I am seventeen and my eighteenth birthday is at Christmas. What also makes me look less than my age is the fact that I don't have any of the trendy clothes that girls of my age would normally wear. Also, I look after the circus children, so I am always with children much younger than myself, and people jump to conclusions. I don't want to keep you in suspense, but I would like to tell you a little about myself first, so that you will understand my situation. Let me pour the tea before I start; it will be going cold." The situation had suddenly become very intriguing and I watched in perplexed mode as Meredith expertly poured the tea into our cups through the silver strainer.

"My mother always impressed upon me never to put the milk in first. She had learned from her own mother that it was bad manners to do otherwise and etiquette demands that ladies adhere to a strict routine. It's always, tea first, leaving enough room for hot water, then milk, from a jug never a bottle. Then comes sugar, with separate spoon or tongs, from a bowl never a packet and then stir gently with teaspoon from the saucer. Finally, one must always pick up the cup and saucer as an item, holding both in the one hand before removing the cup with the other to take a sip. The cup must be held delicately with thumb and first two fingers only, and separating or fanning out the other two. I could go on," she said with a grin, "and give similar instructions in etiquette for eating cake; but I think I've said enough, so here endeth the lesson."

"Goodness me, I forgot the plates and knives for the cake, I do apologise."

Meredith went to a small oak sideboard with drawers and cupboards and returned with two china plates in the same pattern as the tea set. She handed me a beautifully designed cake-fork, again in hallmarked silver with an ivory handle.

The sponge cake was light as a feather and had a tangy fresh lemon flavour – it was mouth-wateringly delicious. While I complimented Meredith on her wonderful cake, in my mind also, I suddenly had a kind of deja-vu experience. It was as if I had been here before – but Meredith was Crocodile … or Crocodile was Meredith, if you see what I mean. Inexplicably, although they were totally dissimilar in appearance, they had the same mannerisms, the same gentle nature, the same way of expressing themselves.

Meredith interrupted my strange train of thought by saying suddenly, "I am sure you must have read about my parents; it was in all the newspapers and on the television news at the time." Before I could answer, she continued, but in a voice now infused with emotion, "They were only thirty years old … it was on the last Saturday of the circus year, in the afternoon. The bosses of the circus had persuaded them to do their trapeze act without a safety net because they could get double the normal price for the tickets ... just as they are doing with Crocodile this Saturday. It all went wrong … one of the trapeze wires snapped. My father was desperately trying to hold onto my mother by his fingertips, but couldn't hold her ... I was sitting in the front row so I saw it all. I am sure that he could have saved himself but he couldn't hold my mother so I think he let go of his own trapeze, even though he had a good grip ... they both fell fifty feet to the ground. They were rushed to hospital and I went in the ambulance with them ... they were unconscious. I was at the hospital for hours while the doctors tried to save them. But they couldn't. A doctor came and held my hand and took me into a quiet room and said that he was very sorry, that the surgeons had done everything possible but they had been too badly injured. He said that if it was any comfort, they would not have remembered anything, they would not have suffered any pain. They both died at the same second. He said he was sure that they would now be together, in peace, in a better place."

I took hold of her hand just as the doctor had done and said: "How absolutely awful for you. That must be something that you can never really come to terms with. I clearly remember reading about it at the time, but I must tell you that by a strange coincidence, I also remember their names. Your father and mother were called Frank and Lily ... Frank and Lily Holt ... and you must be Meredith Holt, if I am not mistaken."

"However did you know that?" she asked in a puzzled voice.

"Oh, it isn't that I have some miraculous memory," I replied. "It's just that my mother's brother was called Frank and he had a wife, Lily. My grandmother's maiden name was Holt, and her brother was called Frank. I was so shocked when I read about the accident, in the newspaper, and it was no more than a coincidence that their names were familiar, but that is why I can remember them."

I saw that Meredith's face had brightened a little and she said, shaking her head, "It's nearly half a lifetime away for me now, and although I will have to bear the pain all my life, the torment has eased a little. Now I don't cry myself to sleep every night, and I occupy my mind with other thoughts and activities during the day. I try to keep busy and when I am on my own in the caravan I read a lot, especially about animals. I think that if I could find a good career, something that I know would have made my Mum and Dad really proud, that would help me a lot. I love animals and I think that more than anything else I would like to work with animals, but not in the way the circus folk do, exploiting them. I think that is cruel because they force the animals to do things that are unnatural and they are beaten if they do not perform the tricks properly and confined in cages for hours on end so they don't have the freedom that is natural to them. My Dad's brother, my uncle Steve, you know, Big Steve, you've met him ... is not a bad man, and really has quite a soft heart. He has done a lot for me since my parents died. He's kind of looked after me, but when it comes to animals ... to him they're just animals. In his mind animals don't have souls; they don't go to heaven. It's only us humans that go to heaven; ill-treating an animal, in his book, doesn't make you a bad person, at least not so bad that you won't get into heaven ... if you see what I mean." Meredith took a really deep breath, "Now, I'll tell you what I've discovered!"

"I now know that the Hartley you were looking for wasn't a dog. He was a crocodile, if I am not mistaken."

Meredith said, looking me straight in the eye with an equally straight face.

My heart missed a beat, but there was no point in trying to pull the wool over her eyes any longer because it appeared that she had already worked things out.

Suddenly her face broke into a big smile and she said, "I want to reassure you immediately that we are on the same side, so I won't keep you guessing any longer; I'll just tell you exactly how I know, and what happened. It was Uncle Steve who told me that they had got the crocodile back. I know that they have been after him for a long time and that they suspected he had been kidnapped by a professor and was living in London. The thing was, that they saw him potentially as the biggest box office draw they had ever had ... even bigger than my Mum and Dad's trapeze act. Uncle Steve said that he hadn't reached anything like his full potential when he vanished. Now they've got him back they're going to make him perform some really clever and some very dangerous tricks, like riding the high wire on a monocycle without a safety net! Steve said that they're going to turn him into a superstar. I knew that he was in the circus when Mum and Dad were performing but the children weren't allowed to go near him when he was out of his cage. They told us he'd eat us for his dinner given half a chance, so we were frightened of him and daren't go near him. I know my Mum and Dad felt sorry for him and they used to take him food if we had anything left over from our dinners. I even suspect that they made things especially for him.

Anyway, after you had gone, I carried on looking for Hartley and I kept calling out his name. As I was passing the crocodile's cage, I couldn't see inside because it had curtains all round, I shouted out '*Hartley!*' again. I heard a voice from behind the curtains call out, 'I am Hartley ... I'm in here'. With some difficulty I managed to pull one of the curtains back enough for me to see right inside and there he was, the crocodile, chained to the railings at the back of the cage. There was only the crocodile in the cage and nobody else around at all. He looked so dejected, crouched in a corner, then he lifted his head and looking straight at me, he said, in a very posh voice, 'I am William Hartley Crocodile. I prefer to be called Hartley rather than William, but most of my friends call me Crocodile, with a capital 'C', reserving the name Hartley for formal occasions. So Crocodile will be fine'."

"I thought it was a hoax, that maybe Uncle Steve or one of the others was playing a trick on me, but I pretended to assume that it was him speaking, so I said, 'I believe that you used to know my Mum and Dad, Frank and Lily, the trapeze artists.'

'Goodness gracious!' he replied. 'They were the only people who were really kind to me when I was here before. I was so very sorry to hear about their tragic accident. My Guardian and good friend, the Professor told me about it. They should never have been allowed to perform their act without a safety net. So you must be their daughter, Meredith. They used to talk about you a lot. Of course they did not know that I could speak or even that I could understand what they were saying, but they used to talk to me as if I could understand, and they were always singing your praises. They were very proud of you. The truth is, I didn't speak to anyone, so nobody except Mercedes, my best friend at the zoo, knew I could speak'."

"I asked him, 'How do you know that I won't go and tell everybody that you can speak?' He replied, 'If you're anything like your parents, and I am sure that you are, then I know that you won't tell anyone. Even if you did I wouldn't speak to them and they'd think that you were telling fibs and making it up, so it wouldn't do you any good. I am a good judge of character and I am sure that my secret is safe with you'."

"I said, 'Please don't worry Crocodile, my lips are sealed. I promise I won't tell a soul and you can trust me completely. Also, I think I have something very important to tell you. If I am not mistaken, I believe that some people you know called Matthew and Kate have been looking for you. I think that they pretended to have lost their dog, called Hartley, but I now believe that it was really you that they were trying to find'."

"Well!" exclaimed Meredith. "I've never seen such a sudden change in anybody, let alone a crocodile. He sprang up so quickly, he quite startled me. 'Oh, how wonderful!' he almost shouted, 'that is music to my ears. Somehow I knew that Matthew and Kate would work out where I had been taken, but when you're locked and chained in a cage it's hard to keep your spirits up'.

'Well', I said, 'I hope this makes you feel even better because I would like you to know that I'm on your side also. My Mum and Dad always had a soft spot for you, and always felt that it was wrong for you to be treated the way you were. I remember my Dad saying that he wished he could find a way to get you away from the circus, to give you a better life. So if Matthew and Kate came here to help you to escape, then I promise that I'll do my best to help them and you. They said that they were coming back on Saturday, but I have a feeling they may return before then. I'll find out what they have in mind to do about your situation, so I can act as go between. I'd better not stay here too long in case somebody overhears us but before I go, I would like to know what sort of food they are giving you.'

He screwed up his face and said, 'Please don't ask me to describe it because it's indescribable. I'm a vegetarian, you know, and I have an extremely sophisticated palate. Everybody who has looked after me, Mercedes, the Professor, Matt and Kate, were all culinary connoisseurs of the highest calibre. I also know that your parents were excellent cooks and they used to bring me all kinds of scrumptious titbits'.

'In that case', I said, 'if you can give me a couple of hours I'll cook you a feast fit for a vegetarian king'."

"As I waved goodbye, I noticed a couple of tears trickling down his long snout. He then said, very quietly, 'I hope that I shall soon be in a position to repay your kindness'."

"I dashed back to the caravan and made him the biggest and best vegetarian pie I have ever made. It was full of every vegetable that I could lay my hands on, potatoes, and carrots, and onions and spinach, and cabbage, and green beans, and broad beans, kidney beans, and celery, the list goes on and on. I made it in a rich cheese, mushroom and mustard sauce, and some sauce in a jug with added double cream, for him to pour over it. I patted the pastry and pricked it and then put his name on the top, 'CROCODILE', in big pastry letters, and baked it to a golden crust. You ought to have seen his face when I pulled the tea-towel off, and the way he tucked into it. He must have been ravenous."

"He then said, 'Are you sure that you don't want to share it with me? It is rather embarrassing to find myself gourmandizing on your magnificent pie while you are just standing there watching.'"

"'I'll let you into a secret', I replied, 'I made another small pie for myself which I intend to have for my supper as soon as I get back to my caravan – so you just tuck in. I'll wait until you have finished so I can take the tray and everything away with me then nobody will get suspicious. Also I am truly enjoying standing here watching you enjoy yourself'."

Chapter Nine — Oxford And The Circus

"Between mouthfuls, Crocodile began to tell me a little bit more about himself; how he was brought up in a zoo by Mercedes, and how she was so kind to him and really put herself out to teach him to speak and to educate him. He then told me how his pride and showing off on his bicycle had led to his undoing; his kidnapping by the circus folk. He went on to describe his great escape in the back of the Professor's car. He said that life was much about chance and hazard. For example he wouldn't be here with me now, and eating my delicious pie if they hadn't kidnapped him, and indeed, if they hadn't kidnapped him for a second time. Moreover, if he hadn't been kidnapped in the first place he wouldn't have met the Professor so he wouldn't be the person he now was, and he wouldn't have met Kate and Matthew, and he wouldn't have met me. In the end, he could only conclude that all's well that ends well and that a little suffering will help to make you into a better person, because it allows you to compare the good with the bad and so get a proper sense of perspective on life. He then went on to say that the professor had taught him that one should always be positive about the likely outcome of a chain of events. Put simply, a jar can be half full and it can be half empty, but in fact the state of affairs is exactly the same."

"He then said that it would be unnatural for him not to feel a little sorry for himself in his present predicament, but he knew that it was not always going to be like this. So, not only was his jar half full – it had just filled up quite a bit more, meeting me and eating my wonderful pie!"

"Suddenly, he cocked his head on one side and said, 'You had better take the tray and everything quickly. I can hear voices coming in this direction', I snatched everything off him through the bars and scooped it all into the bin-liner that I had tucked under my belt. Crocodile just managed to close the curtain when Big Steve and his sidekick, Little John, strolled round the corner. They seemed quite surprised to see me and I think I must have made them both jump. 'What are you doing here, Meredith?' asked Steve with a puzzled frown. 'Oh. I'm still looking for that dog, Hartley. They've promised a big reward for him. You haven't seen anything of him have you? I'll tell you what! If I do find him, I'll split the reward with you, and vice versa. Is that a deal? I'm going back for my supper now. See you tomorrow. Goodnight'."

"I didn't wait for an answer and just strolled quietly away carrying the evidence in the bin-liner."

"I don't know whether to laugh or cry," I said. "On the one hand, poor Crocodile locked up and chained in a cage, but on the other, he has found a true friend to help him and to look after him while he is incarcerated. I know for sure that with your help we stand a far better chance of rescuing him, but that it is imperative that we rescue him on Saturday at the latest now there is the additional threat of them forcing him to ride on the high wire without a safety net. I know from our times with him on the mountains that he has no head for heights, and I think that if they force him to do it without a net there could be a tragic accident."

"Just like with my Mum and Dad? you mean."

"Exactly so! This additional threat means that somehow we have to help him to escape before the finale of his act."

"One thing I can tell you," said Meredith, "is that you won't stand a chance of getting him out of his cage. There are two huge bolts with separate, enormous padlocks on the door, and the cage has two-inch diameter steel bars, top, bottom and sides. It was used for the lions in the past. Big Steve has one key on a chain round his neck, and Little John has the other, also round his neck. The bosses have threatened to sack them both on the spot if they allow him to escape again, so they will be watching him very carefully and not taking any chances."

I didn't really want to tell Meredith about our plan to get him to escape directly out of the circus ring just yet – even though I was as certain as I have ever been about anything or anybody, that I could trust her. I have found that one of life's great mysteries is the unknown factor of the amount of trust you can place in an individual. It is not something you can learn easily from books, although some books can point you in the right direction – it is something you only really learn from experience. That takes a long time – and there will always be surprises waiting round the corner. I just felt that I could trust Meredith, as I could trust Crocodile and as I would trust Mercedes, or the Professor, even though I had never met them. It was simply that circumstances might have changed before Saturday and ultimately we may have no choice other than to involve the police. So I simply said:

"I would like to thank you so very much for what you have already done for Crocodile – it is so good to know that he has a friend on the inside. I am sure that if we all pull together we will be able to rescue him. I think it best that I drive back to London now and give Kate and Emily the good news and find out what they have come up with. Emily is the Professor's niece who now occupies the London house where Crocodile used to live and from where he was abducted. I will be back before Saturday and I promise to keep you posted."

"Don't worry about a thing here," she said, "I promise that I will look after Crocodile and help to keep his spirits up as well as making sure he's well fed. You get off now, you look very tired, and there is nothing more we can do here tonight."

* * *

It was dark by the time Napoleon and I arrived in Bayswater. I drove the Dormobile straight to the garage and made my way on foot to the house, carrying his cage, with Napoleon riding on my shoulder. Somehow I felt more conspicuous walking along a London street with the huge bird croaking in my ear than I would have done in the Lake District, but we arrived at the front door without passing anybody and for some inexplicable reason I was quite relieved.

Kate and Emily both came to the door together, clearly eager to find out what had transpired. I gave them both a hug and a kiss and said, "Would you mind if I freshened up first before telling you what has happened? But so as not to keep you in a state of heightened suspense and concern, I will tell you that, on balance, the news is very good. It's just that I'm pretty much exhausted and a quick shower will go down a treat."

"Of course Matthew, we wouldn't expect otherwise, would we Kate?" said Emily. "We didn't know what time to expect you and we thought it best that we have our meal, but we have kept yours all nice and warm in the Julius' in-house catering unit. We'll wait for you in the drawing-room, but I'll go and put the kettle on now, so that you can have a quick word alone with Kate."

Before I could say a word, Emily had bustled off in the direction of the kitchen.

"We've got lots to tell you as well," said Kate. "Emily has been an absolute brick and she's not at all the timid lady that I took her to be. She's had all kinds of important people jumping to attention. You go and take your shower and then we'll tell you everything."

By the time I was back downstairs a grand fire was roaring away and the room was lit entirely by candlelight. The Professor's catering contraption groaned under the weight of what for most people would have been a banquet.

"This surely can't all be for me!" I exclaimed.

"Well we must first tell you that we're all going back to Oxford in the morning so what you can't manage to eat tonight, we'll take with us for a picnic lunch tomorrow," explained Emily. "Kate and I made everything today, so it's all quite fresh, and I thought that it would save us having to prepare something in the morning. By the way, I don't know if Kate told you, but we will be staying in Julius' rooms at his College. I still haven't had the time to sort out all his documents, papers, essays, dissertations, theses, etc. I am dreading what I'll find, but he was a prolific writer and was involved with a myriad of charities and other organisations and I know that there

275

is a huge volume of paperwork to get through. Julius was very generous to the College both during his lifetime, and in the form of bequests in his will. The Fellows of the College have consented to keep the rooms exactly as Julius left them and for as long as is necessary, in order that his work can be properly catalogued. They have promised not to put any time pressures on me, especially as much of the work is also of great value to the College. I was hoping that Hartley could have helped with some of the work, because he was more involved with Julius' academic pursuits than I was. The College of course will also give me all the help I need, but for the moment the rooms are at our disposal, so we may as well make good use of them. Kate and I both agreed that it makes much more sense staying there than travelling back and forth between London and Oxford."

"Right!" said Kate. "Emily and I are dying to know what else you have found out, so you go first and then we'll tell you what we've done."

I related, as simply as I could, the events of the last twenty-four hours or so. I specifically left out the contents of my dream about trying to rescue Crocodile from a giant hourglass, and the storm, and going down into the cave to get Napoleon. Although I was apprehensive about keeping secrets from Emily, because we would not find, anywhere, a stauncher ally or a truer friend to Crocodile, I felt that it was sensible that his cave should remain a secret, at least until Emily had been inside it and seen it for herself. I suddenly remembered that I had left his saddlebags with Napoleon's whistles and pouches in the Dormobile, but I told them that I had brought them with me. I then described my journey back, with specific mention of the poster that I had seen in Burford, advertising Crocodile's performance in the circus ring on Saturday. I told them that this was the reason I returned to Oxford. Finally I described in detail my long chat with Meredith and the news that Crocodile was a prisoner there, but that the best news was that we now had an ally and a good friend at the circus. I told them that I was absolutely sure that we could trust Meredith completely. I also told them, in some detail, about the vegetable pie with his name encrusted on it, and that she was already responsible for lifting his spirits considerably. I said that I knew she would look after him and, if necessary, help us with his rescue. I concluded by saying that the deadline for rescuing him was still Saturday, but I didn't know if it would be Saturday afternoon or Saturday night. For the time being I specifically left out the fact that the bosses of the circus intended to force Crocodile to ride on the high wire for his finale act on Saturday. I thought that, at this juncture, it would only upset Kate and Emily, and the deadline was Saturday anyway, so for the moment this distressing prospect was better left unsaid.

"That is all wonderful news," said Kate.

"Wonderful news," repeated Emily. "Just what the doctor ordered! "

"Let us tell you now what we have been up to," said Kate. "Firstly, the Professor has a Godson who is Chief Inspector of Constabulary at the Police College at Hendon. Apparently the Professor was always very good to him and helped him with his education and in his career. Emily went to his christening with the Professor and has known him all his life. We knew that we might have to involve the police if everything else failed, but I won Emily round to our way of thinking, that if at all possible, we should try to rescue Crocodile without involving the authorities and everything becoming public knowledge. Emily telephoned Robert at Hendon to ask a big favour of him. She told him that she wouldn't be asking if it wasn't very important, but he would just have to trust her because she could not, at this point, give him the full details or the main reason for her request. She said that the subject was a protégé of the Professor, somebody akin to himself, who had to be rescued from a potentially dangerous and horrible situation. Emily told him that it involved the proprietors of a circus currently performing in Oxford. Some event may or may not happen on Saturday, but a police presence in some form would be very desirable, in case, she said, the event did actually take place. All she could say at this juncture was that she would book seats at the circus for both the Saturday afternoon and evening performances if he would kindly get back to her with the numbers of seats required. Robert did not ask questions; he simply said, 'Leave it with me Emily and I'll report back to you within the hour'."

"True to his word, exactly forty-five minutes later the telephone rang. 'It's Robert', Emily said. She was on for about five minutes and I could hear her say things like, 'Yes twelve of you would be more than adequate. Yes, at both performances. Yes, you are right, Julius would not have wanted the number to be thirteen. I look forward to seeing you on Saturday Robert, and thank you so much for your help'."

"As soon as she had put the phone down, Emily rubbed her hands together and said, 'It's all worked out. Robert had asked for eleven volunteers for an *undercover operation* from his police cadets, making twelve in total with himself. He said that he had simply picked the top eleven from the recent exam results saying that it was a surprise reward for their hard work. They would all attend both circus performances on Saturday, for a reason that was *Top Secret*, and he would also take them out for a meal in Oxford. They would make the journey in a police bus so it didn't matter what time they got away'."

"We made the seat bookings immediately, and Emily booked three seats for ourselves on the front row for both performances. I think she had to pay a premium, but she wouldn't let on. She said that the other twenty-four bookings were a help in getting us the best seats."

"Don't you concern yourselves about money, " Interrupted Emily, "it's Julius who is paying for this and it is for a cause that he would most certainly have approved of."

* * *

By mid-afternoon of the following day we were comfortably installed in the Professor's suite of rooms, at his Oxford college. There was only one bedroom, but Emily had also commandeered her *usual room* just down the corridor. We had honed our plans with some fine detail on the previous night and we had decided, amongst many other things, that we would travel to Oxford in two vehicles. Napoleon and I would go in the Dormobile, and Emily would take Kate in her own car. We had concluded that an extra vehicle might be useful, depending on how things evolved.

Most importantly we had decided that if Crocodile were in fact to perform in both shows – and we knew for certain now that there were only two longer performances, not three, on the last day – then we should plan for him to escape from the first performance.

The reason for my going to all the trouble to bring Napoleon with me was that he alone would have been able to get into Crocodile's cage. I had planned for him to carry messages in his pouch so that Crocodile would be briefed on exactly what to do. He could return messages in the same way, and with luck we could possibly agree a detailed plan for Crocodile's escape from the circus ring. So long as he could make it to the Dormobile and scramble inside before he was seen, he would be safe.

Meredith however had, at a stroke, made Napoleon redundant, but at least I would not now have to ask Napoleon to risk his freedom or his life, because there would always have been the possibility that he could have been caught by the circus folk, who were used to handling birds and animals.

The big question now had become Meredith's involvement and just what we could reasonably expect of her, given her close association with the circus. Our discussion the previous night had ended up being focussed on agreeing exactly what we would ask her to do. We had decided finally that I should go back to see her and ask her point blank if she would be prepared to do it.

Chapter Nine
Oxford And The Circus

With this in mind, very shortly after we had arrived in Oxford, it was proposed that I should go immediately to the circus, on my own and in Emily's car, to discuss our plan with Meredith and to find out if she would give us her full support.

When I got there the fairground was in full swing and the afternoon circus show had already started. Meredith wasn't in her caravan, but I could hear the shouts and laughs of the children from behind the caravans, and peering underneath I could see Meredith playing hopscotch with a group of young girls. I slipped between two caravans and waved in her direction. It took a moment or two before she saw me but as soon as she looked in my direction she waved at me, then she said something to the children and came hurrying over – she was quite out of breath.

"All these games keep me in trim," she said, "and I was skipping for half an hour before we played hopscotch. Do come inside and I'll make you a cup of tea. I've got lots to tell you."

Meredith brought me a mug of tea. "Have you not noticed the design?" she asked screwing up her eyes.

I held the mug at arms length and there, emblazoned on the surface, was an image of Crocodile on his monocycle in full circus dress. "Good heavens!" I gasped. "Wherever did you get this from?"

"Big Steve gave it to me. He said that it was a prototype, but that by Saturday they'd have a least six different designs on sale. Apparently, they're also having T-shirts, coasters, and postcards designed and printed and they'll all be ready for the big show on Saturday. Steve said again that they plan to turn him into a Superstar – they reckon Crocodile will become a circus legend. He said that the bosses are really excited. They think he'll put this circus on the map and make them their fortunes."

"Well, what do you think about all this Meredith?" I asked.

"I think it's shameful," she replied. "Whatever they promise, I know that they'll just exploit him for what they can make out of him. He'll be even more closely guarded, and kept locked in his cage all the time except for when he's in the circus ring. He won't see a penny of the money they make out of him. They'll force him to do all sorts of highly dangerous stunts and work him until he has perfected them. I know this from the way they treated my Mum and Dad. They were paid peanuts for risking their lives, and in the end it cost them their lives."

"What I really wanted to tell you was that I now realise that the only way Crocodile can escape will be when he is unfettered in the circus ring. As soon as he comes out of his cage there'll be bodyguards all round him, and as soon as he's finished his act they'll follow him, like minders, all the way back to his cage. You know, just like a boxer going into and out of the boxing-ring. So I'll tell you what my plan is. I'll mark a line in red dye on the canvas wall of the Big Top. I'll tell Crocodile exactly where the mark will be and get him to finish his act as close as possible to the line. Just before he finishes I'll slit the canvas with a sharp knife so that he can ride straight out of the Big Top. That is all I can do and the rest must be up to you. If you can get a vehicle close enough you could be away with him before anybody realises what is happening."

"You really are a genius, Meredith! I have to tell you that I had already worked out a similar escape for him, but I hadn't thought through exactly how he would get out of the Big Top. I now realise that he couldn't just ride straight out because there won't be an opening for him to ride through until the show finishes. Both time and timing are crucial, so if he can just vanish straight through the canvas wall, then that element of surprise should be sufficient for him to get clean away. Your plan is absolutely brilliant!"

"You're making me blush now, but I thought it was just plain common sense. It's not exactly rocket science," said Meredith, laughing and blushing at the same time.

"My only problem is that if the bosses find out that it was I who helped Crocodile to escape, and it's very likely that they will, then I'm really for the high jump. I have no idea what revenge they'll extract, but I can tell you it won't be very pleasant." Meredith grimaced.

"Then perhaps you'd better leave it up to us." I said, "It is quite unreasonable for any of us to expect you to put yourself into a perilous situation, and I am absolutely certain that Crocodile would not entertain the idea for a second if he thought that you would be putting yourself in any danger."

"The thing is," said Meredith, with a shrug of her shoulders, "I've been wanting to leave the circus ever since my Mum and Dad were killed. It was always their wish that I should have a good education, something that was denied to both of them. I can see them looking down at me now, and saying, 'Go on Girl, take this chance, it might be the last one you have to get away from the circus. Go! Before it's too late. Go and make a career for yourself that would make us proud and make yourself proud. Go on! Do it for us!'."

A sudden idea came into my head; perhaps it was a long shot, so I said – but without telling Meredith exactly what I had in mind, "Well, I am sure that between the four of us, that is Crocodile, Emily, Kate and myself, we can help you to get fixed up with a position that you would enjoy. If I remember correctly, you said that you really wanted to work with animals, but not in something that involved exploiting them. I am sure that we can help to find just the right job. In fact I have something in mind right now. I'll discuss it with Kate and Emily as soon as I get back. The three of us are staying in Oxford now so I'll scribble down our telephone number at the College just in case something unexpected or urgent crops up. I'll come back to see you here on Saturday morning for a final briefing and then we'll decide who is going to slit the canvas, you or me. I want you to be absolutely sure that you are doing the right thing."

"That's settled then!" said Meredith. "But don't forget that I will have to brief Crocodile and I will have to tell him exactly where the red mark will be so that he can see it clearly from the circus ring. It would be disastrous if he cycled to the wrong spot and couldn't get out. I can slit the canvas from the outside anyway, so you don't have to worry about me being seen; it will be much easier for me to do it than you. What I'm really trying to tell you is that this may be my last chance to escape, as well as Crocodile's. The circus is going back to Europe this weekend and I don't want to go with it any more than he does."

"In that case," I said, "Kate and Emily and I will work out something for you this evening and I'll tell you all about it on Saturday morning, and if you still feel exactly the same way on Saturday, we'll go for it."

"That's wonderful," said Meredith, "I feel so much happier already. Goodness gracious is that the time? I promised poor Crocodile another pie for his dinner; I'd better get started on the pastry straight away. Before you go, you'll also be pleased to know that he's bucked up no end. His forlorn expression has been replaced with a cheeky grin when he sees me. He tells me that he's even practising his cycling stunts with a new confidence and energy, to the astonishment of his minders. Even Big Steve says he can't believe the change in him."

When I got back to the College there was a note waiting for me, prominently propped up on the Professor's desk. It read, 'Discussed everything until we are both blue in the face – gone shopping to get our stamina back – invited for drinks at 19.30 with the Dean in his chambers – before dinner in the Dining Hall – see you later, Love, Kate & Emily. X.'

'Splendid!' I thought to myself. 'This intermission would give me plenty of time to relax and recharge my batteries before the evening's entertainment, because I was certain that the girls would not return until well after six. First a cup of tea, then a long shower followed by some gentle relaxing music before getting ready to meet the Dean – that would do nicely.'

True to form, well after six, Kate and Emily burst into the room. A more accurate description would be that a mountain of shopping bags supported by Kate and Emily tumbled into the room.

"So sorry were late," gasped Kate. "We got held up at the last minute and we had to make a detour back to the Shopping Centre because, would you believe it, we both agreed that the dress I had tried on earlier suited me the best, and it was only half the price of the one I was going to buy."

"It was absolutely the right decision," agreed Emily, "I told Kate at the time that it was perfect and the price was so reasonable. We had better get a move on because we mustn't be late for Peregrine; he's a stickler for punctuality, even more than Julius was. I'll be back to collect you at twenty-five past."

"I'm ready now," I said,.

"What a shame," said Kate, when Emily had left, "it would have been nice to have been able to try on a few things and show you what I have bought. I suppose I'll have to leave that for the morning. I am really going to have to hurry. It had completely slipped our minds that we were seeing the Dean at half-past seven." Kate wandered into the bathroom as she spoke.

From there she shouted, "How did you get on with Meredith?"

"Very well," I replied." She's absolutely on our side and she tells me that Crocodile has perked up a lot. She's been very kind to him. I'll give you the details over dinner."

"Emily says that the Dean was an undergraduate here at the same time as the Professor," Kate shouted back through the door." Apparently he's known to the students as The PLC, because of his initials. His name is Peregrine Lancelot Crisp. The Dons and Fellows call him Peri, which Emily tells me was a good, or evil genius in mythology. Emily, of course calls him Peregrine."

At exactly 19.25 Emily knocked on the door to collect us. Kate had just made it by the skin of her teeth. We were punctual and at 19.30, we were greeted by the PLC.

"EMILY! How delightful to see you again!" beamed The PLC, immediately stooping to kiss her on both cheeks. "You haven't developed an American accent during your long sojourn in that great country, have you?"

"Peregrine always teases me," said Emily, looking at us and blushing slightly. "No more than you developed an Australian accent when you were lecturing in Sydney. I'd like you to meet my very good friends Matthew and Kate Worth. They're from one of your favourite parts of the world, the Lake District."

"Ah, William Wordsworth country, a pastoral paradise. Great pity he wasn't an Oxford Man. Shame he went to *the other place*." He stooped again to kiss Kate's hand. "Delighted to make your acquaintance my dear."

Then he took my hand and gave it a very robust shake. "Now that's what I call a good firm handshake, always a sign of a good man and a strong indication that we are going to get on well. Mind you, if it had been weak and limp I wouldn't have mentioned it. Wouldn't like to appear rude to a guest, would just have been noted it in my little black book, on the debit side," he said with a chuckle and a twinkle in his eye.

"See how he's teasing you now?" said Emily, "He just can't help himself. It was even worse when Peregrine and Julius were together, I felt so sorry for some of their undergraduates who often took their remarks quite seriously; that is, until they really got to know them."

"I must apologise in advance for not being able to join you at high table for dinner this evening. Sadly, I have a prior engagement, and duty calls. Now let me offer you a glass of wine. I presume Emily has already informed you that Julius was a *Master of Wine*, if not the *Master of Wine*. This is a particularly splendid Meursault; a quite excellent year," he said handing to each of us a large, fine, antique crystal goblet.

Having swirled, sniffed and sipped the golden contents, followed by indecipherable, mm's and ahs, the Dean then continued in a more sombre tone of voice: "I don't know if Emily has told you, but Julius and I were at this great College together as undergraduates. He was my dearest friend and we remained so all our lives. We took exactly the same examinations every year and even though we never failed to get Firsts in everything we did, he always got the higher mark, indeed the highest mark in every examination. It was only at sport that I excelled, at swimming, running and rowing. It was only in these disciplines that I could beat him. The same situation continued throughout our lives. However hard I tried, he was always better than me at everything we attempted. He seemed to possess not only a brilliant mind but also a sixth sense and these he coupled with a streetwise cunning, and not just in academic pursuits. He simply made a fortune out of everything he put his mind to, be it collecting works of art, or fine wine. For example, our wine cellar at the College is the finest in Oxford. Yet it hasn't cost us a penny. Julius personally bought all the wine, but he bought it as an investment. Over the years some of the Fellows have considered him to be overly extravagant, spending what he did, but he would always sell a large percentage on. His timing was impeccable, and he made a huge profit, sufficient to pay himself back and to stock his own private cellar in Bayswater. All the wine in our cellar, and there are many thousands of bottles, have not cost the College one sou. Some of his colleagues have criticized him for living so well, for exceeding the bounds of reasonableness, but he always gave away a very large percentage of the considerable amount that he earned, and most of it to charitable organizations. The College and these organizations are much the richer for his generosity and will be much the poorer for his passing."

The Dean's voice then took on a more enquiring modulation as he said, "Tell me Emily, and please forgive me for asking, but I have sometimes felt, even though I considered Julius to be my best friend and confidant, that there were a couple of ongoing situations in his life that he wanted to keep secret. The first was to do with an early love affair about which he never spoke, but had alluded to in the distant past. The second was I believe much later in life, when he tutored a secret protégé. Secret from the point of view that this person never attended lectures or tutorials at the University, but nevertheless, and on the recommendation of Julius, was awarded an honorary degree. I have personally read some of his papers and whoever it was had a fine mind and thoroughly deserved the degree, but I wonder, now that Julius is sadly no longer with us, if you would be willing to share any information you may have about these people?"

"Well, Peregrine, you have very cleverly put me on the spot and in front of my dear friends Matthew and Kate. What I can tell you is that the love of his life was called Lydia and she died tragically while he was studying with you at Oxford. He could never bring himself to give me the detail on exactly what happened but I have always believed that he blamed his academic achievements for her death. For a while they became more important to him than his love for her and he realised too late, it was a mistake. He had been both selfish and stupid and he would pay for it for the rest of his life. He could have shared his life with Lydia and had a good career, but he put all his energies into the latter."

"As far as his protégé is concerned, you must know his name because it is on his Degree Certificate and filed in College and University records."

"Hmm, well yes I do," replied the Dean, "It is, William Hartley Crocodile. It's quite the strangest name I've ever heard!"

"What, stranger than Peregrine Lancelot Crisp?"

"I should not like to play poker with you for high stakes," retorted the Dean, "but I'd have you as my partner for Bridge any time!"

"It is my belief," continued Emily, "that Hartley, which is my preferred name for him, helped to lessen the grief that Julius continually suffered. He focussed all his

Chapter Nine — Oxford And The Circus

energies on helping Hartley because he believed that, and I cannot elaborate at this juncture, it was an opportunity to be involved with an enterprise that was truly unique in the annals of the evolution of species. I am sorry that I cannot be more specific at this time other than to say that at this very moment, as we speak, poor Hartley is in mortal danger and fears for his life, and that to tell you any more than I have already disclosed could exacerbate his situation."

"Upon my soul!" gasped Peregrine. "Please be assured my dear Emily, that word of this will not stray outside this room; your secret is securely locked in a steel cage."

* * *

Dinner was a fine affair. The crystal and silver shimmered and sparkled in the candlelight from the grand chandeliers, table candelabras and discreet electric lamps, creating a warm, and cosy, intimate atmosphere, in the vastness of the Grand Dining Hall. As we made our way down to high table, Emily pointed to some of the oil paintings adorning the panelled walls that had been acquired for the College by the Professor. She had requested that we sit together with me in the middle so that we could discuss Crocodile and finalise our plans for his escape. The food was traditional English so I will not go into detail, other than to say, it consisted of soup with warm bread, a choice of main course with fresh vegetables and a choice of pudding. It was nicely cooked, hot and wholesome, and well presented on fine china. The accompanying wines were excellent. Our attention, however, had only one focal point, and a leisurely meal in these illustrious surroundings was a perfect opportunity to concentrate our minds on the task in hand. This most certainly would not have been possible if the Dean had been present, so the fact that he was otherwise engaged, and could not entertain us at dinner, proved to be a blessing.

The conversation started with Meredith, and I told Kate and Emily that I was convinced that she was very serious about leaving the circus for good and that she wanted to look for a position in which she could work with animals but in circumstances in which she would care for them properly, not like at the circus where they were exploited for financial gain. I said that I'd had the germ of an idea that could possibly be a solution at some future point, but we would have to think of something now that would be possible immediately.

"Well I can suggest a good interim solution," said Emily enthusiastically, "She could come and live with me in Bayswater. As you know I'm in that great house all on my own, and I've Julius' papers to get through. Some of these involve animal charities so she could help with them. She would certainly learn something about animals that have had a rough deal in life. Another consideration of course, is that she is a young girl who should be enjoying the companionship of girls and boys her own age. Again I do have friends and acquaintances with teenagers of a similar age, so I do not think that I will have any difficulty in introducing her to some nice friends."

"That sounds like a splendid idea," I said, "and especially because I haven't seen many other girls or boys of her age at the circus. The circus is always on the move, so many of the friendships that do spring up will be transitory. What do you think Kate?"

"I must say that I have some reservations about taking responsibility for planning somebody else's future, but I have to agree that if Meredith desperately wants to leave the circus, then I see no reason why we should not be instrumental in helping her to achieve her goal. So long as we impress upon her that it is her decision and she does not hold us responsible for forcing her to do something that is hasty or reckless, then you certainly have my vote."

"Splendid!" I said, "That is wise counsel from both of you. I suggest then that the three of us go to see Meredith on Saturday morning, both for a final briefing on the detail of Crocodile's escape, and to ascertain if, as an interim move, Meredith will agree to Emily's kind invitation."

"Now, next on the agenda is to agree the exact detail of his escape. I have to tell you that Meredith has, to my mind, come up with a quite brilliant suggestion. You know that I had this idea that Crocodile should escape directly out of the circus ring at the end of his act. What I had not taken on board was the fact that, until the show is completely over, all the exits will be closed off. Meredith also worked out that his only chance is to escape directly from the circus ring because escape from his cage would be an almost impossible feat unless he was Houdini. Meredith says that the cage was formerly used for lions and is constructed from two-inch diameter steel bars, top, bottom, and sides. There is only one steel door with two big padlocks securing it. He is chained and manacled to the bars. Only Big Steve and Little John have the keys for the padlocks, one each, kept on chains round their necks. Apparently they are on pain of death, or at least pain of instant dismissal, if their prisoner escapes a second time. Meredith also says that minders will escort Crocodile to and from the ring. So his only realistic chance is to escape during, or at the end of his act, before his bodyguards surround him once more. Meredith's brilliant idea is that she should mark the canvas wall of the Big Top at a strategic point with a dye or marker of some sort, and tell Crocodile in advance where that will be. Then at the critical moment Meredith will slit the canvas at that very spot so that Crocodile can ride straight out into the open air."

"Gosh!" exclaimed Kate, "It's just as if we were planning his escape from Colditz or Alcatraz! Are they really guarding him that securely?"

"Meredith believes that the bosses see his return as a once-in-a-lifetime opportunity to make themselves a fortune. They obviously know his potential from the time he was with them before and they have never given up in their quest to get him back. Meredith says that this time they plan to turn him into a Superstar, a Circus Legend, if you will. You're not going to believe this but Meredith gave me tea in a Crocodile mug. It was a prototype for the ones they will have ready for sale on Saturday. They'll have six different designs. She says that they are also having T-shirts, posters, and post-cards printed and they will all be on sale at the big show."

"Good heavens!" said Emily. "Whatever would Julius have thought of all this? What I am absolutely sure about is that he would definitely be in favour of our plan to free Hartley. Before we went shopping, Kate and I discussed exactly what we should say to Robert. We decided that the best plan was to write out his instructions with the necessary background information and seal them in an envelope, which he must open only if things go wrong. If Hartley gets to the Dormobile in one piece, and without being spotted, and you can get safely out on to the road, and away from the circus, then we will tell him to destroy the envelope and the enclosed instructions without reading the contents. Kate thought that I should stay with Robert and his men and she would act as go between. Once Matthew has escaped with Hartley in the Dormobile, Robert's job is done and I will bring Kate in my car to meet you and Hartley at a pre-arranged spot. This plan will ensure that Robert will intervene only if Hartley is captured. If he escapes then Robert will be non the wiser about the reality of the situation."

"What a team! "I said. "I believe that the escape plan deserves a triple 'A' rating! All that there is left to do now is to spend some time on the exact wording of Robert's instructions, and I think that the three of us should go to visit Meredith in her caravan on Saturday morning just to make sure that she hasn't had any second thoughts about leaving the circus. This will also give Emily the chance to tell Meredith about her proposal of accommodation in Bayswater and the Professor's animal charities."

* * *

So it came to pass on the Saturday morning, on the final day of the circus' year, that Kate and Emily and I visited Meredith in her caravan in order to finalise the detail for Crocodile's escape. Meredith was delighted with Emily's suggestion of living with her in London and helping with the correspondence for the Professor's animal charities. We decided there and then that Meredith might as well return to London with Emily and that the presence of Robert and his men would ensure she could leave safely, without being apprehended by the circus folk. That would also give Robert something tangible to get his teeth into and Emily would brief him in advance. Meredith had managed to get hold of an aerosol of scarlet red paint in order to mark the exact position on the canvas through which Crocodile would make his final exit from the circus ring. Meredith also showed us the knife with which she would cut the canvas – razor sharp one side and serrated on the other. She told us that she had already tried it out and that it had cut through canvas like a hot knife through butter.

We had brought with us Crocodile's trusty saddlebags containing a whistle to summon Napoleon, together with a hat, a long coat and scarf, and a long bushy beard in case it was possible, or necessary, to disguise him. Just for good measure I had also included a Swiss army knife and a fifty-metre length of thin, but very strong climbing rope. I suggested that Meredith leave the saddlebags on the outside of the Big Top just to the right of the slit in the canvas and to tell Crocodile that they would be there waiting for him to pick up on his way out. I said, as an added precaution, that I would carry an identical set of the disguise with me, and take it to the show.

The final point was to describe to Meredith, as accurately as possible, where we would park the Dormobile. I said that I would hoist a small Union Jack on the roof of the vehicle to make it easier to recognise and that Emily's car would be parked next to it. I had done a precise reconnaissance and had decided to park the vehicles in the field, which was now the main car park, directly in line with the Big Top and the Big Wheel. There was a stretch of open ground between the security fence which surrounded the fair and the car-park. This made the distance to the Dormobile from the other side of the Big Wheel almost identical to the distance from the Big Top to the Big Wheel. When Crocodile cycled out of the Big Top he would head straight for the Big Wheel, and the Dormobile would be the same distance again, on the other side – or at least as straight as it would be possible to go. I had drawn a plan for Crocodile, which I had put on the top of the items in his saddlebags. I had also made a copy, which I gave to Meredith.

I felt that we had now done everything possible to ensure the success of our plan. The stage had now been set – the die was cast – only fate could intervene to thwart our best laid plans.

* * *

There were two performances on the final Saturday; a matinee performance at 2.30 pm and an evening show at 7.30 pm. Common sense told us that we should not delay the execution of our plan until the last performance because, even if Crocodile was billed to appear in both shows, there was always the chance that something untoward could happen to prevent him from completing his act in the evening show – and we would have lost our chance. We felt that we should take the first good opportunity that presented itself, and if something unexpected happened then, to prevent him from making his escape, there was still the evening show left for a second attempt.

We arrived an hour early, at 1.30 pm, so that Emily could meet with Robert to give him his sealed instructions and brief him on the likelihood that he may have to intervene to ensure that Emily could get Meredith safely off the site. When Emily returned she said that she had told Robert that Meredith was going to come to stay with her in London, but that there may be some trouble from some of the circus folk. Robert had now gone off to round up his men who were enjoying themselves at the fair.

We were all bemused by the intensive Crocodile memorabilia sales promotion that greeted us as we neared the entrance to the Big Top. As Meredith had predicted, they were selling Crocodile mugs, Crocodile coasters, Crocodile T-Shirts, and Crocodile postcards, and they appeared to be doing a roaring trade. By the time we finally got to our seats on the front row there was only twenty minutes to go to the start of the performance and a brass band, in a small tiered stand at the side of the ring, was already tuning its instruments.

By 2.25 pm all the seats were occupied and the noise level from the audience rose as the pitch of excitement increased. Suddenly the lights went out and the audience went quiet. There was a long silence broken only by a squeak from a horn, a hollow bang and the blast of a whistle, then silence again. Suddenly a dwarf clown, lit by a single spotlight, ran around the raised perimeter of the circus ring – he had a worried expression on his face and kept looking back over his shoulder. There followed another squeak and a bigger bang – then suddenly an

Chapter Nine   Oxford And The Circus

enormous gorilla with red glowing eyes romped around the ring, abruptly stopping and pretending to jump at some children in the front row, who screamed and huddled up to their parents. The gorilla continued in this threatening way, then vanished in the darkness when the spotlight went out. The brass band struck up again and a bright spotlight followed a tall elegantly-dressed man in a scarlet long-tailed coat, wearing a shiny silk black top hat, and carrying a silver-handled whip. He strode purposefully into the centre of the ring and stopped, standing to attention. The music stopped. Then he cracked his whip and lifted his top-hat and shouted, "GOOD AFTERNOON MY LORDS, LADIES AND GENTLEMEN. I bid you ALL a warm welcome to nothing less than what is undeniably THE GREATEST SHOW ON EARTH."

His voice rose to a crescendo as he uttered the final words – in response to which a great cheer erupted from around the audience and everybody clapped spontaneously. The brass band struck up again at a jaunty pace – only to stop abruptly once more as the Ringmaster raised his hands.

"NOW, on behalf of this Great Circus, I have the honour of introducing to you a selection of the wonderful acts that we will perform, for your delectation, in this afternoon's show. Allow me to introduce first of all one of the greatest juggling acts in the world, a husband and wife team from LATVIA, the one and only, JANI & JANIS."

Jani appeared with Janis at his side. He was carrying a dining chair, which he suddenly tossed in the air and caught by one leg on the end of his chin. Janis then pitched five skittles at him, which he deftly caught and began to juggle over his head and over the top of the chair. A spotlight followed the pair as they made their way round the perimeter of the ring, at the end of which, Jani tossed the skittles one by one to Janis, then flicked the chair over off his chin into an upright position on the floor just in time for Janis to sit on it as she caught the last skittle. The couple took a bow and vanished as the light was extinguished.

The Ringmaster permitted a short ovation from the audience before introducing the next act. He then boomed, "I now present to you the Great Waldo and his dancing bear, Bruno."

The Great Waldo was an Abraham Lincoln look-alike, in a stars and stripes outfit and a tall top hat, carrying a long ebony walking stick. A huge muzzled brown bear on a chain followed him into the ring. The band struck up the tune; *I wish I was in Dixie* and the pair danced to its rhythm all around the ring. As the Great Waldo took his bow his hat fell off. It appeared that the bear was also supposed to bow, but for some reason refused. Waldo started poking the animal with his stick, until eventually, but reluctantly, Bruno took his bow. Unfortunately he then stepped back onto the top hat crushing it flat just as the light went out.

Next into the ring came Fernando the Fire-Eater, a Spanish gentleman dressed as a matador. As he breathed fire through a flaming torch, the Jumping Jiminies appeared and somersaulted around him.

Then came Ali Bongo carrying a large, lidded wicker basket, which he placed in the centre of the ring. Sheik

Mustafa immediately followed him, riding on a camel. As the camel toured round the perimeter Ali Bongo lifted the lid and started to play music on a long flute; then out of the basket appeared a large black cobra swaying to the rhythm of the tune.

Ali Bongo and Sheik Mustafa were followed by a trio of clowns, Coco, wearing a sparkling silver one-piece jump-suit with a tall cone-shaped hat: Cosmo in a bowler hat, black tailed jacket and striped trousers, and Calisto, wearing a flat cap and a boiler suit. Just behind them came an Old Mother Riley figure pushing a baby in a pram. The baby wore a large pink bonnet and had an enormous dummy in its mouth. It looked remarkably like the dwarf clown that had been chased by the gorilla at the beginning of the show. The three clowns crowded round the pram and Cosmo pointed to a large yellow flower in his buttonhole. The baby gurgled and tried to grab the flower, only to be doused in water that squirted from the centre of the petals into the baby's face. Old Mother Riley whacked the clown on his head with her umbrella and was then liberally soaked in water. The sketch ended with the baby pulling out a pair of pistols and Mother Riley pulling out a blunderbuss, and the pair chasing the three clowns out of the ring in a cloud of smoke as the blunderbuss went off.

The Ringmaster strode back into the centre and his voice boomed from the loudspeakers.

"I hope you have all enjoyed this little prelude, this small appetizer, this foretaste of the FEAST, of the EXTRAVAGANZA that is now to follow. Permit me now to introduce the first main act of our great show. All the way from Vienna, I give you the internationally acclaimed brother and sister equestrian act of Rudolf and Maria, riding their magnificent Lipizzaner stallions."

This equestrian act was quite superb, involving dressage and the high art of classical riding techniques. The act finished to tumultuous applause from the audience. Kate told Emily that it took about eight years to train a horse to this standard of precision, and that we had seen them before at the Spanish riding School in Vienna.

The Ringmaster emerged again, clapping as he came. When he reached the centre of the ring he said, "I am sure that you will agree with me, Ladies and Gentlemen, when I tell you that you have just witnessed a feast of riding skills unsurpassed in any circus anywhere in the world. Yet our banquet has barely started! You have already enjoyed the hors d'oeuvres, and the equestrian performance by Rudolf and Maria that you have just been privileged to witness, was but the first course of the sumptuous feast that is to follow."

The show continued in this format until the interval, with the Ringmaster introducing a series of big acts interspersed with small cameo performances. We were treated to a group of Chinese acrobats from Beijing who could build human towers out of themselves; a plate spinner from Brazil who could keep fifty plates spinning on poles, all at the same time; a sword swallower from Russia, who could swallow three swords at the same time; a tribe of Red Indians, who used their squaws for target practice; the world's strongest man, who amongst other great feats of strength could bend iron bars with his teeth; and a seal trainer whose seals could balance and head balls better than any professional footballer.

At the interval Meredith came to visit us in our seats. She had brought a vanity case and a small valise containing her clothes with her. I said that I would put them in the boot of Emily's car, ready for the trip to London. Kate then said that we had all been pleasantly surprised by the quality of some of the acts, to which Meredith replied, "Don't you be fooled! Most of the shows aren't like this. It's just that on the first and last days, and occasionally on some special days in between, the bosses splash out and hire in some big acts, which they then put in their advertising, making people think that all the shows are like this. Generally the audience goes away very disappointed; but they work on the fact that many people have short memories, so three or four years later when the show comes round again most people have forgotten, and the kids push their parents into taking them anyway. It's all down to profit and that is why the bosses love to get their hands on acts like Crocodile, because the returns are high for virtually no outlay."

Finally, Meredith said that Crocodile had been well briefed – he knew exactly where the red mark would be and he would pick up his trusty saddlebags containing his disguise on his way out and head as fast as he could pedal towards the Big Wheel, and beyond it to the Dormobile. He had told Meredith that he did not relish the idea of stopping, even for thirty seconds, unless and until he could find a secluded spot in which to put on the disguise. He said to tell us that he would play it by ear.

Finally, the decision to exit the ring would have to be made by him, and she would have to be ready. Meredith had told him that she would slit the canvas as soon as she saw him make his move.

"Lastly," said Meredith, "and I don't understand exactly what he meant, but he just said to tell you, 'Let's hope it's downhill, all the way to the top'."

The format for the second half of the show was a duplicate of the first; with a series of small cameo acts scattered in between the star attractions. The gorilla appeared again as the lights went out, but this time he came from the back of the Big Top, provoking a mixture of screams and laughter as he lurched along a meandering course down to the ring, climbing over seats and people and creating general mayhem as he cut his way through the audience. Finally, when he got to the centre of the ring, the clowns arrived in an old car with its klaxon hooting and chased him round and round the ring. As they careered about, bits started falling off the car, until finally it collapsed in a heap, with smoke pouring out of the engine. The chase continued on foot, round the ring then back up the aisles. It ended with the gorilla appearing on a swing high above the arena, waving to the clowns and to the audience. We guessed that it must have been a different gorilla, a look-a-like, because it would have been impossible for him to make it up there in the few seconds available.

As soon as the debris from the car was cleared the Ringmaster appeared again to introduce Lara and Lash Laroo. Lara had the unenviable task of being strapped to a revolving board, which spun round while Lash Laroo through knives around the shape of her body. When all the knives had been thrown and she was unstrapped from the wheel, her silhouette remained, with its outline picked out in knives. The second part of the act commenced with Lash Laroo wielding a long bullwhip, which he cracked with a sound like a pistol shot. Lara held sheets of paper, which he cut into strips with the whip. She then held a pair of candelabra while Lash extinguished the candle flames. Finally she held a long cigarette in her mouth, which Lash Laroo cut down to a stump. There were parts of this act that neither Kate nor Emily could bear to watch.

There then followed Nellie the Elephant, and Casandra with two miniature ponies. Nellie picked up Casandra with her trunk and put her on her back. Casandra was able to coax and manoeuvre Nellie into all sorts of positions and stances while the two ponies ran between Nellie's legs and jumped over her trunk. At the end of the act Nellie scooped them up, one at a time, and walked around the ring with Casandra and the ponies on her back.

One of the acts involved the twin Twinkle Sisters and a pair of magnificent shire-horses called Cambridge and Lincoln, whose broad backs made excellent platforms for the sisters' acrobatic skills. This included somersaulting simultaneously from one horse to the other as they cantered side by side around the ring.

The Ringmaster entered once again to a trumpet voluntary, and now he stood at the front of the bandstand.

He removed his top hat and bowed low before coming to attention and announcing, "My Lords, Ladies and Gentlemen, I wish to inform you that you are about to be served the penultimate course from our grand banquet. Without further ado, it is my privilege to present to you, direct from Italy, from Rome the eternal city, one of the greatest, nay, in my opinion, *the* greatest trapeze act in the whole world, none other than ... The Fantastic Flying Fellinis."

As the Ringmaster was speaking safety nets covering the whole of the centre of the ring were being installed. The Flying Fellinis entered the ring and one by one climbed rope ladders up to platforms at least fifty feet above the ring. A hushed silence ensued as the audience gazed up at the six figures perched on tiny ledges so high above their heads.

The Flying Fellinis performed for about fifteen minutes and they were undoubtedly spectacular to watch. Frequently all six of them were flying about at the same time, sometimes with as many as four together on a single swing – somersaulting and changing swings gracefully and effortlessly, with impeccably precise timing. At the end of their act they dropped from mid-flight, in pairs, down into the net.

As soon as they had taken their bow the Ringmaster appeared again at the front of the bandstand, once more doffing his top hat and bowing. Then, puffing out his chest and raising his hat and whip high above his head, he said, commencing in hushed, reverential tones, then slowly but surely raising his voice to a crescendo that must have left him hoarse, "My Lords, Ladies and Gentlemen, we have arrived at the moment you have all been waiting for! The final and finest course from our fabulous feast! Persuaded to return, at vast expense, from a long and premature retirement, with his astonishing repertoire of cycling skills and stunts, trick riding on both two wheels and one, the only animal on our planet that possesses such personality and such skills. I have the privilege and great honour to present to you, after a period of so many years, too many years, I give you, once again, the one and only, the unique, the unfathomable, the unmatched – anywhere … at any time … in any other circus in the world. It is none other than our very own and dearly beloved … CROCODILE."

While the Ringmaster had been speaking the circus ring had been cleared of the safety nets and in their place had been positioned a number of ramps of differing heights. As the Ringmaster vanished from the spotlight the band struck up and Crocodile cycled into the centre of the ring. He was dressed in green, all in green, in a long-tailed coat and trousers; even his bow tie and boots were the same shade of green. He wore nothing on his head so that everybody in the audience could see quite clearly that he was a crocodile. He paused for a moment to acknowledge the applause and cheers from the audience. While everybody was still clapping he did a pirouette on the back wheel and then started to ride at ever increasing speed around the ring. He then jumped the bike onto the raised perimeter section and whizzed round at an even greater velocity, finally raising the front wheel and riding at unabated speed in the classic wheelie position. Still on his back wheel he jumped back into the ring and, in ever decreasing circles, returned to the centre and finished with a pirouette.

As the audience rose to its feet in applause I glanced in the direction of where Meredith had said she was going to mark the canvas with a red line and my heart jumped a little when I saw quite clearly that the red line had already appeared and that Meredith was standing just to one side of it in the shadows. I nudged Kate and Emily and pointed in that direction. They both took a long hard look and then grimaced back at me.

"I don't think my nerves can take much more," whispered Kate.

Crocodile was now into a spectacular exhibition on the ramps, doing daredevil leaps, pirouettes, grinds and spins, as he raced the bike around the course.

At some point he had collected a monocycle, which he held above his head as he cycled round. A second later, and without stopping, he had transferred himself to the monocycle and was cycling round a high table, which had suddenly appeared in the centre of the ring. On the tabletop were some skittles, some hoops and a large ball. These were used in turn by Crocodile for juggling acts, which culminated in juggling the skittles or spinning the hoops whilst heading the ball in the air at the same time and then catching it on the end of his snout.

As the audience stood and applauded once more I glanced again in Meredith's direction. She was now standing directly in the spot where she had marked the canvas so I could not see if she had slit it yet.

Suddenly the Ringmaster appeared at Crocodile's side. He raised his hands in the air and then beckoned the audience to quieten down.

"Ladies and Gentlemen," he boomed, "I have been asked by the Management of this great Circus to make a very special announcement ... For your added pleasure and delectation, the Crocodile has been persuaded to add one last death defying act as the finale to his already magnificent performance. He has agreed to ride across the high wire on his monocycle ... WITHOUT A SAFETY NET!"

There followed a series of *oohs* and *ahs* from the audience, in response to which the Ring-master replied:

"It will take five minutes for the Crocodile to prepare himself, anybody of a nervous disposition will have time to leave the BIG TOP before the commencement of this perilous act. I hasten to add that if you do leave you will miss the opportunity to witness a truly great spectacle."

Nobody moved ... everyone seemed riveted to the seats.

"Oh no," wailed Emily, "I can't bear to look! I dread to think what Julius would have thought."

"I can't bear to look either," said Kate swallowing hard. "Don't you think we should get Robert to intervene and try to stop the show?"

"Listen," I said, "just think about it for a couple of seconds. Crocodile is the biggest asset this circus has ever had. Surely they're not going to risk killing him on his first performance and throwing away a fortune. I have a very strong feeling that they'll be using a safety wire, just in case he falls."

"Then why didn't they do that with Meredith's parents?" Kate argued.

"Fair comment," I replied, "but firstly it would have been much more difficult to make trapeze artists secure without the use of a safety net. More importantly it was the first time it had happened and the circus lost not only its best act but also all the future revenues from that act in one horrible accident. I just think that the bosses won't make that mistake again, unless they consider the artiste expendable. Crocodile is too valuable to them."

"I have to agree with Matthew," said Emily. "I apologise for my panic attack but when the Ringmaster made the announcement I just had a vision of poor Hartley wobbling on the wire then plunging to his death. Now, having listened to what Matthew has just said, I honestly do not believe for a moment that the bosses of this circus would risk their fortune on one performance. Besides, everybody in the audience has already paid, and the final show is booked solid. They're not going to make any more money today, so what would be the point?"

"But just say we are wrong!" said Kate.

"Look!" I said, glancing across at Meredith, "I should have enough time to nip round the ring and get Meredith's opinion."

I jumped up and ran round the raised perimeter section of the ring to Meredith.

"I daren't move," she said, "I had already cut the canvas because I thought Crocodile's act was nearly over, so I've got to stand in front of it and hold it together behind my back. I know exactly what you are going to ask me and I think that I can set your mind at rest. It must have been a last minute decision to get Crocodile up onto the high wire, or Big Steve would have told me about it. The reason for the delay now is that they will be fitting a safety band round Crocodile's waist. The band has a steel eye fixed into it and before he starts to cross the wire one of the stage-hands will loop a safety cable under the wire and attach it to the eye with small safety fixings. There will be somebody already on the platforms at each end. They'll make sure he's ok, because of the money, not for Crocodile's safety."

"Thanks' a million for that," I said to Meredith. "I'll get back and put poor Kate out of her misery before Crocodile starts climbing the ladder. Are you sure you are all right?"

"Don't worry one little bit about me," she said. "My only concern at the moment is keeping this canvas tight so that the light doesn't show through the slit. As soon as Crocodile starts his act all eyes will be on him and then I'll be fine."

I dashed back to my seat and arrived to a roll of drums heralding the start of Crocodile's long climb up the rope ladder. It looked remarkably like the rope ladder in my dream, a recurring, troublesome image in my thoughts.

I whispered to Kate and Emily: "Meredith says Crocodile will most certainly be wearing a safety harness so there is absolutely nothing to worry about."

"Not unless he falls off that rope ladder," said Kate, pointing almost vertically up into the air; "it must be at least fifty feet high and you know how Crocodile hates heights."

A single spotlight followed Crocodile up the ladder – he had his monocycle slung over his shoulder. He kept stopping every few rungs but never once did he look down. His long snout was always pointing upwards. Kate, Emily and I, simultaneously heaved a sigh of relief when he eventually reached the top and scrambled awkwardly onto the small platform. As Meredith had predicted, I could just see the outline of another figure on the platform helping him into position. Very gingerly Crocodile straightened into an upright stance. Fifty feet off the ground doesn't sound very high, but having recently done some exterior painting at home at the top of a twenty five foot extension ladder, and even though Kate and I are very accustomed to walking on the high fells of the Lake District, fifty feet vertically up a ladder is stomach upsettingly high. Crocodile had now climbed onto his monocycle and his assistant fed a long balancing pole into his hands. Another minute or two passed as he rocked back and forth, getting the feel of the machine. The audience was deathly silent. Suddenly he launched himself into space and the audience gasped. He pedalled five or six turns forward, then five or six turns back – then he was off – straight across the wire to the other platform without stopping. A great cheer erupted and people clapped and shouted.

We thought that was it – he had done the daring deed and we could all relax a little. That, I hasten to add, was just the beginning of Crocodile's amazing act. He continued his act cycling backwards and forwards across the wire. Then he discarded his pole and did the same again without it. He then rode to the centre and started to juggle with his skittles and hoops. Finally he juggled his skittles and balanced a football on his head at the same time, and then moved the ball back and forth from the top of his skull to the end of his long snout.

Chapter Nine   Oxford And The Circus

The ovation lasted for several minutes, during which time the spotlights were extinguished. The lights came on again suddenly as Crocodile, still on his monocycle and with the football under his arm and a pole in his hand rode into the centre of the ring. The applause from the audience rose to a crescendo as he took his final bows.

As a finale, Crocodile balanced the ball on the pole, and the pole on his snout. He then rode forward and stopped directly in front of us. With a cheeky grin on his face he flicked away the pole and headed the ball straight at us, just as he had done with the Professor when he last escaped from the circus – so it wasn't totally unexpected. I jumped up and caught the ball.

Crocodile immediately spun round and started to pedal furiously around the raised perimeter of the ring. Faster and faster and faster he went ... then suddenly he flew off tangentially heading directly towards Meredith. At the last second Meredith moved to one side, opening the canvas as she did so. Crocodile vanished into the sunlight. Meredith followed him immediately, closing the canvas behind her as she went.

The audience of course thought it was part of Crocodile's act and they continued to clap and cheer until eventually, the Ringmaster appeared in a confused state and announced that, 'he had been informed by the Management', that there had been a small technical problem and that all the performers would not now be appearing in the Grand Finale. The words were spoken hesitantly and in such a way that some people in the audience clearly did not believe him. What started as a low murmur soon erupted into panic, anger and general confusion. Fortunately the stagehands acted quickly, removing the canvas sheets from the exits around the front of the Big Top. Most of the audience had left their seats and made their way down into the circus ring by the time these exits were open and Emily, Kate, and I had no option but to remain in our seats and then follow the general exodus.

As soon as we were clear of the rush, the three of us held a quick powwow. We decided that Kate and I should go back to the Dormobile immediately to make sure that Crocodile was safe inside, and that Meredith had made it to Emily's car. Emily said that she would wait for Robert and his men to come out and then they would all make their way to the Big Wheel. If it was, *all systems go*, Kate would return to Emily at the Big Wheel and they would give Robert his final instructions to ensure that we got safely away.

Kate and I hurried in the direction of the Big Wheel and straight past it towards the car park. We were then 'literally' stopped in our tracks. The carpark had vanished. We were confronted not by an open piece of land, but by an eight foot high fence, behind which was a fleet of large lorries, together with cranes and other pieces of equipment. There was a rifle range close by so we rushed up to the man in charge and asked where the car park had gone because our vehicle was in it.

"It's not gone anywhere," he chuckled, "it's in the same place it was this morning."

"Well how do we get to it?" asked Kate.

"Through the gate," said the man grinning broadly.

"Exactly where is the gate?"

"Now, if you'd asked me that sensible question first, I'd have told you," said the man, stroking his chin, "but you asked me where the car park was and I gave you a straight answer and told you the truth. It's where it's always been, and I am sure your car is still in it."

Under normal circumstances we would have enjoyed the joke, and we have laughed about it a lot since then, but at the time we were extremely anxious about how Crocodile would have coped with this situation. If he'd had his disguise on he could have asked where the car-park was, as we were asking, and he may have been met with the same response – but if he had not been able to put on the disguise he could not have asked the questions we were asking and he wouldn't know where to go.

"I do apologise," retorted Kate. "Please would you kindly tell us where the gate is?"

"If you mean the car park gate – its about 200 yards up there," he said pointing left, "and unless somebody has pinched it, I think you'll find your car in exactly the same place you left it."

Meredith was not in Emily's car so we climbed aboard the Dormobile to be greeted by excited squeaks and croaks from Napoleon.

"Poor Napoleon," said Kate, "we've neglected him terribly, and as things have turned out there was no point in your bringing him with you."

As Kate was speaking and stroking Napoleon's glossy black feathers I was rolling up the carpet for access to the hidden compartment under the floor. I was already experiencing that sinking feeling you get when you know that something is not quite right. I unlocked the trapdoor and peered inside – the compartment was empty.

"I think we had both better go straight back to the Big Wheel and hope that Emily is there with Robert," I said, "and I think we should take Napoleon with us so that he can help us to find Crocodile."

As we approached the Wheel we could clearly see both Emily and Robert, but they were looking up at the wheel, and Emily was shouting and waving, not at us, but at somebody on the Big Wheel.

As we reached her side Emily gasped, "It's Hartley and Meredith, they're stuck up there at the top."

Kate and I gazed upwards, and sure enough there was Meredith sitting next to a gentleman with a big bushy beard.

"Goodness knows what they're doing up there," said Emily, "but Robert has just told me that the motor which powers the Wheel has broken down or fused, or developed some kind of fault, and they can't get it going again."

Fortunately, they did not seem to be in any sort of danger and it did not appear that they had been spotted by the circus folk.

"Perhaps Napoleon can help us after all," I said, rummaging in the holdall and pulling out one of his pouches. I scribbled a short message on a piece of paper and placed it in the pouch with a pencil. I attached the pouch firmly to Napoleon and sent him flying up into the air – a few seconds later and he had landed on Crocodile's shoulder.

We could just see Meredith opening the pouch while Crocodile stroked the big bird. A couple of minutes later Napoleon had delivered the reply.

Kate opened the pouch and read out the note. "Poor Crocodile got lost. Went on Big Wheel so he could see where the Dormobile was parked and how to get to it. He'll explain the rest later."

Meanwhile Robert had spoken with the engineer working on the Wheel.

"I'm afraid it's not good news," Robert said when he returned, "not only has the motor burnt out, but the Wheel has jammed and they can't turn it manually. They may be stuck up there for some time."

"If they can't repair it within a reasonable period of time I think the only solution will be to involve the fire brigade," said Robert. "If you'll excuse me for a little while I'll go and make a few enquires and put the Oxford Fire Brigade Service on notice. There's no point in taking any chances."

Shortly after Robert had left I happened to notice how close the hot air balloon was to the top of the Big Wheel when it was at its highest point at the end of its fixed lines.

Another thing I noticed was that there was a long rope ladder hanging from the side of the balloon's basket. In my mind I was suddenly transported back to my dream

Chapter Nine   Oxford And The Circus

in which Kate and I were trying to rescue Crocodile from the giant hourglass. I then turned to Kate and said, "Why don't we take a balloon flight? There's no queue at the moment and we'll be close enough to Crocodile up there to be able to shout over to him. It's better than just standing here twiddling our thumbs."

"Would you like to come with us Emily?" asked Kate.

"Oh no my dears," said Emily,."I really don't have a head for heights. I'm bad enough on an aeroplane. You go and I'll wait here for Robert."

"What's the rope ladder for?" I asked the balloon man.

"Oh, you won't be needing the ladder here. It's just for emergencies. We have a safety winch and harness onboard as well, because sometimes we operate quite close to trees and the balloon has got snagged on occasion, but that can't happen here. The flight of the balloon is controlled by this winch," he said, pointing to a device with a big handle. "The balloon is also on four fixed ropes which allows it to go no higher than the top of the Big Wheel, so we just winch it down again as the air in the balloon cools, and it's far enough away from the Wheel not to be in any danger."

I purchased two tickets, Kate and I climbed into the basket, and then up we went, getting ever closer to Crocodile and Meredith. Napoleon was having the time of his life flying backwards and forwards between us.

Suddenly Meredith shouted and pointed, "Look down there that's Big Steve and Little John with a band of men coming this way."

There must have been about thirty of them all brandishing dangerous looking implements which we couldn't identify at first, but as they got closer we saw that they were carrying staves, whips, cudgels, knives, and goodness knows what else.

They suddenly spread out and surrounded the Big Wheel. Big Steve cupped his hands and bellowed up at poor Meredith. "Caught you my girl!" he shouted. "Now you'll have some explaining to do."

I saw Emily go up to him and say something but he pushed her roughly away, and then he and a few of the men started to climb up the Big Wheel, like a motley renegade pirate crew boarding an unfortunate galleon, some with their weapons held in their teeth.

It seemed as if my dream was becoming a reality, only some of the detail was inaccurate – it wasn't an hourglass that we were going to try to save Crocodile from – it was a Big Wheel – and I knew that I had only a few seconds to contemplate and to decide my plan.

Firstly, I knew from my dream that we could use the rope ladder to enable Crocodile and Meredith to escape from the top of the Big Wheel into the basket; but then Big Steve and his crew would simply winch us down and capture them both. Even if Robert came back, by the time he had mustered his men, it would probably be too late to save Crocodile and Meredith.

I had to act immediately and decisively, and not worry about the possible consequences of my actions. I took out my Swiss army knife and sliced through the rope connecting the winch to the basket, thus instantly making the winch inoperable so that the balloon could not be wound down. Then I then cut through the cable that worked the burner. The burner supplied the hot air to keep the balloon afloat. The man on the ground operated it remotely. This meant that Kate and I now had control of this operation and we could supply the balloon with enough hot air to keep it level with the top of the Big Wheel.

I shouted over to Crocodile, "Do you fancy a ride in a hot-air balloon? If you remember, Kate and I promised you a flight, so now's your chance ... get ready to catch the rope ladder! You've only got a few seconds before Big Steve and his gang get to you."

As I rolled out the rope ladder I could see that the men were now halfway up the Wheel.

I hurled the rope ladder towards Crocodile and Meredith, but I was well short of my target. I tried again throwing it as hard as I could – but to no avail, and the men were getting ever closer to the top of the Wheel. Napoleon had just landed on my shoulder again and I heard Crocodile shout, "Give the ladder to Napoleon, he'll bring it over!" I gave Napoleon a beak-full of frayed rope at the end of the ladder and launched him in the direction of Crocodile. In the blink of an eye and a couple of flaps of Napoleon's great wings, Crocodile had hold of the rope ladder.

Instantly and heroically he handed it to Meredith. Meredith climbed the first half-dozen rungs of the ladder with Crocodile hanging onto the end. Big Steve's face suddenly appeared only a few feet from Crocodile.

He reached out and grabbed hold of Crocodile's long beard and pulled it clean off.

Big Steve shouted, "I knew it was you, you won't escape me now Crocodile!"

To our astonishment Crocodile looked him in the eye and replied calmly, "I think you are forgetting something! You're forgetting that I am a crocodile, and I am more than capable of giving you a nasty bite that you won't forget in a hurry."

It wasn't obvious whether it was the threat of the bite or hearing Crocodile speak that was the causal factor, but the effect, nevertheless, was akin to the propulsive action of a catapult and it was only extreme good fortune that saved Big Steve from plunging headlong to the ground. It appeared that the garishly obtrusive braces, which supported the giant pair of corduroy trousers he was wearing, had snagged on some invisible protrusion belonging to the Big Wheel. Big Steve was instantly left dangling helplessly in space, attached to the Big Wheel, by courtesy only of his strong elastic braces.

As Big Steve was bouncing up and down like a lead weight on an elastic band, Crocodile pulled up a few rungs of the rope ladder so that he could get one foot onto the bottom rung, but as he was about to launch himself and Meredith from the top of the Big Wheel, another circus hand appeared just below him and managed to grab hold of his saddlebags. To the dismay of the man, Crocodile suddenly opened his mouth very wide, then with one sharp snap of his powerful jaws he bit clean through the leather shoulder strap, leaving the man gaping dumbstruck as Crocodile and Meredith glided gracefully into space on the rope ladder.

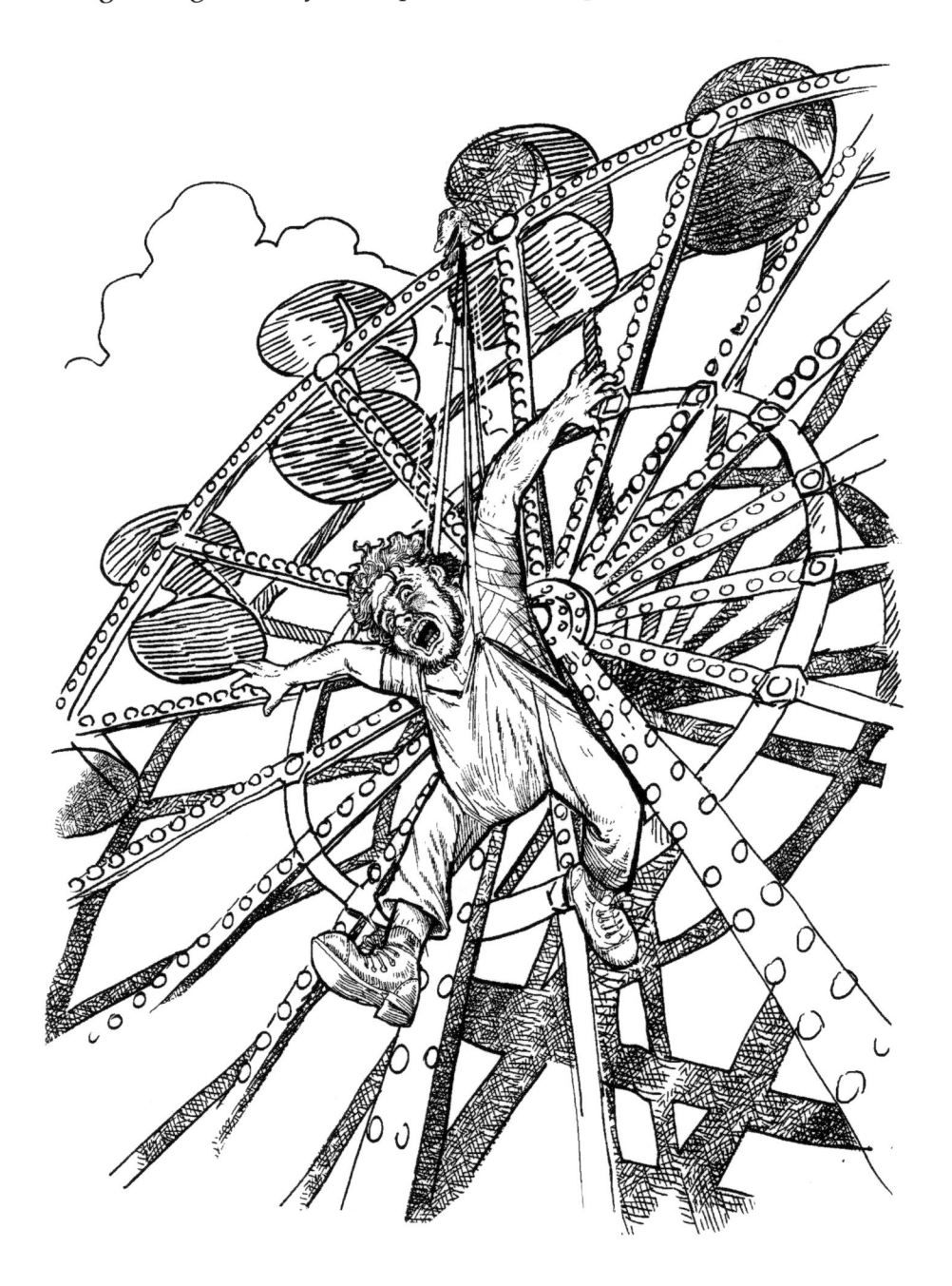

The circus staff on the ground suddenly ran en masse into the balloon enclosure and immediately started to haul on the four ropes that tied the balloon and its basket to the ground. As Kate and I were pulling Meredith and Crocodile into the basket the balloon had started to descend very slowly, as the air in the balloon cooled, and now, slightly faster due to the increased weight in the basket. Suddenly, Kate grabbed my arm and pointed over the side of the basket. I looked over to see that about twenty men led by Little John had surrounded the basket. We heard Little John shout, "Quick Lads, grab the ropes and we'll haul the balloon down!"

Five or six men grabbed each of the four tie ropes and started to haul. Kate immediately responded with a long blast of hot air, but to no avail and the balloon and basket started to descend more rapidly.

"We'll have to cut the ropes!" I shouted.

"I've got my knife ready," said Meredith.

"Mine went with my poor saddlebags," bemoaned Crocodile, "but don't worry, I'll bite through that rope in a jiffy."

"We'll take one each," I said.

The balloon was now being hauled down relentlessly and I could hear Little John shouting, "Heave with all your might Lads. We've got 'em now. They can't escape."

Crocodile, Meredith, and I severed three of the ropes almost simultaneously and the basket lurched violently to one side hurling us all into a heap in the corner. We scrambled up and peered over the side to observe three piles of men where the ropes had been cut. The others still hanging on to the rope, on the last corner, were now several feet off the ground and dangling in mid-air

Kate moved to the burner to give the balloon another blast of hot air.

"Hang on a second Kate," I shouted, "let me cut the rope first!"

"Please allow me," said Crocodile. He leant over the side just as the three piles of pirates were mustering themselves to help their comrades hanging on to the one remaining rope.

One quick snap of Crocodile's teeth and the balloon shot into the air. Peering over the side again we could now see one big pile of men and Little John standing shaking his fist as the balloon took us out of their reach.

"Look, there's Emily and Robert," Kate pointed out. "Poor Emily and poor Robert! They'll be wondering what they've got themselves involved with. I can't begin to think how many laws we are breaking just now, not least of which is stealing a hot-air balloon and endangering human life."

"Yes, but there are very strong mitigating circumstances. I just hope we get a judge who's sympathetic and likes crocodiles," I said, winking at Crocodile.

Unfortunately for Big Steve, the defining image of our escape in the hot-air balloon had to be the sight of that unfortunate giant suspended from the top of the Big Wheel by his own braces.

"Poor Steve," said Meredith, "he'll never live this down. I do hope that the bosses of the Circus aren't too hard on him. After all, it was hardly his fault that Crocodile escaped out of the ring during the show, and looking at him now, nobody could deny that he risked life and limb to try and stop Crocodile getting away."

As the balloon gained height it started to drift towards Oxford; towards, as Matthew Arnold memorably described that hallowed profusion of glorious buildings, *'That sweet city with her dreaming spires'*."

"I remember you telling me about the Montgolfier brothers," said Crocodile, looking at me. "You said that if a genie were to give you the chance to witness any event in the whole of human history, you would probably choose to be there at the very first manned flight, in Paris in 1783, in front of Louis XVI and Marie Antoinette. I don't think that the pilots of that balloon, the Marquis d'Arlandes, and Monsieur Pilatre de Rozier, would have been more overjoyed than I am at his moment. I have regained my liberty once more, and up here in this balloon, I feel as free as a bird."

"I feel exactly the same," said Meredith. "It's as if I also have broken free of my shackles and that this flight in the balloon is both a flight to freedom, and a flight to a new and much happier life."

"I remember you telling me that the Montgolfiers' balloon landed more than five miles away from where it took off in Paris," said Crocodile. "How far do you think we'll get in this one?"

"Well we certainly have a much better fuel than they had, but unfortunately we have only one small cylinder of propane gas and the fuel-gauge is showing less than a quarter full. It was half full when Kate and I first got into the basket and I don't know how accurate it is. I suppose the balloon man would have a rough idea how many short flights were possible on one full cylinder, and even if it ran out it wouldn't matter because the balloon would simply drift back down to the ground. I intend to land the balloon at the first opportunity but preferably not amongst Oxford's dreaming spires."

We had risen to about a thousand feet and we were now drifting directly towards Oxford. I was becoming increasingly concerned that we might not make it to the other side of the city. I decided instantly to aim for Christ Church Meadow, because it was a big expanse of open land with sports grounds and Merton Field surrounding it, and it was also directly on our perceived flight path. I told Kate not to use any more gas and as the balloon lost height we seemed on a good course for a landing in the Meadow.

Down and down came the balloon, but unfortunately I realised too late, the balloon had drifted to the Merton Field end of Christ Church Meadow and we were still about three hundred feet above the ground. I could see Christ Church Cathedral looming directly in front of us as we drifted over Broad Walk and the corner of Merton Field. I was also aware that Deadman's Walk was on the other side of the Field, but fortunately that did not appear to be beckoning us and the balloon was apparently homing in on the very centre of the city. I shouted to Kate for more air and although, thankfully, we instantly gained height, Merton Field, our safe landing ground, was now behind us.

We drifted slowly over Merton College and University College and the target of the balloon now appeared to be the magnificent cupola of the Radcliffe Camera.

CROCODILE   K. Trevor Wigglesworth

As we approached the Camera, I was about to shout for more hot air when we hit some turbulence and the basket started to swing from side to side as we hovered just a few feet above top centre of the cupola.

I called again for more hot air and instantly we were drifting more or less back in the direction we had just come. This time we passed over Oriel and Corpus Christi Colleges and thankfully back towards Merton Field.

My new found optimism was soon dashed as I realised that the balloon's new target appeared to be the roof of Christ Church Cathedral and my heart missed a beat when a quick glance at the needle on the fuel-gauge indicated that the cylinder was empty. I then realised to my horror that we were precisely on a collision course with the Cathedral roof. I had no choice but to tell Kate to give us another blast of hot air and hope for the best.

"That's enough!" I gestured, when I saw that we would just make it over the ridge of the roof.

We cleared the roof of Christ Church Cathedral by no more than a few inches. We were now directly over Tom Quad and I could see the great gate tower, Tom Tower, looming ahead. This huge structure was our next major obstacle. I was about to shout for more hot air but when I looked again, Tom Tower was still more or less the same distance away, and we were hovering above the centre of the Quad where the air must have been very still. Kate and Meredith and Crocodile were peering directly over the side of the basket and I heard Kate exclaim, "Oh my goodness we've arrived slap bang in the middle of a ceremony – they're all there in their caps and gowns and general regalia ... good heavens! I think that's The PLC at the head of the procession!"

As the balloon drifted gently down I rummaged in my bag and pulled out Crocodile's spare beard.

"Quickly!" I said. "Put this beard on and button your coat up, it looks as though you're going to be introduced to the Dean, to the Professor's great friend and colleague, Professor Peregrine Lancelot Crisp."

"Oh, I've met him already, many times, although he doesn't know it," replied Crocodile. "He was a frequent guest at the Professor's dinner parties. If you remember, I told you that I used to hide in the priests' hole and listen to the conversation. Professor Crisp nearly always sat next to the Marquis de Vendance. I believe that I know more about him than he would wish to be known."

"Five, four, three, two, one," – BUMP – "The Eagle has landed!" shouted Meredith.

Under normal circumstances, if these could ever have been described as normal circumstances, I am sure we would all have jumped for joy and hugged each other with great relief. Instead we composed ourselves for the encounter that was shortly to follow. I could now clearly see The PLC. Marching towards us at the head of a bemused body of indignant dons.

"I think you had better fire the first salvo," I said, nudging Kate, "he had an eye for you last night, so you will most certainly disarm him more easily than I could."

"What the deuce do you think you are doing?" bellowed a belligerent PLC as he marched up to the basket.

A demure yet effusive Kate put on an Oscar winning performance, which rooted Crisp to the spot.

Without going into detail and suffice it to say that, having had some considerable experience in the psychology of male/female relationships, I knew instinctively that it was prudent to let Kate and Meredith handle Crisp while I attended to Crocodile's disguise behind them.

"Oh thank goodness it's you Peregrine," purred Kate. "Let me introduce you to Meredith Holt. Meredith, this is Professor Peregrine Lancelot Crisp." Without stopping for a response Kate continued, "By an amazing coincidence, only last night Peregrine was asking about William Hartley Crocodile, Professor Julius Septimus Merryweather's protégé. A refugee from persecution and graduate of this University. We are delighted to inform you, indeed to inform you all," continued Kate raising her head, her arms and her voice in unison as she addressed the wider gathering, "that we have just managed to rescue Mr. Crocodile from his captors. We had intended to land in Christ Church Meadow, but unfortunately we were running low on fuel and were unable to make a controlled landing there. We apologise most sincerely for interrupting your ceremony and beg your forgiveness for this unplanned and untimely end to our flight of mercy. Now, may I present to you Professor Crisp, and to your illustrious colleagues ... our refugee from persecution, and your fellow alumnus, MR. WILLIAM HARTLEY CROCODILE!"

As Crocodile moved forward, now resplendent in a fine beard, and with Napoleon on his shoulder, The PLC raised his hands and started to clap. He had naturally and instantly assumed the role of an informed collaborator in the rescue of

Julius' protégé and now appeared eager to bask in the glory of the enterprise. A great cheer echoed round Tom Quad and as Peregrine raised his cap, the others followed suit.

Crocodile raised his arms and spoke in an emotional voice: "Good afternoon Professor Crisp. Good afternoon ladies and gentlemen. I thank you from the bottom of my heart for your courteous reception in such trying circumstances. I would, however, remind you, that my real identity must, for the time being, remain a secret. I also have a confession to make … that is … and it may or may not surprise you … that this fine beard I am wearing is false and there for the purpose only of concealing my true identity. I hope that you will understand and respect the delicacy of my situation. I am sure that one day the full reality of my unique position will be revealed; until then I humbly crave your indulgence. I know that you are all honourable men and trust that you will grant my request."

"BRAVO!" cried The PLC. "Three hearty cheers for William Hartley Crocodile, HIP … HIP … HOORAH!" Everybody shouted, "Hoorah, Hoorah, Hoorah for William Hartley Crocodile!"

Just at that moment an anxious-looking Emily arrived on the scene followed by an even more perturbed looking Robert.

"Oh thank goodness you are all safe!" said Emily. "Robert and I feared that you would all be killed."

"My Dear Emily," boomed The PLC, "do come and join our little celebration in honour of the heroic rescue of Julius' protégé, William Hartley Crocodile. We have drinks and nibbles laid on in the Great Hall, and you are all most welcome to join us."

I said that Kate and I would just secure the balloon envelope and make things safe, and then we would join them. When we looked up we saw that Peregrine had his arm round Crocodile's shoulder as they walked with Emily, at the head of the procession to the Great Hall.

Meredith said that she would help us to tidy up the balloon. As we were dragging out and folding the envelope I asked Meredith how she had managed to get stuck at the top of the Big Wheel with Crocodile.

"It was that new Lorry Park that created the confusion, and I realised immediately that Crocodile would have had a problem," Meredith explained. "I know my way about the fairground site so I found the Dormobile and Emily's car without too much trouble. As soon as I looked under the Dormobile I knew that Crocodile wasn't in there because I could see that the grass underneath the vehicle had not been disturbed. If he had rolled underneath to get inside the secret door that you told me about, the grass would have been flattened, but it stood proud and untouched. Just to make sure, I banged very loudly on the side of the Dormobile and shouted, 'Crocodile, it's Meredith, can you hear me? Bang on the side if you are in there.' But I was met with complete silence. I decided that I had better go and look for him and as I cut back through the fairground I saw this bearded gentleman at the top of the Big Wheel and knew it must be him. The Wheel was rotating very slowly so I ran up to the man fiddling with the motor and he told me that they were having a problem and that he couldn't get it to stop. As Crocodile came down, I jumped in with him thinking that perhaps if I did one revolution it would be a good opportunity to survey both the whole of the fairground and the circus site, to see if Big Steve and Little John had organised a posse to search for Crocodile. I thought that if I knew exactly where they were and which direction they were heading in I could plan a safe route back to the Dormobile with Crocodile. Unfortunately, the Big Wheel did only another half-revolution and stopped dead with Crocodile and me at the very top ... I think you know the rest."

Chapter Nine

Oxford And The Circus

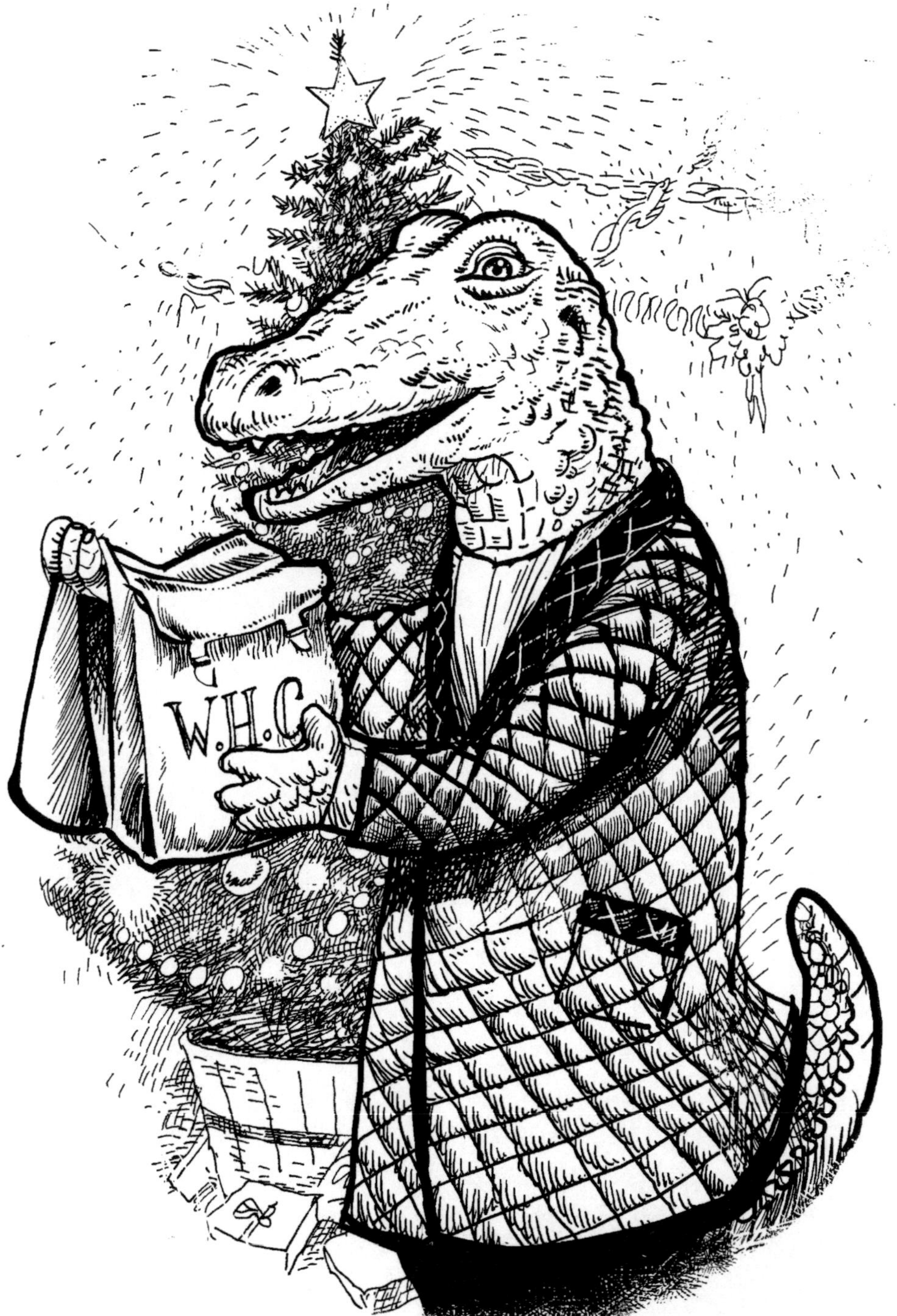
W.H.C

Chapter Ten
Christmas At Windermere

We made the decision to leave Oxford late that night and to return directly to the Lake District with Crocodile. This was made substantially more possible because Robert had instructed a small party of his men to collect the Dormobile from the circus and to drive it to the college. Robert kindly offered to follow us in the bus, with his men, for the first few miles of our journey to make absolutely sure that we were not being followed. We did not want to risk another kidnap attempt, which I felt was a possibility if news leaked out that we had landed the balloon at an Oxford college. Emily had begged us to stay the night but a gut feeling told me to go while the coast was clear. Robert and his men had to leave that night so their protection would not be available in the morning. I discussed my intended route with Robert, which was an exact reversal of the way I had come with Napoleon. We agreed that Robert would escort us as far as Burford, and then they would wait for twenty minutes and check all vehicles that passed through the village to make absolutely sure that we were not being followed. Robert thought that ten minutes would have been long enough, but twenty would be a *belt and braces* approach. We agreed that even if we were being followed, our journey home from Burford would be unknown to any possible pursuer, and given the meandering route I had chosen it would be practically impossible to find us. I couldn't help a wry smile at Robert's use of the word *braces*, and I knew that for the rest of my life, whenever I heard that word it would instantly conjure up the image of Big Steve dangling helplessly at the top of the Big Wheel.

Robert had simply told the balloon man that his balloon had been commandeered by the police, as part of an undercover operation by MI5, to free a political prisoner and that he would be handsomely compensated for his services, and for the use of the balloon. He had given the man his card and telephone number. Emily had already told Robert that she would release the funds necessary to more than fully compensate the balloon man for any loss he may have incurred. She told me that the money would be paid from her joint account with Hartley, the one that Julius had set up. I offered to pay, because the decision to use the balloon for our escape was entirely mine. Emily wouldn't hear of it, telling me, in no uncertain terms, that the balloon was procured, or more accurately, *hijacked*, for the sole purpose of rescuing Hartley – and that was the end of the matter. To this day I do not know if Robert may have suspected what was really going on. He may have linked the two characters in the belief that Crocodile, or Hartley wasn't a real crocodile. On the other hand he may have had no idea that Hartley was the performing crocodile at the circus. He didn't ask, so I didn't volunteer any more information.

Emily had told us at the reception that Peregrine and Hartley had got on, *like a house on fire,* as they had both tripped down memory lane with reminiscences of good times with Julius. When Hartley had finally taken his leave, Peregrine had offered him an academic post at the University, if ever he had a mind to follow in Plato's footsteps, telling him that it would be good to work with someone who had the ability to put a new slant on philosophy. She had concluded by saying, "Isn't it exciting to think that Hartley could one day take over from where Julius had prematurely left off?"

As we said a tearful goodbye to our new and faithful friend Meredith, Crocodile, Kate and I promised that we would make arrangements with Emily for her to come and spend some time with us in the very near future. It was Meredith who had both taken care of Crocodile in his captivity, and had made his escape possible. Without her we would probably not have succeeded in rescuing him, and for that we would be eternally grateful.

Even though, after Robert had left us at Burford, the chance of being followed was infinitesimally minute, I still kept looking in the rear view mirror of the Dormobile all the way home. I had become anxious at times when a following vehicle got too close or stayed for a long time behind us, and I breathed a long and happy sigh of relief when we finally arrived at Bannerigg, beholding once more our beloved Windermere, now partially shrouded in mist in the early morning light. I had awakened Kate and Crocodile as we passed Staveley, and I told Crocodile that this was the first view of Windermere that used to excite me so much, every time I came to the Lake District with my parents when I was young. A great cheer always went up as soon as we got our first glimpse of the lake. Kate said that she used to come with her parents, from Kendal on the bus, and she used to get just as excited at this sudden unexpected sight of the lake. I said that when Alfred Wainwright first came to the Lakes he wouldn't have seen the lake from here because he had arrived by train. Then he went up Orrest Head, which was his first sighting of the lake, and it was that experience that changed his life forever.

Crocodile asked if we could stretch our legs and perhaps walk up to the top of Orrest Head just as Wainwright had done on his first trip to the Lake District.

"I think it's his island he really wants to see," said Kate winking at me.

I brought the binoculars from the Dormobile and the three of us, or rather four of us, because Napoleon didn't want to miss out on some fresh air, made our way up Orrest Head from just north of Windermere Station. When we reached the top, the mist had cleared enough to make Crocodile's Island, just visible in the far distance. I handed the binoculars to Crocodile. He gazed at his island for several minutes without saying a word. Finally, he turned to us and said, "When I was in that cage at the circus I sometimes felt I might never see my island again. Then I remembered the Professor telling me that even if he lost all his money it wouldn't unduly bother him, he'd simply start all over again. Although, when you are locked in a cage and about to be transported to some remote spot on the planet it isn't easy to be optimistic. I remembered reading about all those poor souls who were deported to Australia, and the slaves that were shipped out from Africa to America. I have to admit that I was beginning to think that my cup was much less than half empty, but then on that first visit from Meredith, when she told me that Matthew and Kate were looking for a dog called Hartley, I knew instantly that it was you and that you had come to rescue me. Suddenly my cup was full to over brimming, and I knew that you would find a way to help me to escape. I knew then that it would not be long before I saw my island again."

Half an hour later and we were back home. We parked the Dormobile by the lake and walked down to the boathouse with Crocodile and Napoleon, fully intending to sail over to the island with them, but Crocodile said, "I think you need a very long sleep Matthew. You must be exhausted after all that driving and I need to get back to poor old Sherwood. He'll be thinking I've deserted him. What is eminently more sensible is that I sail over on my own with Napoleon and, if I may ask one more favour of you, that we meet here again in the morning, and we'll go for a walk round Tarn Hows, just as we did on our first outing in the Lake District."

We hugged each other and then Kate and I stood and watched and waved while Crocodile, with Napoleon standing proudly on his shoulder, made his way back home.

It astonished us how quickly life got back to normal after our return to the Lake District. That is, if life with Crocodile could ever be described as normal – but it had most definitely become so for us, and it was now hard to imagine our lives without him. I remembered one of the last things that Emily had said to us when we were discussing Meredith's situation with her, "Goodness gracious!" she had said. "Christmas will soon be upon us and I haven't even thought about my preparations for this year. What with my trip to America, and now all this drama with Hartley coming on top of everything else. I've been up to my eyes trying to sort out Julius' affairs and I haven't given Christmas a thought. Julius started planning in earnest in October and he always endeavoured to make those few special days near the end of December the highlight of our year. He was kept especially busy because of the workload from his charities, so he had to start planning early. Nevertheless, he always believed that life would be a much poorer affair if there was no Christmas to look forward to and to enjoy."

I had replied by saying that Kate and I would love to have Emily and Meredith stay with us this Christmas, and I was sure Hartley would be delighted to make Christmas lunch for us all. I had told Emily that I would get him motivated as soon as we arrived back home, and that it would help to take his mind off his capture, and narrow escape. The likelihood was that Crocodile would want to invite us all to lunch in his cave, but I decided that I wouldn't mention the cave to Emily just yet – for the time being it would still remain a closely guarded secret.

At the beginning of December I had undertaken a mission, an undertaking, which for the time being I wished to keep secret. It involved my leaving Kate to keep an eye on Crocodile, because we felt that it was much too soon to leave him on his own, even for a few days. I had started the necessary research long before our trip to London, and while at first I had drawn nothing but blanks, information that had arrived at home while we were in Oxford had proved much more positive. And so I departed in an optimistic frame of mind, and with the feeling that my mission would be successful. When I returned there was still a week to go to Christmas and enough time to put all the finishing touches to our plans, to make our first Christmas with Crocodile the best Christmas ever.

While I was away Kate and Crocodile had been very busy collecting and foraging for a host of items to use as decoration and for the Christmas table, mostly from the countryside around Crocodile's island. They had decided that Christmas Eve would be spent at our house and Christmas Day in Crocodile's cave. This was to be a complete surprise for Emily and Meredith who were not to be told about the cave until we arrived there on Christmas Day. On my return I was delighted to find that all the decoration and adornment, both in the house and in the cave, was nearly complete.

Kate said that she and Crocodile had agreed that to make Christmas unforgettable, and to make it very special they had decided to include the best ideas that they could find from both Victorian and Edwardian Christmases.

Crocodile told us that the Professor had informed him that the tradition of decorating the house with evergreens was thought by the Romans to bring good luck, and the idea wasn't started by the Christians, but was a part of the Roman festival of Saturnalia. Evergreens generally symbolized everlasting life, but the holly and the ivy had special significance. Holly was sacred to Saturn and its red berries symbolized male sexuality, whereas ivy symbolized female sexuality, fertility and new life. The Professor had told him that ivy was dedicated to the god Bacchus, who wears a crown entwined with ivy. The Christian Church has continued the symbolism, depicting the spiked leaves of holly as Christ's crown of thorns, and the red berries as Christ's blood.

Kate asked what the Professor had said about mistletoe. Crocodile said that he didn't know how the tradition of kissing under mistletoe had started, but mistletoe was considered by the Druids to be a gift from heaven making the tree it inhabited sacred, and especially so if it was an oak tree.

"So there you are," said Kate with a smile, "our mistletoe has come from our own sacred oak tree by the lake, our holly and ivy from our garden, and our Christmas tree from Crocodile's island."

The weather in December had been mild up until the Christmas week, but by the time I went to meet Emily and Meredith at Oxenholme Station on Christmas Eve, there was a sharp nip in the air, tempered only slightly by a watery sun in the clear azure sky, but if you were well wrapped up it was a fine day to be out.

The train from London was on time, though I had arrived early in order to get a parking space. I could hear the noise and feel the vibration when the train passed over my head, as I made my way through the tunnel under the line, to the northbound platform.

"Happy Christmas!" I shouted as Emily and Meredith alighted from the carriage. "Happy Christmas Emily, Happy Christmas Meredith."

"We'll be with you in a minute," Emily called back.

I stood there in some amazement as two mountains of gift-wrapped parcels also emerged from the carriage, seemingly of their own volition, but then with the realisation they were supported on human frames.

"These two nice gentlemen kindly offered to help us down with our luggage and bits and pieces," said Emily.

The men put all the parcels down gently on the platform and then returned for the ladies' suitcases, which thankfully, were of more modest proportions.

Having thanked the gentlemen for their kindness, Emily and Meredith turned all their attention on me, and there followed a warm exchange of hugs and kisses, and Happy Christmases all round.

"It's lucky I came in the Dormobile and not in Kate's little car," I said with a smile as we bundled everything into the vehicle.

"Meredith and I have had a wonderful time in London, buying all our Christmas presents, haven't we Meredith?" said Emily. Meredith nodded, and smiled. "Meredith has been a boon to me in helping to sort out Julius' affairs, and after all the hard work we have done, we felt we thoroughly deserved our little shopping treat, didn't we Meredith?" Meredith smiled again.

"By the way, I had a Christmas card from Robert just the other day. It had a picture of a hot-air balloon on the front and Robert had drawn in a Big Wheel, and a caricature of Big Steve hanging from it. He also put in a note to say that he had squared things with the balloon man, and that he was sure that the matter had now been laid to rest," Emily added.

Just at that moment we were passing Kate's old house on Oxenholme Road, so I slowed down and pointed it out to them. "I have just got to call at the market in Kendal to pick up some fresh fruit and vegetables that Kate has ordered. They should be boxed up and ready, so the detour will only take a couple of minutes," I told them.

I purposely drove back to Bowness the way I had returned from Oxford, in order to surprise the girls with that first view of the lake from Bannerigg. Meredith had never been to the Lake District before, so I knew that it would be a special moment for her when she got her first glimpse of the lake. I imagine that the sudden unexpected view of a lake nestling in a valley, almost anywhere, would quicken the heart. I then drove through Windermere, now bedecked with fairy lights, decorations, and a beautiful Christmas tree. We moved on to Bowness Bay and beheld the wonderful view, down Windermere to Fairfield and its companion fells beyond Ambleside, with the largest island, Belle Isle to the left, and the white boats bobbing about on the blue water.

When we reached the house, Crocodile had already arrived and he and Kate were standing on the doorstep waiting to greet us. Big hugs and kisses were again the order of the day, and such was the excitement that it took some considerable time to get everybody down the stairs into our living room.

"Oh how wonderful!" exclaimed Emily as she beheld a room that looked distinctly like Santa's grotto. Kate and Crocodile had really pushed the boat out with their decorations and the big Christmas tree against the back wall looked magnificent lit up in all its silver glory. A grand log fire was burning merrily, with bowls of chestnuts in the hearth waiting to be roasted.

"What incredible views of Windermere and the mountains," said Meredith, moving towards the windows. "Which ones are those?"

"Directly opposite, is the Old Man of Coniston," I said, pointing, "and to the left of the Old Man is Dow Crag, and to the right, Swirl How, and Wetherlam. The rollercoaster ones are Crinkle Crags, behind which is the highest mountain in England, Scafell Pike. Finally the one to the far right is Bow Fell. Now from upstairs, as you will see from your bedroom window, you can see right down the lake to Fairfield, behind which is Helvellyn. Ambleside nestles at the end of the lake, but is hidden from our view by the trees on Claife Heights just over there. Looking down the lake, it is almost the same view that I showed you from Bowness Bay, but from a higher elevation. You will also see just above the tree-line, to the right of Bow Fell, the tops of the Langdale Pikes."

"You must need to freshen up, so I'll show you to your bedrooms which are back upstairs. People often think that this is an *upside down house*, but it isn't, it's simply that the bedrooms are all on the upper floor along with the main entrance," explained Kate. "Do take your time, and when you come down we'll have a bite to eat. Would you prefer tea to drink or something more seasonal?"

"Tea for me please," replied Emily.

"And for me," said Meredith.

"What about something to eat?" Kate asked.

"We had a good snack on the train, so just a small sandwich or a piece of cake will be fine." Emily replied.

By the time the girls returned Kate and Crocodile had everything ready and loaded onto two large wooden trays.

Emily and Meredith thought that taking the best ideas from the Victorians and the Edwardians and making this a traditional Christmas was a wonderful idea.

"Julius would have been thrilled," said Emily with a hint of sadness in her eyes, "he would have thought it a *capital idea, just his cup of tea*. I am sure that is exactly what he would have said."

"Of course it will be a vegetarian Christmas," exclaimed Crocodile, "but Kate and I promise that you won't miss the turkey or the goose. We have such a variety of wonderful food for us all, some of which can even be carved like a turkey, and the recipe for the gravy is to die for, so I promise that you will not be disappointed."

The two big trays were now set in front of us, with plates piled high with festive sandwiches, warm mince pies dusted with icing-sugar, Christmas cake that I knew Kate had been infusing with brandy and liqueurs since October, together with other delicacies in festive shapes and colours, of which red, green, silver, and white predominated.

As we were about to tuck in, the sound of Christmas carols floated on the air. I looked out of the window to see one of the big boats, The Swan, sailing very close to the shore in front of the house. There was a brass band playing on board, and the boat was packed with Christmas cruisers.

"That was good timing," I said with a wink. "We went to a lot of trouble to lay on the carols for you and with no expense spared!"

The entertainment for the evening comprised for the most part, Charades, and a game called Dumb Crambo, which Emily suggested. Both were guessing games, which had to be acted out, and Crocodile did much of the acting in an array of improvised costumes and beards while the rest of us did the guessing. We also had a singsong around the piano, and as Meredith and Emily were much better pianists than I was, they did most of the playing.

Kate and Meredith, who were Roman Catholics, had planned to go to Midnight Mass in Kendal and I would accompany them to do the driving. Because of this Kate and Crocodile had made an enormous bowl of what, after midnight, when warmed, would become mulled wine, and contained bottles of Crocodile's vintage claret plus many other secret spicy ingredients. So the drinking of alcoholic beverages was to be postponed, at least for Kate, Meredith and myself, until after our return from church, when Crocodile would have supper ready for us.

I can't even remember now what time it was when I finally crawled into bed but I knew that Santa Claus would have nearly finished his rounds. When I went with Crocodile down to the jetty to see him off home I thought we might just be lucky enough to see Santa and his sleigh and reindeer flying down the lake. We had to smuggle Crocodile out of the house very secretively because Emily and Meredith had still not been told about Crocodile's island and had probably presumed that he lived with us. We had all hung our stockings with care on the mantelpiece but in the morning I would have to inform them that Santa had decided to leave all our presents in a cave across the lake.

We awakened to a perfect Christmas Day. Jack Frost had been busy again sprinkling every tree, every bush, and every blade of grass with sparkling crystals of ice. Although there was no snow on the ground, the fell-tops glistened snow-white in the morning sunshine and the surface of Windermere shone.

When Emily and Meredith came downstairs, Kate and I had prepared to make our confessions. We told them that Crocodile did not live with us and that the Professor had constructed a wonderful but rather unusual residence for him on the other side of the lake. We told them that we had kept it a secret until now in order to protect Crocodile and it was of course of the utmost importance that the secret remained within his small group of special friends. Crocodile had invited us all to Christmas lunch and we would shortly be making the trip across the lake in our neighbours' launch, which they had kindly lent to us for the day.

"I always suspected that Julius was up to something like this," said Emily. "He spent so much time away with Hartley that I knew something was going on. Oh I do hope he has made it comfortable for Hartley. He was used to the very best in Bayswater. I do hope he has not put poor Hartley in some detestable garret."

"You can rest assured," I replied, "Hartley lives in a delightfully eccentric, but extremely comfortable ... err, how exactly would you describe Crocodile's abode Kate?"

"I would think that, a grand basement apartment, with some interesting and unique features, would be a good description," said Kate.

"Yes, set in an island paradise," I suggested.

"How intriguing," said Emily. "I should have known that Julius would find something suitable for Hartley."

"Well you will see it for yourself shortly, because we are expected there within the hour."

Before we were half way across the lake we could see Crocodile standing on a rock, waving to us, with Napoleon on his shoulder. As we neared his island we observed that he was dressed in a costume that distinctly resembled one of the Three Wise Men. He had on a long brilliant red gown with an ermine collar and a golden turban on his head, and he held a staff in his hand that was remarkably similar to a bishop's crook.

"Welcome to my island," he said, beaming at us all and hooking the launch with his crook as we pulled in to the shore. "A Merry Christmas to you all."

"Merry Christmas, Crocodile!" we shouted back, with the exception of Emily, who still could only bring herself to call him Hartley.

"A very Happy Christmas to you Hartley," she cried.

"Merry Christmas! Merry Christmas!" Napoleon croaked.

Kate and I were very apprehensive as we approached the entrance to his cave, but much to our relief Crocodile had gone to some considerable trouble with the lighting in the cave, because with the great rock door now fully open, the warm glow from inside was most inviting – in complete contrast to my visit on that awful night when I had returned from Oxford to collect Napoleon.

As we entered the cave we observed that Crocodile had hung illuminated Chinese lanterns everywhere, with brightly coloured festive streamers, intertwined with tinsel, decorating the walls and roof of the cave. The cold stone steps were now carpeted in a rich crimson carpet, which gave an added feeling of warmth.

When we emerged into the cavern it was almost as bright as day, or seemingly so, because Crocodile had used every means possible to enhance the light. The huge chandelier that hung from the domed ceiling now had enormous candles on it and the oil lamps were doubled in quantity. Notwithstanding this, he had decorated almost every surface with tinsel and silver foil, and most of the natural decorations such as pinecones, larch and holly, had been sprayed silver.

"Crikey!" gasped Meredith. "This is the most wonderful place I have ever been in. It sparkles like a cave of diamonds – I am quite sure Santa's grotto would not be more spectacular."

"Well I certainly think Hartley deserves ten out of ten for his Christmas decoration," agreed Emily.

"Please let me take your coats," said a delighted Crocodile, "but I have to confess that a lot of the credit must go to Kate. Many of the ideas were hers, but in the end I got a little carried away and, if I have to be honest, probably over-egged the pudding. I do hope that I have not done the same with the Christmas plum pudding."

He took our coats and then led us to two big sofas that were angled towards each other and placed in front of his fireplace. The wood-burning stove, with its doors open, was blazing away and all the stockings had been hung again with care around the mantelpiece. Santa must have taken them from where we had hung them on Christmas Eve on our fireplace and rearranged them, now bulging with presents, around Crocodile's fine ingle-nook fireplace.

As soon as we had all seated ourselves, Crocodile, with a fancy flourish, presented each of us with a very grand menu.

"I have just described the main courses," he said; "but there are also a few additional surprises which I haven't included."

Opening the menus and with widening eyes and watering mouths we read about the feast that was to follow:

MENU

'CROCODILE'S CHRISTMAS DINNER'

Wild Mushroom and Truffle Bouchees.

Carol Singers' Winter Vegetable and Chestnut Soup
with a selection of home-made breads

Crocodile's Christmas Souffle Tart

Passion Fruit and Lime Sorbet

Nutty Yuletide Log
with Santa's Surprise Christmas Parcels

Accompanied by Parsley Potato Stars,
Light Gratin Dauphinoise Lemony Vegetables,
Crunchy Brussels Sprouts, Whole Baby Carrots,
and Christmas Couscous.

Followed by:

A trio of Crocodile's homemade cheeses with biscuits

Traditional Christmas Plum-Pudding flamed in Brandy

Coffee, Mince Pies and Christmas cake

Each course will be accompanied by Crocodile's personal
selection from his finest Wines

"Goodness gracious!" said Emily with a deep intake of breath. "It's more exotic than dining at Maxim's! And with that number of courses we'll all end up looking like Hartley's Christmas Plum Puddings."

"We have a lot to celebrate," I replied,."This feast is not only about Christmas, it's also a celebration of Crocodile's freedom, so let's give thanks, for we have much to be thankful for. Eat, drink, and be merry."

Suddenly we heard the strains of a familiar tune echoing around the cave. It was the one that Kate and I had heard as we sat on the big rock by the lake on that moonlit night, nearly twelve months ago, waiting eagerly for Crocodile to return. Crocodile with Napoleon on his shoulder walked towards us playing his accordion and singing to the tune of, A life on the Ocean Wave – but the words were now clearly audible as, A life on Windermere – I now knew that I had not been mistaken the first time I had heard it.

Crocodile continued to entertain us with a medley of Christmas songs and carols, which we all joined in. When he eventually excused himself to attend to his cooking, I also made my apologies and asked if I could also be excused for half an hour, because I needed to return to the house to collect his main Christmas present, which was scheduled to arrive that morning, but had not done so before we left.

"I am sorry for the timing but there was simply no other way to arrange the delivery," I explained.

"We'll come and help you in the kitchen," said Kate, but Crocodile wouldn't hear of it, assuring them that everything was safely in hand.

I was only a short distance out from the island before I could see our gift to Crocodile waiting to be collected from the end of the jetty. A quick look through my binoculars confirmed that I was not mistaken and I noted also that the packaging was exactly as I had requested, so that the contents were kept completely secret.

When I got back to the cave I purposely left the package halfway down the flight of steps. As I descended into the cave I could hear whoops and squeals of delight, and as I neared the bottom I could see that the girls and Crocodile had started to open the presents in the stockings. Crocodile was holding a brand new pair of saddlebags above his head, that Kate and I had had made for him at a local saddlery, to replace the cherished ones that he had lost on the Big Wheel.

"Look, Matthew!" he shouted gleefully when he saw me coming down. "They've got my initials, WHC, embossed on the sides! It is the most wonderful present that I could have wished for."

"I am afraid that you are not correct in that assumption," I called back. Then turning round I gestured to the tall dark shape now standing close behind me. The shape moved forward like the Ghost from Christmas Past, dressed in a long black gown and hooded cloak. I held out my hand. The Ghost took it firmly and I escorted the apparition down into the cave.

A hushed silence ensued. You could have heard a pin drop as everyone gazed in wonder and anticipation at the unexpected drama unfolding before their eyes.

The figure followed me gracefully into the centre of the cavern and then towards Crocodile.

In a low curtsey the hood was thrown back to reveal the face of a beautiful lady with long flowing black hair.

"Master Crocodile, I presume?" said the lady, looking straight into Crocodile's face with a wonderful smile.

"Mercedes! it's my Mercedes!" cried Crocodile, his voice breaking and tears welling up in his eyes.

Mercedes put her arms around him and they hugged each other while the rest of the cast looked on. It was a particularly moving moment for Kate and myself who understood, more than anybody, how important Mercedes had been to Crocodile in his early life, both as his friend and guardian, as well as in his education, and in the development of his unique character.

Crocodile began to regain his composure as formal introductions were made. Mercedes said she felt that she knew everybody already because I had given her a fairly detailed account of Crocodile's life since his kidnap from the zoo, and I had spoken at length about the Professor, Emily, Meredith and, of course, Kate.

As the chatter increased Crocodile shouted, "Goodness me! I think I can smell something burning! Please will you all excuse me? I must get back to my cooking."

While he was away in the kitchen Kate and I rearranged the table settings so that Mercedes and Meredith were sitting either side of Crocodile, with Kate, Emily and I seated opposite.

As Crocodile elegantly presented each course, everybody agreed that it was the best food, and the finest wine that they had ever tasted. Apart from the eulogies over the sumptuous feast, conversation initially centred on Crocodile's exploits, to which we each added our own version of parts of the story. Finally, Emily told us that Robert had notified the management of the Circus to the effect that the police authorities were aware of a kidnapping that had taken place from the house in Bayswater and that this was linked to the hot air balloon incident at the fair. In the strongest terms, Robert had informed the bosses at the circus that the authorities would hold them personally responsible if anything like this ever happened again, and that he would personally ensure that their licence for performing with animals would be revoked, and that they would be locked up and the key thrown away, or words to that effect.

"This of course ensures that Hartley can come to visit us in London, in complete safety, whenever he wishes," added Emily. "And I wish to inform you that Peregrine has just proposed to me. I am keeping him on the hook for a little while longer, and I have informed him that I will give him my decision on Saint Valentine's Day. We do get on very well, but I think that he has his eyes set on us living in the house in Bayswater, when he isn't working in Oxford, so life would go on much the same as it did when Julius was alive. We have discussed Meredith's situation and Peregrine says that he will help in any way he can to ensure that she receives a fine education, if that is what she wishes ... so we may have another Oxford graduation ceremony to look forward to in the future. "

"Oh. I am so pleased for you Emily," said Crocodile.

It just so happened that Crocodile was in the process of opening a very special bottle of vintage champagne when

Emily had made her announcement, so he charged our glasses with this exquisite bubbly and we all stood and drank to Emily's future life and happiness with Peregrine.

"To Emily and The PLC," said Crocodile with a wink.

"I haven't said yes to Peregrine's proposal yet," replied Emily, "but I am content to drink to the future happiness of all of us, including Peregrine's, whether we tie the Knot or not ... or should it be, whether or not we tie the Knot?"

"To Emily and to Peregrine," said Crocodile ... whether or not they tie the Knot or not."

Crocodile cleared his throat and then said:

"I think that another toast is called for, although I believe that there are only two of us at this table who will be aware of the reason... Without any more ado, please will you all raise your glasses to Meredith who, unless I am mistaken, is also celebrating her eighteenth birthday this very day!"

I suddenly remembered Meredith telling me that she was eighteen at Christmas but she did not specify which day, and I could not imagine how Crocodile could possibly have known it was Christmas Day.

We all raised our glasses to Meredith, whose cheeks had suddenly turned the colour of holly berries.

"Happy Birthday Meredith!" we all cried.

"Goodness gracious me!" exclaimed Emily. "Why ever didn't you tell us? This is indeed a very special day, and I am sure one that none of us will ever forget."

With a pang of conscience I suddenly remembered

that Crocodile had, shortly after we first met him, told us that his assumed birthday was on the first day of March, and Kate and I had completely forgotten that as well.

Meredith then stood up and said:

"I would like to thank you all so much for everything that you have done for me and to tell you that the happiness that I thought I had lost for ever has been restored to me. If my Mum and Dad are watching us now I know that they will be very proud of me for both helping Crocodile and for having the courage to leave the Circus."

"I also have an announcement to make," she continued, taking a very large Christmas card from its envelope. "Emily advised me to take a post box number in London, so I sent Big Steve a Christmas card together with the box number, and I thanked him for everything that he had done for me since my parents were killed and wished him a Merry Christmas and a Happy New year. I also said that I hoped the bosses had not been too harsh with him. I received this card from him in reply in which he wishes me, and my friend Crocodile, a Happy Christmas. He says he is sorry for what happened, but he was scared that he would lose his job. He says the bosses did sack him but when they received a letter from the police, they had second thoughts about what had gone on and gave him his job back."

"All's well that ends well," said Crocodile raising his glass, "so I think it is only fair to wish Big Steve future happiness as well."

We all raised our glasses to Big Steve and Meredith thanked us for the gesture.

Mercedes then stood up and produced a large white envelope from within her gown, which she handed to Crocodile.

"This is something especially for you," she said with a warm smile.

Crocodile took the envelope and then hesitated, with an apprehensive expression on his face.

"Well, aren't you going to open it?"

Crocodile gently loosened the seal and took out what appeared to be a large photograph.

We all gathered round to take a closer look, and saw immediately that it was a photograph of another crocodile. It was instantly apparent from the soft facial features and the elegant style and fabric of the costume that the crocodile was a lady.

Crocodile himself remained speechless and just gazed open-mouthed at the photograph.

"Her name is Miranda," said Mercedes, "and she was sent to the zoo as your replacement, about a year after you were taken away from me. I have taught her to read and to write and I am pleased to tell you that she is very sweet and very clever. But she can't ride a bicycle!"

When he eventually got his voice back, and still gazing at the picture of Miranda, Crocodile said simply, "I think she is the most beautiful creature that I have ever set eyes on."

THE END.